To Eilid[...]

Hope y[...]

U. Campbell.

Viking Gold

by

V. Campbell

Published by Fledgling Press, 2011
www.fledglingpress.co.uk

Cover design by Joanna Lisowiec

Printed and bound by:
Martins The Printers, Berwick Upon Tweed,
TD15 1RS

ISBN: 978190596290

*I am the master of my fate:*
*I am the captain of my soul.*

*Invictus,* William Ernest Henley

# Part I

# Home

# Chapter 1

If Redknee had known sword fighting was going to be so important, he would have listened to his uncle's instructions. As it was, the heat of the afternoon was getting to him. All he wanted was to escape the training yard and shelter in the cool of the forest.

He tugged at his wool tunic. His shield, big as a wagon wheel, weighed heavy on his arm. He rested it on the ground, lowered his wooden sword and wiped the sweat from his brow. What did it matter if he could fight? He was going to be a woodsman, a tracker. The village didn't need more warriors. His uncle had said it himself many times – the years of raiding were over. The world had changed. Monasteries were no longer the easy pickings they once were.

"Come on," Uncle Sven shouted across the yard. "You give up, you die."

The men watching from the shade of the village oak laughed. Redknee couldn't be sure, but he thought he heard one of them mutter, "Like father, like son."

He'd heard the slur often. Not right to his face, mind. No one would be so brave, with Jarl Sven as his uncle. But he heard the whispers all the same. Redknee did what he always did and turned away.

The skinny youth opposite had sixteen summers – same as Redknee. Harold the Thin was going to be the best warrior in the village. Or so he never tired of telling everyone.

Harold moved his wooden sword from hand to hand.

Taunting him.

Flies buzzed round Redknee's face. Sighing, he picked up his shield, raised his wooden sword and awaited the blow. Might as well get the farce over with.

"Stop there lad."

1

Redknee glanced up. Uncle Sven was marching across the yard. He pulled Redknee aside and spoke in a voice too low for the jeering onlookers to hear.

"Think of your shield like a jug of mead," he said gently. "Keep it high. Don't let your arm drop. If it does …"

Sven stared at the disc of leather-covered yew. Redknee thought he saw sadness in the big man's eyes. But when Sven looked up, he was smiling, the sadness gone. "Come on," he said, slapping Redknee on the back. "Let's try again."

Dust sprayed the air as Harold lunged at Redknee's chest. Redknee heeded his uncle's words and Harold's blow thudded uselessly off his shield. Harold's eyes widened in surprise.

Having the advantage was new to Redknee. Pride flashed through him. *Maybe he could be a warrior.* Thinking quickly he thrust his sword at Harold's belly. But Harold was already out of reach, leaving Redknee's arm floundering at empty air.

Before Redknee could recover, Harold swung his sword low, beneath the protection of Redknee's shield. Redknee fell to the ground, pain coursing through his ankles. Harold stood over him, the sun at his back casting him in silhouette, as if he were Hela, come to drag Redknee to the underworld.

"You're dead," he said, pressing the tip of his sword into Redknee's throat.

"Stop it boys!" Redknee heard his mother call from the door of the longhouse. "That's enough."

Harold sniggered.

"Ach, he has to toughen up," Uncle Sven shouted back. "You'd have him in a bloody dress."

Harold sneered down at Redknee. "It's called the snake-bite. Oldest move there is. But a sap like you wouldn't know that." He twisted the wooden blade into Redknee's throat until he gagged. "Leif Redknee," he said with disgust. "I claim victory over you - shame of the Vikinger, just like your father."

The men's laughter rang in Redknee's ears as he stomped from the yard. He tossed his shield into the long grass. Worthless piece of rubbish – let the dogs sharpen their teeth on the rotten wood. He took the path that climbed the mountainside. He craved to be up in the forest, far above the village. Away from lectures on war-craft and the mind-numbing repetition of military moves. Better to spend a sticky summer day running through the pine-scented darkness. Better to spend it alone.

Things would have been different if his father were still alive. No one would be calling him a coward for a start. He would be the son of the Jarl, a position demanding respect. Oh, Uncle Sven tried his best. But most of the time he was just too busy.

No, Uncle Sven wouldn't come after him. And Harold the Thin, despite his claims to martial greatness, was too afraid of wolves to venture up the mountain. The only person in the whole village who might care was his mother, but she only left the longhouse to work in the weaving hut or wash clothes in the stream.

No, Redknee was on his own, just the way he liked it.

Redknee stood on the edge of a bluff half way up the mountainside. He'd made good progress. Far below, the straw roofs of the longhouses glinted in the sun, as if on fire. Bounded on one side by the silvery-blue of Oster Fjord and on the other by a patchwork of brown fields, the village looked peaceful. Happy, even.

But the summer had been dry. The barley thirsted in the fields, and the mood in the village stank like dung cooking in the midday heat. Redknee turned his back on the view and scrambled on. There was nothing for him there.

After a short while, he heard a soft crunching noise behind him. He ignored it at first, quickening his pace until his deerskin boots skidded on the floury earth.

"You're going too fast!"

He turned to see a hood of copper curls bobbing between the trees. He sighed. "Why are you following me, Sinead? You will be wanted back at the village."

The girl shrugged. "You looked upset."

"Slaves are not allowed to leave the village without permission. My uncle will have you whipped."

Bristling, Sinead folded her arms across her chest. "Well I thought you might really be running away this time. Are you?"

"Don't know." He kicked a loose stone. It skimmed off a tree trunk.

"Can I come with you anyway?"

Redknee sighed. Sinead had asked him about the mountain before. About where the paths led, how far they were from the next village, the nearest big port. She seemed to think him as keen to escape the village as she was. "Look," he said eventually, "even if I am running away, and I'm not saying I am, you couldn't come with me."

"Why not?"

"Because you'll slow me down. And you don't know the ways of the forest. You'd end up troll food in no time."

"Do trolls really live up here?" she asked, her green eyes scanning the tangle of leaves above their heads.

Redknee reached out to a low hanging branch and swung himself up until he was sitting atop it, his legs dangling over the side. He needed to get rid of her to have any chance of tracking the wild deer that roamed the mountain. Her chattering would scare off even the dopiest fawn.

"These woods …," he said, weaving between the lacework of branches "… are swarming with trolls."

"No!" Her eyes widened.

He stood, balancing on a stout branch, stretching his arms towards the canopy. "They are as tall as an oak and as fierce as a bear, with sharp red teeth and fiery eyes."

Sinead snorted.

"It's true," Redknee continued, pulling himself higher. "In fact, they live in tree-trunks, just like this one." He rapped the coarse bark with his knuckles.

"Don't!" Sinead gasped.

Redknee smiled. "Why ever not?"

"You'll wake it—"

A sudden crackle of leaves startled Redknee and he lost his footing. He heard Sinead scream as he crashed to the ground like a sack of turnips. His head pounded and his left arm ached along its length.

4

"Don't move." Sinead's firestorm hair drifted in and out of focus as she kneeled over him.

"Was it a troll?" he asked.

"Shh, don't try to speak."

Ignoring her, Redknee dragged himself up with his uninjured arm. The movement made him feel sick. He turned from her quickly, spewing vomit on his breeches.
She handed him her apron. As he took it, he saw her nose wrinkle at the stench and his cheeks burned with shame.

Suddenly her attention was distracted. Redknee stopped dabbing. His ears attuned to the distant *whoosh – whoosh* of someone, or something, charging through the undergrowth. He listened carefully. Too heavy to be a deer. A bear? No – too fast. Whatever it was, it was coming their way. He turned to Sinead as a spear flashed past her head. Her face went blank and she fell to the ground.

"Sinead!" He scrambled to where she lay. "Sinead, were you hit?"

No reply.

He turned her over. Blood trailed from her hairline and spread, like spindly fingers, over her closed lids.

Closer now, he recognised the rhythmic thud of hooves. Horses! Needing no further warning, he lifted Sinead using his good arm and dragged her beneath a big hawthorn bush. He stayed there, hunkered down in the mud for what seemed like ages, listening to the steady approach of the horses.

A hulking warrior with straggly, piss-coloured hair and a cross-shaped scar over his left eye urged a grey stallion into the clearing. The powerful horse rose onto its hind legs as three other riders joined him. The first warrior motioned the other men forward; Redknee took him to be the leader.

One of the men pulled the spear that had struck Sinead from a tree. Redknee glanced down at her; she was still breathing. It was just a graze.

"Come out, little mice," the leader shouted in accented Norse. "Skoggcat wants to play ..." Redknee watched as a youth, painted head to toe in orange and black stripes, stepped forward brandishing a ball and chain.

5

Sinead stirred. Redknee held his hand lightly over her mouth. One false move and their hiding place would be revealed.

Skoggcat and the other four warriors circled the clearing, getting ever closer to the hawthorn bush.

Sinead was awake now, her eyes alert to the danger. Redknee cradled his bruised left arm against his body. There was no way the two of them would be a match for this lot. Redknee's heart thrummed so loud, he was sure they must be able to hear it.

Skoggcat stopped beside the hawthorn bush, about a man's length from Redknee, and sniffed the air. A smile spread across his face.

Redknee looked down at his breeches. Curdled lumps of sick still clung to the damp leather. *Damn.* He tried to scramble to his feet. But Skoggcat was already under the branches, his claw-like hands grabbing at Redknee's ankles, dragging him out. Redknee wriggled and kicked as hard as he could, aiming for Skoggcat's hard-set eyes and mouth. But it was no good, Skoggcat was too strong.

As soon as they were in the open Skoggcat swung his iron ball at Redknee's head. Redknee ducked, raised his arm and the chain twisted round his wrist. Ignoring the vice-like pain of the links biting into his flesh, he tugged hard, pulling an already over extended Skoggcat off his feet. Locked in battle, the pair tumbled down a fern covered slope.

They came to a stop with Redknee on his back. Skoggcat fought like the wildcat he mimicked, scratching at Redknee's face and baring sharpened teeth. Struggling to hold him off, Redknee tried to use the iron ball still attached to his wrist to smash Skoggcat's nose. But Skoggcat was as agile as he was strong, dodging every blow with a gleeful sneer.

Redknee changed tack. Rather than trying to fight him off, he seized Skoggcat's clawed hands and held them. Confusion showed in Skoggcat's eyes as he tried to twist free. But Redknee held tight, got his foot under Skoggcat's belly and pushed – sending the screaming youth flying over his head. Seizing the advantage, Redknee leapt to his feet and drew his eating knife.

"Redknee!"

He turned to see the first warrior hoisting Sinead onto his grey stallion.

Turning from Skoggcat, Redknee scrambled up the embankment and ran headlong at the big warrior. But the warrior just laughed as he turned his stallion and galloped into the forest. Skoggcat jumped up behind one of the other riders and stole a lift. The men were gone just as quickly as they had arrived.

Redknee kept up his pursuit until he could no longer make out the shadows of the trees. Exhausted, he slumped to the ground. Sinead was gone and he was lost.

Redknee forced himself on, crashing into outstretched branches, tripping on exposed roots. He strained to see in the shadowy, moonlit darkness of the night. There had been no sign of Sinead's abductors since they galloped off that afternoon. Face it, he thought, he was never going to catch them. And even if he did, what, exactly, was he going to do? Attack five warriors with his eating knife?

He rubbed his elbow. He was going to have a bruise the size of an apple. The villagers might as well call him Red-arm as Redknee, for all the difference it made. He was too clumsy to be a warrior. Too clumsy for anything but—

A cry pierced the night.

Redknee's hand shot to his knife. Wolves. He stopped and listened. The animal's mate would reply, betraying their location. He waited, but there was no response. Not wolves, he thought. One wolf. A lone hunter. He drew his knife. Wolves, even a lone one, demanded respect. Each step he took seemed to echo through the forest, so he moved forward on tiptoe, every muscle in his body taut as he eased, quiet as he could, through the maze of branches. The wolf was near, but how near?

He knew he should avoid the wolf – his eye was on bigger game tonight. But then, to be able to wear a wolf pelt – that would show Harold the bloody Thin. *Harold the Bleeding Scared*, more like.

7

Thorns tore at his arms; his legs ached from keeping on tiptoe. One wrong move would expose him. Eventually he slumped, exhausted, onto a fallen log. And that was when he heard it.

A soft mewling.

He peered through the undergrowth, but all he saw was a dark knot of leaves and twigs. He heard the mewling again; this time he crept towards its source. The earth became soft, like butter, and he trod carefully. There must be water nearby.

A fresh hoof print then another, glistened in the sludge. His first piece of luck! Heart racing, and forgetting his fear of the wolf, he followed the horse trail past a tightly packed copse of ash and elder. Suddenly, the ground slid away and he toppled backwards, arms flailing. He tumbled down a mossy slope, ripping his tunic and dropping his knife as he clutched uselessly at the slick earth.

Something large and hard stopped his fall. Unable to get up, he lay on the ground, blood trickling across his face. He grimaced as the metallic taste reached his mouth. He would probably die here, his broken body picked clean by scavengers. Was this how it had felt for his father? Death. Cold, lonely, slow…

They said his father had surrendered. A coward's death. Well, Redknee was not a coward. At least he had the satisfaction of knowing he had died trying to save his friend. Of running into battle, not away from it. Would that be enough to get him to Valhalla, he wondered, the final resting place of the great warriors?

A fine mist began to settle over him. He smiled. The village had been waiting for rain now for weeks. He inhaled the vapour and closed his eyes …

The mewling was much closer now. Right beside him, in fact. Redknee opened his eyes. How long had he been asleep? He looked about. It was still dark. Pain shuddered through him. A welcome pain. He was alive.

As he groped for the rock that had broken his fall, his fingers curled round a sharp object. His eating knife. He slid the knife into his belt, and, summoning all his energy, pulled

8

himself to his feet. He leaned on the stone for a long while, absorbing its strength.

Then Redknee saw him. Cowering in the hollow trunk of an old pine tree was a tiny wolf cub. Its white fur stuck out at odd angles and its nose bore a round grey mark the size of the Arab coins his uncle kept locked in a chest. Redknee daren't move closer. The cub's mother would be nearby. A she-wolf never left her young for long.

Then he heard it. A ragged howl. Like the rush of wind through a cave.

He spun round, bracing himself for the attack. Long white teeth glimmered against black gums. Redknee spread his arms wide. He'd heard wolves could be scared off if you made yourself look bigger. But the she-wolf kept coming. She was almost on him now, growling and pawing the ground, a demon of spit and fangs and blood. A gash the length of a man's forearm cleaved her right haunch. Redknee winced. This was not her first fight of the day either. He edged backwards. She tried to leap at him, but her legs quivered and it was more of a shuffle. A moment later she collapsed to the ground.

The pup crawled from its lair and nudged its mother's nose with its head. A triangle of pink tongue darted over the pup's ears, but the she-wolf was beaten. Her eyes lolled with exhaustion and her head slumped onto her paws.

As the she-wolf took her last, rasping breath, she looked up at Redknee, with, he imagined, relief in her eyes. And he knew what he should do. He edged over to the pup, who was now trying to wake its mother by patting her face with its paw, and gently scooped it up. Pale amber eyes ringed with black stared warily at Redknee.

"Hey, little one," Redknee said, stroking the pup behind its ears. The pup tried to wriggle free. Redknee fished a scrap of bread from his belt-pouch and held it out. After a moment's pause, the pup gobbled it down greedily.

"You're all alone in the world now. I know what that feels like. But don't worry, I'll look after you. We can be a team."

The pup eyed Redknee for a moment then began licking his face. "Ergh," Redknee said, holding the pup at arm's

9

length. "I'll have to teach you to stop that if you're ever going to make a fierce hunting dog."

He tucked the pup into his tunic and trudged through the wet mud until he came to a wide clearing. A torch flickered a short distance off. He ducked down. The fiery image danced across the ground. He'd reached the banks of a mountain lake – one he didn't recognise. More lights joined the first – their reflections shimmering on the water.

He crept through the reeds until he was within hearing distance. Fifteen or so men lounged by a campfire, drinking and cutting strips off a deer carcass they'd suspended over the fire on a stout branch. Redknee's mouth watered. He hadn't eaten since breakfast. The men were loud and drunk. Two were arguing over a game of dice. A few took turns goading a brown bear they had tethered to a tree stump. The poor beast was so tired it hardly responded to their bullying.

Redknee crouched in the shadows and looked for Sinead. A group of horses stood to one side. Redknee recognised the grey stallion. Beside the horses was a wooden cage. Their leader, the big warrior with the bad eye, stalked over to the cage, pulled out a girl and dragged her towards the campfire. Redknee wasn't sure it was Sinead until he heard her squawking on in her usual way. Like a seagull arguing with an ox. Pointless and annoying.

"Let me go, you big oaf," she said.

"Wish granted," he said, pushing her in front of the fire.

The men looked up from their meal. A raven-haired youth in a fine chainmail coat addressed the big warrior. "Ragnar," he asked, "when do we attack Sven's village?"

Ragnar smirked. "First light, son. If we can get this girl to talk. She knows where it is. I know it. But she says nothing."

The youth jumped up, grabbed Sinead's hand and thrust it towards the flames. "Tell us the way to Sven Kodranson's village," he demanded.

Sinead jerked her head back and spat in his eye.

"You little—" The youth brought his palm across her face, knocking her to the ground.

10

At the sound of the slap, every muscle in Redknee's body tensed.

Ragnar sighed. "Calm down, Mord. You must never let a woman rile you. Besides, the point is to make her talk, not shut her up forever. Now put her back in the cage until she comes round."

Sulking, Mord lifted Sinead's limp body, dropped her inside the cage, bound the door shut and rejoined his father by the fire. The rest of the men were happily engrossed in their food and in taunting the poor bear. None, it seemed, were brave enough to tease Mord over Sinead's outburst. There was no sign of Skoggcat. Staying low in the undergrowth, Redknee edged closer.

"Can't wait to see Sven again," Ragnar said as Mord sat beside him on an upturned log. "Bet he'll squeal like a pig when I run him through. Just like his brother did." Laughing, he drew his knife and jabbed the bear in the gut. The animal moaned. Ragnar's eyes lit up.

"My spies have confirmed Sven still has his brother's book," said Mord, ignoring his father's jest with the bear.

"What would I do without you, Mord? You know everyone's secrets."

A smile flashed across the young man's face, then vanished. "They also tell me Sven has finished his longship," he said.

"Then this is the perfect time to strike. Nothing like taking advantage of someone else's hard work, eh?" Ragnar said. "And it is high time I studied the book for myself – Sven has denied me it long enough. Now, have you seen your useless freak of a brother?"

Mord shook his head. "What about the boy? The one who was with the girl."

"What about him?" Ragnar frowned. "He's nothing. We lost him ages ago." Ragnar studied his son for a moment, then said, "You worry too much. Relax. We'll find Sven's village soon enough." Ragnar slapped Mord on the back and turned to talk with his men, who were rowdily debating whether Thor, the god of thunder, or Odin, the god of war, would win in a fight.

11

Mord moved to the edge of the camp, away from the men. He took a piece of ivory from his pocket and began working it with his knife.

The pup squirmed inside Redknee's tunic, Redknee pushed him down, out of sight, his mind spinning as he closed the distance to the cage. He forgot the pain in his arm, the pounding in his head. He'd heard of Ragnar. Uncle Sven had spoken of him. But always in hushed tones. For it was Ragnar who had killed Redknee's father. Murdered him.

The cage was near where Mord worked on his carving. But the night was dark and he didn't see Redknee crawl up behind Sinead, reach through the bars and tap her on the shoulder.

No movement. Nothing. He tried again, this time tugging the ends of her long hair. She opened her eyes slowly, saw him, and winked.

Redknee held his fingers to his lips. "Lie still. Don't draw attention." He used his knife to start sawing the rope holding the cage door closed. From the corner of his eye, he saw one of Ragnar's men approach carrying a bucket.

"Hurry!" Sinead whispered.

"I'm going as fast as I can." Ragnar had used heavy flax and Redknee felt his knife buckle.

Ragnar's man reached the far side of the cage. Redknee hid in the shadows as the man tossed a bucketful of lake water over Sinead and turned to go. Sinead let out a tiny gasp as the cold water hit her skin.

Ragnar's man stopped. He turned just as Redknee looked up and their eyes met through the bars of the cage. Sinead stood in an attempt to hide Redknee. But she was too late. Then, just as the warrior drew his sword and bellowed for help, the rope came away in Redknee's hand. Before Redknee could stand back, Sinead was out of the cage, fleeing for the trees. But Ragnar's man was quick to block her escape.

Redknee grabbed Sinead's hand and pulled her the other way. There was a clear route past the campfire and round the far side of the lake. But as they neared the campfire, Ragnar caught up with them, anger burning in his eyes.

"You again!" he said, drawing his sword and lunging forwards.

12

Redknee sprang back, just dodging the flames. His knife was no match for Ragnar's sword. Thinking quickly, he grabbed a branch from the fire and thrust it in Ragnar's face. The big man flinched, slipped on the ashes, and, twisting to miss the fire, landed at the bear's feet.

Sinead yanked the tether and a moment later the bear was free.

Redknee and Sinead made for the forest. As they wove through the trees, the pup still tucked safely into Redknee's tunic, they tried to close their ears to Ragnar's terrible screams.

They zigzagged through the forest, branches snatching at their faces and legs, the pounding of hooves only a few paces behind. Eventually the sound receded and Redknee felt certain they'd lost Ragnar's men. But like fleeing deer, the two of them tore blindly on. It was only after a long while that he felt Sinead ease her pace.

"Have we lost them?" she asked, gasping.

Redknee motioned for her to stop, as his own heart hammered in his chest. He listened to the darkness. To the sounds of his mountain. The shadows heightened every whisper. Sinead stood rigid beside him. He reached out and took her hand in his. Her skin felt hot despite her soaking.

"It's alright," he said. "I can't hear the horses." The fear in her muscles eased. "But we have to get back to the village. Ragnar and his men plan to attack at first light. And he'll want revenge after your trick."

Sinead snatched her hand away. "You mean untying the bear? What else was I to do? We were trapped."

"All I'm saying is, if Ragnar survived being mauled, he'll be looking for us."

"Oh," Sinead gulped. "We should hide, then. No point heading to the village when we know that's where Ragnar's going."

"What? And leave my mother and uncle to die? Ragnar said he wanted to kill Uncle Sven. Just like he killed my father."

13

"Well they're not my family. I'm just a slave. I don't owe my captors loyalty."

He grabbed her by the elbow. "You owe them your keep and protection—"

"Look, I held my tongue, didn't I? I didn't tell them the way to the village. That ought to buy your precious family some time."

"They'll find the place soon enough – they've got this far," Redknee said, letting her go. "But that *was* loyal of you."

"I was afraid," she said, rubbing her elbow. "I thought Ragnar would kill me if I told him. Once he had no need of me."

"Typical," Redknee said. "A slave thinking of herself first. Especially a Christian one." He sighed. "Look, we're wasting time. You do what you like." He stomped off but paused after a few strides. He had no idea where he was, or even if he was going the right way.

"You've no clue where you're going. Do you?" Sinead called. "Ooh, the great Redknee – jarl of the mountain – totally lost."

"Be quiet!" Redknee spun round. "You might not care about raising the alarm, but I do." The night had already faded to a smoky grey and he could see the outline of individual trees. He ran his hand over the trunk of a tall pine. A fleece of moss shrouded its north side. He turned to Sinead.

"Oster-Fjord lies west; if we go …," he calculated west from the position of the moss, "… that way," he said, pointing towards a bracken-covered escarpment, "we should reach its shores. We can follow the water to the village. Are you coming?"

The pup slid from Redknee's tunic and stretched on the ground.

"What's that?" Sinead asked.

"What does it look like?"

Sinead glowered. "A skinny little wolf cub."

The pup yawned, baring every one of its sharp teeth and its long stretch of pink tongue. Then it sauntered over to Sinead and nuzzled the hem of her dress.

"Hey," Redknee said. "Don't be a traitor!"

14

"Aw, he likes me." She scooped him up and the pup obliged by licking her chin. "Don't be jealous. He just has good taste." She set the pup on the ground. "Where did you get him?"

"Rescued him."

"Really?" Her eyes widened. "Quite the hero tonight."

"Yeah, well," Redknee muttered. "No point wasting more time."

"Does he have a name?" she asked.

He shook his head.

"What about Silver?"

"What about it?"

"Because of the mark on his forehead, and he might bring you luck."

Redknee shrugged. Hunting dogs didn't have names. "Come on," he said, following the command with a low whistle. The pup trotted over. "Good boy," he said, bundling it into his arms and starting to walk. He called over his shoulder to Sinead. "If we make good time, we can still reach the village before sunrise."

"Wait, what am I to do?" she asked.

"What do you mean?"

"I don't want to return to the village."

"Why not? Isn't my mother kind to you? You're her favourite slave."

"Yes ... she *is* kind ... for a pagan. But I ... I don't want to be a slave anymore. I thought we were running away. I want to go home."

*Had* he been running away? He wasn't even sure himself. He sighed. "Look, I *have* to go back. Besides, isn't this your home now?"

"Wait!" Her voice sounded strangled.

He shook his head and kept walking. "I don't have time to waste. It's nearly light."

She scuttled after him, falling into step at his side.

He grinned. "So, you decided to come with me after all?"

She glowered at him. "Not much choice."

He stopped and looked her in the eye. She was still breathless from their run and her skin was flushed the pale

15

pink of the river salmon. "You're wrong, Sinead," he said. "There's always a choice."

Redknee stood on the cliff and stared at the huddle of longhouses below. They'd reached the village at last. Purple light stretched across Oster Fjord, turning the beach a pale lilac. Dawn came early this time of year. *Wavedancer* stood, tall and proud against the gleaming water. A fine oak ship. A fine prize. Finished, save for the dragon figurehead Uncle Sven would attach at the launch ceremony, her curved silhouette contrasted with the squat bulkiness of the longhouses.

Already, plumes of smoke twisted into the early morning sky. Redknee felt his stomach grumble. His mother would have her porridge pot over the fire. He could dry his wet feet. He started to run.

"Come on," he called to Sinead.

She had taken the pup from him, and held it tight as she tried to keep up with his new, faster pace. He tore down the path, skidding on loose stones and half-tripping on exposed roots. But he didn't care. He just wanted to get home. Trees sped past in a blur. Green, brown, orange.

Orange?

He was being followed, and one name flashed through his mind.Before he could do anything, Skoggcat ripped through the trees and knocked him flat. But he had misjudged the distance and kept going, past Redknee, until he dropped over the edge.

Redknee scrambled to his feet and ran to where Skoggcat had disappeared. Sinead was already peering over. About half a man's length below where they stood, Skoggcat gripped a naked root with one hand, his feet dangling in the air. They were still far above the village. A fall from this height would kill a man instantly.

"He must have been following us all along," Sinead said.

Redknee nodded. How could he have missed the signs? Ragnar's threat – fear for his family – had distracted him. That was the only explanation. Even so, Skoggcat must have been quiet as the dead.

"What should we do?" Sinead asked.

Skoggcat stared up at them, terror pinching his tattooed face. He reached for the root with his free hand, but the movement loosened the earth and he slid lower. A tiny noise, barely a whisper, came from the back of his throat.

"He's trying to speak," Sinead said.

Redknee pulled her from the edge. "We should go. He's seen the village. If we help him, he'll only tell Ragnar the way."

Sinead's face turned white. "But—"

"Oh, so this is different to running off without telling my family about Ragnar's attack?"

"*No*... I mean—"

"He was trying to kill me, Sinead. It's not my fault he fell."

"But it's so cruel."

"Life's cruel," he said, walking away.

Sinead caught up with him and placed her hand on his elbow. "Life might be cruel," she said. "But you're not."

"*Please help me ...,*" came the disembodied plea.

"I'm going back," she said, gathering her skirts and turning round.

He sighed. She might see rescuing Skoggcat as an act of mercy, but her charity would only bring death to those Redknee cared about. And yet ...

To slay a man in battle was honourable. To leave him to die slowly—

That wasn't the Viking way.

He turned on his heels and went to where Sinead lay on the ground with her arms stretched over edge of the cliff. The pup sat beside her, watching her every move.

"I can't reach," she gasped.

He leaned over. Skoggcat's hand strained to meet Sinead's smaller one. "He'll attack us as soon as he's up," Redknee said.

Skoggcat shook his head. "I promise I won't."

"How do we know you won't lead Ragnar to our village?" he asked.

"My father thinks I'm useless. He'll believe I didn't find anything."

17

The root Skoggcat clung to began to give way. Sinead screamed.

Reluctantly, Redknee lay on the ground and lowered himself, face first, until he was hanging down the rock face from his waist. He felt the blood rush to his head and closed his eyes while he regained his balance. When he opened them again, he immediately wished he hadn't. The village looked nothing more than a tiny speck, hundreds of feet below. Taking a deep breath, he forced himself to focus instead on Skoggcat.

The youth stretched for Redknee's arm, but he was still too far away.

This was a bad idea. He couldn't help Skoggcat, and now he was going to die trying. He glanced over his shoulder at Sinead's expectant face and sighed.

"Grab my feet," he said. He felt her sit on his ankles. He wriggled further out, over the edge, until he felt his feet lifting off the ground. "Hold on!" he called over his shoulder.

"I am," she replied. "There's nothing else I can do. You're going to have to grab him quickly."

Redknee felt a tug at the hem of his trousers and realised the pup was holding on too. He grinned to himself.

Skoggcat was closer now. Redknee could just brush his fingertips. If he could only reach a bit—

The cliff splintered beneath Redknee's chest, spraying shingle over Skoggcat's head; plunging Redknee lower. Once Redknee steadied himself, he realised it was the boost they needed. He reached for Skoggcat; grasping his hand just as the root came apart and tumbled to the valley floor.

His arm creaked as Skoggcat's full weight swung from his wrist. The youth was heavier than he'd expected. He felt sharp rocks scour his chest. His heart raced; Skoggcat's weight was pulling him over the edge. Redknee tensed his stomach and arms.

"I can't pull you back up," he said to Skoggcat. "You're going to have to climb over me."

Skoggcat nodded and Redknee braced himself as he felt the youth's hands, knees, then feet, grind into his spine.

18

For a terrible moment, he thought Skoggcat would kill Sinead as soon as he was up then push him to his death. The moment he felt Skoggcat's weight go, he scrambled backwards and sat on the path, panting. He felt like he'd been torn apart on the rack.

Skoggcat stood a short distance away. Redknee eyed him warily. Sweat glistened on his painted skin. Up close, he was even stranger than Redknee had first thought. Naked, save for a pair of wool breeches and an amber necklace; black stripes criss-crossed his chest and arms.

"They make me strong ... like a big cat," Skoggcat said, following Redknee's gaze. "I got them in the east ... where they have cats the size of cows."

Redknee nodded. He wanted to be on his way – to warn the village of the impending attack. It didn't pay to talk to the enemy – he didn't want to know someone he might have to kill later.

"Is Ragnar your father?" Sinead asked.

Skoggcat nodded.

"Did the bear get him?"

"I ... don't know ... I was stalking you ..."

"Come on," Redknee said, scowling at Sinead. "We should go."

"Wait!" Skoggcat called after them. "My father is coming to your village to find a book. He says it has more value than anyone knows. Maybe if you give him the book, he won't destroy your village."

"Thank you," Sinead called over her shoulder.

"What are you doing?" Redknee asked. "We've done enough damage. And he's probably feeding us lies."

As Redknee hurried home, people, little more than specks in the distance, were already outside feeding chickens and starting for the fields. Redknee's stomach did a somersault. When it came to it, Harold the Thin had been right. He *was* a coward. He hadn't believed Skoggcat's promises, yet he'd been too weak to let him die.

Now Ragnar was coming, and it was all his fault.

# Chapter 2

Redknee burst into the longhouse as Uncle Sven spooned great lumps of broth into his mouth.

"We have to get ready!" He shouted, running past his startled mother and pulling his uncle's bowl away. "We're going to be attacked at first light!"

"What's this?" Uncle Sven said, snatching his breakfast back. "Where have you been all night? Your mother was worried sick."

The longhouse was empty apart from his mother and uncle. The big fire in the centre of the room crackled with newly chopped wood. His mother stood at her iron pot. She put down her ladle, wiped her hands on her linen apron and bustled over. The scent of fresh rosemary filled his nostrils as she enfolded him in her arms. "I was so worried," she said, raining kisses on his forehead. "I thought I'd lost you, just like—"

"Quit your clucking, woman." Uncle Sven stood. "You fuss too much over that boy. He's nearly a man. A night in the woods will have done him good." He slapped Redknee on the back so hard he almost fell. "Well then?" He looked at Redknee. "What do you say?"

"Sir, we need to—"

"Your night in the woods. Do you good? Toughen you up?"

"Er, yes Sir. But—"

Uncle Sven turned to Redknee's mother who was filling another bowl from her pot. "See. Best thing for him."

His mother rolled her eyes. "Oh yes - what doesn't kill him makes him stronger," she said wryly, handing Redknee the bowl of steaming porridge.

He inhaled deeply then remembered Sinead. He turned to see her hovering in the open doorway. He held out his bowl.

"What's this?" Uncle Sven's eyes narrowed. "The Irish slave girl!" He laughed. "I would never have—"

"Sinead." Redknee's mother spoke quickly. "You're late for your duties. Take your porridge in the milking shed."

Blushing, Sinead took the bowl Redknee offered and retreated hurriedly.

Redknee turned to his uncle. "Sir," he said, more forcefully this time. "When I was in the forest, I came across Ragnar and his men. I overheard him say he was planning to attack us at first light. He intends to steal *Wavedancer*."

Uncle Sven pushed aside his empty bowl. His grey eyes took on a faraway look and Redknee wondered if he was remembering something from long ago. Eventually he asked, "How do you know it was Ragnar?"

"I heard the men talking."

"I see. How many men did he have?"

"About fifteen, Sir. All mounted and armed."

Uncle Sven paced the room, his hands clasped behind his back. "And how do you know Ragnar means to attack us, and not some other village?"

"I heard him mention you by name, Sir ..." Redknee's voice trailed off as his mother busied herself with pots and pans.

Uncle Sven ceased pacing. "Spit it out boy. What else did he say?"

"He said he wanted to ... to run you through, Sir, as he did my father."

The clatter of pots falling to the earth floor filled the room. Redknee's mother gripped a big cooking pan to her chest like a shield. "Oh Sven," she said, her face tensed with fear, "it's not happening again, is it?"

"Mind yourself, woman." Sven leant on the table and his long hair fell across his face, hiding his expression.

Redknee hadn't known his father, but he'd often wondered if he had looked like this man. Six and a half feet of tightly thatched muscle, with wide grey eyes carved in a face the colour of sandstone. Redknee reckoned most of the villagers would do anything for Sven. They would stand their ground and defend the village to the death, if that was what Sven asked of them. Redknee wondered if his father had mustered the same respect when he was jarl.

Sven straightened to his full height and turned to Redknee. "Did Ragnar mention anything else at all? Think Redknee, did he talk about hidden treasure?"

"Er … other than wanting to steal *Wavedancer*?"

Sven nodded.

Redknee remembered Skoggcat's words about the book. He should probably mention that, no matter how crazy it sounded. "Erm … I think he also said something about a book. But I've never seen a book in the—"

Sven slammed his hand on the table. "Damn it, Redknee!"

"Sorry," he said, hanging his head. "Does that mean he really is coming to … to kill you?"

"I thought I'd seen the last of Ragnar sixteen years ago," Sven said quietly. "I should have killed him when I had the chance." He took his battleaxe from an iron hook on the wall, slung it over his shoulder and crossed to the doorway. He paused, his hand on the oak frame. "It seems I've failed."

Uncle Sven stood beneath the village oak and bellowed orders. Everywhere Redknee looked, people were readying for the attack, their faces pinched with fear, their hands shaking. Two boys scurried past laden with scythes, axes and lumps of wood. Makeshift weapons.

Gudrid the Healer and Thora, the Smithy's wife, women Redknee knew as his mother's friends, were gathering rocks and piling them inside the door of the feast hall. Their faces shone with the effort and sweat darkened their coarse brown dresses.

Redknee recalled the fine tempered swords Ragnar and his men had carried and his heart sank. There were only five seasoned warriors in the village. The rest of the free men were just farmers, used only to the occasional summer raid. There were the slaves, too, of course. Wends from the Rhineland and Celts from Ireland. In total Redknee estimated there were maybe twelve male slaves. But they couldn't be trusted. And Uncle Sven would never give them weapons.

22

Add to this the fact that Koll the Smithy had spent the spring helping build *Wavedancer* instead of making new weapons or fixing the old ones. True, the village would have the advantage of numbers – it boasted the thirty free men needed to sail a longship. But everyone knew that, even under Uncle Sven's direction, farmers and part-time raiders, even ones strong and willing to defend their homes, were no match for Ragnar's warriors.

At the edge of the village, just short of the treeline, a group of men were digging knee-deep pits. Redknee watched as they filled them with wooden spikes and covered them with grass – a trap that would lame a horse or snap a man's leg like a twig.

Something soft pressed between Redknee's shins. He patted the pup on the head. "Hey, Silver," he said. The pup nuzzled his hand and he knew the name Sinead chose fit. "There's going to be a fight here this morning. I'll need you to help me defend the village."

Silver blinked and rubbed his cheek against Redknee's boot. "I'll take that as—"

The scrape of iron on granite made him look up. Harold the Thin sat on a big stone sharpening his dagger, his hard blue eyes trained on Redknee. Harold uncoiled and swaggered over. "Where'd you get him?" he asked, pointing at Silver with his dagger.

"The forest," Redknee said, pushing Silver behind him.

One of the younger boys came over too. "That's a wolf pup," he said, eyes widening in his round face. "Did you take it from its mother? Did you kill her?"

"Maybe." Redknee shrugged, his eyes focussed on Harold's dagger.

Harold sneered. "You didn't kill a wolf."

"Its mother's dead," Redknee said, challenging Harold to disagree.

Harold beckoned the pup over. "Let me see him."

Silver squashed between Redknee's legs and began licking Harold's fingers.

The younger boy laughed. "He's friendly," he said, and tried to pat Silver himself.

23

Harold pushed the younger boy away, grabbed Silver by the neck and squeezed. Silver whimpered and his big paws went floppy.

"Stop that!"

"Make me," Harold said, grinning.

Redknee shoved Harold to the ground and grabbed Silver. The pup looked at Redknee with confusion in his amber eyes. He was too trusting by far.

Harold scrambled to his feet. "I'm watching you," he said. "And your stupid mutt."

The muscles in Redknee's right hand clenched into a ball of anger. He knew he had to show Harold or the teasing would never end. But he couldn't start a fight here, now …

The younger boy hurtled down to the shore, to where the men were pulling a sheet over *Wavedancer's* bow. "Redknee killed a wolf! Redknee killed a wolf!" He shouted, over and over, as he tore along the sand. Redknee cringed at the false credit.

"Stop fighting!"

Redknee turned to see Uncle Sven bearing down on them.

"We'll see how you fare in a real battle," Harold said. He tucked his dagger into his boot and scuttled off towards his father, who was overseeing the digging of the pits.

Redknee looked up to see Uncle Sven looming over him. "What am I going to do with you?" He folded his arms across his chest. "You warn me Ragnar is making an imminent attack, then I find you mucking around. Why aren't you helping with the defences?"

"I, er …"

"Look at Harold. He's helping Olaf prepare the ditches."

"I was—"

"You were just doing nothing, as usual. Go help Magnus ready *Wavedancer*."

Redknee trudged down to the beach, Silver trailing at his heels. He didn't notice Sinead walking towards him, a basket of arrows balanced on her hip, until she was right beside him.

"How's your arm?" she asked.

Redknee moved his elbow to show he could still use it. "Not as bad as I thought. Gudrid gave me a paste. It stinks of mustard, but it seems to be working."

She nodded then asked, "What did Harold want?"

She must have seen his telling off. "Nothing," he replied, ashamed.

Sinead looked doubtful. "I think you'd better watch your back during the attack."

Redknee glanced over to the pits. Harold was knee deep in mud, his skinny frame taut as he drove his spade into the earth.

"Don't worry," Redknee said. "I'll be ready for him. Besides, this is all my fault."

"With Harold?"

"No – Ragnar. If I ... if we, hadn't helped Skoggcat, none of this would be happening."

She shielded her eyes from the rising sun. "You saved a life. No one can criticise you for that."

Redknee shook his head, "Look, you won't tell anyone about it ... will you?"

"Who would I tell?"

He studied her for a moment, her face half-hidden by her hand, inscrutable. In truth, Ragnar would have found the village by himself eventually. Redknee nodded, dismissing her.

Redknee hurried down to the beach where he found Magnus pushing *Wavedancer* into the fjord. He already had a few slaves helping him. "We taking her out?" Redknee asked.

"We'll leave her just past the headland," Magnus said. "It'll keep her safe from attack. Will you follow me in a rowboat?"

Redknee took one of the rowboats and followed Magnus to the centre of the fjord. Only a couple of years older than Redknee, Magnus already had the unblinking gaze of a steersman. He guided *Wavedancer* expertly to the calmest part of the fjord and dropped anchor. Redknee brought his rowboat portside and waited while Magnus unhooked the sail.

As he waited, he ran his hand along the overlapping strakes of *Wavedancer*'s hull. Sixteen on each side – one for each summer since his birth. It was only a coincidence, but he fancied it linked them. Her keel was made from an oak as tall as twelve men. It was the longest he'd seen. Tonight was to have been her launch ceremony. They had been saving their food for weeks. He doubted it, but maybe the village would be as proud of him one day.

"Come on, dreamer."

Redknee jumped as Magnus chucked the rolled up sail into the rowboat and leapt in after it. The slaves followed, their arms filled with oars. Once they were back on the beach, they dragged all the rowboats into the shallows and filled them with rocks. Better to scuttle them than let Ragnar destroy them.

They waited. Each man, woman and child prepared as best they could. Some hid, praying to Odin that hiding places would not become graves. Hunched and tensed, their hands clutching a jumble of farm tools, rusty axes and wooden clubs. Only a few lucky men owned swords.

As the sun marched across the sky, Uncle Sven kept his lookout through a flap in the side of his longhouse, his eyes scanning for the smallest movement in the trees, his muscles ever twitching.

Redknee watched as he ran a finger along the blade of his battleaxe. If Redknee didn't know him better, he would have thought his uncle was looking forward to settling the score with Ragnar once and for all.

By nightfall, Redknee's muscles ached. He'd been crouching at the far end of his uncle's longhouse all day. Huddled between the old women and the cows, he couldn't decide whether the stink came from the shaggy-coated longhorns or the old crone whose papery skin hopped with lice. He stretched his left leg and sighed with the relief, then repeated the exercise with the right one. The old crone flashed him a toothless smile. He quickly returned to peering through a crack in the wall.

He could see across the open ground to the mantraps and treeline beyond, his eyes trained on the dark spaces between the bushes. But nothing, nothing at all, had moved in the forest and he was beginning to doubt he'd heard Ragnar correctly.

26

Then he remembered Skoggcat's words of warning and he knew, deep in his bones, the attack was coming.

People began moving about the main part of the longhouse. Redknee heard Harold's father, Olaf the Bear, challenge Uncle Sven.

"Come on Sven," Olaf said. "The boy was wrong. Ragnar isn't coming. Not tonight, not ever."

Redknee got to his feet and let himself through the wattle gate that separated the animal pens from the living quarters. The room was full of angry freemen. Redknee quickly realised they were fed up waiting for an attack none believed would come.

"Ah, Redknee," Uncle Sven said. "You finished guarding those heifers?"

The men laughed.

"What a pong!" Harold gripped his nose between his thumb and forefinger and made a face.

Redknee ignored the taunts and faced Olaf. The big man carried one of the few swords in the village. "I know what I heard," Redknee said. "Ragnar *is* going to attack."

Olaf stroked his pale beard thoughtfully. He possessed the same hard blue eyes as his son. "Why are you so sure?"

Everyone was staring at Redknee now. "As I said . . ." His voice trembled, but he squared his shoulders and spoke up. "I *know* what I heard."

"But Ragnar doesn't know this part of the coast," Olaf said. "He'd need to be lucky to find us."

Redknee pushed the image of Skoggcat running into the woods to the back of his mind. He opened his mouth, a lie already formed, but Uncle Sven cut in.

"Come on, Olaf, Ragnar is no fool. If he looks, he'll find us."

"Maybe, but doesn't the boy have a vested interest in all this?"

"How so?" Sven asked.

"His father's death."

"That was a long time ago." Sven cast an awkward glance at Redknee. "Come, Olaf, we mustn't talk about such things in

27

front of him." Sven clapped his palm on Olaf's shoulder and directed him towards the door.

Grudgingly, the villagers returned to their lookout posts. They were learning that waiting was hard.

As a second peaceful night gave way to a new day, Olaf continued to argue Ragnar wasn't coming. There was no need, he said, for the whole village to stay on alert. Eventually Sven agreed.

The village buzzed with relief as people crawled from their hiding places. Olaf said the launch ceremony for *Wavedancer* should go ahead that night. The villagers cheered – their spirits needed lifting. Sven approved the feast but quietly placed six extra men on guard duty.

From the way they scowled at him as he made his way to the feast hall, Redknee assumed most of the villagers thought he'd made the whole story up. Inside, the longhouse heaved with big, sweaty bodies. It seemed everyone in the village was there. Uncle Sven sat at the top of a rectangular table loaded with plates of boar, venison and hare. The men tore pieces of meat with their teeth; tossing the bones to the floor. The women moved about the table, bringing more food; filling the men's drinking-horns with mead.

Redknee sat at the bottom of the table, beside Koll the Smithy. Silver sniffed Koll's boots then curled up at Redknee's feet and closed his eyes. Koll smiled at the pup and slipped him a slice of ham. "Hear you killed this one's mother, he said.

"She was injured."

Koll nodded and offered him a gull egg. Redknee shook his head, grabbing a chicken wing instead. As he ate, he noticed a white-haired woman slip into the hall. He recognised her as Brynhild the Old who lived in a mud hovel, a day's walk from the village. It was unusual to see her at a feast.

Beside him, Koll peeled the gull egg, swallowed it whole and washed it down with a long slug from his drinking horn. He grabbed a serving maid by the waist. "More mead,

28

woman," he said, burping and wiping his greasy face with his hand. The slave rolled her eyes and left. He turned to Redknee.

"Bad business with that toad-licking coward. Would have liked to get my hands on his neck."

"You mean Ragnar?" Redknee asked.

Koll nodded and mimed a throttling action, his fleshy upper-lip curling with intent. "But no matter, for we put *Wavedancer* into action tomorrow. And about time too – my hands are raw with popping rivets. By Thor's hammer, the men could do with a bit of cheer."

No one had spoken to Redknee about setting sail. Had his uncle forgotten he was nearly of age?

His face must have betrayed surprise, for Koll laughed. "You really are in a world of—"

A dagger split the table beside Redknee's hand. Harold pressed his face up to Redknee's cheek. His breath stank.

"Got your trunk packed for tomorrow?" he said.

"I've … still got that to do," Redknee stammered.

"Mine is full of the best Frankish weapons." He pulled his dagger from the table and waved it in front of Redknee's nose. Redknee recognised it as the one he'd seen him sharpening the other day. It had a distinctive ivory handle carved with interwoven snakes.

"My father bought it for me when we were in Kaupangen with Sven," Harold said. "Layered steel – heated 'til it's hotter than the sun then cooled in Saxon blood."

Redknee snorted. "Aye, pig's blood, more like."

Harold flicked the blade against Redknee's throat, anger flashing in his eyes. "What was that?"

The sound of wood scraping against the floor echoed through the hall as Olaf rose to his feet. "My son," Olaf boomed from Sven's side at the top of the table. Everyone turned to watch. "Now is not the time. Save your energy for a worthy adversary."

Harold grudgingly slid his dagger into its scabbard.

Olaf looked at Redknee. "I hope you will be on the beach tomorrow to wave us off."

"With the girls," Harold sniggered under his breath.

Redknee felt his cheeks redden and hung his head lest everyone should see. He would show Harold. Just give him time.

"Now Olaf," Uncle Sven also stood. "It's not been decided we sail tomorrow."

The whole room watched Olaf's face. As Sven's right-hand-man, Olaf was usually the jarl's strongest supporter.

"But there's been no rain for weeks," Olaf said. "The lands are dry. If the harvest fails we will have to find food elsewhere."

A nod rippled through the hall.

Uncle Sven made his way down the table, placing his hand on the shoulder of each man in turn. When he reached the end, he ruffled Redknee's hair and turned to face the room. He spoke loudly so all could hear.

"Olaf, you're right to fear for the crops. But it's too soon. Ragnar could still strike. And it's not certain the harvest will fail. Why, there was a little rain only a couple of nights ago."

"Nothing but a miserable dribble!" Olaf said. "Besides, we need gold. When we were in Kaupangen last month, the price of grain was low. Even if our harvest is good, it won't be enough. The abbey at Jarrow is rich in new coin from Rome. We should raid it now, before others hear of the consignment."

"And leave our women and children alone?" Sven asked.

Magnus piped up from the back of the room, "They could come too."

"There isn't space on *Wavedancer* for everybody," Sven replied.

Redknee saw his uncle's fingers twitch round the hilt of his dagger, wary of the unprecedented challenge to his authority as jarl.

All the boys longed to know whom, out of Olaf and Sven, would win in a fight. They didn't call Olaf *the Bear* for nothing. Rumour had it he once killed a full-grown brown bear with only his hands. But while Sven was a celebrated warrior, he was an even greater tactician. He'd often used his fox-like cunning to outwit his enemies. The village boys loved to hear the story where he gained access to a walled Christian town while hidden in a coffin.

"You want to go a-Viking," Sven continued. "But the days of raiding are over for us Northmen. The soldiers of the White Christ are everywhere now. The abbeys and monasteries are not left unprotected as they once were. The King demands taxes from honest farmers. Things are not as they were when we were young. We must look to our future, to the future of our children."

"You've led many a raid before," Olaf said. "Would you deny these men the chance to find riches?"

A murmur went round the room. Redknee suspected the villagers were fed up with the hard toil of farmers – the idea of easy wealth appealed.

Uncle Sven nodded. "In my younger days, no. But look how that ended."

"It's not my fault," Olaf lowered his voice. "Nor the fault of these good men, that you lost your brother fighting Ragnar. That was a long time ago. You … we all … must move on."

Olaf addressed the gathered men. "Who will sail with me on the morrow?"

The sound of chewing stopped. Silver looked to Redknee, confused. Redknee pushed the pup back under the table.

"There is no one willing to risk their life for your folly," Sven said, turning back to take his seat at the head of the table.

"I will come with you!" Everyone in the hall turned to see Karl the Woodcutter raise his axe in the air. Short and stout, like a boar, and with a quiet manner, he looked surprised at his own outburst.

"I will come too!"

"Aye!"

A string of voices echoed Karl's. Soon half the men were standing, excitement gleaming in their eyes at the promise of adventure.

"So, we have some takers after all," Olaf said.

"You're making a mistake," Sven replied in a low voice. "Wavedancer was built for a greater purpose than stealing coin from helpless nuns."

Olaf laughed. "A great ship, for a great voyage. Is that it? Well, the Jarrow monastery is ripe for the plucking – but if you have proof of a better target, you should share it."

31

"I've only rumours to go on."

"We risk our lives for rumours now?"

"You must trust me—"

"Why, when your judgement at home is so flawed? If you think that boy of yours will lead us when you're gone—"

"You're hasty in expecting the worst, dear friend. My body is strong and my heart will beat for many years yet. As for the boy, I wish only to say that my brother's son is *my* son. And, with Odin's guidance, I have raised him as my own. But fear not. Before a boy can voyage with me he must be master of the oar, the sword, and himself."

A murmur rose from the room. Many of the assembled feared they would only pass this test on a good day.

"Too true," Olaf said laughing. "As you say, the boy is not suited to being a Viking. By the gods, we have all seen that he cannot wield a sword. Why, my own pup took him for a fool but the other day." He pointed to Harold, who grinned and nodded like a pampered cat.

Redknee shrank behind Koll's deerskin-covered shoulders. He wished Thor would strike a hole in the ground to swallow him.

A growing murmur rose from the tables. One drunk shouted, "To Olaf the Bear and his son!" A few of the men drank to this toast.

Redknee wished he hadn't come to the feast.

Uncle Sven looked shaken, but he spoke again, "It takes more than a strong forearm to be a leader of men."

"But it helps!" Someone shouted from the far end of the table.

"Let us ask the rune-reader," Thora, Koll's wife said. She put down her jug of mead and pulled Brynhild the Old forward.

Brynhild's half-blind eyes blinked in the firelight. She tapped her walking stick on the floor three times. Silence fell over the room. The reading of the runes was a serious business. "Show me the boy," she said.

Thora grabbed Redknee, pulled him in front of Brynhild and stood back. The old hag sniffed the air round Redknee's face. Then she circled slowly, closed her eyes and began chanting.

"What is she doing?" Thora asked. "I thought she was going to read the runes."

Brynhild's watery eyes flew open. "This is no good."

"She said the boy is no good!" Thora shouted.

"No, I did not say that. This place – it's no good, there are too many people—"

"Just read the runes," Thora said.

"Very well." Brynhild held a dirty leather pouch in front of Redknee. "Pick three stones."

Redknee nodded. He didn't believe any of this. Life held so many things even the gods couldn't explain. But then, he was interested to hear what she had to say. He felt inside the pouch, picked three smooth stones and placed them in Brynhild's gnarled hand.

She squinted at them. "For those of you who know your *futhark*," she began, "the first is raidō, the rune of travel. The boy will journey far." Everyone nodded solemnly, for what Viking did not travel far ... eventually?

She grasped the second stone and held it to her face. "This is fehu, the stone of wealth. The boy will have riches one day." There was a murmur of discontent, for who likes to hear of another being rich when you work the fields for twelve hours a day just to stay alive?

Olaf stood. "This is rubbish. The hag can tell us nothing. I tell you – the boy is no leader."

"Be quiet," Thora said. "The rest of us want to hear this."

Brynhild hovered over the last stone then snapped it up between her fingers. "I think you will be pleased," she said. "This is othala – the leader of men."

A cheer went up round the room and Redknee felt his heart beat in his chest like a caged bird.

"Shh," Brynhild said. "I have not finished. This stone has two sides. It can mean leader, or ... slave."

After the standoff between Sven and Olaf, the feast spluttered out like a campfire in the rain. The men who had chosen to sail with Olaf withdrew to his longhouse at the far end of the

33

village. Those who elected to stay with Sven trudged to his longhouse for a night of fitful sleep, for Sven still insisted on keeping a lookout.

Redknee slumped on a bench outside the feast hall while the womenfolk cleared the remains of the meal. It was a good spot to keep watch. The night was chilly, and he was glad of Silver's warmth curled at his feet.

"Psst. Redknee."

He turned to see Sinead poking her head round the door, an old broom in her hand. Her soft features sagged with exhaustion and her apron was splattered with drops of fat.

"What is it? Want me to lift something for you?"

"No." Sinead glanced nervously over her shoulder, then crept outside and joined him on the bench. "Look, I think I know why Ragnar really wants to attack the village. When I was kidnapped, Mord, Ragnar's eldest son – the one with the chainmail tunic—"

"I remember him."

"Well, I heard him discuss a book with Ragnar – it must be the same one Skoggcat told us about."

"I heard him mention a book too, said my uncle had it, but … I thought he was crazy. There are no books in the village—"

"Oh, sometimes I can't believe I'm *your* slave. I've seen so many books. When I worked in the apothecary at the monastery I used medical texts all the time."

Redknee was silent. Sinead had a way of making him feel stupid. After a bit, he asked, "Do you know if it's a book of healing they're looking for?"

Sinead shook her head. "The book Mord discussed with Ragnar is about a voyage by an Irish monk to an island many days sail to the West. You know, the Irish are just as good at sailing as you Northmen."

"I doubt it."

"Ragnar wants to follow the monk's voyage."

"Why?"

"The island it talks of, the one the monk sails to, the book calls it the Promised Land."

Redknee had heard of Iceland, a rocky island recently settled by outlaws and thieves seeking to escape King Hakon's new laws. He didn't think any true Northman would need a book to find it. Just sail west for several days and—

"I think we should look for it."

*"What?"* Redknee said, his voice rising. "Go find Iceland?" Silver glanced up startled. Redknee patted him on the head and he went back to sleep.

*"Iceland?"* Sinead looked confused. "No, the book, you fool – Iceland has nothing to do with it."

Redknee shook his head. "Assuming this book really is in the village, searching for it could be dangerous"

"But if we found it, we could give it to Ragnar, stop any bloodshed."

"Oh, so *now* you care about my family."

"That's unfair. I'm sorry I ever suggested running away."

Redknee shrugged. What did it matter now?

Besides, his mind kept slipping back to his uncle. Sven had been reluctant to believe him about Ragnar. Reluctant, that was, until he'd mentioned the book.

"Does the Promised Land have treasure?" he asked.

"I don't know. Why do you ask?"

"It's just something my uncle said when I told him about Ragnar."

"What was that?"

"He asked if Ragnar had spoken of hidden treasure."

"Do you think that's what Skoggcat meant when he said *'The book has more value than you know?'"*

"Maybe."

"It sounds like your uncle knows more than he's telling."

Redknee shrugged. His uncle had known Ragnar for a long time – even before he'd killed his father. Did Sven know why Ragnar wanted the book? If he did, he wasn't telling anyone.

And if Sven did have the book, he was keeping it well hidden. Redknee sighed and ran his hand through his hair. None of this made sense. His uncle couldn't even read.

"Sinead! Get back to work. There are still three boar carcasses to clear away, and ten times as many chicken bones." Redknee's mother loomed in the doorway. Despite the late hour, her corn-coloured hair was tucked neatly under a white linen cap, but her rosy skin shone with exertion.

Sinead rolled her eyes and ducked back inside the feast hall.

"Leif, why aren't you asleep?" his mother asked, taking Sinead's place beside him on the bench.

Redknee shrugged.

"You're not still worried about Ragnar?"

"I *know* he's coming."

"But it's been so long," his mother said gently. "They are old, forgotten scores."

"But that's just it, I don't think it has anything to do with the past. I think Ragnar wants something he knows we've got."

At the sight of the conviction on Redknee's face, she sighed and stared at the night sky. After a long silence, she smoothed her apron over her dress and turned to him. "I see I can't convince you. But please, if Ragnar does come, I forbid you to allow the rot of an old blood feud to infect your young life. I forbid you to seek vengeance for what happened to your father."

"But that's just it. I don't know what happened to my father, other than it was Ragnar who killed him. But why? I'm nearly sixteen, I've a right to know. You can't make me promise if I don't know."

"But Leif, darling, it's pointless to relive the past," she said, shaking her head as if to dispel the pain that burned in her eyes. "Besides, you know what happened. There was a fight over plunder. Erik ran away, and Ragnar threw his axe, which struck him in the back. It was dreadful."

"Were you there? Did you see this happen?"

She shook her head. "I was sleeping."

"But that still doesn't explain why."

"I think you're looking for reasons where there are none."

Redknee sighed. Maybe she was right. Maybe Harold and the other boys were right too when they called him son of a coward. "How could you do it?" he asked.

"Do what?" she said.

"Give me a father like that – a coward?"

36

"Oh Leif, I'm so sorry. I do hear the snide remarks. But you're nothing like Erik. He thought the world owed him something – why, he could start a fight in an empty longhouse! And he had strange ideas. Such strange ideas. Whereas you …" She studied him for a moment and he shuffled awkwardly under her gaze. "Brynhild is right," she said, nodding. "You're not meant for this place. I think that's why you're friends with the girl."

"With Sinead?"

"Oh, maybe this is just a mother talking … all mothers think their children are special, you know."

Redknee wondered if the lateness of the hour had affected her mind. "Is it Sven?" he asked.

"Is what Sven?"

"Is it because of Sven that you can't tell me what happened to my father?"

She looked shocked. "I've told you everything I know. Your uncle has been a good father to you. You must always remember that. It's not every man who will take in his brother's son and raise him as his own."

"Yes, I'm very grateful," he said stiffly. "It's just … well, I just wondered, that's all. I think Uncle Sven knows why Ragnar is coming. Has he ever shown you a book?"

"A book! Goodness me, why do you ask such a thing?"

"I think that's what Ragnar wants – a book that belongs to Uncle Sven."

"Oh dear, I think you've been spending too much time with that Irish imp. It doesn't do any good to talk about these things, you know. Bringing up the past – it can only cause harm. But I do wonder if it was the right thing to keep it."

"Keep what – a book?"

His mother fidgeted with the cord of her apron and looked away, as if she was about to return inside. Instead, she lowered her voice. "I have to finish cleaning the hall. But after that, come and find me. I have a gift … it might go some way toward helping you."

# Chapter 3

The low sun cast a cool, pink glow across the water. Redknee had slept fitfully on the hard bench. Someone had placed a wool blanket over his shoulders, but the chill had still seeped into his bones. The model of loyalty, Silver had huddled at his feet the whole night.

"You're learning where your food comes from," he said, giving the pup a gentle nudge. They ambled down to the beach together. He needed to find his uncle. He'd decided he would just ask him about the book.

Olaf's men were already up and preparing *Wavedancer* for their raid on the Jarrow monastery. They had brought her back onto the beach. She held her new dragon figurehead high, like a haughty Arab stallion. Painted red with gold leaf, her figurehead gleamed, eager to meet the smooth mercury of the fjord.

Twenty or so brightly coloured shields decorated the gunwale. Men busily loaded supplies – weapons, oars, dried food and furs. Each man had his own chest to sit on while he rowed. The chests contained their belongings and any plunder they were lucky enough to steal. Agreement as to each man's share would have been reached last night. This would depend on prowess with a sword and fearlessness in front of the enemy. The more you fought, the larger your pot.

Karl the Woodcutter shuffled across the deck, a rope coiled in his hand. He looped one end through the corner of the sail and tied the other to the gunwale. Even at sea, the big square sail could be raised or lowered in seconds. Coupled with the power of the oars, *Wavedancer* would be quick, easily able to skip over to Jarrow in two days. Maybe less.

"Not tempted to join us?" Redknee looked up to see Karl laughing good-naturedly.

"She's a fine ship," he continued. "Your uncle has done us proud. She'll be a joy to sail."

Before he could answer, Olaf appeared carrying a bundle of oars. "Where's your uncle?" he asked.

Redknee squinted into the morning sun. "Don't know," he said.

Olaf handed Karl the oars. "There's six there," he said. "Mind, I've counted them."

Karl nodded and disappeared to the other side of the deck.

Olaf turned back to Redknee. "Still worried about Ragnar, boy? It'll do you no good. Now take my lad, he doesn't waste time thinking about things that might never happen. He just gets stuck in. That's why he's coming on this raid. I know I can trust him to focus. I won't find him mooning about the woods with some silly slave girl."

Redknee stared into Olaf's hard eyes. He'd never understood why Sven chose him as his right-hand-man. Was his uncle *afraid* of him? "Do you …" he asked, "do you have something to say to my uncle?"

"Nah," Olaf said, slapping *Wavedancer's* hull with his hand. "We'll bring this slippery fish back to him in a few days. See if he still wants to go on his adventure."

"Adventure?" Redknee asked.

"You really don't know?" Olaf said.

Redknee shook his head.

"Your uncle wants to take *Wavedancer* north to the ice sea."

"Why? Is it because of a book?"

"A book?" Olaf said laughing. "You've been spending too much time alone. All that thin mountain air has fuddled your head. I've never heard your uncle talk about a book. No, I think he's dreamt up the whole trip. But I say there's no gold up there. Fat monasteries – that's where we should be going. But why do you ask? Has he shown you a book?"

"I need you now, Leif!"

Redknee turned to see his mother hurrying down to the beach, her goatskin boots slipping on the wet pebbles.

"Come on," she called, puffing heavily.

39

"Aye," Olaf said, waving his hand. "Go help your mother with her chores."

His mother led him to her weaving hut at the far end of the village, behind the feast hall. It was dark inside and she lit a whale-oil lamp. The hut was little bigger than a rowing boat, and smelled of damp wool and pine kernels. The loom stood against the far wall. A length of drab brown fabric hung from the crossbeam, the warp threads held taut by hooped stone weights. Large baskets of raw wool crowded the earth floor. She picked a small bowl off the only table and held it out.

"Take some," she said. "You'll need breakfast."

Redknee took a handful of the roasted pine kernels and stuffed them into his mouth. They'd always been his mother's favourite. He remembered her teaching him to count with them when he was little more than a babe in arms. He held out a second handful for Silver.

His mother smiled and turned towards the far wall. At first, he thought she was looking for something on the floor, then he realised she had opened a secret door beneath the loom. He peered over her shoulder and saw the door hid a shallow compartment hewn in the dirt.

She pulled out a long, thin bundle of rags. "I didn't want the men to find this," she said. "And what man ever comes into the weaving hut?"

Redknee smiled, for it was true.

She unwrapped the parcel and Redknee gasped. A blade as long as a man's leg and straight as an arrow, shone in the lamplight. The sword was the finest he'd ever seen. As he took it in his hands, heat surged along his arms and spread through his body. Every nerve tingled. He made a sweeping motion with the steel blade that seemed to split the air in two. Silver's amber eyes followed its every move.

"Was it my father's?" he asked.

His mother tilted her head to one side, studying him. "Your father used it for a while," she said eventually. "But it belonged to *my* father – your grandfather."

Redknee inspected the workmanship more closely. A pattern of interlaced copper decorated hilt and pommel. He turned it in his hand. A shallow groove ran the length of the blade, the better to collect blood and aid withdrawal from spasmed muscles.

"It's yours to keep."

"Mine? But you've heard the men, I'm no fighter—"

"You're my only child. And, much as I wish it wasn't true, I've a feeling you're going to need it. But you must promise me you will never use it in vengeance." Redknee nodded.

"No," she said. "You must say the words, for it will not be easy."

"Alright," Redknee said, shrugging. "I'll never use it for revenge. But what about Uncle Sven?"

She folded her hands beneath her cloak. "What about him?"

"He would have more use for it."

"My father didn't want it to go to Sven."

Redknee digested this. From the stories he'd heard, he couldn't understand anyone favouring his father over Uncle Sven. Strong and clever Uncle Sven who had taken Redknee under his wing as his own son and who led the village so ably. *"Why?"* Redknee asked. "Why did grandfather not want the sword to go to Sven?"

"I don't know," she said, tensing. "But it belongs with you." As she said these last words, her eyes darted towards the door.

His mother knew more, but he nodded slowly, in a kind of understanding. She had kept the sword for him – she *believed* in him. That was enough. Perhaps his grandfather had too, though he didn't remember the old man.

He thought about pushing her again for answers about his father. But her pinched face warned him not to. He would bide his time – ask her again when the time was right. Eventually, he asked, "Does the sword have a name?"

"If it does," she said smiling, clearly more comfortable with this question, "I don't know it."

Redknee held the sword aloft. Sunlight streamed through a crack in the door and reflected off the blade. "I shall call you *Flame Weaver*," he said, "after this place where you have hidden, waiting for me."

Shouts came from outside the weaving hut. "Wait here," Redknee said, pushing Silver into his mother's arms as he sped through the door.

Women and children were running for the longhouses, their faces pale with fear. Equally terrified men ran towards the approach road. He saw Magnus struggling into his leather breastplate and grabbed his arm. "What's happening?"

"Ragnar is coming," Magnus said, fumbling with a complex arrangement of straps. "Will you help me into this damn thing? My hands are shaking."

Redknee secured the tapes at Magnus's waist.

"How long?" he asked, glancing across the open ground separating the village from the forest. He got his answer before Magnus could reply.

Hooves thudded against dry earth; the riders emerging from between the trees as one. They sat high on their mounts, driving them on, their hair and clothes streaming behind them, their heavy weapons clanking at their sides. Dust enveloped the pack like a shield wall as it crossed the open ground. Ragnar pulled to the front, the morning light sparkling on his pointed helmet and breastplate. He held a shield painted red and blue on one arm, and a spear in the other. And even as his grey stallion tore across the scrub, his eyes scanned the villagers like a greedy hawk.

Redknee held his breath – if only one horse fell into the pits, their order would be broken. But Ragnar led his warriors along the curve of the road, and they charged into the centre of the village, beneath the oak, without casualty.

Redknee counted twelve heads. Skoggcat was at the rear but his brother, Mord, was absent. Redknee caught the smug look on Skoggcat's face. He had betrayed them after all.

Ragnar halted his stallion in front of the feast hall. He stood high in his stirrups, the sun pouring across his face and Redknee saw the damage the bear had done. Angry furrows scoured his cheek from brow to chin. Redknee hoped Sinead had the sense to stay hidden.

The villagers stood shoulder to shoulder, facing Ragnar's men. None had had the chance to mount, and only Magnus had donned armour.

42

Koll stood on Redknee's left, a hungry grin on his broad face. "Fun at last!" he said and winked.

Redknee shuddered in horror. He would rather be anywhere else. He felt *Flame Weaver* in his hand. His uncle would expect him to use it if things turned bad. Where was his uncle? He looked round. Sven was nowhere to be seen.

Ragnar shouted, "Sven, Son of Kodran the Wolf, brother of Erik the Fearful, I call on you to show yourself."

The villagers waited silently to see what Sven would do. For a moment, Redknee thought his uncle had run off. Then he heard the familiar deep voice and the tension in his spine eased.

"Who asks?" Sven boomed from the far side of the village. He stepped forward slowly, his battleaxe in his hand.

Ragnar pulled his horse in tight. "Come, old friend. You know me."

"I knew a Ragnar Hrolfson once. I know not this so-called Overlord of the Northlands that stands before me."

"I must speak to you, Sven," Ragnar said, his voice sweet as willow sap. "In private."

Sven strode up to Ragnar and looked him in the eye. "I've nothing to say to you."

"Come friend—"

"We're not friends. You killed my brother."

"A curious thing … such a shame he died of his wound – most unlucky."

Sven raised his axe to strike—

"Come," Ragnar said, raising his hand peaceably. "You know it was unavoidable … and very long ago. Now, will you spare a few moments for one who has travelled far to see you?"

"As I said—"

"I ride under King Hakon's colours." Ragnar pointed to the red and blue stripes on his shield. "It is on his authority that I seek you."

At this, Sven's body seemed to slacken, and he sighed. "You have ten minutes," he said. "Tell your men to dismount and hand over their swords."

43

Ragnar waved his arm to indicate his men should comply. Magnus darted forward to collect their weapons.

Sven led Ragnar to his longhouse. "Come inside," he said. "Grown men should not chatter in public like silly maids." But when Ragnar's men made to enter, Sven raised his arm to bar their way. "Just you," he said to Ragnar. "Your men can take refreshment outside."

Ragnar froze in the doorway. "My men must accompany me. I've nothing to say which they can't hear."

"Very well," Sven said, and waved to Olaf, who had been watching from the beach. Despite their disagreement, Olaf ran forward with Karl the Woodcutter and two others. It seemed Olaf was still Sven's right hand man.

"These men will join me," Sven said. "You may bring three of your men inside. The rest must wait here."

Ragnar nodded and the group entered the longhouse. The village breathed a sigh of relief as the door slammed behind them. Most went back to work, but some, including Koll and Magnus, stayed to watch the rest of Ragnar's men. And Redknee too, stayed close, for he'd seen an uncharacteristic tremble in his uncle's hand.

Magnus wiped the sweat from his brow. "That was a close one," he said.

Koll laughed. "Thought you were going to faint. You might have a year or two on this little one," he said, prodding Redknee in the shoulder, "but he stood fast, didn't you, lad."

Redknee said nothing – he'd been shaking inside.

"What's happening?" a female voice asked.

Redknee turned to see Sinead standing a little way off. He went over to her. "Did you see Ragnar's face?" he asked.

She shook her head. "I was hiding."

"You've got to stay out of sight … if he sees you—"

"But I want to know what's happening."

Redknee watched as Ragnar's men joined some of the villagers drinking mead on the beach. Koll and Magnus followed them, their weapons drawn and ready. Satisfied the men were well guarded, Redknee waited until they were settled, then whispered to Sinead, "Alright, I know how we can find out."

44

He led her into the grass at the back of the longhouse. "There's a loose board here," he said, crouching. "I used it to watch for Ragnar's men before. When no one believed they were coming."

"I believed you," she said, kneeling beside him.

"You don't count."

"Why not?"

"You were there, you *knew* they were coming. Besides, you can't fight."

"The men don't think you can fight either," she said, folding her arms across her chest. "Guess that makes you no better than me."

"Shh, they might hear us. Besides, I have *Flame Weaver* now." He pulled his sword from its scabbard.

"Where did you get that?" she asked, quickly adding, "it doesn't make you a warrior."

"Maybe not," he said. "But you might be glad I have it one day." He returned the sword to its scabbard and eased the board open. A longhorn stuck its nose through. "Away with you, stupid beast," he said, pushing it back.

They pushed their faces through the gap and stretched their necks until they could just see the men moving about the far end of the longhouse.

Ragnar spoke first. "I must raise the, ahem … *delicate* … matter of an *unpaid debt*."

"I owe you nothing," Sven replied.

"Sit down, old friend, and hear me out." Sven remained standing, but Ragnar continued anyway. "Now, if I remember rightly, your longship got to that monastery first—"

"First?" Sven sniffed. "I didn't know it was a race."

"*Come,* let's not fight over old scores. You won, after all. But I hear you went back this spring – why?"

"How do you know that?"

"Ah well, nothing, it seems, remains secret forever," Ragnar said, a sadness in his voice. "But I would like to know why you returned."

"Slaves – it's an easy target."

"Come now, you're an experienced raider. You can get slaves anywhere. There must be more to it."

"What does all this have to do with King Hakon?" Sven asked. "We're allowed to raid who we like, so long as it doesn't affect him."

"He's been baptised."

*"So?"*

"The religion of the White Christ is … different. It frowns, unfortunately, on the raiding of abbeys and monasteries."

Sven snorted. "My heart bleeds—"

"Yes, well. He believes the spoils from any religious institutions should go to a true Christian. This brings me to the, *ahem*, point of my visit. There are rumours you have … *a book.*"

"A book?" Sven asked. "What interest does a book hold, compared to gold and silver?"

"Funny question. This one tells of a land where the rocks are made of sapphire, the flowers of ruby, and every raindrop – a pearl! A land promised to the followers of the White Christ."

Sven laughed. "Pure fantasy."

Ragnar slammed his fist on the table, his tone suddenly changed. "You forget, Sven. I know what you did. And I want the plunder that's rightfully mine. I want … *the book.*"

The scrape of swords being drawn filled Redknee's ears.

Sinead's eyes widened. "They're going to fight!"

"Shh," he held a finger to his lips and listened. Silence. "Something's wrong."

"What?"

"Not sure." He looked to the treeline. Where was Mord? The question had been gnawing at him since Ragnar arrived. "Listen."

"I don't hear anything."

Silver bounded round the wall of the longhouse and began tugging at Redknee's tunic. "I'm busy," Redknee said, gently pushing him away. "Go back to my mother."

"He wants you to follow him," Sinead said.

Reluctantly, Redknee followed Silver to the front of the longhouse and stopped. Was he imagining things? No. It was faint, but unmistakeable: the sound of oars rowing across water. His eyes met Sinead's as realisation dawned – Ragnar had been *stalling*.

"Stay out of sight," he said to Sinead as he raced down to the beach, waving his arms in the air and shouting "Attack! *Attack!*" as loud as his lungs could bear.

A black warship crept from behind the headland. The villagers on the beach drew their weapons. But Ragnar's men had hidden swords beneath their cloaks and were already bearing down on their stunned hosts.

Redknee drew *Flame Weaver*, energy and fear coursing through him. *This is it,* he thought, as one of Ragnar's men charged at him with an axe. He ducked to the left and the blow screamed past his ear. He spun round, ready for the second blow.

It never came.

Koll was on top of the brute with his axe. The man's legs buckled, he stumbled forward, skidded on the wet pebbles and fell to the ground, dead.

As Redknee stared at his attacker's blank and bloodied face, everything slowed. The fury of metal on metal screeched all around him, but he was frozen in the eye of the storm. Nearby, Koll dispatched another foe, and another. Redknee shook himself from his stupor. Amazingly the villagers were winning. They pushed Ragnar's men back till the sea suckled their ankles and there was nowhere for them to go but Valhalla.

Everything was about to change.

The black longship cut through the shallows and rose onto the sand. It was then Redknee realised it wasn't painted black at all, but clad in iron. Mord stood at the prow, his sword aloft as his men leapt ashore.

"Take what you want!" he yelled, "but bring the book to me."

A horde numbering more than twenty swarmed up the beach, hacking at everything that moved. Knowing they were outnumbered, the villagers ran, sweeping Redknee along with them. But Mord's men were quick to the chase, cutting down stragglers as they flooded into the heart of the village.

47

Women and children were running in all directions. Redknee's heart slammed against his chest. It was going to be a bloodbath. He had to get to his uncle. Something was keeping him and he had to find out what. As he sped towards his uncle's longhouse, he saw Brynhild the Old felled by a blow to her stomach. The woman clawed the ground as her body breathed its last, her runestones scattered across the mud. He hoped his mother had stayed hidden.

Redknee stuck to the sides of the buildings. He passed Thora in the door of the feast hall, a stone in her hand. She was frantically trying to choose a target.

"Forget it," he said. "Just stay out of the way."

She nodded and slunk inside the building, apparently grateful to be told what to do. Redknee thought he saw a pair of hard, blue eyes stare at him from the darkness of the hall. Was Harold, the great warrior in training, hiding with the old women?

Sven's longhouse was across the yard from the feast hall. Redknee spotted a cart piled high with barrels sitting in front of it and made a dash for its cover.

As he rounded the cart, a giant with tattooed arms and black teeth blocked his way. "Where do you think you're going?" he grinned, pointing his sword at Redknee's chest.

"Nowhere," Redknee said. Trying for distraction, he asked, "What's this book Mord's looking for?"

The giant swung his sword. It just missed Redknee's face and he fell, dropping *Flame Weaver*. The giant kept coming. Redknee scrambled backwards, saw an empty barrel and pulled it into the giant's path.

Smiling, the giant brought his sword down with dizzying speed, crushing the barrel as if it were made of straw. "Damned if I know," he said amiably. "Can't read."

"Don't kill him, Toki."

Redknee turned to see Mord striding towards them.

"Why not?" The hulking brute seemed to deflate.

"He might know about the book." Mord's chainmail glistened with fresh blood. "Tell me," he said, grinding his foot into Redknee's chest, "where Sven keeps the book he stole from the Irish monastery."

"I don't know what you're talking about."

"It would be better for you if you did," Mord said.

Redknee tried to think of something clever to say, but he had nothing. Maybe Sinead had been right. Maybe they should have looked for the book.

Mord studied him with unblinking eyes. "Very well," he said. He drew his knife and pressed it against Redknee's cheek. "Have it your way."

Redknee felt his skin dampen with blood. "I already told you. I don't know where it is," he said, and spat into Mord's face.

Mord wiped away the phlegm. "You little bastard. You'll pay for—"

"Stop – I know where it is." Sinead stood nearby, her face strangely calm.

"It's that girl again," Toki waved his sword in Sinead's direction.

"Don't!" Redknee yelled to her. "They'll kill you."

"Shut up!" Mord said, kicking him in the guts. Then he turned to Sinead. "This better not be a trick."

She shook her head and started towards the weaving hut. Mord and Toki followed her.

Redknee lay in the mud, cradling his belly. He felt a cool hand caress his forehead. It was his mother. He tried to heave himself upright.

"Shh, don't move," she said, concern in her eyes.

He felt the ground for his sword.

"Is this what you're looking for?" she pushed *Flame Weaver* into his hand.

"I thought I'd lost it," he said, lurching to his feet. "I have to stop Mord. He's got Sinead." The pain in his stomach was more bearable when he had a purpose.

His mother shook her head. She had lost her linen cap and her blonde hair fell untidily round her face. "You're in no condition— " she began, then froze.

Mord had returned. He was dragging Sinead behind him, a goatskin parcel under his arm.

At that moment, Sven burst from the longhouse and stumbled into the fray. He had a gash on his left shoulder but

49

he still looked strong. Redknee felt like punching the air. His uncle had won through. Olaf and the others followed, their tunics splattered with blood. There was no sign of Ragnar. Redknee's spirits soared – his uncle had killed him. The day would be theirs.

Just then, Ragnar's blood-soaked face appeared in the doorway. He leaned against the frame, gathering his strength while his men joined him. Redknee's heart sank. Uncle Sven had failed.

Seeing his father, Mord held up the goatskin parcel and shouted, "I have served you well, father – I have the book!"

Ragnar's eyes flashed. "Do it," he called to Mord. "Do it now."

Mord nodded and turned to his men. "Burn the village!" he shouted. "Spare no-one."

A cheer rose from the attackers. Someone hurled a blazing torch at the feast hall. The straw roof caught fire immediately. Soon the whole village was alight. Those who had been hiding staggered out of the burning houses gasping for breath. Redknee gagged as the smell of cooking flesh, like roasted pig, filled his nostrils. He tore off his cloak and wrapped it round a girl with flames crawling over her skin. Pushing her to the ground, he rolled her in the mud. Her skin sizzled like crackling as the flames died.

Everything was in chaos. Through the smoke, he heard Mord shout, "To the longship! The day has been won!" and, almost as suddenly as they had arrived, the attackers disappeared. Some villagers chased them – as if vengeance could be exacted by a few lucky flesh wounds. Others looked to their own, scrabbling about for buckets, pans, anything to kill the flames.

Bewildered, blackened faces stared back at Redknee as he searched the smoke. For what, he didn't know. *His mother? His uncle?*

Suddenly he found himself beside Ragnar. The surprise on Ragnar's face quickly changed to scorn as Redknee levelled *Flame Weaver* at his breastplate.

"Out of my way boy," he said. "If you want to live to grow a beard."

Redknee adjusted his grip and rooted his feet to the ground. He wasn't going to let Ragnar pass.

"Stand back, lad." Sven said, appearing through the smoke.

Ragnar's face twitched with fear.

"Been left behind?" Sven asked, swinging his battleaxe in a figure of eight.

Before Ragnar could reply, Redknee's mother ran forward and grabbed Sven's arm. "Just let him go, Sven," she pleaded. "There's been enough killing."

"Away with yourself, woman," he said, shaking her off. "This isn't your concern."

Seeing Sven distracted, Ragnar lunged at his belly, but Redknee's mother had moved between them and the blade pierced her chest. She slumped forward, surprise and confusion in her eyes. Ragnar withdrew his sword and she staggered to the ground.

Redknee rushed forward, "Mother!" he cried, gathering her in his arms.

Blood soaked her dress and her lips had turned white. "So cold," she mouthed as her eyes flickered closed.

"Don't go!" he said, clasping her hand to his cheek.

Sven knelt beside them, his face lined with shame. Redknee looked round. Ragnar had gone.

Her eyes opened. "My son," she said, her voice cracked. "There is something I must …"

"Yes?" he leaned in, pressing his brow to hers. Her face took on a calm, serene expression. After a moment, she whispered:

"Find your father."

51

# PART II

# VOYAGE

# Chapter 4

Redknee stood, ankle-deep in mud, his tunic charred with smoke and stained with his mother's blood. He turned to his uncle. "Where did he go?"

"Who?" Sven's face was grey with shock.

"Ragnar."

"The horses," Sven mumbled and shook his head. "He took the horses."

Redknee looked at the devastation. Timber skeletons blackened the sky where once longhouses had stood. Ragnar and his men were gone. A piebald mare rooted in the dirt. It must have belonged to one of the attackers. Redknee staggered across to the mare, pulled the reins over her head and leapt onto the saddle.

"Stop!" Sven said. He reached for the mare's reins, but Redknee drew the horse away.

"This is your fault," Redknee said. "She was trying to protect you."

Sven reeled back, horror plain on his face. "It wasn't meant to happen like this."

"You knew Ragnar was coming?"

"No. Of course not. But I should've known he'd never let it rest."

"Let what rest? A fight over some stupid book? Is that it, is all this because of a book?"

Sven lowered his gaze. It was all the answer Redknee needed. He spun the mare towards the path and dug his heels into her ribs.

"Where are you going?" Sven called after him.

"I'm finishing what you began," he said, urging the mare into a gallop. "Ragnar lives and so, apparently, does my father."

Redknee took the narrow trail that followed the fjord to the sea. Low branches raked his face and chest as the piebald thundered along the treacherous path. The ground fell away steeply to his right. Below him, the water glittered between the trees.

The outline of the black ship flickered in the corner of his eye. His heart raced as the snake figurehead drew level with him, jet eyes glinting in the sun. He heard Mord shout to his men to row faster and the wooden beast edged ahead.

He had to get to Ragnar before Mord was able to come ashore and rescue him. They likely had a meeting point. A big, sandy bay, where their ugly ship wouldn't be forced to navigate treacherous rocks. He dug his heels into the mare and hunkered down. The sound of the oars cutting the water fused with the thud of the mare's hooves. Hull to nose, nose to hull, they went, each tree trunk a marker.

The mare was lazy, trying to slow, but he pushed her back into a gallop. Her rough gait jarred his bones, but soon the trees sped past in a blur and it seemed to him like the swish of the oars began to recede.

Redknee knew this coast almost as well as he knew the mountain. It wasn't far until the jumble of cliffs opened to the chalk-lined safety of Cave Bay. He pressed his heels deeper into the mare's sides. He'd played in Cave Bay as a child and an idea was forming in his head.

Only, he had to get there before Mord and his rescue party.

The path swung away from the water, rising steeply until Redknee could look down on the heads of Mord and his men. Steel helmets glittered like silver coins. They were nearing the mouth of the fjord. As soon as they reached the open sea, Mord would order up the sail and the black ship would slide through the water faster than Redknee's reluctant mount could run. His only chance was to cut across country. Aim for Cave Bay, and pray he'd guessed their plan right.

Redknee turned the mare from the path and into the woods. She hesitated at first, slowing to a trot as she picked her way through the bracken. He shouted at her, dug his heels into her sides. This was no time to be prissy. Cutting across the headland would only save time if they kept pace.

◊

They came out of the woods high above a sandy bay sheltered on three sides by white-faced cliffs. He'd reached Cave Bay. Redknee peered at the horizon; wind and rain tore at his hair. The black ship was rounding the headland. It would reach the bay soon. He'd been right, but he didn't have long. The mare puffed heavily.

"Well done," he said, patting her mane.

He dismounted and stayed low, using the yellow jewelled gorse that crowned the bluff for cover. He saw the horses first. Three brown mares and a grey stallion tied to a piece of driftwood bedded in the sand. The stallion harried one of the mares – biting her neck and kicking her legs. Ragnar's horse was vicious as its master.

He couldn't see Ragnar and his men, but the presence of the horses told him they must be nearby. As a child, Redknee had hidden in the maze of caves that pocked the soft rocks. Ragnar must be sheltering in one of those now.

Redknee crept back from the cliff edge. He would have to use his plan. He rummaged in the undergrowth. He needed to be careful; these cliffs were deadly if you didn't know what you were doing. If only he could remember—

A hole emerged from between the leaves. He pulled the grass aside and listened. Nothing but the rumble of waves.

He looked out to sea. The black ship turned into the bay; he had four minutes, maybe five. He scavenged around, tearing at roots; sticking his face into the dirt like a hungry pig. But the ground was bound tight. There were no more openings.

Yet he remembered the place so clearly – a deep chamber in the rock that led to the caves below. Why couldn't he find it now? Nettles stung his hands as he wrestled with the undergrowth. Then, beside an old rowan tree, he found a hole the size of a big porridge pot. He pressed his ear to the dark.

Laughter echoed off the walls. He'd found Ragnar. He should have remembered the rowan marker – the tree that protected against witches. Forgetting had cost vital moments.

He eased into the void. The shaft was narrower than he remembered. Or maybe he was just bigger. He pressed his feet against the wall, bracing with his back, and began shuffling down. Soon the daylight was no more than a pinprick above his head. The dark below endless. He thought about going back. Returning to his uncle to let him sort things out. But anger drove him on; his mother's final words spinning through his mind:

*Find your father.*

The father he'd never known. Been deprived of these sixteen years past. Murdered by Ragnar – she'd said so herself.

And now ...

Now nothing made sense. His past was a lie. The only thing he knew for sure was Ragnar *had* killed his mother. He'd seen that with his own eyes. And he was going to exact revenge.

Everything he'd worried about before – Harold's bullying, his uncle's expectations, suddenly it all seemed foolish. Petty. The worries of a boy.

He must have shuffled down twenty feet, maybe more. His thighs ached, his back felt raw. It had been easier when he was a boy hunting gull eggs. The chalk down here was damp and pulpy, and as he moved lower, it started to crumble beneath his toes. He scrambled against the tunnel sides with his hands, tried to dig his elbows, his knees, anything into the soft walls. But still he slipped into the darkness, his cloak twisting round his shoulders, over his head. He kicked out, fought with the wool, clawed at the walls. *Flame Weaver* got caught between his legs, he kicked it away, wedging it in the wall and gradually his fall slowed.

When he came to a stop, he had no idea how far he'd fallen. The tunnel opened above a cavern and it had been his plan to jump the last ten feet to the floor. But he needed to judge it right. Too soon, and he'd break his legs. He unclipped his cloak pin and tossed it into the void, counting *one, two, three*, in his head before he heard the telltale rattle. He gulped. *Three.* He reckoned ten feet for every number. Jumping thirty feet onto hard rock was madness. Suicide in the pitch black.

He looked at the pinprick of light above. Maybe he could climb back up. But by the time he got to the top Ragnar would have escaped. Above him, something moved across the tunnel entrance. He froze. Had one of Ragnar's men spotted him? There was no going back now. He peered into the darkness.

That meant only one thing …

Light from above pierced the tunnel, bleaching the rocks white. The flash stunned Redknee, sending him flailing blindly downwards. He reached out with his hands, grabbed at *Flame Weaver*, and was left dangling in mid-air. He heard a deep rumble. Thor was charging across the sky, wielding his hammer in anger.

Moments later, the next flash lit the tunnel. Redknee heard whinnying and looked up to see the old mare peering down. He laughed. It hadn't been Ragnar's man at all. Fear played tricks on you. Had to be conquered. Stay calm. That's what he had to do. He stuck out his left foot, there was no more rock, just air. He'd reached the end of the tunnel. Time to jump.

When the next flash of lightning came, he loosened his muscles and slid, blind, into the gloom. It was hard to land safely when you couldn't see. But he kept his knees bent and hit the floor on all fours, like a frog, tumbling into a forward roll, then the floor disappeared and he was spinning out of control through the blackness, towards the bowels of the earth, head first into hell. He braced for the impact that never came …

The water welcomed him, streaming into his nose, his mouth, his eyes. Still he fell, but slower now and he fought it. He kicked, stretched out and now he was going upwards, slowly at first, then he broke the surface, gasping for breath. Air had never tasted so good.

He bobbed in the waves, struggling to get a sense of things. He'd forgotten at high tide the sea filled the cavern almost to the brim. But it wasn't quite high tide yet – there should still be a dry ledge – leading to a way out, and, hopefully, to Ragnar.

He pulled himself from the water and felt his way in the darkness. Relief filled him as he realised he'd found a big, flat platform with a passage heading off it. He listened at the entrance and heard laughter. Ragnar was still here.

Just as he'd remembered, the walls and floor were thick with seaweed. Quickly, he gathered up armfuls of the stuff, teasing the oily yarns through his fingers, separating and flattening each strand. All the while, the storm roiled overhead, lighting the cavern as he worked. Finally, he wound the seaweed about his head and body until he was unrecognisable.

He found his sword lying on the ledge, and followed the laughter till the passage became so narrow he had to hold his breath to squeeze through. It was quieter here. The howl of the sea was far away, replaced by the tinkling of water through a thousand unseen cracks.

A flash of lightening showed Ragnar and four men sitting round a campfire in a cave beyond the passage. Redknee shuffled forward and crouched behind a rock.

"Three cheers for Ragnar!" one of the men shouted, raising his drinking horn and glugging the contents.

Redknee saw Toki, the giant with black teeth, raise his horn for a moment, before stumbling backwards and collapsing in a drunken heap. The others laughed.

Ragnar stood. "Thank you, but you brave men must take your share of the credit. And so must my fine son, Mord." The men nodded and raised their horns to this toast, while Ragnar continued. "It's true I've promised you great riches. But there's still much to do. King Hakon has charged us with unravelling the secrets of the *Codex Hibernia* and the treasure of which it speaks. We must go to a place the Christians call the Promised Land, which lies many days voyage to the west. There will be danger. But we are Northmen, and we do not shirk at the prospect of a little sea spray."

The men roared at this. As they raised their horns again, lightning struck, ripping apart the darkness. Without thinking, Redknee leapt into the light and snarled, "I am the cave troll. Thor is my master."

The men gaped in horror.

Redknee went on. "You have wronged Thor by attacking a village under his protection. He demands satisfaction."

60

"We're done for!" one of the men shouted, throwing down his horn and running away. As the others fell about in confusion, Redknee ploughed into the mêlée, swinging *Flame Weaver* before him. Lightning flashed off the blade, chased by the ever-gaining thunder.

"There's no such thing as a troll," Ragnar called. But his men ignored him, their terrified shouts filling the cave. One ran straight into the wall, knocking himself out cold. Another burned himself tripping over the fire. Redknee caught the edge of a man's cloak with his sword, scratched another's arm. One by one, the men fled, leaving him alone with Ragnar.

"Such brave warriors," Redknee said. "So skilled at butchering women and children."

A bolt of lightning lit Ragnar's mangled face. "You're not a troll," he said, shielding his good eye from the glare.

Darkness fell again and Redknee skirted past him. "How can you be sure?"

"I met one once."

"Really?"

Thunder shook the stone rafters.

"Yes … I killed him." Ragnar lunged forward, but Redknee was behind him. "Where are you? Is this some sort of magic?"

Redknee stifled a laugh. His keener eyes gave him the edge. He swung his sword at Ragnar's back. But the older man dipped forward at the last moment and the blade nicked his hair.

Ragnar spun round. The lightning came thick and fast as Redknee fended off a barrage of iron. He felt himself being pushed out of the cave, towards the beach. He tried to hold his ground, but it was difficult just meeting the speed and strength of Ragnar's blows. The mouth of the cave yawned above them, and then they were outside, in the full cauldron of Thor's fury.

Ragnar's men circled them. He heard someone shout, "It's just a boy!" The others laughed and he realised his seaweed mask had dried out. The men crowded in, banging their shields. At first Redknee ignored it. Then he tried to gain strength from their taunts. Energy crackled all around him.

61

The sea air whipped his hair and lashed his skin. He felt strength rise inside him, age-old strength. He *could* do this. He was fighting the man who killed his mother, and he would take him down.

A foot shot out from the circle, knocking Redknee onto his back. Faces teemed above him, mocking. Ragnar pressed his sword against Redknee's throat. "Who are you?" he demanded, kicking *Flame Weaver* from Redknee's hand.

"Your nemesis."

Ragnar laughed. "I like your pluck, troll boy. Reminds me of myself at your age." He flicked away the last strand of seaweed covering Redknee's face. His smile faded. "I know you. You're the boy who rescued the slave girl in the woods. Look what that bear did to my face." He tilted his cheek, showing Redknee the curdled flesh. "You'll pay for this." He signalled to two of his men. They dragged Redknee to his knees and tied his hands. "If I'd killed you in the fight," Ragnar whispered into his ear, "you would've gone to Valhalla as a warrior. Instead, I'm going to execute you like the whelp you are, and you'll go to Fólkvangr, with the cowardly and weak."

Redknee heard the scrape of a sword being sharpened behind him. He clenched his muscles for the impact and stared at the horizon. The black ship was only a short distance from the shore. Behind her, the heavens swelled like an angry bruise. The dark silhouette of a ship off her stern caught his eye. He squinted through the dim light and his heart quickened. It was following her.

*Could it be Wavedancer?*

He turned to Ragnar, who had stopped sharpening his sword and was admiring the gleaming blade. "Mord won't share the treasure with you," Redknee said.

"What?"

"When I was in the forest, I heard Mord talking about his plans. I heard him say to Toki there," he nodded toward the giant, "that once he had the book, he didn't need you. He was going to keep the treasure for himself."

"Hold your gibbering tongue and prepare to die," Ragnar said, raising his sword above Redknee's neck.

"Wait!" Redknee searched for something to say, anything. "If I'm about to die, can I ask one last question?"

Ragnar paused. "Alright."

"Did you kill my father?"

"I've killed many people, troll boy. You'll need to give me a better clue than that."

"My father was Erik, son of Kodran the Wolf."

"I didn't know Erik had a son," Ragnar said, lowering his sword. "This changes things."

# Chapter 5

The black ship rose onto the beach. Grinning, Mord leapt from the bow and splashed through the surf. He held the goatskin package he'd taken from the village high out of the water.

Ragnar turned from Redknee and opened his arms to greet his son. They hugged and slapped each other on the back. "Come now," Ragnar said, his face glowing with excitement. "Let's see the map."

"I've searched through the *Codex*," Mord said. "But there doesn't appear to be one."

Ragnar's shoulders dropped. "Then it's all been for nothing."

"Maybe not. I've brought the girl who can speak book words." Mord snapped his fingers and Sinead stepped out from behind him. The wind flattened her dress against her body and her green eyes shone like steel. Redknee looked away. She was a traitor.

"Please father," Mord said. "We must go. Sven and his men are nearly upon us."

Ragnar nodded. He dragged Redknee across the sand and aboard the black ship. "You'll be of use to me yet, troll boy," he said, pushing him onto the deck.

Ragnar left Redknee where he was sprawled and went to stand with Mord at the prow. He slung his arm casually over his son's shoulder and began giving orders to the men. Father and son looked easy together. Happy. Even murderers, it seemed, showed affection to their sons. Skoggcat hovered near them, a sunstone in his hand. On seeing Redknee he scowled, and slunk towards the stern.

As soon as Ragnar turned his back, Redknee tried to free his wrists. But the rope was bound fast. All he could do was wait. He hunkered beneath the gunwale and watched as

Ragnar's men pushed the black ship into the water. She bobbed for a moment as they climbed aboard. Then the drum started. The men rowed in time and the black ship charged, battle ready, through the surf.

Sinead scurried over and knelt beside Redknee. She had the book under her arm. "You all right?" she asked.

He ignored her and stared out to sea. *Wavedancer* was about three ship-lengths off their starboard side. He could just make out his uncle's bulky silhouette behind the dragon figurehead.

"Answer me," she said, this time grabbing his shoulder.

He spun to face her. "Good people are dead – my *mother* is dead. Did you strike a deal with Ragnar when he kidnapped you in the forest? Agree to give him the book. Is that it? Traitor!"

"No! You have it all wrong," she said, her face paling. "I gave them the book to make the killing *stop*."

"Your lies make me sick," he said, scrambling to his feet and pushing past her, but there was nowhere for him to go on a ship filled with enemies. So he turned to confront her again and froze as a lone arrow pierced the deck between them.

"By Odin's eye!" he exclaimed, gaping across at *Wavedancer* as the men prepared to release a second volley. "My uncle can't know I'm here."

"Or he doesn't care," she said.

Before he could argue, a cloud of arrows darkened the sky, blotting out the sun. He ducked under the gunwale as best he could, while Sinead huddled at his side, Mord's precious book raised above her head.

Ragnar's men hid beneath their shields and, moments later, the sound of steel tips thrumming into upturned wood drowned out the waves. Three more volleys followed. The rhythmic *whoosh – thud, whoosh – thud* only punctured by the occasional cry of the stricken. Yet most of Ragnar's men survived the onslaught unscathed. When it seemed that the last of the arrows had landed, Ragnar lowered his arrow-studded shield and called to Redknee.

"Troll boy," he said. "Your uncle thinks pissing on us will make us cry. It's time to show the old dog this ship has teeth."

65

With a nod, Ragnar ordered his men to push their rowing to full speed. The black ship cut through the water, heading straight for *Wavedancer*. Timbers groaned as the black ship rammed *Wavedancer's* starboard side, the iron hull of the black ship shattering her soft wooden boards. Iron hooks flew across *Wavedancer's* bows, binding her to the black ship in a reluctant embrace.

Uncle Sven took the initiative, boarding the black ship before Ragnar's men boarded *Wavedancer*; slashing at anything that moved with his axe. Koll and the rest of the villagers followed, met by a wall of Ragnar's men. With his hands tied, Redknee knew he was easy meat. He tried to push onto *Wavedancer*, but it was impossible.

He saw Sven wield his axe against a terrified oarsman then change direction in one smooth move, swinging his axe towards Redknee. He watched, open-mouthed, as the steel blade whizzed through the air, headed for his chest. His uncle was going to kill him and all he could do was stand and watch. Only when he looked down did he realise his hands were free, the piece of rope that had bound them curled at his feet.

"Get out of here lad!" Sven said. "You've done your bit."

He didn't need to be told twice. But before he could do anything he felt a dizzying lurch as the ships came apart. Someone had cut the hooks. Men crashed beneath the waves, still locked in combat. It was his last chance. He saw Sinead cowering amidships. An arrow pinned her skirt to the deck. He ignored her tugging. She didn't deserve his help. Instead, he seized the book from under her arm, tucked it beneath his tunic and flung himself into the air.

*Wavedancer's* side slammed into his chest. Winded, he clutched at the rail above as the sea crashed over his back. But the wood was slick and it was hard to get a grip. He felt himself being tugged below, his lungs filling with water ...

# Chapter 6

A hand reached out, pulling him up and onto *Wavedancer's* deck.

"I thought you could swim better than that, lad." Koll smiled down at him. "But I didn't know you could fly."

Redknee held the book away from his dripping clothes and squinted up at Koll.

"By Odin's eye! What's that?" Koll asked.

"Ragnar called it the *Codex Hibernia*."

Sven marched across the deck. "Give it here, lad." His uncle took the book, satisfied himself the goatskin wrapping had protected it from water damage, and locked it inside a wooden chest.

Redknee heard the patter of small feet behind him and turned to see Silver bounding across the deck. He knelt and bundled the pup into his arms.

Koll smiled. "I knew you'd want us to bring him."

"Thanks," Redknee said, as Silver covered his face in slobbery licks.

Sven grunted. "We can go now," he said, turning to the men. "Every hand to an oar. Let's teach Ragnar a lesson in seamanship."

They rowed until blisters split their hands and their arms felt like lead. And still the black ship followed; a menace on the darkening horizon. Redknee pulled his oar with every muscle in his body. In front of him, Koll did the same, his biceps flexing with each stroke. Sven ordered the sail raised, but kept them rowing, eking every last drop of speed from *Wavedancer*. She was lighter; longer than the black ship – and should have been faster – but her hull was taking in water and they daren't put into shore or Ragnar and his men would be on them like a swarm of locusts.

As night fell, and the black ship receded, Sven allowed them to take turns rowing. When his break came, Redknee flexed his stiff fingers. He felt as if his hands had been melded to his oar.

"You did well today," Sven said.

Redknee turned to see his uncle looking down at him. Blood stippled his cheeks and his brow glistened with sweat. The gash to his shoulder had been roughly bandaged. "I'll take your oar now," he said.

"I can manage," Redknee answered, adding, "You fired at the black ship when I was onboard."

Sven laughed. "When you scampered off on that old nag, I didn't think you'd actually catch up with Ragnar." He ruffled Redknee's hair. "Don't look so serious. If I'd known you were onboard, I'd never have given the order. I'm impressed, though. I can see I underestimated you, but you mustn't be so foolish in future. Now move over and let me have a go. You must be dog-tired."

"Is this it?" Redknee asked without moving. "Are these all the survivors?"

He glanced round the deck. Olaf, Koll, Harold and Karl were rowing, as was Koll's wife, Thora. Magnus held the tiller. There were a few men from the outlying farms Redknee vaguely recognised, and the Bjornsson twins. But that was all.

"A handful of women and children live," Sven said. "I sent them to old Knoffson's farm. They'll be safe there." He paused, laying his hand on Redknee's shoulder. He seemed stiff, formal. So different, Redknee thought, to Ragnar's easy way with Mord.

"I'm sorry," Sven said eventually. "I'm sorry about your mother. I'll miss her too." He took a deep breath. "Ingrid and I were … great friends. Did you know she and I were betrothed once? Before she met your father. When he died—"

"You don't care about her," Redknee said, pushing Sven's hand away. "You don't care about any of us. All you care about is that stupid book."

"That's not true."

"My mother said my father is still alive. Do you know about that?"

"Oh lad. The poor woman was dying. She was delirious; she had no idea what she was saying."

"So my father *is* dead?"

"I'm sorry if she gave you false hope. Your mother was at his funeral. Lit the burial pyre herself. There's no reason why she should think he is still alive. By Thor's blood, I saw my poor brother killed by Ragnar with my own eyes. There's no question what happened. I'm only sorry people have been so reluctant to talk to you about it over the years. We were trying to be sensitive – my brother was killed running away from a duel. I'm sorry to say that he was a coward. We wanted to spare you that – I can see now it was a mistake."

"But—"

"There *is* no secret. You have to forget what your mother said and get on with your life – live in the present."

Before Redknee could reply, Olaf came over and stuck his head between them. "Why's Ragnar so bent on chasing us?" he asked.

"You know Ragnar. Always looking for trouble."

"We're risking our lives for you, Sven. We should know why."

"They're only hounding us because of that stupid book," Redknee said, pointing to the wooden chest where Sven had locked it earlier.

"What's so special about it?" Olaf asked.

"Ragnar believes it holds the key to treasure," Redknee said. "He means to use the book to find it."

Olaf frowned. "Does your boy speak the truth?"

Sven frowned. "When I went to Kaupangen last month, an old merchant there didn't have the silver to pay me what he owed. Gave me the book instead. I laughed at first, for what would I want with a book? But he said it was worth more than all the gold in Christendom."

Olaf let out a long, low whistle. "And when were you going to tell us this?"

"What was there to tell? When I returned home, I realised how foolish I'd been and hid the book away – I didn't know until now that Ragnar wanted it. I'd come to think the stories about the treasure were just that, stories."

69

"Well," Olaf said. "I'm not dying over rumours. I say we toss it to them and scarper home. It's already soaked in blood, no point adding ours."

"Home to what?" Sven asked. "The village is gone, our families butchered. I say we find this treasure for ourselves. Must be truth in it if Ragnar wants it so bad. Think about it - avenging our dead by denying Ragnar what he most wants."

"But none of us can read it."

"Wait until you see this," Sven said. He went to the chest and, unlocking it, brought out the parcel. Nearby, the others were starting to listen in on the conversation and a small crowd had begun to cluster round them, headed by Koll and his wife, Thora.

Sven removed the goatskin wrapping. Inside was what looked like a stone block covered in decorated leather. He opened the book to the first page and a cream-white unicorn with cornflower blue eyes stared out. Redknee didn't think he'd ever seen anything more beautiful in his whole life. The unicorn sat on a bed of snowdrops and above its head were five large ivy leaves filled with gold writing that shimmered in the failing light.

"Coloured runes?" Koll asked.

"Not runes," Sven said. "It's the words of the churchmen. They spend all day copying this stuff, growing hunched and wan."

"Why?" Koll asked.

"They're rich," Sven said. "They have a powerful god. They don't need to farm. Or fight. And some clever ones have hidden the secret of their wealth in here." Sven turned to the next page; it was filled to the edges with tiny black writing. "Most of the pages are like this," he said, flipping past many more sheets bearing the same spidery hand. "But then I saw this one," he said, stopping at a page decorated with an ornate compass, the western point of which was filled in with gold leaf and bore a neat inscription in the strange script, "and knew their treasure must lie to the west."

The small band gasped.

"We've been listening," Thora said, indicating the group behind her. "And we all want to help you look for it. None of us have families to return to. What do we have to lose?"

"Aye, woman," Sven said. "I'm with you on that."

Suddenly the men were energised by the prospect of this strange book and its treasure. A chorus of "Ayes!" went up and the men began talking excitedly amongst themselves. Sven raised his hand for silence and the noise died out.

"There's nothing we can do tonight. We're tired and outnumbered. Most of us have lost loved ones. We cannot turn around to attack Ragnar, it would be suicide. We will make our repairs at sea as best we can and head for the Sheep Islands, four days sail to the west. I have a cousin there with a good farm. He will give us shelter." He glanced sideways at Olaf who was standing at the side with his arms folded across his chest. "Anyone who wants to return home can do so then."

The sea obliged for the four days and four nights it took to reach the Sheep Islands. North westerly winds fed the big square sail ensuring its belly was always full.

At night, they huddled down in sheepskin sleeping bags. Redknee shared his with Silver, glad of the extra warmth. But even in a fair wind, sleeping at sea was akin to threading a needle while on the back of a galloping horse. Redknee wedged himself between two chests, but still woke each night to find he'd been swept half the length of the deck.

He wasn't used to living in such close quarters with the others. Back at the village, his uncle's longhouse was unusual in only sleeping the three of them and a couple of slaves. He was quickly learning to keep to himself. His adventure with Ragnar and knowledge of the book had given him a sort of fame. Thora asked him repeatedly to tell the story of how he surprised Ragnar in the caves. He was growing tired of it and wasn't the only one. He'd seen Harold's resentful looks. The balance of power between them had shifted and Harold crackled like pig rind on a spit.

It didn't help that, at dawn on the third morning, Harold slipped on a hot, steaming pile of Silver's mess. Redknee had been waterproofing the boards with sheep fat when Harold

71

woke. Drowsy and barefoot, Harold stumbled out of his sleeping bag to take a pee over the rail when he stomped right through a big green turd the texture of porridge.

"Get that bloody mutt away from me," he'd said, jumping around, trying to wipe his clogged toes on the smooth boards. "Before I skin and eat it."

Redknee scooped Silver into his arms and left Harold to it. But from then on he started training the pup to go over the side.

They ate as well as could be hoped. Their bread gone by the end of the second day, they were forced to catch herring with sinew fishing lines which they cooked in a fire lit in a metal trough filled with sand. Silver helped chase the thin, scraggy seabirds that landed on deck, but he was too young and slow to catch them. Thankfully, Karl's bow didn't have the same problem.

There was a shortage of fresh water, but Olaf had loaded five skins of Koll's mead, and these were doing a sound job of keeping the men happy. Normally only allowed buttermilk, Redknee got a kick flouting Sven's rule under his nose. Not that he sought Sven's nose, mind. He did his best to avoid him. A difficult task on a longship. It seemed wherever he turned, his uncle was there, ready with advice on whatever mundane task he was doing.

Working kept Redknee sane. While the others lounged on deck playing *hneftafl* and discussing how they would spend the treasure, Redknee kept his hands busy fixing ropes, gutting fish and cleaning the boards. Work stopped his mind wandering across the wide, boring expanse of sea. Stopped him thinking about his dead mother. Stopped him wondering if her death really was his uncle's fault. But it didn't stop him plotting against Ragnar.

Always, the black ship was on their tail. At times, she dipped below the horizon and Redknee would think they'd finally lost her. But, just as surely, her yellow sail with its crimson snakehead would jut back into sight.

Good.

Ragnar would not give up easily. That was his weakness. Redknee would use it against him.

72

On the fifth morning, they passed granite rocks that rose from the water like giant swords of the sea-gods. Redknee spotted a small hovel atop one of these cliffs. "Who would live there?" he asked Koll, as he helped mend a torn piece of sail.

An old man with nothing but a piece of ragged linen wrapped round his middle had come to look at the boat from the cliff edge.

Koll shrugged. "No idea. These rocks can't supply much meat or ale." He shivered in the damp air. "You'd have to be crazy to live out here."

"He's a hermit," Sven said, coming to stand beside them.

Redknee ignored him.

"What's that?" Koll asked.

"A loner monk – who spends all day on his knees talking to the White Christ," Sven said.

"That one looks like he needs fattening up – and the company of a good woman, if you know what I mean." Koll winked and jabbed Redknee in the ribs. "His God can't be up to much. Not a patch on Thor, if you ask me." The smithy rubbed the hammer pendant he wore around his neck and slunk away, leaving Redknee alone with his uncle.

"Your mother came here once. To the Sheep Islands, I mean. Not to these meagre rocks."

Redknee spun on his heels. "Don't you speak of her! It was your book that got her killed!" The words, festering on his lips for days, exploded off his tongue.

Sven began to reply, when the lookout called, "Land Ahoy!" and everyone on the ship strained to see.

Redknee pushed past his uncle. Three mountains stood proud against the sea, their peaks helmed in mist. Rough meadows, peppered with black-faced sheep, swept down to a wide, silver beach where a single longhouse surrounded by outbuildings nestled in the dunes.

Yet there was not a soul to be seen.

# Chapter 7

A man ran across the beach towards them, his dark cloak flapping in the wind. Sven drew his sword and the others did the same. But the lone man kept coming, unaffected by the slicing rain or the steel of the welcome party. As the man neared, Redknee saw his avian features stretch into an enormous grin.

"Sven!" he shouted, his words carried by the wind. "I can't believe it! How long have I waited for this visit?"

Sven lowered his sword and embraced the man in a bear hug. "Ivar! My cousin. How long has it been?"

"More than sixteen summers," came the quick reply. "Too long – I'm no longer a young man. I won't be able to keep up with you."

Sven laughed. "It *has* been too long. But you speak ill of yourself. You're no old man. And it was *you,* not me, who thought up pranks to torment the wenches!"

"Ach! Little boys' games. Matilda won't allow them now." Ivar batted the air with his hand. "But tell me, what brings the great Sven Kodranson to my little island?"

"Bad news. Jarl Ragnar burned our village. Ingrid is dead."

Ivar's face paled. "I'm sorry—"

"He's chasing us. I fear, if you give us shelter, he'll attack you too."

Ivar squinted at the horizon. "I see the top of a sail."

"That's Ragnar's ship."

Ivar looked thoughtful. "Matilda won't like it, but I know where you can hide. It'll be like old times! Come on boys. There's no time to waste."

Ivar leapt aboard *Wavedancer*, an excited gleam in his grey eyes. He directed them through a channel at the far end of the bay, hidden on all sides from the sea. They sailed north until they reached a canyon of polished basalt. It was as if Thor himself had slashed a path through the cliffs. Ivar pointed to the opening.

Olaf scowled. "We'll be dashed to pieces."

"I'll show you how," Ivar replied.

Sven nodded and ordered Magnus to guide them into the canyon. The cliffs grew, looming overhead until they almost touched, making the sky seem a long, long way off. There was no room for oars. The water was strangely tranquil and *Wavedancer* stalled, unable to go on.

Ivar perched on the rail and pushed against the rocks with his feet as if he was walking sideways. "Now boys," he shouted. "Copy me."

They squeezed along like a great millipede, each man shuffling an inch at a time. Yellow-beaked gulls circled overhead, attracted by the gentle slap-slap of water as the ship edged along the canyon. After a while, Redknee's backside grew numb. He dropped his legs and rocked from cheek to cheek, easing each buttock in turn.

"No slacking!" Sven shouted down the line.

Harold sniggered from his lookout post.

Redknee resumed pushing off from the rocks. He'd got his uncle his precious book, what more did he want? Couldn't he just leave him alone for once?

"Beach ahead!" Harold's tinny voice called out.

Redknee craned his neck. A short way off, the canyon widened to a lagoon framed by amber sands and high, vine-clad walls. No sound from the sea breached this citadel. The men whispered, as if afraid to waken some ancient monster long hidden beneath its emerald depths. Magnus guided the ship to the beach and they spilled onto the sand.

"This lagoon can only be entered from the sea, or by that path," Ivar said, pointing towards a wall of twisted vegetation that rose from behind the beach.

"We'll have to swim out," Olaf said. "And we'll be killed doing it."

Vines as thick as a man's arm slithered up the bank in a knotty dance, but Ivar just drew his sword and charged forward. "Time to work up a sweat, boys!" he said, diving into the fray and hacking wildly.

75

Redknee tore at the vines with his hands, while Silver barked at his feet. Soon his fingers were drenched in blood and sap. A short way off, Harold chopped methodically with his ivory-handled dagger.

"What happened to your sword?" he sneered. "A big boy take it away?"

"I don't need a weapon to fight a plant," Redknee replied. But losing *Flame Weaver* gnawed at him. Just one more thing Ragnar had taken.

They continued for some time, slicing and tearing at the vines as if they were the corpse of some loathsome dragon. Ivar broke free first, closely followed by Redknee.

Visibly exhausted, Ivar plunged his sword into the ground. "I'm not as strong as I used to be," he said, shaking his head, then added, "You're like her."

"Who?" Redknee asked.

"Ingrid – same sandy hair. Same blue eyes. Same chin. Would've recognised you even if you'd turned up without Sven."

"Did you know her?" he asked, desperate to hear any crumb about his mother.

"Ah, she was a fine woman. An accomplished swordfighter in her own right, you know. Now, take my Matilda, while she's—"

Sven stumbled through the overgrowth. "What's that about your Matilda?" he asked, joining them.

Ivar hesitated. "My Matilda … that's right. She's a good cook. Best on the island." He started to walk away then paused. "You'll need those seen to," he said, indicating Redknee's bloodied hands.

Smoke rose from Ivar's farm. "Ah, my wife is cooking!" Ivar said, rubbing his belly.

Koll licked his lips. "A home-cooked meal," he said, starting down the hill towards the smoke.

"Wait!" Sven shouted. "Ragnar and his men may be there."

Ivar reached for his sword.

"Not yet, Ivar," Sven said gently. He turned to his men. "We need a volunteer to check the farm."

76

Redknee stepped forward. "I'll go."

"Don't be daft, lad," Sven said. "It's too dangerous."

"I'm the fastest on my feet. I'll be there and back before you, or anyone else, know about it." He didn't add that he'd spent a lot of time creeping around recently and was getting good at it. Besides, if Ragnar was there, he wanted to be the first to know.

"The boy's right," Olaf said.

"Ah ... very well then," Sven said. "But mind and take care. I don't want to have to rescue you again."

Harold sniggered.

"I didn't see you volunteer," Redknee called over his shoulder to Harold as he ran down the hillside, Silver scampering at his heels.

He hunkered down as he neared the longhouse. Apart from the blueish wood smoke coming from a hole in the turf roof, there was no sign of life. Heart sinking, he pressed his body flat against the longhouse wall and peered round the corner. A young boy sat in the yard playing with a tabby cat. Seeing the cat, Silver made as if to yelp. Redknee grabbed his snout and held his finger to his lips. The pup seemed to understand. Redknee exhaled slowly.

He squinted through a crack in the wall. Grain sacks reached the ceiling. Ivar was well prepared for winter. Redknee shuffled further along towards the living quarters. The door of the longhouse was ajar. Careful not to attract the toddler's attention, he crawled over and squinted into the dark interior. He expected to see Ragnar holding the women hostage. Instead, he saw a pair of thick, bear-like arms pour steaming water into a wooden tub.

*Had Ragnar demanded a bath after his days at sea?*

He waited as the woman sprinkled herbs on the water and pinned her hair behind her ears. The scent of myrtle reached his nose as she began to unclip the copper brooches securing her pinafore. Suddenly he realised the *woman* was bathing. Not Ragnar. Panicking, he stumbled backwards, knocking over a barrel of water. A group of startled brown geese flew, squawking, into the air.

77

All round the yard, people appeared. Hard eyes staring. He tried to explain but when he opened his mouth nothing came out. A shadow passed over the sun. He looked up to see the bear-woman glaring down at him. She held her under-dress tight about her sturdy body, her eyes bulging with fury.

"You were watching me as I took my bath," she said, her fist mashing into his cheek, not waiting for a reply.

Laughter rang in Redknee's ears as he tried to dodge her anger, but the blows came fast and he was slow to his feet. He heard Silver barking, but the pup was no match for this brute of a woman.

"Someone stop her before she kills him!" The voice came from across the yard. It sounded distinctly mocking.

A hand grabbed his ear, pulling him upright. The brute had him against the wall now, her stale breath curling his skin as she barked insults into his face.

"I wasn't looking at you," he managed to whisper through the onslaught. "Ivar sent me ... to make sure the farm ... hadn't been attacked." This seemed to have a moderately calming effect, and she loosened her grip while she digested this information.

"How do I know you're telling the truth?" she asked.

"Because I confirm it," Ivar said hurrying across the yard, followed by Sven and the rest of the men. He turned to Redknee, laughter twinkling in his eyes. "I see you've met my lovely wife."

That night Ivar ordered the slaughter of two fine black-faced sheep and they feasted with Ivar's family in the warmth of the longhouse until their bellies ached. Matilda reluctantly forgave Redknee's spying although she still cast him an evil look whenever she didn't think her husband was watching.

After the feast, Redknee lazed on the rushes in front of the fire, Silver curled across his stomach. Matilda's skill had not been exaggerated, and the taste of fragrant meat still lingered on his tongue. Stewed fish and scrawny sea birds could not compare to land food. He half listened, eyelids slowly closing, body still rocking to the rhythm of the sea, as Sven told Ivar the story of Ragnar's attack.

78

Ivar waited until Sven finished, and asked, "So why don't you just give Ragnar the book and be done with it?"

Uncle Sven sighed. "It's not so simple. Ragnar is working for King Hakon. I fear he will have our heads on a spike no matter what we do. We're behind with our taxes. We've lost our homes and families. We've nowhere to go. If we give Ragnar the book, what hope would we have?"

"But you can't run forever. It's not like old times. King Hakon has men everywhere."

"I know. The only thing I can think to do is to keep going west, to Iceland. I think that's what the book wants us to do. We'll leave first thing in the morning so as not to put you and your family in any more danger."

"My daughter is in Iceland," Ivar said. "Astrid married one of Iceland's great lords. He has his own differences with King Hakon. And she'll give a warm welcome to any friend of her father's. Iceland's a big place. You could over-winter there while you decide what to do."

"What to do?" Olaf cut in. "We should go home. Anything else is madness."

Ivar looked thoughtful. "I have something I want you to take to my daughter. A gift, if you like."

"We've little room on the ship for such things," Olaf said.

Ivar smiled and clapped his hands.

A small, stooped man in long brown robes hobbled into the room. "I'm not here to join your pagan rituals," he muttered. "I've told you this before."

Ivar laughed. "We have guests, Brother Alfred."

The monk peered round the fire-lit hall. "More heathens, no doubt."

"Brother Alfred was on his way to convert the Icelanders to Christianity, but got lost and ended up here. We didn't tell him he wasn't in Iceland for nearly two months."

"Most uncharitable," Brother Alfred sniffed.

"So, Sven, will you repay my kindness and take this fool with you? My family have no use for him. The boys merely throw stones … and I won't even tell you what the girls do!"

Sven nodded, a look of satisfaction glinted in his eye.

79

Redknee took a gulp from his drinking horn. It would be a *long* journey to Iceland.

Later that evening Sven let Brother Alfred examine the *Codex Hibernia*. The little monk's eyes lit up when he saw the picture of the unicorn with the five ivy leaves above its head.

"Does it say how far we should sail to the west?" Sven asked.

The little monk nodded enthusiastically. "Yes, yes. It says right here," he said, pointing to the page opposite the picture of the unicorn. "Oh, now, this is very complicated language. But it says the treasure you seek is buried in a land far to the west. Er, with high mountains and er, green forests and er, big rivers." He looked up from the book, his pale features all squashed and serious in the firelight. "Are you going to take me away from this godforsaken place?" he asked.

"If you help me find this treasure," Sven said.

"Oh, I can do that," the little monk replied. "So long as you take me with you."

After they had looked at the book for some time and Sven was satisfied the treasure did indeed lie further to the west, he took the book from Brother Alfred and locked it away in one of the oak chests at the back of the longhouse.

Everyone dozed together, head to foot in a circle round the fire. Sleep eluded Redknee. He wanted to ask his uncle why he'd hidden the book if he hadn't thought it valuable. But he hadn't had the chance. Instead, he filled his time trying to block out the sleep noises of the men, and when the grunting and snoring and farting became too much he quietly let himself out of the longhouse. Silver followed him down to the beach.

"Hey there little one," he said, ruffling the pup's thick collar. "I suppose you couldn't sleep either."

Silver dipped his head in what Redknee took to be agreement.

"You and me both," Redknee said, selecting a smooth round pebble from the sand and skimming it across the still water of the bay. It bounced four times before disappearing beneath the surface.

"So much for that," he said. "You know what I don't understand?"

Silver gazed up at Redknee with dark, golden eyes.

"Well, what I don't understand is this – I'd never heard Uncle Sven even mention the *Codex Hibernia* before, and now he knows all about it. He's determined to find its treasure, that's for certain. No matter what the cost. And he knew the book was valuable before Ragnar came, otherwise why would he have kept it hidden?"

"I used to be good at that."

Redknee spun round to see Ivar standing in the moonlight, a flat, grey pebble between his thumb and forefinger.

"Shall I see if I can beat you?"

Redknee nodded, though he hadn't really been trying before.

Ivar snapped his hand back and sent the pebble skating over the water, it bounced once, twice, three, four … five times before plopping beneath the surface.

"Bad luck," Ivar said. "You know, I used to do this with your mother, the summer she came to stay with us."

"Why was she here?"

"You know, I can't really remember, but I think she was expecting you."

Redknee wasn't sure why, but he felt himself blush. "You were going to tell me something about her back at the lagoon, before my uncle came upon us."

"Oh, that. It was nothing. Only that my daughter, Astrid, has something that once belonged to your mother. When Ingrid was here, she spent time with Matilda, embroidering. They made beautiful things – caps, gloves, belts, everything. But your mother had a special talent. She gifted Astrid, who would only have been one or two at the time, a lovely cloth decorated with flowers. When Astrid married, she took it with her to Iceland, but I'm sure she would let you have it. Considering."

"Thanks," Redknee said, not sure what else to say. "I'll ask her when we get there."

81

"Jarl Ivar!" A shepherd boy ran towards them from the direction of the hills. He had a bow in his hand and his face was pink with exertion. "They're here!" he shouted.

"Where?" Redknee asked, his heart pounding.

"At Whale Bay," the boy said, trying to catch his breath. "Hundreds of them!"

"Let's go," Redknee said to Ivar, "while we still have the advantage." He charged towards the longhouse to wake the others, but before he went more than five steps, the door flew open and Sven burst out dressed in full armour, his battleaxe in his hand.

Redknee turned to Ivar. "How far is Whale Bay?"

"We can row there before sunrise," Ivar replied. "But it's not Ragnar this shepherd boy comes to warn us of ... but the *gungiger.*"

Redknee must have looked confused, because Ivar explained, "*The gungiger* – the little whales."

Sven visibly relaxed, sliding his battleaxe through a loop on his belt. "You're going on a whale hunt?" he asked.

Ivar nodded then turned to the shepherd boy. "Have you told the other farms?"

"Yes ... I've lit the beacons."

Sven tensed. "Ragnar will see them."

Ivar looked thoughtful. "But he won't know to what ... or where we go."

Koll came up beside Sven in the doorway. He was also wearing his leather armour and carrying his axe. "Fresh meat for breakfast!" he said, grinning. "And if Ragnar shows up, we'll cut him down in the shallows with the whales." He emphasised this with a series of crude slashes.

Sven nodded and stood aside to allow the rest of the men, who had now woken and dressed, to filter into the yard. Redknee went to stand beside them. He had no weapon for the hunt save the eating knife Matilda had given him. But when Sven saw Redknee he motioned for him to go inside.

"You should let the boy join us," Ivar said. "It will get him used to killing."

"It's too dangerous. He needs to learn the difference between being brave and being downright foolish."

82

"But he's the son of a great warrior—"

"We do not speak of that," Sven snapped. He turned to Redknee. "You stay here and guard the *Codex*."

Redknee waited until the rowing boats bobbed out of sight. Everyone had gone, even the women and children. But not him. No, he had to stay and watch the stupid book. He kicked a pebble, watched as it plopped beneath the surface of the water, then he turned, head bowed, to go back inside the longhouse, Silver trotting quietly at his heels.

Damn his uncle for refusing to allow him on the whale hunt. His uncle's censure echoed in his head. *He needs to learn the difference between being brave and being downright foolish.* His cheeks reddened. Downright foolish. That's what his uncle thought of him chasing Ragnar.

He turned to Silver, who'd already settled himself by the dying fire. "But I nearly killed Ragnar," he said. "*And* I got the book, didn't I? Eh, little pup? What's so foolish about that?"

Silver looked up, a quizzical expression on his face. Cursed book. He was with Olaf there. They were never going to find the treasure, even with Brother Alfred's help. Sven was an idiot for even trying.

If only he hadn't grabbed the book from Sinead. Let Ragnar piss away time looking for some poxy treasure. By Odin's eye, it probably didn't even exist. *They* should be avenging their dead. First Ragnar then King Hakon. Nothing foolish in that.

The longhouse stank of sweat and mead. He joined Silver beside the fire, giving the embers a prod with the toe of his boot. It would be a long night. Suddenly, he wanted another look at the *Codex*. When Brother Alfred had been turning the pages, he'd seen the picture of the unicorn again, with its cornflower blue eyes and gold mane. Next to it, the pages with words looked drab. But it wasn't just that. There was something very real about the unicorn, its sad eyes staring from the page, as though ...

Redknee shook his head. He was going mad if he thought that. As mad as his uncle. He raked the fire with his toe again, orange sparks danced in the half-light. His stomach grumbled. If he looked, maybe he could find some leftover bread.

He got to his feet, but even as he started to shuffle round the room, he knew he wasn't looking for food. It was the eyes that troubled him. They were beautiful, yes, but it wasn't that. It was the way they looked as if they held a secret.

He found the chest against the back wall of the longhouse. He tried the lid, but found it locked. He supposed it made sense.

"You stealing?"

He spun round to see the shepherd boy staring at him. Silver trotted over and started sniffing the boy's mud-caked boots. "No … I thought I was alone."

The boy had a quiver full of arrows slung over his shoulder and he carried a slender yew-wood bow in his hand. He smiled.

"Clearly."

"Actually, I was looking for the book my uncle put in here. But it's locked."

"I see," the boy said. "Don't you want to go on the hunt?"

"My uncle said I should stay."

"Oh. I suppose that's that then."

"Why haven't *you* gone?" Redknee asked.

"I was just leaving."

The boy didn't move. He was smaller than Redknee, thinner, but Redknee reckoned they were about the same age.

"Well," Redknee said. "Don't let me stop you."

"My name's Olvir," the boy said. "I can show you where they've gone."

Ivar's advice about killing came back to him. If he was going to take his revenge on Ragnar, he'd need to do a better job than he'd done at the caves. He'd killed before – fish, chickens, a pig – nothing that would actually fight back. And what, after all, did he care about guarding the book?

"Alright," he said. "Show me."


The rowing boat slid through the calm sea like an eel. Redknee had left Silver at the longhouse with strict instructions to behave. The pup had whined a little, scraping his paws down the inside of the longhouse door as he'd been shut in, but

84

Redknee was firm. Silver was still too small for the dangers of a whale hunt.

Olvir proved an excellent navigator, for a shepherd, and they came upon the other boats while the moon was still full in the sky.

The rowing boats formed an arc closing off the head of a shallow bay. Beyond them, flumes of water spurted into the air.

"Whales," Olvir said, pointing to the spurts. "The men will circle them and drive them ashore. No one will see us if we join the end."

Redknee nodded. Soon boats arrived from the other farms and they were lost in their number.

The boats crept forward in tight formation, forcing the whales towards the beach. As many as a hundred of them thrashed in the surf, each as long as four men, their waxy black fins catching the moonlight, churning the water to a milky soup. One tried to escape by smashing its tail against their boat, knocking Redknee flat. They were going to capsize. But a man waded over, plunged a long metal hook into the whale's shiny skin and dragged it into line.

When they were only yards from the beach the men leapt into the water and dragged as many of the whales ashore as they could. Redknee and Olvir copied them, but without one of the long hooks, they couldn't gain purchase on the whales' smooth contours.

"Here," a toothless old man said, handing Redknee a spare hook, "stick the metal end in the blow hole and pull. That'll hook 'em good and tight." He laughed. "Hook 'em … get it?"

He waded off, still chuckling at his own joke. They took turns hooking the whales and dragging them ashore. Redknee felt the muscles in his arms and shoulders being worked.

When there was no space on the beach, the men took out their knives. With probing fingers, they felt for the jugular vein and sliced it open. Blood seeped into the sea, weaving round Redknee's legs.

Olvir's face drained of colour.

"What's wrong?" Redknee asked.

Olvir didn't reply, instead he fell forward, disappearing beneath the surface of the waves. Redknee shot over, hoisted him up and carried him ashore, laying him on the sand. His face was grey, expressionless. Redknee lifted his head and slapped his cheek. Olvir spluttered awake.

"I thought you were dead."

Olvir reddened. "I hate the sight of blood."

"No slacking, boys!"

Redknee turned to see Ivar shouting at them. His tunic was soaked in blood and splats glistened, like pimples, on his face.

"We've got to make this harvest before sunrise." He squinted in the half-light. "Is that Olvir?" he asked. "Faint again?"

Olvir nodded.

"You stick to your bow and arrow, son," he said, shaking his head and wading back into the sea.

"I've failed," Olvir held his head in his hands. "Ivar will never let me go on another whale hunt."

"Why did you come when you knew there would be blood?" Redknee asked.

"I *so* wanted to prove myself."

"Look," Redknee said, his voice softening. "I think it's best if you wait here for a bit. Keep an eye on those dunes," he pointed to the low grass-fringed hills behind them. "Ragnar is out there and all this noise is going to attract his notice."

Olvir nodded. Redknee left him and made for the water.

Stupid boy, nearly getting himself killed just to impress Ivar. It was an insult, being left to nurse such a … a weak-stomach. Anger coursed through Redknee's veins as he grabbed the nearest whale, tilting it onto its back to reveal a snow-white belly. This would be easy. He'd seen the men do it many times. He placed his knife between his teeth and let his fingers probe for the jugular. But everything under the coarse, blubbery skin felt the same.

A short way off, Harold and Olaf hacked frenziedly at the remains of a large bull, their blood-splattered faces twisted with pleasure. Redknee looked away in disgust. There was a skill to this that meant the beast didn't have to suffer. He gripped his knife firmly, readied himself to make a good clean

86

cut, but at the last moment, he saw his face reflected in a big glassy eye, and hesitated. The whale fluttered her dorsal fin and a tiny calf darted from under her, twisted between his legs and disappeared out to sea.

Nausea rose in his throat. He fought it down. He would *not* be weak. The muscles in his arm extended and jerked back as if some outside force controlled him. Her skin made a ripping noise. Blood stung his eyes; he fought to contain the spurts by pushing her beneath the water. The wound bubbled, fizzed, died. He let her bob back to the surface. Her white belly had turned salmon-pink and she felt limp. He wiped the blood from his eyes and began to move quickly, slotting the hook into her blowhole and pulling her onto the fat-soaked beach. He skidded on some yellow gore and lay exhausted on the sand, little pieces of flesh and guts crusted to his face.

Scavengers circled overhead. Little children ran along the beach batting them with oars. This sea-harvest was vital for the island. Ivar would divide the kill equally among the many farms. Every part of the haul would be used, and the black meat would feed them through winter.

The whales hadn't stood a chance. Their bodies lay along the beach in neat lines. Battle dead. Their black livery shining in the fading moonlight, each with a stripe of honour cut into its breast. Redknee had never seen or smelt so much death in one place. Not even when Ragnar had come to his village.

He sat up and scanned the low hills enclosing the beach. Clumps of silvery grass blew in the wind. There were no trees. Not even in this sheltered bay. A shadow flickered between the dunes. A moment later, a lapwing waddled out. He rubbed his eyes. Tiredness was playing tricks on him.

He found Olvir sitting on his own some distance from the others, his head in his hands. Redknee hunkered down beside the shepherd boy.

"It's not your fault if you can't stand the sight of blood."

"I'll always be left alone with those damn sheep if I can't fight like a man."

There was nothing brave about the dispatch of the whales. Still, though, he recognised the outsider in Olvir.

"I'll bet you're a sure shot with your bow."

87

Olvir sniffed. "Yes ... but the others say it's a coward's weapon. You don't get up close. Don't see the blood."

As Redknee listened, he saw a figure move between the dunes. This time he wasn't imagining things – it was the clear profile of a man. He motioned to Olvir to get down as, a moment later, a hail of arrows purred through the air and landed on the sand. A group of more than twenty heavily armoured men charged from behind the dunes towards the main part of the beach where the others were dismembering the carcasses.

Ivar and the other farmers mustered quickly, meeting the attackers blow for blow. Not one to be left out of a fight, Sven was fast to wade in, crunching flesh and bone beneath his axe.

"Should we help?" Olvir asked.

"We're unarmed ..." Redknee said through gritted teeth. "We should stay where we are."

Olvir picked up a stone. "I'll never be a warrior," he said, pulling back his arm to throw it.

"No!" Redknee said, catching him. He took the stone from between Olvir's fingers and chucked it away. "I've another idea." He grabbed Olvir's wrist and pulled him towards the bloodied water. "If you know this island so well, you'll know where Ragnar has left his ship."

# Chapter 8

They came upon Ragnar's camp in a secluded bay as the first streaks of dawn stained the sky. High, jagged rocks protected the bay on three sides, affording only a narrow opening to the sea. The black ship was anchored in the shallows. Without Olvir, Redknee would never have found such a perfect hiding spot.

"I'm afraid," Olvir whispered as they snuck ashore under cover of a rocky outcrop.

"I was afraid once too ..." Redknee said, sliding his eating knife from his belt, "... still am. But just think of it like looking for one of your lost lambs. You might come across a wolf, but it's still got to be done."

"But there's so many of them."

"It's easier if you don't think ... hang on, what do you mean?"

Olvir stabbed a dirty finger in the direction of the camp.

Redknee paused to take a proper look. He'd been so busy staying quiet as he docked the rowing boat and crept ashore that he hadn't surveyed the camp. About twenty men lay in fur sleeping bags round a fire.

"How did they get back so quickly?"

Olvir shrugged. "Maybe they were never at Whale Bay."

"That wasn't Ragnar who attacked us?"

"Ivar has a running feud with the jarl of a nearby island. They're always fighting over the whale harvest. They used to split the haul. But the other jarl said he should get more because it was harder to raise sheep on his piddling rock. Said his family would starve."

"What's Ragnar been up to while we've been playing at fishermen?" Redknee asked worriedly.

Olvir shrugged. "What about your plan?"

"Its not going to work now, is it?"

89

"How should I know? You never told me what it was."

Damn right, Redknee thought. Competent navigator, maybe, but Olvir was no strategist. "By Thor's hammer, you're even more annoying than the girl."

"What? I found this place for you. It's not my fault I can't stand blood."

Redknee bit his tongue before he said anything he'd regret. One wrong move and they'd have the whole of Ragnar's mini army on them. He eyed Olvir as he cowered behind a lump of granite. Maybe the boy just needed a chance ... someone to give him confidence ... someone to believe in him.

"You know ...," Redknee said gently. "It's not the sight of blood that makes you faint."

"It is."

Redknee shook his head. "That's just what you've been told."

"I'm thinking about blood now, and it's making me queasy." To emphasise this point, Olvir swayed a bit and reached out to support himself against the rock.

"Don't be daft," Redknee said. "If you tell yourself you'll be fine, then you will be."

Olvir looked thoughtful. "So ... you're saying if I try and forget about blood and guts and gore ... and all that stuff ..."

Redknee nodded.

"... then I won't faint... and I'll be a great warrior!"

Redknee hesitated. "I wouldn't say it will happen at once—"

"Alright!" Olvir's eyes shone with excitement. "I'm ready to take on Ragnar and his men single ... sorry, double-handed."

Redknee sighed. "We should bide our time ... wait for the right moment."

"But look, they're leaving."

Redknee looked over at the camp. Olvir was right. The men were standing, rolling up their sleeping bags and getting their weapons together. He watched as they began marching towards the hills, leaving the black ship guarded by a sleepy looking Mord and Toki who'd already resumed their places by

90

the fire. Now was indeed the time to strike. He'd show his uncle he was good for more than guarding a stupid book.

"Where are they going?" Olvir asked.

Redknee shrugged. "I don't know."

"What about your plan then?"

"Oh. It's quite simple. All we need are some sheep. Think you can find me a few of those?"

Olvir nodded. "If there's one thing I know about, it's sheep."

"What's that infernal bleating? Toki rubbed his eyes and sat up.

"It's just some herd passing," Mord said. "Go back to sleep."

"I fancy some mutton," Toki said, staggering to his feet. "You coming?"

"Can't you kill a lamb on your own?"

"If I do, I won't share it."

"One of these days I'm going to have you beaten for insolence," Mord said, sighing. He put down the piece of bone he'd been carving and picked up his sword. "Not sure I should leave the girl," he said, glancing to where Sinead slept near the fire, her hands tied behind her back.

"Bah, she'll be fine … get it?"

"What?" Mord frowned.

"Never mind," Toki said, leading the way towards the dunes and the bleating. "Anyone would think you're sweet on that girl."

"Don't be stupid … I need her, that's all."

"That's what they all say."

Redknee watched as first Toki, then Mord, disappeared behind a grass-fringed dune and out of hearing. It was time to make his move. He looked to where Sinead lay on the sand; someone had given her a rolled up tunic to prop her head, and her chest rose and fell in the slow rhythm of sleep. Waking her would risk alerting Mord and Toki. Besides, she seemed to be doing just fine on her own.

91

He scuttled across the sand on all fours like a crab. The black ship sat high in the water, buoyed by the gentle swoosh-swoosh of surf. Jet eyes stared down at him from the snake figurehead, all-seeing, like Odin's ravens. He shuddered. Still, as precious stones, they might be worth good coin. He would remove them with his knife later.

Moving quickly, he dislodged the anchor, gave the ugly iron-clad bow a mighty push and scrambled on board. Olvir's diversion wouldn't give him long. With some effort, he raised the big square sail, but the morning was calm and it sagged wearily against the mast.

He eyed the oars. He could never row such a large ship out of the bay on his own. He glanced towards the dunes. What was keeping Olvir?

A scuffling sound came from the other side of the hull. Olvir's call was the *churr-churr-chirruc* of the reed warbler. He heard the clank of metal against wood, the soft thud of leather boots scrabbling to find purchase against smooth, sea-polished planks, but no birdcall. He drew his knife. It would give scant protection against a sword, but he had nothing else. A hand reached over the rail and groped about for something solid to hold. He rushed forward and stamped on it.

"Argh! Why did you go and do that?" Sinead's pain-twisted face popped above the gunwale.

Redknee stood speechless.

"Well?" she said, pursing her lips into a thin line, "don't just stand there like an overgrown turnip. Help me up."

"Why should I? You betrayed me. You went with Mord of your own free will. You only want to come back because I've got the book."

"I'll scream."

"No, you won't." He shot forward, pulled her onto the deck and pressed his hand over her mouth. She twisted like a feral cat, but he held her tight. "I'll let you go if you promise to behave."

She shook her head.

"Fine," he said. "Then I'll push you over the side. It's quite a drop."

92

Her eyes widened, she tried to stamp on his toes and bite his fingers, but he clamped her jaw shut and hardened his grip. She kept on wriggling, but when her face went pink, he released his hand for a moment allowing her to gasp for air.

"You need me as much as I need you,'she said between breaths.

"How?"

"To read your damn treasure book."

"Don't actually. We've got a monk."

Something flickered in her eyes. Redknee wasn't sure what. Jealousy? He tightened his hand over her mouth and whispered into her ear. "Now," he said. "Do you vow to stay quiet?"

She nodded slowly and he released his grip.

"I don't know why you want to come with me anyway. Uncle Sven will have you whipped for giving Mord the book."

"And wouldn't you like that?" she asked, anger flashing in her eyes. "But you're wrong, because I know something about the *Codex* Sven doesn't."

"Well, I hope for your sake you're right. Otherwise you can wipe that stupid grin off your face."

"It has to do with King Hakon – he's dying."

"What do I care about King Hakon's health?"

"You should, it's why he wants the book."

"So? I'm fed up with talk about this book. I'm with Olaf. I think we should go home."

Sinead smirked. "Just shows how little you know. I also heard Ragnar mention your father."

"What did he say – tell me!"

"Got you interested now," she said, a smile tugging on her lips. "Take me to Sven and I'll tell you what I know about Erik Kodranson and the *Codex Hibernia*." Then she turned from him, sashayed across the deck, picked up an oar, slid it through one of the ports in the side of the hull and sat down, ready to row.

Redknee sighed. "We need to wait for Olvir."

"The scraggy blond boy with the sheep?"

"How—"

"You'll be waiting some time."

"Did they get him?" he asked, panic in his voice.

"He's run away."

"Never . . ."

"The boy's a coward ... now, are we going?"

"I already said—"

"If we don't go, Mord and Toki will be back. Wasn't this your plan?"

"Yes... but I thought I could sail it."

"In these conditions?" She tilted her face towards the rising sun, the rose-hued dawn illuminating her pale cheeks.

He shook his head. She was really annoying him. He wished she'd stayed put. If he'd wanted her help, he would've wakened her. Why'd she have to be so damn ... contrary? And now this story about his father; he could swear she was toying with him.

He sighed. "You sure Olvir's gone?"

She nodded vigorously.

Shoulders sagging with defeat, he picked up an oar and slid it through the oarport opposite Sinead.

"Pull when I say. It's important we go together."

"Aye, captain!" She winked at him then stared forward, a look of mock seriousness on her face.

He gave the order and they pulled together, dipping their oars into the water just enough to move them away from the beach.

"The wind will pick up once we leave the bay," he said, glancing over to the spot between the dunes where he'd last seen Mord and Toki. They would be back soon. It wouldn't take them long to realise the sheep were a diversion. He willed the black ship to move faster – but it crept on slowly under their scant power, carried as much by the ebbing tide as their effort – while his heart raced like a startled deer. Nothing but a great burst of wind would give them the speed they needed. Eventually they drew level with the high rocks marking the exit to the bay.

"We're nearly there," Sinead said.

"Just keep rowing!"

Before she could answer, a figure dropped from the rocks above onto the deck with a heavy thud. Redknee leapt to his

94

feet as Toki staggered upright. Blood seeped from a gash in
the giant's right arm and he was wheezing, breathless.
Redknee eyed him warily. He seemed to have lost his sword.

Redknee grabbed his oar and held it across his chest.
"Run," he said to Sinead. She nodded, hurrying towards the
stern.

"Naughty pup," Toki said, wagging his finger. "Didn't
your mother tell you stealing is wrong?"

"Ragnar *killed* my mother," Redknee said, charging.

As Toki ran forward to meet him, a second figure dropped
onto the deck. The movement distracted Toki, and as he turned
his head, Redknee smacked the flat of the oar into his skull.
Redknee wheeled round, ready to fight the second man. It was
only when the newcomer started tearing into Toki that he
realised it was Olvir.

"You came back!"

"Yes ... but I could do with help here ..."

Toki had fallen to his knees but he was still fighting,
lashing out with his fists every time Olvir got close. Redknee
shot between them, bringing his oar sharp across the giant's
face. This time Toki collapsed flat onto the deck, blood
trickling from the corner of his mouth, the fight smashed out
of him.

Redknee turned to Sinead. "Quick, bring some rope."

They bound Toki's hands and feet then tied him to the
mast. His head slumped onto his chest, saliva dripping down
his chin.

"Is he breathing?" she asked, pressing her hand against his
forehead.

"Why'd you care?" Redknee asked.

"It's just ... he looked after me."

In answer, Toki groaned and coughed up yellow bile.

"You're capable of looking after yourself," Redknee said,
going back to get his oar. He turned the length of ash in his
hand and slid it through the oarport. "You said Olvir ran
away."

Sinead flushed scarlet. "I thought he had."

"No way!" Olvir grinned. "Led this oaf and his friend on a
merry dance, didn't I? Said I knew my way round this island

95

like the back of my hand. Well, I got them to follow the sheep, just like you wanted. Fools were so intent on filling their bellies they didn't notice the ravine. This one here was lucky – he managed to land on a small ledge. But the one with the shiny mail coat went flying right over the side. Probably gull food now."

"Mord is dead?" Sinead asked.

"Don't know," Olvir said. "But he won't be bothering us for a while, that's for certain."

"I knew you could do it," Redknee said, slapping Olvir on the back. Silently, he wondered what he'd unleashed in the boy.

Their captive remained unconscious while they sailed back to Ivar's farm.

"What shall we do with him?" Sinead asked as they neared the entrance to the bay, Ivar's farm almost in sight.

Redknee shrugged.

"Sven won't kill him … will he?" She looked at the big lump slouched against the mast and bit her lip. "I mean …" she said, smoothing her face into a mask of indifference, "it'll just cause reprisals."

"By Thor's hammer, why should you give a goat what happens to that outsized ogre?" Redknee asked, trimming the sail to catch the shifting wind. "You'd do better to concern yourself with your own position."

"It's just …" her voice trailed off as a movement on the cliffs grabbed her attention. "Look," she said, pointing, "someone's waving at us."

Redknee squinted into the distance. Harold was running towards them, leaping around like a frog on hot coals, arms flailing wildly in the air.

"What's he doing?" Olvir shouted from his position as lookout up on the prow.

"Damned if I know," Redknee said warily. "But I'm in no mood for his stupid tricks." He decided to ignore Harold's flailing, focusing instead on steering a true course. Hopefully Harold would get the message.

"He looks desperate," Sinead said. "Like he wants to warn us." She stood on the rail and waved to him.

"—What are you doing?" Redknee said, grabbing her flapping skirts and hauling her onto the deck. "Are you crazy?" he demanded. "You could've fallen … do you want to get yourself killed?"

She laughed in his face, a hollow, hysterical hack. "You didn't seem to care when you threatened to drop me over the side."

Heat flooded his cheeks. "We were inshore—"
She shoved past him, lurched for the tiller, jamming it hard and sending the ship careering towards the rocks.

"You'll ground us!" he said, pushing her out the way as the ironclad keel scraped noisily over a granite outcrop. Then he swung them out to sea so violently the ship tilted onto its side, sending loose barrels flying about the deck before he was able to steady their course.

"How dare you manhandle me like that!" Sinead said. "You don't know it's a trick. So you want to show your uncle how grown up you are – you've done well, stealing this ship. But unless you listen to others, you'll put us all in danger."

Anger boiled in his veins. He wasn't going to let Harold spoil his success. Wouldn't give the little turd the chance, no matter what Sinead said, or how much she riled him. For once the glory was all his, and he was going to take it … giving Olvir his due, of course.

"Hey, you two," Olvir said. "Stop bickering. You're like an old married couple." He motioned to Harold. "This lunatic, is he a friend of yours? Because he really wants us to go over. What's the worst that can happen? There's three of us and only one of him."

Redknee sighed. He didn't like to admit it, but Olvir's logic made some sense. Feeling outnumbered, he took hold of the tiller and reluctantly steered them as close to the rocks as he dared.

Harold shimmied down the cliffs until he was almost at sea level, cupped his hands over his mouth and yelled into the wind.

"Sail to the next bay. Don't go to the farm."

97

"Why?" Sinead called back.

"Ragnar is there!"

Sinead turned to Redknee, a look of *"I told you so"* on her face.

"He's lying." Redknee tried to sound unconcerned.

Olvir strained to see past the headland and into the bay.

"What's happened?" he asked, "while I've been playing at raiders with you?"

"Nothing's happened," Redknee said, ignoring Harold's warning and setting them on course for the farm. "I'll bet he wants us to take the black ship to a quiet bay so he can wrestle her from us and claim this success as his."

They slid round the headland and for the first time the full sweep of the bay came into sight. Olvir gave a cry of horror. In the distance, flames ripped into the sky where Ivar's farm had stood.

# Chapter 9

Redknee ignored Harold's warning and set the black ship on course for the farm. It must not be a repeat of Ragnar's attack on his village. So much death. It couldn't happen twice. He wouldn't let it. He'd save those now where he'd been unable to before. *And he'd left Silver in there.*

As they reached the beach, he leapt from the ship, wrapped his cloak round his face and charged across the sand towards the burning longhouse. There was no sign of Ragnar or any of his men. *Was he too late?* As flames licked the pale, summer dawn, memories of charred, blackened skin flashed through his mind. He nearly retched. *It was happening again.* Smoke clawed at his throat, he held his breath, afraid of finding the terrible, terrible smell of roasting flesh.

Sinead grabbed his arm. "What are you doing?"

"Seeing if anyone is inside."

"You'll be killed," she said.

*"By the Blessed Virgin, I didn't mean it."*

Redknee turned to see the little monk they'd met the night before. He knelt on the ground; hands clasped together, eyes shut. His lips moved quickly, silently, as if chewing something distasteful, like a bee.

"What's he doing?" Redknee asked.

"Praying," Sinead said. She went over and put her hand on his shoulder. His robes were singed with ash. "Is anyone inside?" she asked.

Brother Alfred's eyes flew open. "Oh praise be! You have come for me. It was an accident. I—"

"Is anyone inside?" Redknee said, stopping the monk mid rant.

The little monk shook his head.

"What about a wolf cub?"

The monk looked blank.

Redknee stared at the burning longhouse. The turf roof had collapsed and angry, red flames escaped from between the rafters. He sank to his knees and closed his eyes.

"I shut him in," he said, "he wanted to come with me and I shut him in." He felt Sinead place a hand on his shoulder, but he received no comfort from it.

"Who did you shut in," she asked, nudging his cheek.

He turned to face her, to explain how he'd left his pup to die, and was greeted by a paid of amber eyes. "Silver!" he cried, bundling the pup into his arms, "I thought you were dead."

He glanced up at Sinead, who was standing a little way off, a smile tugging on her lips. "Why didn't you tell me?"

She shrugged.

Then he remembered his uncle's order. He turned back to the little monk. "What about the book?" he asked. "Did you get that out?"

Brother Alfred shook his head. "It all happened so quickly. I didn't think."

Redknee sighed. "Uncle Sven charged me with the *Codex's* safekeeping," he said to Sinead. "Is it true what you said earlier – about it having a connection to my father?"

"That's what Ragnar said."

"What, Sinead? You have to tell me *exactly* what he said."

"He said it belonged to your father – well, that your father stole it from an Irish monastery."

"*What?*" Redknee's mind spun out of control. "Sven said *he* was given it by a merchant in Kaupangen just last month."

Sinead shrugged. "I'm only telling you what Ragnar said."

Redknee started towards the longhouse.

"Where are you going?" she called after him.

"If what you say is true, I've no time to waste."

The chest where Sven stowed the book had been against the back wall of the longhouse. Rather than fight through the inferno, Redknee skirted the flames, making his way round the outside to the rear of the building. The fire was even more intense here, its roar deafening. But he spotted a gap in the timbers, covered his mouth and slid through.

100

Heat seared his skin. He saw the chest; the pale oak blackened under the caress of the flames, but otherwise undamaged. He tried the lid. It didn't budge. Damn. He cast around for something to break the lock.

He saw, not too far away, an iron-headed hammer wedged beneath fallen rafters. *Perfect.* But as he scurried across the room to reach it, the last remaining rafters crashed down. He raised his arms to protect his head as he was pummelled to the floor in a cloud of smoke and dust. Everything hurt.

He tried to move. Found he couldn't. Something, a rafter maybe, had fallen on his leg, trapping him amongst the blackened debris. He closed his eyes. He couldn't die here trying to save a damn book. By Thor's hammer, he only had Sinead's word it had *any* connection to his father. No, he had to go on.

He couldn't quite reach the hammer from where the timber pinned him to the floor. Summoning all his strength, he tried to tug his leg free. The effort moved him a couple of inches closer to the hammer, maybe less. *Was it enough?* He lay flat on the floor and stretched his arms out until his joints clicked. His fingertips brushed the end of the hammer. *Just.* He closed his eyes. Another inch was all he needed. Gathering the last of his energy, he yanked his trapped leg again. This time it didn't budge. Not an inch. Nothing. By Odin's eye, he *was* going to die here.

He saw a white hand with neat fingernails reach down for him. It must be Freya, he thought. Come to take him to Valhalla. But she didn't touch him, instead she picked up the hammer. It was then he realised it wasn't Freya, but Sinead, come to help him.

"Hurry up," she said, handing him the hammer. "This place will collapse any moment." She helped lift the timber from his leg, which was cut but not broken, then they hastened to the chest.

The rusty old lock came away easily using the hammer. Redknee quickly opened the lid and reached inside for the book. But the chest was empty save for a yellowed piece of linen.

He turned to Sinead. "Where is it?"

101

"How should I know? Come on," she said, pulling on his tunic, "we have to go."

He looked frantically about the remains of the longhouse.

"But it must be here. I've *got* to find it … I promised my uncle …"

"It's gone, and we should go too." Sinead grabbed his arm and began dragging him towards the opening they had come through. They ran outside as the building collapsed behind them.

Brother Alfred had been joined on the beach by a pink-faced and breathless Harold.

"What happened?" Sinead asked Brother Alfred.

"You spilled your oils," Harold said sharply to the little monk. "Didn't you?"

Brother Alfred nodded slowly. "Yes," he said. "I … I was sending prayers to the … the Blessed Virgin and knocked over my incense burner. In the name of all the Saints, I … I truly didn't mean to do it …"

"So it wasn't Ragnar?" Redknee asked.

Brother Alfred shook his head.

Redknee glared at Harold. "You lied."

Harold shrugged. "I thought I saw him up on the hills. I was just trying to help."

Redknee scanned the hills for movement. Ragnar and his men *could* be lurking in the shadows. He'd seen them leave their camp some time ago. Yet, there was something odd about the way Harold was acting. He seemed unusually on edge.

"Know anything about the *Codex?* It's gone missing," Redknee asked.

"Nothing – I just got here."

"Why did you leave the whale hunt?"

"There was a skirmish between Ivar and one of the local jarls—"

"So you ran away?"

*"No…"*

A bloodcurdling scream pierced the air. Matilda ran along the beach towards the burning farm, followed by a rag-tail bunch of children. "My house!" she cried, falling to her knees,

102

tears streaming down her broad face. "My beautiful house – who did this?"

Harold pointed a skinny finger at Brother Alfred who was cowering a little way off. "It was him."

Matilda struggled to her feet and lumbered towards the monk.

"I didn't do it on purpose, I swear! On the life of the Blessed Virgin, it was a mistake."

Matilda pulled back her mighty forearm ready to bash the little monk squarely on his soft cheek. Redknee winced inwardly. He knew what it felt like to be on the receiving end of her anger. But, as if from nowhere, a hand shot out, grabbing Matilda's arm and spinning her round.

"What's happening here?" Ivar asked his wife in the gentlest of tones.

"Our house!" Matilda moaned. "That stupid monk has burned our house. I told you to get rid of him ages ago."

Sven, Olaf and the rest of the men splashed through the shallows to join Ivar on the beach.

"Oh, thank goodness," Ivar said. "When we saw the flames, and then the black ship in the bay, we thought Ragnar was already here. He was spotted heading this way with a large number of men-at-arms. The fire only serves to reinforce my decision - we're going to leave with Sven. Visit Astrid in Iceland. We'll deal with Brother Alfred's crime later."

Redknee blocked out Matilda's cries for Brother Alfred's blood as he turned to see his uncle running up the beach towards him. Beside the black ship stood *Wavedancer*, sleek and proud in the morning light. His uncle had brought her from the hidden lagoon, a sure sign they were going to leave rather than stand and fight. Redknee's heart sank. He was going to have to explain about the book.

"How did Ragnar's ship get here?" Sven asked.

Redknee shuffled forward. "I stole it from him."

"You?" Sven looked confused. "But you were to stay here and guard the book."

Redknee gulped down the bile rising in his throat. "I ... yes, I was. But I thought Ragnar might have left his camp unguarded."

Sven looked thoughtful. "Well done," he said eventually. "You're turning out to be quite resourceful. I assume you got the book out of the longhouse before the stupid monk set it on fire."

"I ... yes, I'll—"

"Well then – go and get it. We're leaving now, not next week."

"Yes," Redknee nodded, without moving.

"Here it is." Sinead stepped forward, the goatskin package under her arm.

Redknee was speechless.

Even Sven looked taken aback. "Didn't you run away with Ragnar?" was all he found to say.

But Sinead didn't get the chance to respond, because at that moment, Ragnar and his men mounted the ridge separating the beach from the mossy peak beyond.

# Chapter 10

Wavedancer was easier to sail with the extra strength of Ivar's family and the slaves on board. They also had the rations they took from the black ship before they set it alight, and some of the whale meat. And they didn't have to worry about being followed; the last they saw of Ragnar was him trying to douse the flames devouring his precious ship.

Olaf was angry they weren't returning home. But even he had to agree it was their duty to take Ivar to the safety of his daughter's household. Five days' easy sail, that was how long Ivar said it would take to reach Iceland. And eventually Olaf agreed they would have enough food and water to last them, provided they weren't held up in bad weather.

Matilda wanted to hang Brother Alfred right away. But Sven stopped her.

"I'm in charge on this ship," he said. "And while it is Ivar's right to seek justice for the burning of his farm, I say there'll be no hanging, or retribution of any sort, until we reach Iceland." He turned to Ivar who stood beside his wife. "You know I need Brother Alfred to read the *Codex*. But I also know I cannot ask you to put off punishing him indefinitely. All I will ask, dear cousin, is that you give some thought to coming with us on our quest beyond Iceland."

Ivar nodded solemnly. "I will think about your offer."

Matilda folded her arms huffily across her ample chest. "Call yourself a man?" she said derisorily. "And yet you do nothing."

"Calm down, dear," Ivar said, stroking his wife's broad shoulders. "I'll deal with Brother Alfred when we reach Iceland."

Brother Alfred had been cowering at the far side of the longship during this exchange. As Matilda was led away by

Ivar, she turned and spat in his face. "You'd better be a light sleeper!" she hissed.

"How did you find the book?" Redknee asked Sinead as the sun went down on their first full day at sea.

"Oh that. I thought there might be another chest. I ran back inside and saw there was."

"So it was in there all along?"

Sinead nodded.

"I'm going to ask my uncle how he got the book again. He said he was given it by a merchant in Kaupangen last month. But if what Ragnar says is true, about my father taking it from a monastery, then the book might have something to do with my father's … disappearance."

"I thought your father was dead."

"My mother told me he is still alive."

Sinead's eyes widened in surprise, "Oh – so you think the book might have something to do with … *him*?"

Redknee shrugged. "Maybe. I didn't put the two together until you told me what Ragnar said about my father taking it from a monastery. And if what you say is right, then my uncle is lying. I need to ask him about that."

Sinead looked afraid. Very afraid. "Oh, please don't ask him."

"Why?"

"If he's trying to hide something, and he thinks … Oh, I don't know. Please don't."

"I have to, Sinead. This is important."

"But he'll punish me."

"You never seemed afraid of my uncle before."

"But this is different – I think we might have stumbled on something we're not supposed to know."

"What do you mean? Do you know something you're not telling me?"

Sinead shook her head.

"Well, I'm going to ask him. It's the only way I can find out."

"Don't – I'll … I'll tell him how you led Skoggcat to our village!"

Redknee stood in silence. She wouldn't dare. Would she? Well, it cut both ways. He didn't think his uncle knew she'd given Mord the book. If he told Sven that, it would surely be the death of her.

"How are my two favourite young people?"

Redknee turned to see his uncle coming over to join them. He mumbled something about being just fine.

"Well," Sven continued. "It's really you, Sinead, who I need to speak to."

Sinead nodded silently. She looked terrified.

"I need to know why you ran away with Ragnar."

"Please Sir," Redknee said. "She didn't run away. Mord took her."

"I see," Sven said. He turned to Sinead. "Is that correct?"

She nodded.

"And you are unhurt?"

She nodded again.

"Good," he said smiling, and he started to leave.

"Sir," Sinead said, her voice small and high-pitched. Not at all how Redknee was used to hearing her.

"Yes?" Sven asked, pausing.

"When I was at Ragnar's camp, I overheard him talking about why he wanted the book, why King Hakon wants the *Codex*."

"Really? Why you're quite the little eavesdropper."

Sinead smiled.

"And how do I know you're not sent by Ragnar to spy on me now?"

Her smile quickly faded.

Sven laughed. "Relax, I'm just teasing. So tell me, why does our esteemed king seek the *Codex*?"

"King Hakon is ill. Some say it is leprosy and that he is dying. This book, the *Codex*, it is about an Irish monk, Saint Brendan, who lived many years ago. The book tells of his journey to the Promised Land – a place far to the west – where he found great riches. But, more importantly, according to the *Codex*, the Promised Land is a place where death has been conquered."

107

"I see," Sven said. "So he isn't looking for Saint Brendan's treasure. He wants to go to the Promised Land where he will be able to live forever."

Sinead nodded. "That's what he believes."

"And he has sent Ragnar to find this place for him."

"Yes. But Ragnar's son, Mord, he wants the treasure for himself. It is to be their reward for helping King Hakon."

Sven stroked his beard. "Well this puts a different slant on things. King Hakon wants my head on a spike for non-payment of taxes. But then the fox *will* keep putting them up."

"He is spending a lot of money trying to find a cure for his illness," Sinead said.

"Well, well. Perhaps there is a way I can get back on his good side. If we were to find the Promised Land first, then we could legitimately claim the treasure for ourselves, and also save King Hakon from his terrible death. Thank you, Sinead," he said, starting to leave again. "If we do indeed find this Promised Land, I shall personally see to it you are given your freedom."

Redknee watched as his uncle made his way up the deck, speaking to each of his men in turn, giving them encouragement. He stopped beside Brother Alfred and motioned for the little monk to sit with him.

Satisfied his uncle was out of earshot, Redknee turned back to Sinead. "Why didn't you tell my uncle you can read?" he asked. "Then we'll find the Promised Land sooner – Brother Alfred is taking ages with his reading."

"I don't know … I'm afraid."

"You?"

Sinead nodded. "I don't want them to kill Brother Alfred. I don't think he caused the fire."

"Neither do I. But if it wasn't Ragnar, and if it wasn't an accident, where does that leave us?"

"Maybe someone started it deliberately."

"But who would do such a thing – and why?" As he said this, his eyes were drawn to where Harold sat, busily sharpening his ivory- handled dagger on a slice of granite.

Sinead followed his gaze. "The thought had occurred to me too," she said.

108

"But why try and warn us?"

"But *was* he warning us, or was he trying to keep us away – blame someone else?"

"We can say what we like, but it means nothing without proof. And if we can't prove it, Brother Alfred will hang, or worse, when we reach Iceland. Matilda will see to that."

He glanced over to where Brother Alfred was sitting beside Sven on a thick bundle of furs. They were going through the *Codex* – with Sven turning the pages, the little monk reading them aloud. Something Brother Alfred said made Sven frown. He asked the monk to repeat it, which he did. This time Sven grinned.

"Do you think we should listen?" Redknee asked.

Sinead nodded and they went over to join them.

Redknee spoke. "Please Sir," he addressed his uncle, "can we listen too?"

Sven's eyes widened in surprise and for a moment, Redknee thought he was going to say no. But he nodded and motioned for them to join him on the furs.

Sinead knelt beside Brother Alfred. He narrowed his strained eyes. "Please sit still," he said, "and no fidgeting. I need my concentration."

Redknee sat beside Sinead and nodded.

"Continue," Sven said, "You were getting to the good bit, where Saint Brendan first sights the Promised Land."

"Yes, yes," Brother Alfred said, and began reading again. "When Saint Brendan first saw the Promised Land his eyes lit with delight – for never before had he seen such a well-formed shore-line. Perfect for ships of all sizes to dock. And … and studded with well-formed bays, perfect for ships of all sizes to … to drop anchor and to protect them from the vagaries of the weather – storm, tempest, gale."

While Brother Alfred spoke, Sinead had been peering over his shoulder at the spidery black script. Brother Alfred stopped and glared up at her. "You're putting me off," he said. Sinead pursed her lips and sat back down properly.

Brother Alfred frowned and began reading again. "Yes, and, er … when Saint Brendan, who was a strong Irishman,

109

with flame red hair and arms as long as oars and legs as thick as oak trunks—"

"I don't remember that bit from before," Sven cut in.

"Well, that's what it says," the monk blustered.

"And what about magic animals?" Sven asked. "Are there any?"

Brother Alfred paused for a moment while he studied the text. "Yes," he said. "It says further down here there are people who run well-organised farms, but they have the heads of … dogs."

Sven gasped. "Then it is true!" he said, his eyes brightening with excitement.

Sinead had raised herself onto her heels again, trying to get a good look at the place on the page where Brother Alfred was pointing with his finger.

"Show me," she said. Brother Alfred looked startled. "Show me," she repeated, "where it mentions dog-headed people."

"There," Brother Alfred said pointing quickly to a knot of thick, spidery writing before slamming the book shut. "Really," he said, rubbing his temple with his thumb and forefinger, "that is all I can do for today. The light is fading and reading takes it out of me. I'm not a young man."

Sven smiled and slapped Brother Alfred on the back. "Not to worry. You have done well. We shall do more tomorrow."

Sinead grabbed Redknee's arm as Sven and Brother Alfred moved away. "I don't think he was reading from the book," she whispered.

"What?"

"Well, I tried to get a good look at the text, but I couldn't see any of the things he was saying. I can't be sure, but I think he was making it up."

"Why would he do that?" Redknee asked.

"I don't know. Maybe he doesn't want us to find the Promised Land and its treasure. Maybe he thinks it's only for Christians, not heathen Northmen."

Redknee watched as Brother Alfred joked nervously with his uncle while his uncle locked the book safely inside his iron-riveted chest. Was she right? Was the little monk really leading them on a wild goose chase? If he was, he was taking a big risk with his life. Uncle Sven was the only person who would protect him against Matilda's wrath. Redknee turned back to Sinead.

"Well, there's only one way to find out if he's telling the truth. You're going to have to get hold of that book and take a proper look at it."

Redknee watched Sinead saunter over to Brother Alfred while he ate his dinner and offer him a second helping of boiled whale-meat. Redknee could just hear what they were saying. She asked him which monastery he came from.

Brother Alfred smiled as she spooned the dark meat into his bowl. "I come from Winchester in Sussex, my dear."

"Oh," Sinead feigned interest. "I come from the great monastery of Rock Fells … in Ireland."

The little priest grinned. "I used to know the Abbot well. He kept pigeons."

Sinead rolled her eyes. "Hundreds of them. They made *such* a mess."

"And what did you do at the monastery?" he asked.

"Various things: I worked in the kitchen garden, planting herbs, weeding. I also helped the apothecary make his medicines."

"Really my dear? What a responsible job. And how did you end up here, with these … these heathens?"

"They came to Rock Fells this spring and took me, along with many others. Most of the others they sold, but Jarl Sven's sister-in-law, Redknee's mother, she took a liking to me. I've worked for her ever since. She was a good mistress – fair. But she was killed when Ragnar attacked our village."

"I'm sorry to hear that. And I'm sorry to hear that you have not had the opportunity for Christian fellowship these last months past. Perhaps we can pray together?"

Sinead nodded. "I would like that. I also enjoyed hearing you read from the *Codex*. I should like to listen to you again."

Brother Alfred grinned. "Why thank you. I'm delighted you are so interested. It's a very special book – about one of your countrymen, if I'm not mistaken. A man of great faith."

111

"Yes," Sinead said. "You know so much about it. Shall we pray now?"

Redknee watched as they knelt together, clasped their hands and closed their eyes. He hoped Sinead chose her words carefully.

There was one mouth onboard *Wavedancer* Olaf refused to feed. "We have few enough rations to last us," he said, "without having to fill our enemy's belly."

Redknee had deferred to his uncle.

"Don't look at me," Sven had said. "Olaf is in charge of provisions. Toki is *your* captive. If you want him to eat, you'll need to feed him from your own portion."

"Of course, we could just drop him over the side," Olaf said.

At this, Sven threw his hands up and said, "It's up to you, Redknee. I've questioned him, he claims to know nothing of Ragnar's plans. But he's a big, strong man. Maybe you can sell him as a slave when we reach Iceland, though his teeth are black from too much mead."

Matilda turned out to be a beautiful singer. She knew all the old sea-faring ballads and sang long into the night about Siegfried and Orla. The men listened; awed such a lovely sound could come from such a foul-tempered woman. Even Thora, Koll's wife, listened in silence, a rare occurrence for her.

It was the afternoon of their third day at sea. Redknee watched as Sinead and Brother Alfred huddled beneath their cloaks, hands clasped together, eyes pressed shut. They looked strange, their pale lips moving in sync. Like sleep-talkers.

"You look funny," Redknee said, standing over them.

"Be quiet," Sinead said irritably. "He won't hear us over your jabbering."

"Who won't?"

"Do you know nothing? God, of course."

"You've been sitting like that for ages. Are you sure He's going to reply?"

Brother Alfred opened his eyes. "It takes time," he said. "Why don't you sit with us?"

Redknee hesitated. As part of her plan to get a good look at the *Codex*, Sinead had been spending a lot of time with Brother Alfred over the last three days. Of course, Sven had kept the book locked in his chest for that whole time, so the exercise had been pointless so far. But Sinead seemed to be enjoying herself – too much for Redknee's liking. He was beginning to think she *wanted* to spend time with the strange little monk, doing her God-talking and generally acting strange.

"No one is watching," Brother Alfred said, seeming to read Redknee's reluctance.

Redknee slumped down on the deck beside Sinead. There *was* a great deal he could learn from the monk – after all, he was the only person apart from Sven who had seen the book properly.

"You look like there is something you want to ask me," Brother Alfred said.

Redknee thought about the book – he had so many questions. Like what it said – if it mentioned anything about his father. It was a stupid thought, but it had occurred to him nonetheless. Then he remembered Sinead's theory that Brother Alfred was a fraud and he bit his tongue. Instead, he asked about the God-talking.

"The praying thing you were doing just there." Brother Alfred nodded. "We saw some hermits living on top of a tiny rock off the coast of the Sheep Islands. Uncle Sven told me they do the God-talking all day long. Do you know if that's true?"

"Yes, it is. They are very spiritual men."

Redknee let out a long, low whistle.

"You are surprised?" Brother Alfred asked.

"Don't they get bored – talking to themselves all day long?"

"You liked to go up to the mountain on your own," Sinead cut in. "Didn't you ever get bored up there?"

"It's not the same thing. I was busy – hunting, looking for good bits of wood, that sort of thing. Even if I let my mind wander, my body was always at work."

113

Brother Alfred chuckled. "Perhaps we have found an ascetic in training."

"What did you call me?" Redknee asked.

"Nothing … nothing. I just meant you could be like a hermit, going into the forest on your own."

Redknee wasn't sure what to make of that, so he changed the subject.

"Are you worried about landing in Iceland?" he asked.

"Redknee!" Sinead said. "What a terrible thing to ask."

"No, child," Brother Alfred said. "He's quite right to ask." The little monk turned to Redknee. "I am not afraid of going to the next world, if that is what you mean."

"But only great warriors have an honoured place with the gods."

"Those are your beliefs. But they are not mine. The way to heaven, the equivalent of your Valhalla, is not through fighting and killing, but through loving your fellow man and believing in Jesus, the son of God." With these last words, Brother Alfred gazed skyward, as if this heaven place he spoke of was somehow located above, with the birds of the air.

"That's stupid. Isn't it competitive to get a place? Just being loving is too easy."

Brother Alfred chuckled again, a habit that was beginning to annoy Redknee. "That's where you are wrong, my child. It is the hardest thing, to love. Quite the hardest thing of all."

By the end of their fifth day at sea, Sven still hadn't brought out the *Codex* for Brother Alfred to read again and it was driving Redknee crazy. All he could think about was the possible connection between the book and his father. He had to know what it said. So he confronted Sinead after their dinner of smoked fish.

"This isn't working," he said. "I need to ask Uncle Sven if he knows the book once belonged to my father."

"No," Sinead said, dragging him as far as she could from prying ears. "You mustn't. Something is wrong. I don't know why Sven hasn't brought the *Codex* out for Brother Alfred to read again. Maybe he has his suspicions about the monk's motives too. But you mustn't ask Sven about the book's

114

connection with your father. He'll know the information could only have come from me – I'm the only one Ragnar could have told."

"I don't understand how Ragnar would know that."

Sinead shrugged. "Neither do I. But he did. And I don't think anyone here knows about the history of the book, not even Olaf."

"Alright," Redknee said. "If you won't let me ask that, I'm going to tell him you can read."

"But Brother Alfred – that's as good as killing him."

"You heard the silly monk. He's accepted his fate – is even looking forward to going to heaven. If he didn't start the fire, then he's a fool to cover for whoever did. It's not our problem. We need to know about the book. If what my mother said is to be believed, my father is out there somewhere. Alive. And I've a growing feeling he may need my help."

# Chapter 11

The following morning Redknee found his uncle going over the remaining food supplies with Olaf.

"Ah, there you are, lad," he said when he saw Redknee approaching. "It'll be half rations from now on if we don't reach Iceland soon."

"This trip has been madness from beginning to end," Olaf grumbled behind him.

"Thank you Olaf," Sven said. "But I don't remember anyone asking your opinion."

Olaf slunk away with a frown on his face, leaving Redknee alone with his uncle.

"Please Sir," Redknee said. "I need to talk to you about the *Codex*." He *so* wanted to ask where his uncle first got the book – if he'd gotten it from his father. But he remembered his promise to Sinead.

"Yes," Sven said. "What do you want to say?"

"Well, it's just Sinead doesn't think Brother Alfred is telling you the truth about what it says in the *Codex*."

"Really?" Sven looked intrigued. "And why does she think that?"

"Because ..." he glanced over to where Sinead was helping Thora and Matilda mend a tear in the sail. She frowned at him. Ignoring her, he turned back to face his uncle. "Because," he went on, "because she can read."

*"Land ahoy!"* One of the Bjornsson twins shouted from up on the prow. Everyone ran forward, eager to sight Iceland. Redknee started to follow the others, but his uncle grabbed him by the elbow and pulled him back.

"Not so fast," he said. "Are you sure the girl can read?"

Redknee nodded. "Well," he said, less certain now. "I think she can. She said she used to help the monks in the

116

apothecary with their medicines. They taught her so that she could read the formulas."

"It's strange how she returned to us, don't you think? I can't help wondering if she's a spy. But then, you're good friends with the girl. You would know if she were a traitor."

Sven's blue eyes seemed to pierce Redknee's soul. If he was going to tell his uncle that it was Sinead who gave the *Codex* to Mord, then this was the time to do it, or forever be labelled an accomplice. His throat felt dry. But before he had the chance to speak, his uncle went on:

"Well," he said, shaking his head. "I do believe I'm becoming overly suspicious. Why would a slip of a lass like that want to double-cross us? And how would she even begin to do it? So yes, perhaps I will let her have a look at the book. Of course, this does mean one good thing."

"What's that?" Redknee said, almost afraid to ask.

"It means we no longer need that annoying little monk."

Redknee watched in amazement as the dark pip on the horizon ripened to a hot, angry orange. The fiery kernel the populace rather ironically called *Iceland* was at war with the gods. The belligerent rock puffed its cheeks and spat a brew of smoke and fire at the sky. As they drew closer, burning ash speckled their tunics; terrifyingly, these incendiaries appeared to be coming from the land up ahead. Sven ordered the sail lowered before it caught light. Silver whimpered. Redknee bundled the pup into his arms and brushed the hot flecks from his fur. The fiery air seared their faces, leaving them gasping, inhaling the sharp, unmistakable smell of sulphur.

Brother Alfred's hand trembled as he crossed himself. "We've been condemned to hell!" he whimpered, and began to pray.

"Oh shut your trap!" Ivar said. "My daughter has told me of this fire mountain." Then he grinned mischievously. "You're not in hell little monk … *not yet*."

Ivar laughed at Brother Alfred's terrified face. The little monk continued his praying in silence, but it didn't escape Redknee's notice that his book-shrivelled eyes kept darting towards the fiery peak of the mountain, as if a terrible dragon

117

was about to soar forth at any moment and drag him, screaming, to the pits of hell.

Reykjavik, big and messy, lumbered into view. More than thirty longhouses stood between the sea and the volcano, their inhabitants seemingly oblivious to the escalating fire show.

They docked *Wavedancer* alongside an assortment of fishing boats and merchant vessels in Reykjavik's busy port. Ivar and Matilda took Uncle Sven up to the town to find their daughter, leaving the rest of them at the docks under Olaf's charge.

A row of wooden pontoons stretched into the sea like fingers. Traders selling everything from juicy apples to cured meats and fresh fish crowded these narrow walkways plying their wares. But instead of shouting out their prices clearly, as the traders had done when Redknee visited the market town of Hedeby, here they coughed into scarves tied round their mouths as flakes of ash swirled in the air like grey snow. Redknee wasn't sure he wanted to stay in Reykjavik. Not even for the night.

"This place is bad," Koll said, holding his hand over his mouth. "The air tastes like poison."

"We've been told to wait here," Olaf said. "And that's what we'll do." But even he glanced around uneasily as the smoke cloud creeping over the town seemed to thicken.

Brother Alfred shuffled nervously, his leather-soled boots making a scuffling noise on the deck.

"Not long now," Harold said, sniggering as he drew his finger across his throat.

Sinead glowered at Harold then laid her arm on the little monk's shoulder, whispering something that seemed to calm him. Redknee turned his back on them; the Christian's problems weren't his. He hopped from the ship and motioned for Silver to join him in a walk along the black sand. He'd had enough of being cooped up.

Ivar and Uncle Sven returned a short time later with a small group of armed men. The men were led by a young woman in a pale grey dress; a colour that Redknee fancifully imagined shimmered like ice. He knew from the way the fine silk hugged her graceful figure that she was rich. Years of work had not made her hunched and coarse, like most women. And yet, despite the easy life she'd led, and all the things she obviously had, including this reunion with her parents, her face seemed empty. Blank. The woman made a delicate sound in her throat, like a cough, and began to speak.

"My name is Astrid Ivansdottr," she said, her voice a curious mix of fragility and brittleness, like a highly polished shell. "My husband is Gunnar the Sailor, Jarl of Reykjavik. I'm sorry to hear your homes have been destroyed. But you're welcome here; you'll each be given quarters with one of our good families. I hope you will consider us friends." She paused, fidgeting nervously with the tassels on her belt. She looked unused to directing a longship full of men.

Ivar nodded for her to continue.

"My husband is away," she said, a shadow crossing her face. "I'm uncertain when he'll return. In the meantime, please consider the resources of my household at your disposal. There will be a feast at my longhouse this evening to celebrate your safe arrival."

A satisfied murmur went round the ship. Koll let out a belch and rubbed his stomach. The big warrior would sleep well tonight. There would be no such luck for Brother Alfred. Astrid's men put the little monk into stocks and led him, stumbling, towards the town.

Sinead went over to Sven. "Excuse me, Sir," she said. "What are they going to do with him?"

"They're going to keep the fool locked up tonight, and try him tomorrow," he said. "As luck would have it, there's a meeting of their high court, the All-thing."

"Please sir, I don't think Brother Alfred caused the fire at Ivar's farm."

"Neither do I," Sven replied. "But this isn't my jurisdiction."

"What about the *Codex?*"

"Ah, still thinking about your freedom, little one?"

Sinead blushed. "I only want to know who will decipher the book if we no longer have Brother Alfred."

"You're very keen to save his life."

"I'm only thinking of the success of this voyage."

"Then why haven't you told me before that *you* can read? *Eh?*"

Sinead glared at Redknee, but he said nothing. What had she expected? The monk wasn't his problem. He needed to know what the *Codex* said. She'd told him it'd once belonged to his father. Now the pages might hold the key to where his father was.

No, not *might* ... they *did* hold the key. He felt it in his gut. Finding his father depended on it.

Redknee followed Astrid through the mud-soaked streets. He'd never seen so many people in one place before, hadn't known there could be so many different faces. Stalls selling hundreds of goods lined the narrow streets, from soapstone bowls, to copper brooches, to thick bear furs the colour of snow, to great steel swords, to reams of linen and wool in every colour from the palest buttercup yellow to the deepest blood red. He stared openly, drinking in the sights, the smells. Everywhere, people jostled with each other, competing to find the best bargain. Redknee ran his hand across a display of seal-fur hats, luxuriating in their perfect softness. The stallkeeper glowered at him and he quickly shoved his hands into his pockets. He must look filthy after five nights at sea.

He ran to catch up with Astrid, who, used to the throng, had struck out ahead. A young swineherd slipped about in the mud, trying to drive his hairy black charges into their pen. But the pigs had minds of their own. Curses flew from the mouths of nearby stallholders as the pigs charged between them, threatening to overturn their wares. Redknee grabbed Silver by the scruff of thick fur at his collar and held him steady against the assault of greedy snouts.

Astrid stopped and stared back at Redknee, her blonde hair rippling in the breeze.

"I'll only be a moment," he shouted. He saw a piglet running towards him and deftly nipped out the way. Pleased with his dexterity, he grinned up at Astrid as a boar with huge tusks smashed into his calves, tossing him into the air.

120

Redknee thought he'd died; that the boar had pierced some vital artery in his leg. To be fair, wrestling with a pig was not the way he'd hoped to go. He doubted the Valkyries would let him enter Valhalla. Then he heard roars of belly laughter followed by a squelch as he landed in a pile of pig shit. Valhalla, he realised, would have to wait. Astrid's lips curled into a wry smile.

Avoiding her gaze, he picked himself out of the mire and muttered to Silver. "Come on," he said. "We must keep up with the lady." His faithful companion, however, was keen to stay at a distance. This time the crowd cleared to let Redknee pass, and he could have imagined himself a great king, but for the sniggers and pinched noses.

A stone wall enclosed the yard to waist height. Redknee shivered in the wind. He was keen to change his stinking clothes. But all he could see leading off the yard was a door hewn into the hillside.

Astrid saw his puzzlement. "Covering our houses in grass keeps them warm in winter." She smiled, but the warmth didn't reach her eyes. "And there are no trees on Iceland with which to build proper roofs."

He nodded as if he knew that already.

She paused in the doorway and pointed to Silver. "He stays outside."

"Why?"

"Bleyðra doesn't like dogs."

"*Who*?"

"My cat."

The longhouse was a strange mix of luxury and decay. The main room was large, but felt dark and underground, which, of course, it mostly was. Although fine tapestries hung from the roof, they were old and worn and did little to disguise the plain mud walls. A big pine bed strewn with thick furs, the ultimate in comfort, stood at the far end of the room, a white cat nestled between its folds. This, no doubt, was Bleyðra. Redknee eyed it with envy. After many nights at sea, such a bed would bring sweet dreams. But the room was dusty and cold, warmed only

121

by the pitiful embers of a half-dead fire. Perhaps the absence of Astrid's husband explained the air of neglect.

Astrid crossed the floor and pulled a fresh linen tunic and pair of wool breeches from a chest. Redknee took them tentatively, glancing round for a private place to change. There was nowhere.

"You're not shy?" she asked.

Redknee blushed furiously. He was used to dressing in front of others. He just didn't want Astrid to see him wipe pig shit from his body. That was all.

"There's a curtain over here," she said, lifting a tapestry from a dark corner to reveal a small alcove. It was tiny, but it would have to do. Replacing the curtain behind him, he shrugged off his stinking tunic and screwed it into a ball.

The curtain twitched. Astrid stood holding a bowl of steaming water. "I thought you might want this," she said, smiling.

He took the bowl, and, aware of his nakedness, snapped the curtain back into place. He heard a giggle, and, a moment later, a hand snaked round holding a square of fresh linen. Redknee grabbed the cloth with a mumbled, *"Thank you."* After he'd given himself a good wipe and a quick sniff just to be sure, he pulled on the fresh tunic and breeches.

When he came out, Astrid was lying on the bed, a wolf fur draped over her shoulders, her silk dress glimmering in the half-light. "Those clothes suit you," she said.

"They do?" He examined the too long sleeves and the rolled up trouser legs.

"They were my husband's," she said, rolling onto her back and raising her arms above her head, so that the wolf fur slid from her shoulders. She stared up at him, blue eyes wide, lips slightly parted. He didn't want to think about her husband, so he perched on the edge of the bed and tried to think of a change of subject.

Eventually he said, "I left my dirty clothes on the floor." He knew he'd said the wrong thing as soon as the words left his mouth.

122

"Oh," she said, her mouth puckering with distaste. "I'll get one of the slaves to wash them." She sat up then, and the moment was broken.

"Aren't you worried about the volcano?" he asked.

"Oh ... that! Mount Hekla is always blowing off. We don't bother about it at all. The bile from her guts feeds our crops. Makes them grow strong. Frey treats our farmers well – gifting us the earth's own gold. As long as we keep him happy, that is."

"You're lucky. In my experience, Frey is a fickle god, difficult to please. The crops were dying in my village, yet Frey did nothing. We must have offended him, but we don't know why."

Astrid tilted her head thoughtfully. "Here, we are careful to always keep Frey ..." she paused, seeking the right word, "... *satisfied*."

The door opened and a blade of yellow light severed the gloom. Ivar and Matilda stomped in followed by Uncle Sven and Sinead.

Matilda went straight to the fire and started turning her meaty arms over the cinders like roasting hogs. "This is no good," she scolded her daughter. "You must have a proper fire."

Astrid rolled her eyes and turned away from her mother to where Ivar and Sven had settled themselves at the wooden table that ran the length of the room. "There is mead in that pitcher," she said, pointing to a big jug sitting on the table.

"Thanks," Ivar said, and began pouring. "Would you like some, darling?" he asked Matilda.

Matilda grunted.

"We'll have food soon, dear," Ivar said. "I know you're starving."

Redknee noticed Sinead hanging back in the doorway.

Astrid spotted her too and scowled. "What's that slave doing here?" she demanded.

Sinead turned the colour of raw beetroot.

123

Redknee shifted awkwardly on the edge of the bed. Suddenly he didn't want Sinead here, talking about the stupid monk, spoiling things for him.

"Oh, her?" he said carelessly. "She can sleep in the barn—"

Uncle Sven cut him off. "This is Sinead. Our house-slave. We take her everywhere."

Astrid pursed her lips. "Well, it's most irregular to have a slave sleeping in the jarl's house. My husband will not be pleased." She held out a basket of bread. "The slave will have to make herself useful. She can start by serving this."

Sinead looked at Uncle Sven. He nodded and she scurried forward, head bowed, and proceeded to offer the basket round the small group. As she passed Matilda, Redknee saw the older woman stick a fat ankle under Sinead's feet. She stumbled, jarring her knee. Ashamed, he avoided Sinead's eye when she served him.

"We won't impose on your hospitality for long," Uncle Sven said, biting down on a chunk of black bread. "We'll be away in a couple of days."

"Where are you going?" Astrid asked. "Your son told me you offended Frey."

Sven flushed. "*My nephew,*" he corrected.

Redknee blushed too. He supposed he did have the same colouring as his uncle. It wasn't a difficult mistake to make.

"You are right about one thing, Astrid," Sven continued. "We must have offended Frey because the rains didn't come this spring and the wheat turned to dust before mid-summer." Sven went on to explain about Ragnar's attack and the promises made in the *Codex*. "So," he said finally, "we're going to find Saint Brendan's treasure, and, we hope, a new place to live."

"How exciting," Astrid said. "My husband is on a voyage of discovery too. He's gone to a beautiful island to the west called Greenland. Have you heard of it?"

Sven shook his head.

"Crystal waterfalls feed valleys overflowing with golden corn, and animals so fat they can't walk. The sun bathes the fields in honey and the rain falls soft as a baby's feet. It's a

124

renowned paradise." Astrid's face glowed with excitement as she described Greenland.

The description bore some resemblance to the descriptions of the Promised Land in the *Codex*. But Redknee decided to stay silent.

Matilda stirred beside the fire. "Enough of that crazy talk, daughter. Your husband's not coming back."

Astrid jumped to her feet, spilling her food on the floor. "That's a lie!" she said, tears pricking her eyes. "Gunnar *is* coming back for me. And he's going to make me Queen of Greenland." With this, Astrid turned and ran out of the house.

Redknee jumped to his feet, ready to go after her.

"I wouldn't do that, lad." Ivar said. "Our daughter's always been a bit weepy. She'll be back soon enough."

Redknee hovered, unsure what to do. Uncle Sven motioned for him to sit down. Reluctantly, he sank back onto the bed, watching dumbly as Sinead picked the spilled food off the floor.

"We'll execute Brother Alfred tomorrow," Matilda said, picking seeds from her teeth. "By *blood eagle*, I should think." Everyone nodded; everyone except Sinead who had become absolutely still.

*Blood eagle* was the most horrific method of death known.

125

# Chapter 12

Astrid returned that afternoon in a better mood. "I want to go to the hot springs," she said to Redknee. "They're just outside Reykjavik. Won't you come with me? Be my protector?"

Uncertain, Redknee looked to his uncle.

"Don't look at me, lad." he said. "I'll be spending the afternoon buying supplies and making repairs to *Wavedancer*. The pup can keep me company. I don't need you here."

The road to the hot springs wound round the side of the volcano. Ash peppered the sky. Redknee tied his scarf over his face to block out the stench of sulphur. The soil here was black. His old nag nearly unseated him each time she stopped to chew on the stunted shrubs that clung to the desolate slopes.

"Give her a good kick the next time she does that," Astrid grinned down at him from her sleek grey mare.

Redknee grunted. They rode on in silence. Why had she chosen him to accompany her? Couldn't be for protection. There were plenty of bigger, stronger men. Besides, she had her own guards. Why not bring one of them? He opened his mouth to ask, when Astrid turned her horse into the yard of a neat looking longhouse and dismounted.

"I thought we were going to the hot springs," Redknee said.

Astrid smiled. "We are. But I wanted to bring you here first."

Redknee glanced round. Several horses were tied to a bridle post, their masters obviously inside. "What is this place?"

"It's a tavern."

His uncle had warned him about taverns. He hadn't been allowed inside the taverns the time they went to Hedeby. "Dens of liars and pickpockets," Uncle Sven had said. Then

126

he'd left Redknee outside while he went in to complete his business.

"What's wrong?" Astrid asked. "Never been inside a tavern before?"

"Of course I have," Redknee mumbled.

Warm air, carrying with it the smell of good ale, roast meat and sweaty bodies greeted them as they entered the tavern. "Let's find a table," Astrid called above the noise. They pushed past several groups of men before they found a small table at the back of the room. Redknee noticed more than one set of eyes turning to stare. Apart from the serving maids, Astrid was the only woman.

"Is this a good idea?" Redknee asked in a low voice. "I mean, is it safe for —"

"Oh, don't be such an old goose. I've been here before. Most of these men know who I am."

Redknee relaxed. He didn't fancy fighting off any of these brutes. A girl with straggly hair and broken teeth came over.

Astrid put a coin on the table. "Two ales, wench. And be quick about it."

The girl put the coin in her pocket without saying anything and left. She returned a few moments later with two wooden tankards filled to the brim, handing Astrid's to her carefully, and plonking Redknee's on the table.

Redknee took a careful sip. He hadn't had ale before.

"How does it taste?" Astrid asked.

"Good – sweet."

Astrid's ale sat untouched in front of her.

"Aren't you drinking yours?" he asked.

"Later, I have to find someone first." Astrid stood and waved to a small boy sitting near them on the floor. The boy hurried over. He was barefoot and dressed in rags. Astrid whispered something in his ear. The boy looked doubtful. "There's a coin in it for you," she said, loud enough for Redknee to hear.

The boy nodded and scurried away.

"What was that about?" Redknee asked.

"He's going to find the man I'm looking for."

"You don't know him?" Redknee asked, surprised. "We're meeting a stranger?"

"Not exactly, it's someone I used to know. But before we meet him … before *you* meet him, I need to know I can trust you. So can I? Trust you, that is."

Redknee stared into his tankard. "I suppose you can. Though it depends what you mean. I won't have to do anything, will I?"

Astrid laughed. "So gallant!"

"I didn't mean it like that."

"No," Astrid said. "You won't *have* to do anything. But I think you'll be interested – really interested in what Ulfsson has to say."

The small boy returned and held his hand out for the coin.

"Where is he?" Astrid asked.

The boy jabbed a dirty finger over his shoulder. Behind him, in the shadows cast by the whale oil lamps, was the outline of a tall, thin man with long dark hair. Astrid gave the boy the coin and shooed him away.

The man stepped into the light. Although he was tall and well built, his face was hollow and his skin hung loose on his bones. He looked haunted.

"Please," Astrid said, pushing her ale across the table. "Sit down. Drink." There was a spare stool at their table and the man took it. Astrid continued. "This is Redknee," she said. "He's a friend of mine. He can be trusted."

The man nodded, but his eyes kept darting round the room, as if afraid others might be listening.

Astrid went on. "I want you to tell him what you told me. I want you to tell him why my husband might still be alive, and why it's worth my while looking for him."

Redknee stood. "You don't need to tell me this. I believe you. It's your mother who needs convincing."

"Sit down," Astrid said. "You're being a fool. This will interest you. I promise." Reluctantly, he did as she asked.

Ulfsson spoke quietly. "It began two years ago. Astrid's husband here, Jarl Gunnar – we called him Gunnar the Sailor – heard tales of a land far to the west where there was treasure to be had, and easy living. He got a couple of ships together and

128

enough men to sail them; promised us all great riches if we found this place. Greenland, he called it."

Redknee sat up. This bore a close resemblance to the stories in the *Codex*. "Did you?" he asked, excitement in his voice. "Did you find this Greenland?"

Ulfsson slumped in his seat. "We found no land matching that description. We did find a vast island, rich in soil and rain, but populated by fearless warriors who can vanish and re-appear at will."

Redknee let out a snort.

"What?" Ulfsson asked. "You doubt me?"

"Vanish and re-appear at will," Redknee said incredulously. "You expect us to believe you?"

Ulfsson shrugged and continued. "We left Reykjavik on a fine spring morning with two ships and more than seventy men. *Fighting men.* Of those seventy, only myself and Jarl Gunnar remain."

"Really? And how is that?" Redknee asked.

"I was lucky. I caught a fever. The others left me to die. But I recovered and made my escape on one of our abandoned longships."

"And what of Jarl Gunnar?" Redknee asked.

"That's easy," Ulfsson said. "*He* went native."

The men at the next table had stopped playing their game of dice. One of them stood and came over. He put his hand on Astrid's shoulder. "That husband of yours not coming back?" he asked.

Astrid frowned and tried to remove his hand, but he just tightened his grip and leaned in so that his wine-stained lips nearly touched hers. Astrid tried to twist her head away, but he only leaned in further. Ulfsson chose this moment to taste his ale. A moment later, he was on his feet, yellow liquid shooting from his mouth, spraying the leery stranger in the face.

"By Odin's eye," Ulfsson shouted. "That's not ale – it's piss!"

The stranger wiped the foul-smelling liquid from his face, drew back his fist and punched Ulfsson square on the nose. Ulfsson staggered back into a table of drunken sailors. The biggest of them leapt to his feet and took a swing at Astrid's suitor. A moment later men from two other tables joined in. Soon the whole bar had erupted. Astrid and Redknee stood with their backs to the wall as stools and tables flew about in front of them. There was no way they could make it through the mêlée to the door without being floored, or killed.

Redknee felt a sharp tug on the hem of his tunic. He looked down to see the small boy who had found Ulfsson. The boy motioned for them to follow him. He led them out through a back door. When they reached the front of the longhouse, the fighting had spilled outside. Ulfsson lay on the ground, his head split open. Redknee stared at his body in horror. He might have been a deluded liar, but there was so much Redknee had wanted to ask him.

"We're here," Astrid said, sliding off her horse and looping its reins over a jagged black rock.

Redknee blinked. He'd never seen anything like it before. Steam rose in great white clouds from a lake of the palest milky blue.

"Come on," Astrid said, slipping her tabard over her head. "Don't tell me you can't swim."

Redknee dismounted and kicked off his boots. The sharp rocks cut into his feet.

Astrid was already at the water's edge wearing only her under-dress. "Turn round," she said.

"What?" Redknee asked, confused.

"You can't expect me to disrobe with you watching."

Redknee blushed and turned his back. How long should he give her? He bit his lip. If he turned round too soon …

"Alright," Astrid shouted.

He spun round. She was submerged up to her neck. Her pale hair dark with water. Disappointment coursed through him. He rebuked himself. What had he expected?

"Aren't you coming in?" Astrid's voice interrupted his thoughts.

He quickly shrugged off his tunic and threw it over a rock. But when he reached down to untie his breeches, he froze, suddenly unsure what to do. Should he keep them on? He glanced up at Astrid. She was swimming further into the lake, her back to the shore.

Damn. It was his decision.

Leaving his breeches on, he hopped over the sharp rocks and submerged himself slowly beneath the warm waters. Every muscle in his body relaxed. Astrid had been right; this was a truly wonderful place.

She had swum almost to the centre of the small lake and he started to swim after her. She was treading water when he reached her.

"You decided to join me after all," she said.

"Why are we here?" he asked.

She raised an eyebrow.

"I'm being serious. Why did you bring me to meet Ulfsson? What does your husband's voyage, and the ramblings of a mad man, have to do with me?"

She dipped her head below the surface and rose with water spouting from her mouth. "Kiss me," she said.

She was playing games. It felt dangerous.

*Good dangerous, or bad dangerous?* He didn't know. She looked up at him with her clear, blue eyes and, before he could change his mind, he was leaning forward.

Astrid giggled. "Follow me," she said, turning and diving beneath the surface.

Taking a deep breath, he plunged after her, kicking as hard as he could. Astrid's dark shape snaked through the milky waters. Eventually she surfaced, and Redknee followed, his lungs gasping for air. She laughed, water streaming down her face. "You swim well," she said.

He looked round nervously. She'd led him out deeper still. Past a small island made of the brittle black stone that seemed to cover Iceland. "What do you want?" he asked.

She circled him slowly, her skin glistening in the strange light. "Why do you think I want anything in particular?" she asked.

He shrugged. "I don't, I just thought …"

"I'm going to tell you a story," she said, winding her hair into a knot on top of her head. Myriad droplets streamed

131

across her neck and shoulders. He looked away. "Do I displease you?" she asked.

He shook his head. His tongue felt weak, like soggy bread. He doubted his ability to speak.

"I needed you to hear Ulfsson's tale so you didn't think me mad. It's a shame he was killed in that brawl. He could have been useful to us." She tilted her head thoughtfully to one side. "No matter, we shall do without him - back to my story. Not long after I was married to Gunnar, a ship arrived here in Reykjavik, carrying a band of Norse warriors much like yourself. They came seeking a great treasure. A treasure said to be worth more than all the gold in Byzantium. They knew this treasure existed because, they said, it was spoken of in a famous book – a book written by monks. They also had a scribe with them, a hermit monk, I think. He'd studied this book well. He said it spoke of the treasure being hidden in a vast land to the west. He called it the Promised Land.

"Naturally, my husband's interest was aroused. He asked if he could join them on their quest. They said any strong, honest man was welcome to throw his lot in with theirs. He sailed with them on midsummer, taking two ships and more than seventy of our best men with him. That was two years ago."

Redknee listened to her tale in silence. The book she spoke of had to be the *Codex Hibernia*. But was it too much of a coincidence?

"You look pale, like you've seen a ghost."

"These men, these Norse warriors that came to Reykjavik; was one of them called Erik Kodranson? Their leader perhaps?"

Astrid shook her head. "I don't remember that name. But there were quite a number of them. Why do you ask?"

"I think," Redknee said, his voice growing hoarse. "I think one of them was my father."

# Chapter 13

"They say my husband is dead. But I don't believe it," Astrid said. "I will help you find your father if you will help me find my husband."

"How can I do that?" Redknee asked.

"I want to go west with you. Will you take me?"

"I'm afraid it's not up to me. You would have to ask my uncle. He isn't keen on having women on the ship."

"Pah! My mother went with you – and there's that slave girl. And the coarse one, the wife of your blacksmith."

"Thora," Redknee provided.

"If you say so, come on." Astrid said, smiling again. "It'll be fun. We'd be a team. And who knows, we might even find this treasure for ourselves!"

"I'll ask my uncle," Redknee said. "But I can't promise—"

"Oh, by Thor's hammer, I've seen the way your uncle treats you. Like a son. He'll grant you this request. Now, come on, I'll race you to the shore."

As Redknee followed her retreating figure, he wondered just what, exactly, he had promised to do.

Astrid laid on a magnificent feast for them in her longhouse that night. Having had his fill of meat and preposterous stories, Redknee had escaped outside with Silver. He was planning which direction to take his walk: along the beach or into the town, when Sinead caught up with him.

"You disappeared this afternoon," she said. Her cheeks were flushed, and her auburn curls were escaping from beneath her linen cap.

"I was with Astrid."

"Oh, *right*."

"Why do you ask?"

133

"I wanted to speak to you about Brother Alfred. I can't believe they're going to execute him by *blood eagle*," she said, her voice shaking.

Redknee had never seen anyone actually killed this way. But he knew the method. First, they opened the victim's back and cut the ribs away from the spine with a sharp sword, fanning them out so they resembled the blood-stained wings of an eagle. Then they fished out the lungs and placed them on the victim's chest for the birds to eat while the still conscious victim watched in horror. It usually took several hours for the man to die.

It was a torture of last resort – reserved for those guilty of the worst crimes. It surprised him they were going to use this most heinous of devices for Brother Alfred. The fire hadn't even killed anyone.

"It's harsh. But it's not my problem," Redknee said. "Aren't they giving him the benefit of a trial at the All-thing tomorrow?"

"Matilda is baying for his blood. Do you really think he'll get a fair hearing?"

"I don't know Sinead? What's fair? Was it fair that you helped Mord slaughter my village?"

She blanched. "You know I gave Mord the book to *stop* the killing."

"I've been thinking. How did you know where the *Codex* was hidden?"

"I looked for it – like I said I would. Found it hidden beneath the old loom in the weaving hut. Most likely your uncle, being a man, didn't know the women used that space to keep spare scraps of fabric. There are lots of things us women know that pass you men-folk by."

A group of drunken men spilled out of the longhouse. Olaf, Magnus and the Bjornsson twins were among them. They disappeared between the buildings, returning moments later with a mangy chestnut stallion.

"They're too drunk to ride," Sinead said.

Redknee shrugged. "If they want to break their necks, I'm not going to stop them."

The drunks formed a circle.

134

"You'd better stand back!" Magnus shouted cheerily. "That is, if you value your skulls in one piece."

Redknee and Sinead moved away as Olaf led the stallion into the ring. Scars criss-crossed its mud-spattered coat. Seeing the small crowd, the horse snorted, drew back its lips and sunk its teeth into Olaf's hand.

"By Odin's eye!" he cursed, smashing his fist into the soft, pink tip of its nose. The horse staggered, its hooves skidding in the mud. It took a couple of juddery steps to regain its balance. But as soon as it did, Olaf dragged it back to the middle of the circle. Olaf's blow had angered the creature; rage glittered in its eyes as it pawed the ground.

"What's happening?" Sinead asked.

"Don't know," Redknee said as one of Astrid's men led a grey stallion, a hand or so smaller, towards the chestnut. "I think they're going to make the horses fight."

The grey's eyes shone with fear as it whinnied and tried to back away. But its handler dragged it by its mane until it cowered before the big chestnut. The crowd had swollen to more than forty. Voices clamoured for attention as one of Astrid's men took bets.

"Talking about the book," Redknee shouted above the noise. "Have you been able to get a look at it? See if what Brother Alfred said about the Promised Land is true?"

Sinead shook her head. "Your uncle has kept it locked away on *Wavedancer*, guarded by the Bjornsson twins. I don't know how I'm supposed to get a look at it when you're flouncing about with that snooty cow. I need your help."

"I'm sure my uncle will ask you to read from the *Codex* soon. Besides," Redknee said, pulling Sinead to one side so they were standing on the fringes of the crowd, "I was making good use of my time. I found out valuable information from Astrid. Two years ago a ship of Northmen came here searching for the Promised Land. They even spoke of a book. Astrid's husband left with them."

"So?" Sinead said. "We know Ragnar wants this treasure, why not others?"

"Because I think one of those men could have been my father."

135

A weary sort of sympathy flashed across Sinead's face. "*Oh Redknee*," she sighed. At that same moment, a hush came over the crowd. All bets had been placed. Harold rushed out, made a line in the mud with his dagger, and retreated. A whip cracked through the air and both horses reared, their powerful front legs clattering together mid-air.

Sinead looked away. "I can't watch this." She turned to go then paused, laying a hand on Redknee's sleeve. "I know you want to believe your father is still alive," she said softly. "And I know I fed that desire when I told you Ragnar spoke of a connection between your father and the book – that he'd owned it at some point. I regret that now. It was just idle talk. Even if there was some link, your father is dead, Redknee. He's been dead to you for years." Then she disappeared into the crowd, taking Silver with her.

Redknee stayed a few moments longer. Perhaps Sinead was right. Certainly, if his father *was* alive, he'd abandoned his mother to raise a baby on her own, hardly the act of a hero. He pushed the thought from his mind. That he would find his father had been his mother's dying wish. A wish he would honour.

He watched as the chestnut snapped at the grey's ears; blood spurted across the smaller horse's flanks onto the ground. The crowd roared. Harold was at the front, urging the chestnut on, his face delirious with pleasure. Redknee sensed something different about Harold.

The cross in the mud. What a clean cut his dagger had made. That ivory handle was Harold's pride and joy, he was always cleaning it. But now, it looked dirty, black. *The dagger.* That was it!

He turned and pushed through the crowd after Sinead. She had been right about Brother Alfred's innocence after all.

"Redknee!" He heard someone call his name.

He looked round to see Ivar waving to him from the door of the longhouse. Damn. He had to find Sinead quick.

"Come here, lad," Ivar shouted. "I've something for you."

Redknee sighed and crossed the yard. Sinead and Brother Alfred would have to wait. Ivar beckoned him inside the longhouse, which was eerily quiet with all the men outside watching the horse fight.

"Remember I told you that your mother lived with us for a few months before you were born?"

Redknee nodded.

"Well, she was a very skilled craftswoman. She made many beautiful gifts for us." Ivar had crossed the room and was looking inside a big linen chest. He brought out a yellowed square of cloth and held it to the light. "I think this is it," he said squinting. "Yes, superb workmanship." He looked up at Redknee. "Come here lad, and see for yourself."

Redknee went over to him and took the cloth. True enough, the embroidery was exquisite. A border of white snowdrops encircled a rather self-satisfied looking unicorn. Above the unicorn were five ivy leaves picked out in gold thread. It looked exactly like the page from the *Codex* that had so beguiled Redknee just days before.

He couldn't believe it. His brain struggled to digest its import. After a long moment, he glanced up at Ivar who looked pleased with himself, and a bit drunk.

"This embroidery," Redknee said, his voice shaking with incredulity. "It was made by my mother before I was born?"

Ivar nodded. "She finished it while she was, you know, expecting you."

Redknee stared at the cloth again. It was fine, soft linen, perfect for covering a small table, or adorning the cradle of a newborn. If his mother had sewn this design, it meant she must have seen the *Codex* – been familiar with the image of the unicorn. And if she'd spent the time embroidering this image, there must have been a reason. It must have been important to her.

However he looked at it, this scrap of cloth was proof of his family's connection to the *Codex*. And it began before he was born.

"Thanks," he said to Ivar. "This means more to me than you can know."

He turned and ran from the longhouse. Sven claimed the *Codex* had been given to him only last month, by an old merchant in Kaupangen. Claimed that it was the first time he'd

137

seen it. Redknee now knew he had lied.*But why?* He had to find his uncle and make him speak the truth.

He found Sinead at a jewellery stall. Some of the local merchants, sensing an opportunity, had brought their wares out for the visitors. Sinead picked a soapstone cross and tied it round her neck.

"The green complements your eyes," the stallholder said.

Redknee came upon her quickly and he saw a flash of embarrassment on her face.

"Have you seen my uncle?" he asked. "I must speak to him."

Sinead hurriedly untied the pendant. "No," she said. "I was just going to visit Brother Alfred. Will you come with me?"

Damn. He wanted to speak to his uncle right now.

"Please," Sinead said. "He's innocent and he needs our help. Time is running out."

Redknee sighed. His uncle could wait. "Where are they keeping him?" he asked.

"He's in the barn with Toki. Does this mean you'll come?"

"It's no favour," Redknee said. "I've seen something that could save his life and make mine a lot easier."

"Well then," Sinead said smiling. "There's no time to lose."

They pushed through the crowd, past four burly men carrying away the grey's broken corpse. Magnus and Olaf were collecting their winnings. Magnus waved as they passed, both he and Olaf were splattered with blood. Not for the first time, Redknee shuddered at the fine line between life and death.

Sinead averted her gaze and hugged Silver close. He curled his lips and growled at the smell of the blood.

"Shh, little one," she said, then turned to Redknee, a look of disgust in her eyes. "How can men be so cruel?" she asked.

A man led another horse past them, towards the big chestnut killer. Redknee shrugged. "They're worse to people. At least they don't subject horses to *blood eagle*."

Sinead shook her head and started walking towards the barn. "When I became a Christian I thought I was entering a

138

kinder world. But one day, when I was at the monastery, I heard the local Bishop condemn an old woman to death. She was burned as a witch; the villagers claimed she'd summoned the devil to blight their crops."

"Maybe she did. Brother Alfred believes this Christian devil is powerful."

She sighed. "It was no coincidence the old woman owned rich land next to the Bishop's farm." She paused beside the barn door. "This Promised Land your uncle seeks ..."

"Yes?" Redknee asked.

Her voice hardened. "I go there not as a slave, but as an equal."

"My uncle has already promised you freedom, if we find it."

She smiled. "I should know better than to trust a Northman. Now," she said, motioning to Silver to wait outside, then pushing the barn door open. "Tell me what you know."

# Chapter 14

Someone was already visiting the prisoners in the barn. Whoever he was, he didn't see them enter.

"Who is it?" Sinead whispered.

"Shhh," Redknee said, holding a finger to his mouth. He peered through the darkness. The man stood at the far end of the barn with the prisoners, the hood of his cloak masking his face. Brother Alfred and Toki sat tied back to back against an oak pillar.

"I can't see. Let's wait there," Redknee said, pointing towards an empty stall. They crouched down in the wet hay and waited, putting the stink of manure from their minds.

The visitor spoke. "I know you understand the book. Tell me what it means or you'll feel my boot in your face." His voice was so low as to be unrecognisable.

"Bless you," Brother Alfred said. "For you know only violence."

"Don't try me, monk," the man said, and began pacing up and down the barn, cursing under his breath. "Look, I know you're lying. You'll be dead by sunset tomorrow, unless you tell me. Come on … *talk*. Are you protecting someone?"

Brother Alfred stayed silent this time. Presumably afraid of a boot in his face.

"Is it the Irish girl?" the visitor asked. "I know there's a traitor. There must be, Ragnar's attack was too much of a coincidence. It could be her. You're close to her, you would know. And by Odin's eye I've never liked Christians."

No answer.

The visitor sighed. "I see I'm wasting my time. I'm going to go. Give you time to think. But I'll be back soon. If you have any sense, any at all, you'll make the right choice. Just think … we could do this together. You and me. Split the treasure between us. Forget the rest of those fools. I'll leave

140

you now, but when I return, I expect you'll crow like a cockerel on the first day of spring."

Redknee and Sinead huddled in the shadows as the visitor swept past them. The barn door opened and Redknee caught a glimpse of the visitor in the moonlight. He didn't need a second look to recognise the battleaxe at his belt.

It was Uncle Sven.

Redknee and Sinead sat in the dark for some time, afraid to move in case the visitor returned. He didn't think Sinead had recognised his uncle, and he wasn't about to tell her. Besides, she had some answering of her own to do.

"Do you think I'm a traitor?" she asked, so quietly he almost thought he hadn't heard.

"Someone does," he replied.

"Do you?"

"Honestly?" he said. "I don't know. I'm not even sure I know what the word means anymore."

"Right. Well I'm not. Just because I'm different, it doesn't mean I can't be trusted."

"I agree," Redknee said.

"Do you think it's safe for us to move now?"

"Yes. The longer we leave it, the sooner he's coming back. And I don't think we should be found here."

They crawled over to the prisoners. Brother Alfred had a burst lip and black eye. Sinead swooped down on him and began dabbing at his cuts with the edge of her apron. "Oh, what have they done to you?" she said, tears springing to her eyes.

In contrast, Toki looked well, the wounds from his fight with Redknee and Olvir nearly healed. His lips curled into a grin at the sight of Sinead's ministrations. "Is it my turn next?" he asked, a mischievous glint in his eye. "A man could get used to that kind of treatment."

"Be quiet," Redknee said, kicking dust in Toki's face. "I don't know what you're smiling about. You'll be next."

Toki grinned, flashing a row of coal black teeth. "If you say so, *Master*."

Redknee ignored him and knelt beside Brother Alfred. "I've information that will save your life."

"Brother Alfred looked piously towards the roof. "My life is but God's to save," he said, then refocussed on Redknee. "But I'm listening to what you've got to say."

"Courage deserted you, little monk?" Toki asked. "Where's your God now?"

"I've already told you to be quiet," Redknee said. He turned back to Brother Alfred. "You didn't cause the fire at Ivar's farm. But you knew who did, and yet you said nothing. Why?"

The monk looked thoughtful for a moment. "I wanted the person responsible to come forward on his own."

"I know him, and he won't," Redknee said. "But worse than that, this person you've protected – he's dangerous. I think he could do it again."

"You really know who did it?" Sinead asked.

"I should've realised earlier," Redknee said. "The first clue should have been the events of that night. Harold's behaviour was strange. But that wasn't enough in itself. His precious dagger gave him away; the one with the ivory handle. When he brought it out to cut the centre mark at the start of the horse fight, I saw the hilt was black, like it had been dropped in a fire."

Brother Alfred nodded solemnly. "I came across the boy sharpening his dagger in the grain store. I told him, one spark in that place and the whole farm would go up in flames. But he didn't listen to me. It was like he was under a spell. He was talking to someone who wasn't there, a girl I think. Yes, that's right, the name he said, over and over, was Aud."

"Aud was his sister," Redknee said.

Sinead let out a long, low whistle. "We have to tell someone."

"Who would believe you?" Brother Alfred asked. "Everyone is convinced I'm to blame."

"We can't confront Harold on our own," Sinead said. "He'd deny it. We have to go straight to your uncle. Ivar's judgment is clouded by Matilda's anger."

142

Toki snorted. "You think Sven Kodranson will treat the monk fairly?"

"Stop listening," Redknee snapped. "This is no concern of yours." But he feared Toki uttered the truth.

He spoke to Sinead in a low voice. "I don't think we can go to my uncle on this one. It wasn't his farm, it's not his decision. He won't want to tread on Ivar's toes."

"Then *what*?" Sinead asked.

"We confront Harold ourselves. But first, we need to get a promise from Brother Alfred."

"What can you mean?" the little monk asked.

"Tell him, Sinead."

"I don't understand," she said.

Redknee stood. "It's quite simple really. Sinead thinks you're not actually reading from the *Codex*. So, if we do this to help you, we want your word that you will read from the book truthfully."

Brother Alfred nodded furiously. "Yes ... *yes* ... " he said. "I give my word."

Before he lost his nerve, Redknee dragged Sinead from the barn. Outside, the festivities were still in full swing. Silver hadn't waited as asked. The daft pup was probably trying to catch gulls on the beach. They had no time to look for him. The crowd had grown bored of the horse fighting and were shouting at two youths wrestling. Olvir called to them as they pushed through the revellers.

Redknee kept his head down. "Don't stop," he said to Sinead. "The fewer involved the better."

But Olvir was like a dog with a bone. "Hey!" He called again. "Where are you going?"

"We could do with the extra help," Sinead said to Redknee.

Perhaps she was right. He'd seen the frenzied look in Harold's eyes when the chestnut stallion tore the grey apart. Redknee stopped. "Alright, he can come."

Redknee scanned the crowd for Harold while Sinead explained the situation to Olvir.

143

"I saw him go down to the beach after the horse fight," Olvir said. "He was carrying a torch and some brushwood."

Sinead glanced anxiously at Redknee. "Do you think—?"

"The violence," Redknee said, starting to push through the crowd. "It's what sets him off."

They pressed through the drunken spectators towards the beach. The crowd thinned as they approached the bluff. "I think he's been obsessed with fire," Redknee said, scrambling down the steep path, "ever since Ragnar burned our village."

"There he is!" Sinead pointed to a figure at the far end of the beach heading towards a crop of jagged rocks. "He's dragging something behind him."

It looked like a sack, filled with … with something that seemed to be *moving*.

Redknee vaulted the last few feet and ran across the beach, oblivious to Sinead's screams to wait for help. But by the time he reached the spot before the jagged outcrop where they'd spotted Harold, Harold had vanished.

Redknee tore on. He leapt the rocks and skidded to a stop in front of a large pyre with a stake in the centre. Harold had tied the sack to the stake; he held a lit torch in his right hand.

"What are you doing?" Redknee asked.

Harold glanced up, his eyes feverish with excitement. "Stand back," he said, "this is none of your concern."

The sack squirmed. Something inside was alive. "By Thor's blood," Redknee said. "What have you got in there?"

"Nothing."

Redknee circled the pyre, his eyes trained on Harold. "I know about your obsession with fire," he said steadily. "This is not the way."

Harold snorted. "What do you know? You didn't see your sister melt beneath the flames. Her skin black and curling like old leather." Despair lined his face. "She was only nine."

Redknee blanched at the image. He hadn't known Harold had lost his sister. "I saw my mother die," he said.

Harold's eyes shone with interest. "How did it feel to hold her?" he asked. "As she took her last breath?"

Redknee shuffled uncomfortably. It was clear Harold had gone mad. "You relive it, don't you? Over and over."

144

Harold nodded slowly, lowering the torch a little. Redknee saw his chance. He leapt across the pyre and drove his fist into Harold's nose.

Harold fell, blood trickling from his nostril. The torch landed in the sand. Redknee kicked it away and was on him in a flash. Fists clenched, he rained blows on Harold's ribs. Harold twisted and clawed like a drowning stray but Redknee fought him down.

"Stop!" Sinead screamed. "You'll kill him!"

Redknee turned round. Harold kneed him in the groin and followed with his fist in Redknee's face. He flew backwards onto the sand. Harold came at him. Something shiny glinted in his hand.

*The dagger.*

Harold pressed the blade against his throat. As Redknee pushed back with all his strength, wisps of smoke reached his nostrils. The torch had made contact with the brushwood. He saw Sinead and Olvir running to help him.

"No!" he tried to shout, although his voice came out raspy and hoarse. "See to the fire first."

Sinead nodded and began tugging on the ropes attaching the sack to the stake while Olvir fought the growing flames.

"I want to see your face when you die," Harold sneered, madness shining in his eyes.

"Get off me!" Redknee shouted, squirming beneath his grip.

Harold laughed. "Will you cry, when I kill you? Like they say your father did when Ragnar killed him."

Anger seared through Redknee. How dare Harold speak of his father? Blind with fury, he spat in Harold's face. Harold thrust the dagger with new vigour. The blade nipped the soft skin at the base of Redknee's throat; then the pressure was gone. Harold was being lifted off him and he had a clear view of the night sky and its endless tapestry of stars. Redknee took great gulps of air.

A moment later, Astrid's pale face blocked the view. "You saved my darling Bleyõra," she said, holding her white cat up to her cheek. "I'm forever in your debt." She bent down and placed a kiss on his forehead. He felt himself blush as he wondered at her sudden appearance.

Uncle Sven stepped forward. "You all right?" he asked. It had been Sven, then, who had saved him.

Redknee nodded. He explained his theory about the fire at Ivar's farm.

"It was the violence of the horse fight that set Harold off tonight," he finished. "On the Sheep Islands it was the whale hunt."

Uncle Sven's face was a sombre mix of acceptance and sadness. "This will cause trouble with Olaf," he said, as Astrid's men led a sobbing Harold from the beach. "Which is all I need since Karl the Woodcutter has just been found with his throat cut."

# Chapter 15

Karl the Woodcutter lay behind the longhouse in a pool of his own urine, a gaping red smile parting the frigid skin of his throat. Redknee, Uncle Sven, Astrid and Ivar stared at the body. No one needed to ask what Karl had been doing before he was killed.

"Who was he last seen with?" Sven asked.

"With your men," Astrid said. "I don't know their names."

"He was sitting with Magnus and the Smithy at the feast," Ivar said. "But I saw him leave the longhouse alone, not long before the horse fight started."

At this moment, Magnus and Koll appeared, their faces almost as white as that of their dead friend.

"Did he get in a fight?" Sven asked them. "Do you know if anyone had a grievance with him?"

Koll shook his head. "Not that I know of. Has he been robbed?"

Sven pointed to the silver Thor's hammer still round Karl's neck and the bronze ring on the third finger of his right hand. "No thief would leave items of such value."

"They may have been disturbed in the act," Magnus offered.

"True," Sven said eventually. "But I think there's more to it than that."

"Reykjavik is such a busy place," Magnus continued. "Karl was drunk. Any lowlife could have slit his throat hoping to line their purse."

"No," Astrid said, shaking her head. "My men aren't murderers. It could just as easily be one of your men, Jarl Sven. A dispute brought with you from home, perhaps?"

"This is a sorry day," Sven said. "I've known Karl for more than twenty years. He was a good man. I will find whoever did this and see he pays."

147

"Aye," Koll said. "I'm with you on that."

Sven turned to Astrid. "Will you ask your women to see to Karl's body?"

Astrid nodded and left. Heads low, the rest of the men followed her, leaving Redknee and Sven alone with the body.

"This wasn't a robbery or a fight," Sven said. "Someone murdered Karl. There's a traitor in our midst, I can feel it in my bones. Whoever it is, they're in Ragnar's pay. It's how he found our village."

Skoggcat's face flashed through Redknee's mind. Traitor? What traitor. *He* was the traitor. "Sir," he said, taking a deep gulp. "Maybe that was just bad luck."

"No, lad," Sven said, shaking his head. "You want to believe the best of people, and that's a good trait. But if you're going to survive in this world, you've got to be smart. You showed brains and mettle with Harold tonight, unwise though it was to go confronting him on your own like you did. I'll not have you behave so recklessly again, you hear?"

Redknee nodded.

Sven crouched so that he was level with Karl's face. Gently, he untied the silver Thor's hammer from round Karl's neck and closed it in his fist.

"Karl's wife will be glad of this," he said. "By Odin's eye, I'm going to find the traitor. He has blood on his hands – the blood of many. And when I find him … or *her*, I'm going to make them pay."

Harold's bones shook in his skinny frame as the whip cracked across his bare back. It had taken four full-grown men to restrain Olaf. But Ivar had believed Redknee's story when he saw the charred ivory dagger and after hearing Astrid tell of the near burning of Bleyðra on the beach. Ivar had given Redknee Harold's dagger as a reward. Despite the fine workmanship, Redknee doubted it would bring him luck. Still, better in his hands than Harold's.

It was only the respect Uncle Sven had for Olaf, and his years of loyal service, that had spared Harold from a worse fate. In the circumstances seven lashes was a light punishment. Redknee would have liked to say he couldn't bear to watch,

148

that he didn't relish each desperate scream as the leather flayed Harold's soft white skin to a pulpy pink mush. But it would be a lie.

Redknee watched through a crack in the door as Thora prepared a hot poultice for Harold's back. He was in a bad way. He had not coped well with the lashing and had developed a fever. Redknee suspected it was a fever of pride. Olaf, worried his son wouldn't last the night, maintained a vigil at his bedside.

Thora left the longhouse. As she passed Redknee, he whispered, "Will Harold live?"

Thora glanced behind her, into the half-lit room. "I hope so. If he dies, you will have made an enemy of Olaf for life."

"Aye," Redknee said, "and if Harold lives, I fear I will have made two."

Thora nodded and left. Redknee turned to follow her, he needed to find Sinead, reassure himself she wasn't the traitor, when he heard Olaf start to speak.

"You did well, son," he said, stroking Harold's damp brow. "Took the lashings like a man, just as I knew you would."

"I tried my best, father," Harold mumbled. "Did I do good?"

Olaf nodded and took his son's hand in his. "Yes," he said. "You did just as I told you."

At that moment, Bleyðra sidled up to Redknee and began purring at the door. Olaf and Harold both looked up. Redknee pressed his body flat against the wall and edged away.

Redknee learned from Koll that Brother Alfred had gone into the foothills of the volcano to thank his God for his release and Sinead had gone with him. He wanted to speak to her before his uncle did; reassure himself she wasn't the traitor. He thought of the gash in Karl's throat. Could a woman, nay, one little more than a girl, really do that? Uncle Sven seemed to think so – if the conditions were right. Karl had been drunk, that was true. Whoever killed him had caught him while he

149

was off guard. Maybe, under those circumstances, a woman really could kill a full-grown man.

But Sinead?

He shook his head. She'd helped him out of the fire at Ivar's longhouse. Hadn't she? A little voice at the back of his head told him she'd been looking for the book – saving him was only an afterthought.

No. He wouldn't believe it. No matter what his uncle thought, Sinead was his friend. Surely he could trust her. *Couldn't he?*

# Chapter 16

As he walked up the lower slopes of Mount Hekla, Redknee cursed whatever madness had driven Brother Alfred to thank his God in such a place. What greenery there had once been was long dead – the skeletons of water-starved shrubs and grasses littered the edges of the path. The brittle black earth burned hot beneath his feet. It was like walking on the embers of a dying fire. Above him, flares of hot orange lit the night sky. He wrapped his cloak round his head, fearful a stray flash would fry him alive.

Silver whimpered.

"You're right, little one," Redknee said, "venturing up here is *exactly* what my uncle would call downright foolish."

Redknee found them praying. Two small figures kneeling before a wooden cross. Silver bounded forwards, licking Sinead's face until she opened her eyes and gave him a hug.

"Karl the Woodcutter has been found dead," Redknee said. "His throat cut."

Brother Alfred shook his head. "Well, don't look at me. I was tied up in the barn."

"That's what I wanted to talk to you about. You see, my uncle thinks there's a traitor among us. Someone who is working for Ragnar. My uncle thinks this person murdered Karl."

"That is most terrible," Brother Alfred said, frowning. "I will pray for Karl's soul, certainly I will, even though he was a pagan. But I fail to see how this connects to me."

"Sinead and I, before we spoke to you in the barn, we overheard," he glanced awkwardly at Sinead. She nodded for him to continue. "We overheard my uncle asking if you knew who the traitor was. You didn't answer. But if you do know,

151

no matter who you were protecting, you *must* tell me now because my uncle thinks it is Sinead."

Sinead let out an involuntary gasp. "It was your uncle in the barn?" she said, covering her mouth with her hand.

Redknee nodded.

"Oh, I will hang for this if the real murderer cannot be found!"

"Stay calm," Redknee said, placing his hand on her shoulder. "*I* believe you didn't do it. Brother Alfred can repay the service you have done him."

Brother Alfred shook his head. His face had turned pale.

"I wish I could help you, child," he said, looking at Sinead. "I truly do. But I don't know what your friend is talking about. You see, it wasn't me Sven Kodranson was questioning in the barn, but the other prisoner. The big pagan one with teeth like coals, Toki, I think his name is."

As Redknee digested this new information, a burning rock flew from the mouth of the volcano landing with a hiss close to where they stood. Silver leapt sideways with a yelp.

"We can't stay here," Redknee said, tugging Sinead's sleeve as a second flaming rock crashed into the earth, this one shattering in a spray of orange sparks. He turned to Brother Alfred. "We must go *now*."

Brother Alfred shrugged him off. "You go and see to this Toki, I have not finished the litany. God has kept me safe today. He will continue to keep me safe while I pray."

Another rock landed next to them, the dry grass at their feet crackled before erupting in flames. Brother Alfred looked surprised but remained kneeling.

"Sinead?" Redknee grabbed her hand as the grass fire began to spread. "Don't be foolish. Come with me *now*."

As Sinead hesitated, a rock struck her head, knocking her to the ground. Like a ravenous beast, the fire closed round her, trapping her in its jaws. Redknee pulled his cloak over his head, leapt through the flames and lifted her across his shoulder. The fire was already hot, and getting hotter. Sweat trickled down his spine as he looked for an opening. There were no gaps.

152

"You have to jump!" Brother Alfred had stopped his praying. *About bloody time*, Redknee thought.
Taking a deep breath and closing his eyes, he ran at the flames as fast as he could. Heat scoured his body, then cool air hit his lungs; he fell to the ground and rolled in the mud. He came to a stop. Sinead's dress was singed at the edges, but she was otherwise unharmed. He shook her gently while Silver and Brother Alfred looked on.

As Sinead stirred, her hand shot to the cut on her forehead. Blood smeared her fingertips. "What happened?" she asked groggily.

"A flying rock from the volcano hit you. But I think you won."

A smile flashed across Sinead's face, but it was short-lived. The fire had gathered pace now, fed by a hundred smaller blazes and a new burst of flying rocks. Redknee pulled her to her feet. She staggered a few steps before collapsing against him.

"Come on," he said, tugging hard. "We have to race the fire. Think you're up to it?"

She nodded cautiously. Silver yapped encouragement.

Redknee turned to Brother Alfred. "Your God has given up for the day," he said.

The little monk winced, but he followed Redknee all the same.

The four of them tore down the mountain pursued by a twisting knot of flame. By the time they reached Reykjavik, the volcano's caldera had burst and sheets of scalding ash were falling thick and fast. The longhouses nearest the mountain were ablaze. A group of men were trying to douse the flames. Redknee ran up to a young man carrying a wooden pail and tried to tell him it was pointless, that they must leave. The young man shrugged him off. It was the swineherd from the first day on the island.

The town was in chaos. People running everywhere. Some huddled under blankets, trying to avoid the falling ash. Others just stood there, staring at the sky. He held his scarf over his

153

mouth. They would all suffocate if they didn't get out fast. He turned to Sinead. Her eyes were wide with fear.

"We must get to *Wavedancer*," he said. "And quick, there won't be enough boats for everyone."

Astrid stood outside her longhouse, her silk dress smeared black. She was with a group of her warriors. They stood in a circle round a young woman. The woman's hair had been shaved off so her head looked strangely deformed. One of the men pushed the woman to her knees and held her still.

Astrid stepped into the middle of the circle and raised her hands aloft. The breeze whipped her golden hair about her face as she turned to face Mount Hekla.

"Frey, god of farming, protector of Iceland, as a sign of our loyalty, we give you this sacrifice."

Sinead gasped. "They're going to kill her!"

Suddenly Redknee knew what Astrid meant by *keeping Frey satisfied*.

"Oh dear, oh dear," Brother Alfred said, "this won't do." He knelt and started to pray.

"Stand up, you fool," Redknee said. "You're as bad as them. We need action, not more praying."

Redknee charged forward as the warrior holding the girl drew his dagger. He didn't see Redknee's fist. The blow, delivered square on the chin, sent the man flying into the mud. As he hit the ground with a squelch, Redknee heard twenty swords drawn in unison. He froze. He hadn't exactly thought of an exit strategy.

"What are you doing?" Astrid asked, her voice high and panicky. "We must pacify Frey or the whole island will be devoured by his wrath."

"You think slaughtering this girl will help?" Redknee asked.

"The sacrifice of a slave has always worked in the past. What else would you suggest? Dousing the lava with buckets of water?"

Redknee shook his head. "We must leave," he said.

Astrid laughed. "There aren't enough boats for even half the people of Reykjavik."

154

Sinead stepped forward. "We're wasting time. We must go."

"Listen to the slave girl," Astrid said, "before I sacrifice her instead."

"This is stupid," Redknee said. "There's space on *Wavedancer* for you, your men, and many more besides."

Astrid shook her head. "We will stay and make the sacrifice. It will pacify Frey. Anyone who leaves, I shall regard as a traitor."

"You're sentencing these people to death if you force them to remain," Redknee said.

One of Astrid's men stepped forward, his face white. "If there's a space for us," he said trembling, "we should take it. Save our sacrifice for when we really need Frey's protection."

Suddenly the rest of the men were agreeing.

Redknee sighed with relief. He wasn't going to be cut to pieces just yet.

Most of the longhouses were on fire now. Astrid looked around her and then at the cowering slave girl. A scowl of disappointment marred Astrid's pretty features. "Very well, then," she said. "To the beach!"

The warriors began running through the town towards the harbour. Redknee pulled the slave girl to her feet. She had no more than thirteen summers to her pitiful frame. "You're free to go," he said.

The girl stared at him with terror in her eyes. She seemed not to comprehend. Then Sinead spoke to her in a strange, lilting tongue. The girl nodded and started running towards the beach. Redknee stared at Sinead.

"She speaks the Irish," Sinead said, shrugging.

Redknee turned to Brother Alfred. "You must take Sinead and Silver to *Wavedancer*."

"Oh, yes," Brother Alfred said, springing to life. He took Sinead by the elbow and began leading her towards the beach.

"Are you coming too?" she called over her shoulder.

"I'll be right behind you. There's one thing I must do first." He turned and started across the yard towards the barn. Silver followed him.

"No – you go with Sinead." He spoke sternly.

155

The pup glanced towards Brother Alfred's retreating figure.

Redknee sighed. "I need you to look after her."

Silver hesitated, gold eyes wide, before darting off, quickly catching up with the mis-matched pair.

The barn sat on a small hill behind the longhouses. The fire had not reached it yet, if he was quick, he could make it there and back in time.

The barn was hot and dark inside. Redknee peered through the smoke. He heard a cough. Toki was still in there. He kept his head low where the smoke was thinnest and found Toki tied to the pillar where he'd left him the night before.

"Waste of time," The big man said when he saw Redknee.

"What do you mean?"

"Coming back to kill me."

"Don't worry. You're not so lucky. I'm here to speak to you."

"Really? You mean I have my uses. What's in it for me?"

"If I like what you say, I'll release you. If I *believe* what you say, I might let you come on *Wavedancer*."

"So sure your uncle hasn't already left."

Redknee shrugged. "You should trust me. I'm the only chance you've got."

"All right. What do you want to know?"

"I heard my uncle questioning you last night."

Toki nodded slowly. "Coward gave me this." He tilted his head so Redknee could see his bloody lip.

Redknee winced. He didn't like to think of his uncle dealing out brutality. "So you didn't answer his questions?"

Toki shook his head. "Matter of fact, I thought you were Sven, back to put an end to me."

"Why would my uncle want to kill you? Apart from you being one of Ragnar's lackeys."

"'Cause of what I know."

"Go on."

"You Erik Kodranson's boy?"

Redknee nodded.

"I knew your father."

156

"You lie."

"It's true. I knew both your parents. I grew up with your mother as a guest in her father's house. She was a good friend."

"And yet you attacked me – and my mother too."

Toki shook his head. "If I'd wanted to kill you, or your mother, I would have succeeded. My time with Ragnar was done."

"You *let* me capture you? On *purpose*?"

Toki shrugged.

Redknee eyed Toki with disbelief. He didn't know what to think. "I don't know," he said, "your story could be a trick to get me to trust you."

"Lad, you ask the wrong questions. You can't afford not to trust me. Did you know your mother almost married Ragnar?"

"That's a lie."

Toki laughed. "Oh, your uncle never mentioned that? And neither he would. You see, he was in love with your mother too."

"Stop it … stop these lies. Just tell me why Sven was questioning you about the book. What is it you know?"

"I'm telling you – if you'll listen."

"Get on with it then."

"Your uncle was jealous of your father," Toki said, coughing. The smoke was getting thicker. "I suppose he told you your father was a pathetic warrior. You don't need to answer. The look on your face says it all. Well, it's true he wasn't much of a fighter.. But that doesn't mean he wasn't brave. Before you were born, your father, Sven and Ragnar raided an Irish monastery. They stole many great treasures from it, not least a precious book, the only one of its kind in the world."

"The *Codex Hibernia?*"

Toki nodded. "Your father became obsessed with the book – with decoding its secrets. But there was a falling out – that's when your father fought Ragnar. Afterwards, Ragnar ran away with the loot and set himself up as a warlord, buying in mercenaries to enforce his rule. He didn't get the book though

– Sven, the canny old fox, must have taken it for himself in the commotion."

"Damn," Redknee said. "I *knew* the book was linked to my father. But why was my uncle questioning *you* about it?"

"Back then, I was your father's closest friend. Your uncle believes your father, in his obsession, decoded the exact location of the treasure. Sven thinks your father told me where this was."

"Did he?"

Toki laughed. "I wish. Do you think I would be serving that maniac Ragnar as the hired help if I knew the secret to riches beyond imagination? I don't think so."

"Do you know if my father yet lives?"

Toki shook his head. "I don't know. I never saw him again after his fight with Ragnar."

"You saw the fight?" Redknee asked, surprised. "Is it true my father was mortally wounded?"

A rafter crashed from the roof, setting fire to the straw at Toki's feet. "Come on," Toki said. "I'll answer anything you want once we get out of here. I've kept my side of the bargain. Now untie me before we're both killed."

# Chapter 17

The beach heaved with people trying to squeeze onto the few remaining vessels. A dozen rowing boats and a couple of larger fishing crafts groaned beneath many times their normal load. Yet still the panicked islanders piled on.

*Wavedancer* had broken her moorings and was wedged in the shallow waters near the beach. Koll and Uncle Sven were trying to push her free as yet more people clambered onboard. She looked fit to topple.

"By Thor's hammer," Redknee said to Toki as they arrived on the scene. "They'll sink *Wavedancer*. We've got to help my uncle push her free."

Redknee and Toki hurried across the beach. Sinead and Brother Alfred were among the mass of people wallowing in the shallows. Brother Alfred was trying to raise Sinead high enough to grab an oarport, while a man on the deck tried to stamp on her head. Olvir was a little further off. He couldn't see Silver anywhere.

"Forget that," Toki said. "It's every man for himself." He stretched his long legs, charging at the pack of bodies, bounded across their backs and onto the deck before anyone could stop him.

So much for gratitude, Redknee was on his own. He splashed into the water and jammed his shoulder under the hull next to Koll. He pushed with all his might, but the weight of all the people had crushed the keel into the sand. She was stuck fast.

"We'll never move her like this," Koll said, wiping the sweat from his brow.

Uncle Sven's face turned pink as he pushed harder. "We need more men down here, and fewer lording it on deck."

"They're scared to help," Koll said. "In case they lose their place."

159

Redknee had an idea. He splashed through the shallows until he reached Olvir. He tugged on his friend's shoulder. "We need your help up front," he said.

Olvir nodded. Sinead and Brother Alfred followed too, the pudgy monk waddling awkwardly as his cassock fanned in the surf. They took up positions on either side of Redknee.

"Now," Sven said and they pushed their weight against the keel as one. The ship creaked and scraped a short furrow in the sand before lodging itself in the seabed once again. She was sinking deeper into her sandy grave with every effort they made.

"It's no use," Sven shouted above the clamour. "We need more strength."

"Praise be to the Lord!" Brother Alfred huffed. Redknee turned to see him dragging a large wooden plank across the beach, his weedy eyes popping with the strain. "Will no one help me with this blasted thing?" he wailed.

Redknee rushed from the water and lifted an end.

Uncle Sven looked doubtful. "How will we get that under the hull?"

Brother Alfred looked round in anticipation of a volunteer. When none was forthcoming, Redknee raised his hand.

"I'll do it," he said. He didn't want to, the tide was strong, but someone had to, someone small enough to get right under the hull, and strong enough to wedge it there, or they would all die on this forsaken beach.

"No!" Sinead gasped. "You'll be crushed."

Ignoring her, Redknee hauled the plank into the water and swam out, avoiding the churn from flailing limbs. It was too deep to stand at the prow so he trod water as he filled his lungs with giant gasps of air. Taking one last breath, he started to descend beneath the waves when Sven grabbed his arm.

"You're beginning to take after your mother," he said, sadness in his eyes. "She was afraid of nothing."

Redknee nodded. He hadn't known his mother was brave. He only knew her as the woman who darned his socks and cooked his porridge. Unsure what to say, he took one last gulp of air and plunged beneath the waves, the board tucked firmly under his right arm. As the quiet of the water cocooned him,

160

he thought he heard his uncle urging him to be careful. But he couldn't be sure.

He kicked hard until he was beneath the sloping underside of the hull. As he struggled to get deeper, the sea flattened him against the strakes. Barnacles gouged his skull. He clutched at seaweed, his cursing muffled as the stalks came away in his hand. He had to wedge the plank tight under the keel for the plan to work.

Something slid past his calf. His heart quickened; roared in his ears. Panicking, he lashed out with his feet in a frenzy of bubbles. The force sent him crashing into the hull. Blood trickled into his eye and he blinked in the half-light as an eel slithered past. He relaxed. An eel he could deal with.

But his relief was short-lived. In his terror, he'd let go of the board. He saw a dark shadow floating towards the light. He kicked after it, reaching it just before it popped through the surface. Damn. He had to start again. Kicking like a frog and pulling at the hordes of barnacles clinging to the hull, he inched his way along. Eventually, he made it deep enough. Faint with lack of air, he fought to wedge the board under the keel. Summoning the last of his strength, he pushed as hard as he could until the board was jammed tight between the ship and the soft seabed.

His fingers tingled. Yellow spots swam in front of his eyes. He had to reach the surface. He kicked, forcing the water to carry him faster towards the light. Every nerve in his body ached for air. Craved it ferociously, like a parched man craves water. He was nearly there: his delicious drink of air in reach. And then, nothing …

He woke, coughing and spluttering in Uncle Sven's arms. "We thought we'd lost you there. You were gone for some time."

"I got it under," Redknee said, quickly composing himself. He was still in the water, but it was shallow enough that he could stand. He found his feet and moved away from his uncle. "Someone needs to get those people out the way."

"I'll do it," Sinead said. She stood waist deep in the water, strands of hair plastered across her face like trailing vines.

161

Sinead did her best to convince the stricken islanders to stand back while the men tried to push *Wavedancer* free. A couple of the islanders came to help them. But still nothing happened. Redknee sighed. His efforts were in vain. They were all going to die. Clouds of black smoke had reached the beach now. People covered their mouths as lumps of ash rained down, blotting out the sun.

"We'll all choke to death!" Koll said, wiping a pulpy mixture of ash and water from his face.

Suddenly, a great explosion rent the air. Redknee covered his ears as the seabed shook beneath his feet. He staggered. A large wave slammed into his side, knocking him under the water. When he surfaced, a jet of orange fire shot hundreds of feet skyward from the top of Mount Hekla, hurling a torrent of rocks in all directions. A vast plume of black ash crowned the fire, and it appeared to be coming their way.

Brother Alfred stood, his mouth agape. "Dear Father in Heaven," he said, trembling, "the whole island will be swallowed."

"Come on," Redknee said. "We need to push, NOW!"

It must have been the tremor, or strength born of panic, for this time, *Wavedancer* slipped free of the sand. But the people on board lost no time. As soon as the ship was free, someone gave the order to begin rowing and twelve sets of oars struck the water at a brisk pace.

"Those ungrateful dogs," Sven said. "They're leaving without us!"

Redknee powered through the waves after them, followed by his uncle and hundreds of desperate souls. He heard his heartbeat echoed in the rhythmic splash of *Wavedancer's* oars. He didn't know what he was doing; swimming after a ship? Damn stupid. *Wavedancer* had been built for speed by some of the finest craftsmen in all the Northlands, and she cut through the waves faster than any swimmer could hope to follow. He would never catch them, but then, what else could he do? He couldn't turn round.

His heart bounced in his ears as he forced his limbs to keep going in disregard of the odds. He'd rather drown trying to escape than be fried alive ashore.

Then it struck him. He could no longer hear the rhythmic thud of the oars. He stopped to look up. Oars flailed randomly, splashing water into the air, like the legs of a drunken caterpillar. In their panic, and without the leadership of his uncle, they'd lost their rhythm. *Wavedancer* would not make good time unless her oarsmen worked together. His heart soared. This was his chance. He tucked his head down and ploughed forward.

Redknee reached *Wavedancer* right behind his uncle. Seeing a place where the oars were still, he slid underneath and scrabbled to grab hold of the hull. But the wood was slippery and his fingers failed to find purchase. His uncle fared better; being tall enough to reach an oarport, he hauled himself bodily over the rail and onto the deck.

The hysterical voices of those onboard rose above the waves, punctured by the sound of drawing steel. The crowd fell silent. Redknee looked up, expecting to see Sven's body tossed over the side. Instead, he heard a man shout above the din:

"We can't take anymore people on board. This ship is full."

The man hadn't asked a question, but Redknee waited, hoping to hear a response in his uncle's familiar voice. After what seemed like a long time, he heard his uncle reply.

"We must all work together," he said. "You cannot sail this ship without the knowledge of the men who built it." Redknee breathed with relief. His uncle's voice was strong and true. He was unhurt.

"Ach, they're all much the same," the man who'd spoken before shouted. "Any more people and this tub will sink."

"Aye!" Someone else shouted. "Throw any newcomers overboard."

The clang of steel on steel echoed through the hull. Redknee struggled to see if Ivar or Olaf were there to help his uncle, but his hand kept slipping and he feared being swept beneath the keel.

Other swimmers started arriving at the longship, circling out of reach of the oars. Koll was among them. Redknee motioned to Koll to swim under the oars and join him. Just as

163

Koll's head disappeared beneath the surface, a hand appeared over the side of the hull and dragged Redknee upwards, out of the water and onto the deck.

"Couldn't leave you to drown, after you saved my life," Toki said, smiling.

Redknee shivered in the cold air. Fighting had broken out between Sven and the Icelanders. Sven wasn't alone. Olaf, Magnus and the Bjornsson twins had come to his aid. But the ship was packed, leaving scant room to swing a sword. Fearful women and children huddled together, stamping on the hot ash that singed the deck. Astrid stood at the prow, her beloved Beyõral curled beneath her cloak. She was protected by four of her men-at-arms. They seemed to be biding their time before choosing a side. Redknee had no such luxury.

He turned to Toki. "I suppose you're unarmed."

Toki grinned. "These big fingers can be light as a feather." He pulled an old twin-edged sword from his belt and handed it to Redknee. "I prefer to fight with an axe," he said, producing a short-handled hatchet from beneath his tunic.

Redknee shook his head. "I won't ask who you took these from."

"Can't reveal any more secrets today," Toki said as he turned to meet a charging Icelander head-on.

Redknee gripped the hilt of the rusty sword and glanced round. Sven and his men were outnumbered by the rabble of Icelanders by as much as six to one. But the mob fought carelessly, panic in their eyes. Sven's men stood a slim chance.

His uncle swung the great Dane-axe above his head. It whirred through the air, terrifying the two men who'd been about to attack him. Sven growled savagely, baring his teeth at the pair, and they scampered away. Redknee was about to join the fighting when a fiery rock struck a rolled-up sail. The wool erupted in a flash of orange. Silver darted out from under it, his amber eyes wide with fear.

Sven's display did not deter the ox of a man who stepped up next. The beast lunged at Sven with an iron-tipped spear, the muscles in his vast arms snapping with every thrust. Sven brought his axe crashing down on the man's hand, but the

164

blade skittered off the spear, causing only a flesh wound. Sven dodged the next jab. But the deck was slick with ash and seawater; he faltered. His attacker took the advantage, lunging at Sven's chest. Redknee heard a strangled cry. It could have come from him, he couldn't be sure as he tore across the deck to where his uncle first convulsed and then stiffened against the spear.

Redknee hurled himself between them. The old sword suddenly felt smart as an arrow as he propelled it towards the attacker's shoulder. The spearman, still wallowing in his early success, moved slowly. Redknee felt bones crumble and splinter as the blade made impact. The man staggered. Redknee pushed him to the ground and raised his arms for the final blow. The man closed his eyes and a tear trickled down his cheek. Redknee wavered. This wasn't what he'd intended. The ship would be witness to a bloodbath and *none* would escape the volcano alive. The fighting had to stop now.

He pressed his foot into the spearman's chest. "Submit, or I'll fillet you like a cod."

The man gripped the lesion at his shoulder and nodded. Redknee saw the ship's horn dangling from a hook on the mast, grabbed it and blew as hard as he could.

The fighting continued. So he seized his captive by the collar, pressed his sword against the man's throat, and blew again.

"Stop!" he shouted. "I have your leader."

A couple of heads jerked round, but there was no let up in the fighting.

"Stop fighting or I'll kill him!"

Reluctantly, a few of the Icelanders lowered their weapons. Redknee took this pause as his cue.

"We're not your enemies," he shouted. "All we want is to escape the volcano, just like you. There are hundreds of your fellow Icelanders still in the water, and not a few of my uncle's men."

"Aye, and they'll sink us if we stop for them," a woman shouted.

"Which would you prefer?" Redknee asked. "To die by the sword or to help your fellow man? This ship is strong, she can

165

easily take more. And if you let me, I'll tell you how we can carry every last person floundering in the water to safety."

At this, most of the men lowered their swords. Many still had loved ones in the water and were willing to listen to any plan that might save them.

# Chapter 18

They neared the islands as dawn eclipsed the night. Tongues of sharp, white light licked the heavens clean. Redknee lifted a hand to shield his eyes. Morning made everything depressingly real.

He pulled his sheepskin tightly about his shoulders and went to check on his uncle. Sven had lost a lot of blood from his injury. Though the spear seemed to have missed any major organs, it had re-opened the shoulder wound Sven had suffered during his fight with Ragnar. Last night Redknee had ripped his woollen cloak into strips and bandaged his uncle's shoulder. Blood now showed through, a dark patch on the brown wool.

"Ach," Sven grunted, pulling himself upright, "I'm fine. Look," he said, raising his left hand, "I can still move my arm. It's the others you should worry about; the ones who have been in the sea."

Redknee lifted the bandage gently. The wound was clean and it had started to clot. Satisfied, he nodded, left Uncle Sven to rest and went to see the ropes.

*Wavedancer* had never been so full. People lay everywhere on deck, huddled together against the cold, propped upright against the mast, even sitting on the gunwale, a sea of pink faces, crushed together in adversity. Yet these were the lucky ones. Redknee pushed past them and leaned over the rail; a blast of tart air caught his face. They had entered colder seas. They would be lucky if anyone in the water had survived the night.

The water was glassy smooth, devoid of life. He slumped against the rail. The sea had taken them. Beaten the fires within, doused their will to live. He punched the blistered wood. They had tried so hard to save those *Wavedancer* could not carry. The ropes had been their only solution, to drag the wheezing, spluttering, half-drowned husks in the water to the nearest island, a safe distance from Mount Hekla's wrath. It was a crazy plan, but it was the best they could do. In the end though, it hadn't been enough.

A dark fleck near one of the ropes caught his eye. *A head?* He called out, but it didn't move. His heart sank. It had been too much to hope.

Sinead joined him. "We should pull the ropes in," she said, her voice flat as the millpond surrounding them.

He looked round the deck. His uncle still dozed, as did most of the others onboard. No one had truly slept last night. But it was time. Koll was out there somewhere, and Redknee had to know if his friend lived. He took the end of one of the thick ropes slung round the gunwale and pulled. At first, it slid along easily, but soon he felt resistance. He tugged hard, but it was stuck. He glanced at the water. Several objects, visible now as heads, bobbed nearby. One of the heads looked up at him and opened its eyes.

*They were alive!*

"Hang on to the rope," he yelled, pulling for all he was worth. "I'll get you out."

Sinead placed her hand on his arm. "Bring that poor soul in. I'll swap my place."

"No. It's too cold."

"If *they* can survive the night, I can make it to the islands. We'll land before the sun has fully risen."

Redknee nodded. The choice was hers to make.

Sven, Olaf and many others came to help Redknee pull out the survivors. They rescued more than thirty people. He didn't know how many had clung to the ropes when they left Reykjavik last night, but he thought it more than twice that number.

For each shivering wreck they hauled aboard, one brave volunteer from the ship traded their place. The exchange was performed in silence, without knowing the sum of who lived and who had died. Both an answer and a question, each sodden being brought a queasy sort of relief, for every family had spent a sleepless night, unaware if their father, brother or

168

son would endure. The final toll, they knew, would be known only upon landing.

Joy and sorrow warred in Redknee's heart as they plucked the last survivor, trembling and blue, onto the deck. Koll grinned shakily at him, his clothes plastered against his body.

"Anything worth eating?" Koll asked, rubbing his belly with a trembling hand as Thora ran forward to hug him.

Redknee stared at the water stupidly, hoping to conjure more faces from the blankness. But nothing came of it. Despair burned in his guts. Must death follow him everywhere?

Brother Alfred shuffled over to the rail and rested a plump hand on his shoulder. "We have done our best," he said. "It is as God wills."

"How can you say that?" Redknee snapped back. "You prayed to your god all night. You said he is powerful; more powerful than all our gods. Stronger even, than Odin. So why did so many die?"

"Oh, it is not the fault of my god," Brother Alfred said, shaking his head sadly. "Yesterday's fire mountain is only the beginning. The end of days comes fast upon us. The Son of God will soon return to destroy the earth and claim the faithful as his own. That is why I first came to these Northlands, to spread the Good News before the final reckoning."

"What rot you talk! We have our own stories for the end of days. A great battle, known as Ragnarok, will rage across the world. There is no mention of a fire-spewing volcano. Why should I believe you? Why should I believe the end of the world is upon us because one measly fire mountain kills half a town?"

"Oh yes, that is a very good question," Brother Alfred said screwing up his face. "It is the year, you see."

"I'm afraid I don't."

"This is the nine hundredth and ninety-ninth year since the birth of our Lord Jesus."

"So?"

"Well, it is thought by many revered monks, indeed by the Pope himself, that Christ will return to earth on the year marking the one thousandth anniversary of his birth. That year, my child, is but six months away."

"I can't listen to this anymore," Redknee said, slamming his fist against the rail. "Your story doesn't explain anything. It is next to useless. What use are stories anyway? They can't wield a sword or sail a ship or feed a starving family. Do stories clothe you when you're cold, or nurse you in sickness? Can a story build a village, or forge a river, or make the living from the dead? Even the greatest tales of gods and heroes are, in the end, nothing but words that wander in the wind. It is men, and only men, that keep them alive."

Brother Alfred blinked in astonishment. "How well you speak for a boy of sixteen summers. You are moved by your experience, no doubt. Yes, that is the explanation. But I tell you, the end of days *is* near. You should heed my warning. We must all prepare. Christian or no, it is not too late to convert. I tell you, this spring shall see the one thousandth anniversary since the birth of our Lord. Christ will return. We are lucky to be living now."

Redknee snorted. He did not feel lucky.


Soft, pliant sands wreathed the islands off the coast of Iceland. Those *Wavedancer* towed were able to walk the last few miles ashore with ease. From here, Mount Hekla's fiery rage was nothing but an ember on the horizon.

Redknee sought Sinead among the hysterical families on the beach. He found her kneeling in the shallows, her curls flattened against her face; her eyes pressed shut in prayer. Goosebumps crinkled her pale skin.

He pulled her to her feet and pressed his warm body against her cold one. "You're alive," he gasped.

Her eyes flashed open in response and he felt a surge of pure bliss. In that moment he forgot his sorrow and despair. Hope is a simple animal. It will take the most meagre scraps and invent a banquet.

"Do you still think I'm a traitor?" she asked.

He cupped her head in his hands and stared into her eyes. "I never thought that," he said. "We must find who really killed Karl and prove it to my uncle."

170

Thirty-six townspeople had survived the sea; together with the sixty who'd managed to stow aboard *Wavedancer*, it was a sizeable catch. With the smaller boats also heading for the coastal islands, Ivar volunteered to stay with the Icelanders as their temporary Jarl. This would allow Astrid to sail west with *Wavedancer* to find her husband, Gunnar. Matilda agreed to look after Bleyðra.

They lit fires along the beach and huddled round for warmth. The Icelanders kept to themselves, leaving Sven and his men alone to discuss the next step in their voyage.

"This is madness," Olaf said when he heard Sven still intended to press further west. "Our supplies are low. The *Codex* is lost. We should put an end to this stupid quest and return home, where we know what awaits us. By Thor's hammer, if we sail too far we could fall off the end of the world, right into the jaws of Jörmungandr, the great sea-serpent! He waits for foolish travellers like us, you know, and can swallow a longship whole."

Sven shifted uncomfortably. "Olaf, you've always been my right-hand-man and I hear what you say about Jörmungandr. It's a risk. But your son is ill and ... well, it seems you've lost your thirst for adventure. I will understand if you want to remain here, with Ivar. I won't see it as you giving up."

Olaf turned red. "I'm *not* afraid. I would gladly face Jörmungandr, Fenrir and all the monsters of Middle Earth if I thought there was any point to this stupid quest of yours."

"I never said you were afraid," Sven said mildly. "And while your concern about the serpent is valid, we're unlikely to have to face the giant wolf Fenrir at sea. I merely meant that I know the value of family and I will understand if you want to look after your son while he recovers from his ... ordeal."

Olaf stood, upsetting his bowl of fish stew. "You're obsessed with the legend of the Promised Land," he said, jabbing his finger in Sven's face. "You can no longer see the stories about it are preposterous. Have you heard the crazy tales the men tell to keep their spirits up? With each passing day of hardship, the stories become more ridiculous, more insane. Thora thinks she's going to bathe each day in asses'

171

milk; Magnus thinks there will be emeralds the size of duck eggs; Koll thinks every meal will be a feast to rival midsummer; and, silliest of all, that slave girl thinks we will let her go free." He sneered at the last.

"You are wrong about one thing, Olaf." Sven said, a smile tugging at his lips. "I still have the book. I hid it on *Wavedancer* before that volcano blew its top. I tell you, we *will* find the Promised Land. We *will* avail ourselves of its riches."

"Pah," Olaf said. "You have no idea. Karl has already suffered for your madness. I for one am not going to throw my life away on rumours, or lose my only son, the last living member of my family, under the leadership of a fool."

Magnus stood. Redknee noticed his hands shook. "I agree with Olaf," he said, his voice feeble, like watered mead. "We don't really know much about the Promised Land, or even if the book is reliable. If Ragnar wants the treasure, maybe we should leave him to it; not go seeking more danger."

A few insipid "*Ayes*" trickled round the campfire.

There was a time Redknee would have sided with Olaf and Magnus. If it wasn't for the prospect that his father might be out there somewhere, he would have stood and been counted with them. But as it was, the chance, albeit remote, that he was following in his father's footsteps, was enough to spur him on. Ulfsson's words had been enough to convince him of that.

Redknee spoke as Magnus sat down. "What the book says is true. I know this because I have met a man who I believe has been to the Promised Land."

"When?" Olaf shouted

"In Iceland; Astrid took me to him. The man, Ulfsson was his name, had sailed with her husband. They left Reykjavik two years ago looking for Greenland. Instead they reached a land far to the west where the people spoke no known language." He thought of adding the bit about the disappearing warriors, but decided it would not help the case.

"Where is this man now?" Olaf asked, his voice dripping with derision. "Find him, and let him speak for himself."

"He can't," Redknee said. "He was killed in a tavern brawl."

172

"How convenient," Olaf said. "Tell me, how do we know this Ulfsson's land, if Ulfsson even exists, is the same as the Promised Land of the *Codex*?"

Redknee had no answer to this, but Sinead saved him from providing one by climbing onto a rock and coughing.

"Some of you might not know me. I'm the servant girl you took from the monastery of Rock Fells in Ireland."

Oh, by Odin's all-seeing eye, Redknee thought, she might be pretty, but why did she have to stick her nose into everything? Others agreed, because a murmur went round the group, peppered with insults about her slave status. At least no one called her a traitor.

Sinead ignored the remarks and went on. "Olaf says the rumours about the Promised Land are lies. But I often heard the monks talk of the place. About how Saint Brendan was said to have visited it. There are no more learned men in the whole world than the monks of Ireland. We can trust their judgment. If they say the Promised Land exists, I believe them."

"She lies!" Someone shouted.

A rotten apple sped towards her from the midst of the group; striking her on the forehead. She staggered; Redknee thought she was going to fall. He dashed forward, but Astrid was quicker. In a flash, she had stepped up and offered her arm for balance. She stared at Sinead the way a fox eyes a chicken. This was no act of charity.

"May I?" Astrid asked, nodding at the rock, though it didn't sound much like a question.

Disoriented, Sinead nodded dumbly and stood down.

Astrid ascended the rock that had become their *de facto* hustings. Her cool stare silenced the hecklers. She began confidently, with no trace of the hesitation or anxiety she'd shown on their arrival at Reykjavik. The contrast thrilled Redknee; it should have terrified him.

"As some of you may know, my husband is in Greenland. It is my belief that this is another name for the Promised Land of your legend. My husband is a great man – a respected leader and fearless warrior. I want to help him settle there and

173

I will give a thousand coins of Arab silver to each man who helps me."

Chatter rose from the crowd. Astrid's offer had captivated them.

But Olaf wasn't finished. He stood in front of her. "Are we going to take orders from these, these … *women*?" He spat the last word as if it was a piece of indigestible gristle.

Doubt twisted, knife-like, into the assumptions of every man present. Redknee could see it in their faces, the desire for riches, for adventure, for glory versus the safe, easy route that would preserve their lives but end forever their dreams of immortal renown.

In the end, Sven, who was the better diplomat and still held the respect of his men, saw his opportunity writ large in the big, simple faces before him. It was not bravery they lacked, but clarity. He would give them that.

"Astrid will grant a thousand coins of Arab silver to each man who will search for her husband. I will join her, but I will add this promise – that each man who helps me reach the Promised Land will receive forty acres of fertile land and as many jewels as he can carry."

A cheer went up from the men. The decision had been made. They would continue on. Redknee prayed that hope had not, after all, fooled them into eating scraps.

# Chapter 19

Olaf placed the alcohol-soaked rag across his son's back with care. Harold juddered in pain. Olaf grabbed him to his chest and stroked his hair. The sway of the ship seemed to soothe the father but not the son. Harold's eyes had withered. They were devoid of hope, like those of an old man. Death-bed eyes.

Redknee let the tarpaulin fall back into place and turned away. He still had Harold's ivory-handled dagger hanging from a loop on his belt. It didn't feel a like a prize now. It felt like a warning. Had revenge played a part in Olaf's eventual, and somewhat reluctant, decision to continue on with them? It wasn't like the big man to give in. It wasn't like Harold to forgive a trespass. When Redknee had asked his uncle, he just laughed.

"Olaf is still my most trusted man," he'd said. "He understands his son did wrong so I'm sure he harbours no grudge against you for Harold's lashing. But he's been through a lot. He needs time, and space, to see what an opportunity the Promised Land is. The fact he's decided to join us, when he could have stayed with Ivar and Matilda, means he's starting to come round."

Redknee had nodded at Sven's explanation. Privately he wondered if his uncle's desire to find the Promised Land hadn't begun to curdle his brain.

Dismissing these thoughts as best he could, Redknee tucked the dagger into the folds of his tunic and wandered along the deck. It was three days since they'd left Iceland. The seas grew colder. Frost dusted the planks, even at midday. When he woke in the mornings, he could see his life-breath floating in the air. Sinead reassured him the chill wouldn't leach his inner vapours unless it became *much* colder. She delighted in puffing shapes from between her pursed lips and watching as her life-breath disappeared into the frigid sky. Wasteful, Redknee thought. And not quite believing her, he huddled up to Silver at night all the more.

As he approached the stern, Redknee saw Astrid exchange a word with Magnus at the tiller. The presence of Astrid and her four men-at-arms had upset the on-board dynamic. They kept to themselves near the stern; had their own rations of pickled mutton; duck eggs; even turnips and a small pouch of horseradish. But they didn't share. This annoyed the rest of the men forced to survive on the scraps Olaf had scavenged from the tiny island where they'd sheltered from the volcano.

Seeing Redknee, Magnus gave Astrid a curt nod and turned to stare back out to sea, his eyes shuttered; blank and impassive as the dull waves.

Redknee avoided Astrid's cool stare – she still hadn't forgiven him for stopping her sacrifice to Frey – and turned back towards the prow. Thora sat with Koll and the Bjornsson twins, swaddled in bear furs, only the pink tip of her nose peeking out. The wind caught a scrap of their conversation. They were discussing the treasure. *Not again*, Redknee thought, when he heard Thora declare she would have brooches of jade and five slaves just to braid her hair.

Koll saw him. "Join us," he said, waving. "We have a chunky fish stew."

Redknee shook his head. It was time he spoke to Sven about the origins of the *Codex* and its links with his father. The unicorn and ivy embroidery on his mother's cloth was evidence enough of a connection. Toki's story about how Sven believed Redknee's father had worked out the location of the Promised Land, perhaps even found it for himself, if Ulfsson was to be believed, made speaking to Sven critical. Since they'd left Iceland, the tale had burned in Redknee's mind, hotter than the flames of Mount Hekla.

Redknee clenched his hand. Everything pointed to Sven having lied. How dare he keep the truth from him? His uncle was nothing but an interloper in his father's longhouse, living, as he had done for the past sixteen years with Redknee and his

176

mother. Living as *jarl* in his father's stead. He'd put off speaking to his uncle long enough. Long enough by far.

Sven stood at the prow, his arm slung over the red and gold dragonhead, cloak billowing in the wind. His desire, nay, Redknee thought, desire wasn't a strong enough word. Obsession, *that* was it. His uncle's obsession to reach Greenland, lest it be the Promised Land, had made him impatient. Redknee could almost picture saliva dripping from his uncle's mouth as he watched for that first glimpse of Greenland's famous lush hills. Sven hadn't sat, hadn't slept, hadn't turned his eyes from the horizon since they'd left Iceland. He even took his whale stew standing, oblivious to the brown liquid sloshing over his fine blue tunic.

As Redknee approached his uncle, Toki crossed the deck ahead of him and tapped Sven on the shoulder. Redknee paused. He would know what Toki had to say to his uncle. Until now, the big warrior had kept his distance from Sven, fearful, Redknee had assumed, of retribution for defecting to Ragnar's band.

But when Sven saw it was Toki come to join him, he smiled and threw his arm round the younger man as if they were long lost brothers. Redknee halted. It was not the reception he'd expected for Toki, given Sven's threats to him in the barn.

"You have to hear this!" a female voice called.

Redknee turned to see Sinead beckoning him to join her. Sinead, Olvir and Silver were sitting with Brother Alfred, listening as he told one of his stories. Green, blue and gold eyes wide, watching every hand gesture the little monk made as he wove his story in the air, like the weaver threads the weft into the warp.

"Come on," she said. "It's really good."

Redknee glanced back at his uncle. He and Toki were deep in conversation. Redknee sighed. He supposed he could wait. Where, after all, could his uncle go on a longship?

Redknee joined Sinead on one of the thick furs. Silver nuzzled close. Try as he might to focus on the monk's tale, Redknee couldn't help straining to hear the conversation going on behind him. But the wind stole the meat. More

177

disturbingly, Redknee could picture two sets of eyes further down the ship, father and son, marking his back.

Brother Alfred was wittering on about some land of milk and honey. Apparently, it was promised by Brother Alfred's God to his favourite people many summers ago. Sinead was enthralled by the tale, but it left Redknee cold until the monk reached the bit about a sorcerer who caused a great sea to part, allowing him and his people to escape the evil king's army.

"Once Moses and his people had passed safely through the Red Sea," the little monk went on, "the waters came rushing back, drowning the pursuing soldiers."

"Were the chosen people freed?" Sinead asked. "Did they find their land?"

Redknee huffed. Typical. It had to be a story about slaves to keep Sinead interested.

Brother Alfred shook his head. "Not quite yet, little one. For the people didn't appreciate everything God had done for them. They took to worshipping false idols made of gold and precious jewels. This enraged God and he banished them to forty years of wandering the desert."

"So they never got their milk and honey?" Olvir asked with disappointment.

"Well, they did eventually. After their forty years of wandering were finished and they'd learned their lesson. But Moses, their leader, and the one who'd set them free from slavery, never got to see the new land."

"Why not?" Sinead asked.

Brother Alfred shrugged. "He'd done his part. It was time for him to join God."

"That's stupid," Redknee said. "Moses put in all the effort – he should have got the reward."

The little monk pressed his hands together as if in prayer and tilted his head thoughtfully to one side. "Sometimes," he said carefully, "a reward is not exactly what you expect it to be."

Once Brother Alfred had finished his story, Sinead pulled Redknee aside. "I've been thinking about Karl's murder," she

178

said in a low voice. "I'm worried your uncle might still accuse me."

"But Karl was killed around the time of the horse fight," Redknee said, placing a hand on her arm in an attempt to reassure her, "and you were with me then."

Sinead shook her head. "No," she said. "I wasn't. You went off to speak to Ivar in the longhouse."

Redknee remembered Ivar calling him inside and giving him the cloth embroidered by his mother. "I was only gone a moment."

"Long enough to leave me open to accusations. So, I've been thinking. What if we ask everyone what they were doing then and double check their stories?"

"Too difficult."

Sinead tilted her face up to his, a strange mix of fear and determination shone there. Redknee bit his lip. He'd been thinking about Karl's death himself and had come up with a vague plan. But could he *really* trust her? How did he know this wasn't all part of some act? As she'd said herself, there was a big hole in her alibi. He sighed. What choice did he have? Besides, if he played it right, his plan would work just as well on her. He cleared his throat.

"As you know, Uncle Sven thinks Karl discovered a traitor among us – sent by Ragnar – and that's how he got his throat slit. Of course, there could be another explanation. A fight over a debt, a woman. But if Sven is right, all we need to do is flush out the real traitor."

"Er, how is that easier than my plan?"

"You're forgetting we already know one important thing about him, or her."

"What's that?"

"We know they probably want the book more than anything. That's their weakness, and we can use it to trap them."

The more Redknee thought about it, the more he became convinced the book was the key to everything. If he played his pieces wisely, he could use what he knew to trap the real traitor, flush out Karl's murderer and get to the truth about the

179

whereabouts of his father. He no longer doubted that his father yet lived, so convinced was he of the depth of his uncle's lies.

Redknee had watched as Toki took his leave of Sven, a smile playing on his lips. It occurred to Redknee that Toki had been lying when he'd confronted him in the burning barn. Or least hadn't told all he knew. But that didn't matter now. He knew how he was going to play it.

Redknee heard a low moan. He turned to see Harold's pale face poking from behind the tarpaulin.

"*Please,*" Harold said, "*help me.* My dressing has burst." Redknee looked round. Everyone else was busy preparing food, trimming the sails or trying to catch a fat, yellow-beaked gull that had landed on deck.

"Alright," he said reluctantly. "What do I have to do?"

Harold led him inside the tent. It stank of raw flesh. Bloodied linens covered the floor; a bowl of salt water sat by the makeshift bed. Harold turned away and Redknee saw the linen bandages wrapped round his back were soaked through with blood.

"It isn't healing," Harold said. "I need to you change the bandages."

Redknee slowly unwound the sodden linens, wincing as half-congealed blood and blackened skin came away with the cloth. He'd never been this close to Harold before, other than in a fight. He kept thinking Harold might suddenly draw a knife, or punch him in the face. But then he would catch sight of the injuries Ivar's whip had inflicted, and he knew he was being stupid. Unfair, even. The boy was in so much pain. He could almost have been sorry. But wasn't that what Harold wanted by calling him in? No, he thought. Harold wasn't going to play him that easily. He knew what Harold had done, of what he was capable. True, the punishment had been harsh, but people could have died in the fire at Ivar's farm. Harold had known the consequences of his actions.

Harold interrupted Redknee's reverie when he handed him a fresh length of linen. Very carefully, Redknee wound it round Harold's torso, securing it in a knot at his hip. "That's it," Redknee said. "I've done what I can."

Harold laughed. "More than that, I think."

180

Redknee stood to leave, but Harold grabbed his wrist. "I saw you," he said.

*"What?"*

"I saw you help the cat-boy."

Redknee didn't understand him initially. Then it dawned. He meant Skoggcat.

"I didn't realise the importance at first," Harold continued. "But then I saw him again when Ragnar attacked the village. I know you're the traitor, and I'll tell Sven unless you convince him to turn *Wavedancer* round and go home."

Redknee stood motionless. This was the real reason Harold had called him in. Eventually he said, "I'm not the traitor." It was all he could think to say.

"We both know you are," Harold said. "And I want to go home."

Before Redknee could reply, the tarpaulin flew back. Olvir stood wide-eyed in the opening. "You'd better get out here," he said. "The stew has been poisoned. Koll, Thora and the Bjornsson twins are sick."

A crowd had gathered midship. Sinead stood in the centre.

"But I haven't been *near* the stew," she said, her shoulders thrown back, face held high. Redknee saw her hands trembled.

Sven stroked his chin thoughtfully. He'd ordered a barrel to be filled with sea water. "I know there's a traitor among us," he said. "Whoever it is, I believe they killed Karl because he knew their identity. And now the traitor is trying to sabotage this voyage by poisoning three of my best men." He stared directly at Sinead. "*You* gave Mord the *Codex Hibernia* though you knew it to be of great value. Then you left with him of your own free will."

Sinead shook her head. "Mord took me with him. I had no choice—"

"Silence woman!" Sven said. "I haven't finished." He paced the inside of the circle. "I allowed you to rejoin us because of your ability with the book words. But I have found myself unable to trust you. And now I hear you were alone at the time Karl was murdered."

181

"I was browsing the market, was all," Sinead said. "Tried some of their wares. I *saw* Karl's body. A woman couldn't inflict such wounds on a grown man."

"She could if the man was drunk," Olaf said, stepping forward, his face set hard, accusing. Others in the little group began nodding in agreement. "Karl had had more than his share of mead and sweet ale."

"Indeed," Sven said. "Likewise, you had the opportunity and the ability to carry out the poisoning. You worked in the apothecary at the monastery where you lived in Ireland. You would have learned all about herbs and poisons there."

"But when would I have gathered them?" Sinead wailed.

"When you went up the fire mountain with Brother Alfred," Olaf said with satisfaction.

Sinead laughed hysterically. "Even if that were my intention, that mountain was black and bare, strewn only with dead grass. There were no herbs of the kind I knew in Ireland."

"Then you brought them with you," Olaf snapped. "A conceited slave like you is always scheming to kill her masters." He turned to Sven. "I say we do it now. Get her confession quickly."

Redknee stared at the barrel of water standing before them.

Sinead saw it too and shrank back in fear. "*I swear,*" she whispered, "on the life of the Blessed Virgin, I did not murder Karl or poison the stew."

Sven appeared to think for a moment then he nodded to Olaf, who grabbed Sinead by the wrists, dragged her to the barrel and forced her head under the water. She struggled, kicking and flailing her arms. Water slopped onto the deck. But Olaf held her fast, a smirk tugging at the corner of his mouth. Sven nodded again and Olaf let her up, gasping for air.

"Ready to confess?" Sven asked.

She coughed, defiantly shaking her head. "I won't admit to what I haven't done."

Olaf started to plunge her under again—

"*Wait!*" Redknee shouted. It was too much. He knew Sinead wasn't guilty, knew deep in his bones. He'd been with her right after Karl's murder. She hadn't seemed worried or

182

out of sorts in any way. And most importantly, there had been no blood. "She's not the traitor," he said. "Whoever killed Karl would have been soaked in blood. I saw her - her dress was dry."

Olaf's hand hovered, holding Sinead's head just above the surface of the water. Sven nodded for him to wait and he relaxed his grip.

"Go on then," Sven said, "though if this is a ruse to help your little friend—"

"No, no," Redknee said. "I speak the truth. Though I know nothing about the poisoning."

Sven sighed wearily. He turned back to Sinead. "I'll ask you one last time. Did you have anything to do with the stew?"

Sinead shook her head.

"Did *anyone* see who prepared the stew?" Sven asked.

Blank faces stared out from the little crowd. Eventually Magnus spoke up. "Thora made it herself."

Sven groaned. "Well, we can hardly ask *her*." He waved his arm to where Thora lay on the deck, shaking with fever, Brother Alfred hunched over her trembling form, dabbing her brow with a cloth.

"*I* would start by looking in Astrid's pouch," a male voice said evenly.

Everyone turned to see Toki standing a little apart from the others. He leant casually against the rail, his arms crossed loosely about his chest. The low sun behind him cast his face in silhouette.

"Look inside the pouch she carries on her belt," Toki went on, "and you'll find the poison."

The ship fell silent as everyone stared at Astrid. Her men-at-arms had fallen in around her, but there were only four of them. No match for Sven and the others.

"Is this true?" Sven asked.

Astrid shook her head. "Why would I want to sabotage our voyage? I've as much interest in its success as anyone."

"Because you don't want to pay the coin you promised?" offered Toki.

"Oh, this is nonsense."

183

"Then turn out your pouch," Toki said simply.

"Will you allow us to have a look?" Sven asked.

Astrid nodded reluctantly. "I've nothing to hide," she said, untying the ribbon holding the leather pouch to her belt and handing it to Sven.

He tipped the contents onto an upturned barrel. Little black seeds spilled out.

"See!" Astrid said. "Nothing but horseradish for flavouring meat."

"Can I see those?" Sinead asked.

Sven nodded and Olaf held her while she peered at the seeds. A frown creased her forehead. "These aren't horseradish," she said. "They're *wolfsbane*. I know it well. We used it in the apothecary to treat rheumatism. But it's only safe if rubbed on the skin in small doses. This amount," she said, her voice catching, "taken internally, could kill the entire ship."

"No!" Astrid shouted. "She lies. It's only seasoning."

"Swallow it then," Sven said calmly. "Gulp down a handful of these harmless-looking little black seeds and we'll believe you."

Astrid hesitated. "I'd rather not," she said eventually. "Someone must have swapped my horseradish for this … this *wolfsbane*." She stared accusingly at Toki. "How did you know of this?" she asked.

"Yes," Sven said, joining in. "How *did* you know, and why didn't you mention it before?"

Toki shrugged. "Simple. She was showing her men what food she'd brought. I saw then. I didn't realise what it was until now. As Sinead said, the two are similar and I only saw them from a distance."

Sven turned to Astrid. "How could anyone have changed the seeds in your pouch?" His voice had taken on a harder edge.

Astrid stared at him through the wall of her men. "I did *not* poison the stew."

"It's hard to believe you when you are *caught* with the poison."

184

Astrid's chief man-at-arms, one Egil, began to slide his sword from its scabbard. Redknee saw the telltale twitch of his uncle's cheek. Anger. Olaf pushed Sinead aside, reached for his own sword—

Magnus stepped forward. "*I* can swear that neither Astrid, nor any of her men, left the stern all morning." The quiet steersman stood, unblinking, beneath the onslaught of stares. "I have been at the tiller all day. None of them went forward; none could have poisoned the stew."

Sven studied Magnus. The creaking groans of the ship filled the silence. Timber chaffed against timber, a discordant echo. "Very well," Sven said eventually. Sighing, he tipped the poisonous seeds overboard. "But whoever is responsible for this, mark my words: you will not make me turn back. I *will* find the Promised Land and its treasure." He looked at Redknee. "Come, lad. We shall see how Koll and the others fare."

As his uncle turned to go, Redknee saw Astrid mouth a silent *"Thank you"* to Magnus.

As Redknee followed his uncle to the foredeck, Harold appeared, hunched and pale, at the opening to the tent. He stared at Redknee with pink-rimmed eyes. Redknee shuffled uncomfortably. He knew what Harold wanted him to do.

Harold stumbled forward, hands outstretched to clutch at Sven's arm, mouth open, ready to spew forth his twisted truth.

"*Wait*," Redknee said, glaring at Harold. Then he turned to Sven. "Do you think it wise, uncle, that we continue our quest when we don't know who is killing us off?" From the corner of his eye, Redknee saw Harold smile. *The manipulating toad.*

Sven just laughed. "Oh, don't worry lads," he said, addressing Harold too, mistaking his pinched expression for concern, "we *will* find whoever is doing this. And when we do, I'll personally see to it they're hung, drawn and quartered ... *as slowly as possible.* I'm not turning back."

Harold scowled, but Sven was moving quickly down the deck towards Koll and the other poison victims: too fast for Harold's mangled body to keep pace.

185

Koll, Thora and the Bjornsson twins lay side by side on the deck, their bodies pale and motionless. Brother Alfred sat by Koll; he held his head in his lap. The big warrior looked small, shrunken, somehow less than his six and a half feet. His fair hair was dark with sweat and plastered to his forehead. Brother Alfred dabbed his brow, his clothes, like Koll's, were splattered with greenish-yellow vomit. Sven nodded in the direction of Thora and the Bjornsson twins.

Brother Alfred shook his head slowly. "I'm afraid they've given up the fight."

*"And Koll?"* Sven asked.

As if in reply, Koll began wheezing, trying desperately to suck air into his mouth as fast as he could. Suddenly his breathing shortened, his face turned blue as convulsions twisted his body off the deck.

"He's choking," Brother Alfred said. "It's what killed the others. We must do something to help him."

Redknee glanced up at his uncle. "Sinead will know."

Sven stared dully at his best warrior gasping and spluttering for his life. It was no way to go. To be denied the halls of Valhalla was a cruel end. "Get her," Sven whispered, so quietly Redknee wasn't sure he'd heard correctly until Sinead was actually there and Sven was urging her towards the patient

Sinead knelt beside Koll, pressed her ear to his chest and listened. "There's no antidote for wolfsbane," she said. "Our only hope is that he's strong and hasn't taken too much of it. All we can do is try to keep him breathing."

Redknee and Sinead sat with Koll through the night. They kept him cool with water-soaked rags and held up his head so he wouldn't choke on the stinking green vomit. With each breath, his chest rattled like dice in a cup but still he fought on. Eventually, as a small yellow sun rose on the horizon, Koll took his first clear breath. He had passed the worst.

Two more days were spent bringing Koll back to health. Sinead was a good nurse; efficient and kind. All thoughts of the Promised Land, of outing the traitor by baiting them with the *Codex*, vanished from Redknee's mind as he assisted her in tending to his friend.

When Sven told Koll of Thora's death, he roared like a mother bear with a dead cub, smashing two barrels against the side of the ship. In his grief, he refused to allow Thora to be buried at sea. Sinead eventually managed to persuade him of the sense in it by giving him a length of fine lemon coloured linen she'd embroidered with flowers to use as Thora's shroud.

After the burial, Redknee found his uncle standing alone at the prow. He looked older. His skin hung heavy across his cheekbones. Redknee sensed it was the wrong time to ask about the *Codex*, but he had to know; couldn't wait any longer.

"Uncle," he said in what sounded, even to him, to be a pathetically feeble voice. "May I speak to you?"

Sven turned to face him fully. "Of course."

Redknee gulped down his nerves. "When the old man in Kaupangen gave you the *Codex*, was that the first time you'd seen it?"

Sven nodded.

"Then what about this?" Redknee took his mother's embroidered cloth from his pouch. "It has the pattern of five ivy leaves, the same as surrounds the unicorn in the *Codex*. My mother stitched it shortly before I was born as a gift for the infant Astrid."

"Give that here," Sven said.

Redknee handed over the yellowed square.

Sven turned pale. "Where did you get this?"

"Ivar gave it to me," Redknee said defensively. "He thought I should have something of my mother's."

Sven crumpled the cloth into a ball, turned to face the sea and drew back his arm. Redknee felt the blood drain from his face.

"Stop!" he shouted, dashing forward and snatching at the cloth. As Sven shrugged him off, he heard the rasp of snapping fibres. He stumbled backwards, staring at the ragged fragment between his fingers: it contained just two ivy leaves

187

and a curl of green foliage. He looked up; anger coursed through his veins as his uncle calmly dropped the rest of the cloth into the sea.

"Why did you do that?" Redknee shrieked, gripping the rescued portion to his chest. "That was all I had left of my mother."

Sven shook his head sadly. "It's years since I saw that cloth. I'd forgotten it existed. I remember her sewing it quite clearly. It was high summer. Her belly was full with you and she found it hard to move quickly or to travel far. She used to berate herself for being so slow, for spending time in such womanly pursuits. She longed to be out in the forest, or on the mountains. Even training with her sword. Her spirit was wild. A bit like yours ..."

His voice drifted off and Redknee was reminded of the time in the training yard when the same faraway look had come over him.

"I'm sorry I reacted the way I did," Sven said, collecting himself. "It was a shock, seeing the cloth so suddenly."

"So it's true," Redknee said. "My mother *did* see the *Codex* many years ago."

Sven sighed. "I knew this time would come."

"You did?"

"Yes," Sven said, looking him full in the face. Sorrow clouded his grey eyes. "I don't see what harm it does to tell the truth now. It was all so long ago and much has happened since. You're right about the Kaupangen merchant. I didn't get the book from him this spring. It was plunder from a monastery I raided with my brother about a year before you were born. We took our ship up the Irish coast. Times were different then. The monasteries were unprotected. Yet we heard tales they contained great wealth. It was too tempting. The place where we got the book; it is the place Sinead hails from."

"Sinead says she heard the monks talk of the legend of Saint Brendan when she was a child. She's desperate to read the *Codex*."

A thin smile crossed Sven's face. "About Sinead:. I doubt she poisoned the stew, but I still don't trust her. I fear, as a

Christian, her loyalty will always be to the monk who wrote the book – if there are Christian secrets within it, she will seek to keep them from us. And I suspect her links with Ragnar. Her departure with Mord and return to us was too convenient."

"I've heard Ragnar was with you when you plundered the monastery. Is that how he knew about the book?"

Sven nodded slowly. "We were good friends once, Erik, Ragnar and I. But Ragnar double-crossed us. He ran off with the plunder. He thought he'd taken the book, but he made a mistake. It was the only thing he left your father and me."

"Is that what started the feud?"

Sven nodded. "I took the *Codex* to your mother in the Sheep Islands. That was when she made the embroidery. Then I left her to find Ragnar and settle the score. But Erik found him first, with tragic consequences."

Redknee took this in. His father had hunted Ragnar down to avenge his double-crossing. "So, my father wasn't a coward?"

"Erik?" Sven asked.

Redknee nodded.

"Not if you look at it like that. Though it's true he ran when he found himself losing."

"But why did you keep the book hidden for so long?"

"The monks said it told of a voyage to a fabulous land. They were very angry when we took it. Tried to beg with their lives." Sven laughed. "Even offered us their secret hoard of gold. But we thought a book *that* valuable must be worth taking. To be honest though, I didn't really believe their stories. And what could I do with it? I couldn't read the book words. So I hid it away. I didn't tell anyone about it because I knew Ragnar wanted it, and I didn't want him to get his hands on it. Not after what happened to Erik."

Redknee nodded. He could understand that.

"But," Sven continued, "when the harvest looked like failing this year, I thought maybe it would fetch some coin. I took it to the merchant in Kaupangen. The man I went to is no ordinary trader. He has travelled in the lands of the Gaul and the Rus. He is master of their languages and expert in their folk tales. He even speaks the words of Rome. When he saw

189

the *Codex*, with its fine leather cover and bright pictures, he nearly collapsed. He said it was the lost book of Saint Brendan and he knew a man who would pay handsomely for it in gold."

"Was that Ragnar?"

Sven nodded. "After your father died I put it about that Ragnar had double-crossed us. I acted angry, saying Ragnar had stolen everything we'd taken from the monks. If Ragnar believed we didn't have the book there was a chance he wouldn't come after us. It seemed to work. I know he used the coin he stole from us to employ mercenaries. He took his new men-at-arms raiding down the Volga. It was only when I went to Kaupangen last month that I realised he was back and he was looking for the *Codex*."

"Why didn't *you* go after him to avenge my father's death?"

Sven sighed. "Lad, I just didn't have the stomach for it. Your mother rejoined me and we moved north, beyond the Oster Fjord to a remote part of the northlands. Then Ingrid gave birth to you, and, well, things changed. Life moved on." Sven smiled weakly; slapping Redknee on the back. "Come on," he said. "I've had enough reminiscing for one day. It's time for your training." He took two Dane-axes from an armoury chest and handed one to Redknee.

Redknee turned the axe in his hand. This was how his father died. Felled by an axe in his back. "I have one last question. Before we start."

"Go on," Sven said, moving into position opposite. "But it better be quick, I fear the daylight will not last long."

Redknee looked at the horizon. Crimson streaked the pale sky. He sighed. He didn't want to ask again. But felt he had to. "Did—"

*"Yes?"*

"Did Ragnar *really* kill my father? It's just, my mother, before she died, she seemed *so* sure—"

Sven lowered his axe, leant his big frame on the helve and sighed. "Alright lad. It's time you knew the truth. I banished my brother from our village."

*"What?"*

"It's true. He didn't die fighting Ragnar. I sent him away."

190

Redknee's mouth turned dry. *"Why?"* he croaked. "Why did you do that to my father?"

Sven circled Redknee, axe in hand. He no longer looked so weary. "My brother was a restless man."

"All Vikings are restless."

His uncle smirked. "He became obsessed with the *Codex*. The fool got as far as Iceland. When he returned empty-handed, the failure sent him mad. He killed a man he thought was trying to steal his precious book."

"You lie."

Sven shrugged. "Believe what you like. But it is time you knew. My brother, Erik Kodranson, is not your father."

# Chapter 20

The impact sent Redknee flying forward. At first, he thought he'd been struck from behind. Then he saw everyone else was sprawled on the deck too. *Wavedancer* creaked to a stop. Redknee looked round, confused. They were in the middle of the ocean with no rocks in sight. He scrambled to his feet and peered over the rail. Lurking beneath the hull, twice the length of *Wavedancer*, was a huge grey fish.

Olvir joined him. "What is it?"

They both ducked as a mighty tail fin rose from the water and smashed against the rail, showering the deck in splinters.

"It's a sea monster," Sinead cried. "Come to eat us!"

"It's just a fish," Redknee said. But his words lost their conviction as another terrible blow crashed against the side, propelling him backwards into his uncle. Silver started barking from the perceived safety of the deck tent.

"*Shh*," Redknee said, holding his finger to his lips, but Silver ignored him.

"It means to sink us," Sven said, his face white with fear. He turned to the dazed crew. "To the oars," he shouted. *"Now!"*

They rowed hard. But the creature sped after them, weaving its dark shadow through the water at terrifying speed, thrashing its tail, making a fast clicking noise as if exhilarated by the chase. When it drew level with the tiller, it blew a flume of water into the air then tipped its big square head beneath the waves, diving down until they could no longer see it.

"Has it gone?" Sinead asked, looking round.

Sven motioned for everyone to stop rowing. Redknee listened to the telltale clicking as it receded into the depths. By Odin's eye, they'd out-run it! A smile leached across his face. Then the sound changed, growing louder until it became almost deafening – click, Click, CLICK! Redknee braced himself for the inevitable: *Wavedancer* shuddered as the monster surfaced beneath her, then tilted towards port.

Redknee plunged, head first, across the deck. Barrels crashed into his ribs. Feet struck his chest. Buttocks crushed his face. Just as things began to settle, *Wavedancer* tipped the other way. Sinead flew past, her skirts about her head. He fought to grab hold of something, but the deck had become a whirling mass of debris. An armoury chest burst open, sending a lethal spray of swords skittering across the boards. He gritted his teeth as a blade carved his thigh.

Through it all, he saw Olaf's stone-like grip circle the mast, holding Harold safe; the eye in the centre of the storm. Eventually, the rolling stopped and he landed softly against Brother Alfred's belly. He examined his thigh. It was only a flesh wound.

The ship was in chaos.

Sven stood first. Blood dripped from a gash on his forehead, the bandages around his shoulder had unravelled, but he still gripped his Dane-axe in his hand. "We must attack now," he shouted, waving his axe in the air. "Every man find a weapon and follow me."

Redknee grabbed a spare sword and followed. He froze when he reached the rail. The monster resembled a huge *gungiger*, with its tiny, beady eyes and slippery skin caked in barnacles. Sven leant over the gunwale, hacking into it, spraying blubber and blood into Redknee's face, exposing crater after fleshy crater. The others joined Sven in attacking the monster and its back soon became a slimy mash of gore.

"*Come on*, lad." Sven said between strokes. "Get stuck in."

Redknee nodded mutely and jabbed at a section of knobbly skin with his sword. His head still spun from the revelation about his father. He wanted to ask Sven more—

The monster reared out of the water; the sudden movement caught Redknee off-guard and he toppled overboard into the pulpy red swill. Foam rushed his nostrils. He pushed up, broke the surface. The monster's huge head loomed over him. Coughing and spluttering, he grabbed at an oar port and dragged himself above the waves.

193

The monster had one of Astrid's men in its half-open jaw, between teeth as long as a man's leg and sharp as ice-daggers. Redknee recognised him as Ragi, her second-in-command. He must have been knocked overboard too. Ragi leant forwards and Redknee stretched to grab him, but his belt was caught on its teeth.

"Undo your belt," Redknee called.

Ragi nodded and fumbled with the clasp, but his fingers were too slow; the monster tossed its great head and he disappeared forever.

The man-eater turned and stared at Redknee. He flattened himself against the hull. Its eyes were small and black, like sheep droppings. Its breath stank of rotten flesh. Then, without warning, it dived beneath the waves, resurfacing three boat lengths off. Redknee breathed a sigh of relief

"Get out the way!"

He looked up to see Sinead calling him from the deck, her hand pointing out to sea. He followed the direction of her gaze and froze. The monster's bulbous form powered towards him, intent on smashing him to pieces. He tried to uncurl his fingers, to slide effortlessly beneath the waves where the worst of the impact would pass over his head. He heard someone shout *"Move!"* from above, but the beast was coming fast – he was trapped.

Sven threw a harpoon over Redknee's head, it plunged deep between the monster's eyes. A high-pitched squeal echoed across the water, but the monster charged on, preceded by a terrifying surge that distorted its face, amplifying it to grotesque proportions, exaggerating the glare of its beady eyes. A second harpoon joined the first. But to no avail; the monster had Redknee in its sight and would not be stopped. Sven leapt from the deck into the sea, pushing Redknee aside with such force he smashed into the water face first.

Redknee turned round to see his uncle slip beneath the waves just as the monster rammed its ugly great head square into *Wavedancer's* hull. The monster sank from view as suddenly as it had appeared.

There was no body to bury. They'd waited for hours, Redknee plunging, again and again, beneath the waves in a vain attempt to find something, anything of his uncle. But in the end he had to accept the truth – Sven had died saving him.

The monster had knocked two large dents in *Wavedancer's* hull. Water seeped in, slowly at first, then in huge, noisy slugs. *Wavedancer* limped along, her desperate crew bailing as fast as they could with their meagre collection of buckets, chests and bowls. Even cupped hands were used when the light started to fade and fear really took grip. Then a miracle occurred. At least, Brother Alfred proclaimed it such. Great white cliffs jutted, saw-like, from the horizon. Land.

Sinead came to Redknee as they neared the cliffs, which he now saw were made of ice. They rose straight from the water with no beach to mediate between their naked glow and the sea. The cliffs groaned as huge chunks of ice crumbled away, landing with a mighty splash.

"If this is Greenland, it doesn't look very green," she said, scooping the water at her feet with a bowl.

Redknee watched as lumps of ice, fluffed into fantastical peaked shapes, like whipped cream, floated past. The sea was calm; the floes moved slowly, but a brush with one of their jagged edges would surely sink them.

"It looks like the end of the world," he said, using an oar to fend off a nasty looking edge.

They eventually found a thin, grey beach strewn with sharp rocks. Exhausted, and too low in the water to go further, they docked and hauled their injured ship as far up the beach as they could. *Wavedancer's* timbers seemed to slump into the rough sand. Redknee knew how she felt. Fatigue gnawed his bones. His legs felt like lead, his arms worse. Cold and wet, he collapsed to the ground and closed his eyes.

At first, he was too tired to think. Then, slowly, his thoughts began to order themselves. His uncle had banished the man he'd known as his father from the village. This first revelation had enraged Redknee, so that, in the moments before his uncle's death, Redknee hated him more than he'd

195

ever hated anyone. And then, just when he thought he finally knew the truth, Sven had spoken those six simple words:

*Erik Kodranson is not your father.*

Redknee's hate for his uncle had faltered, smashed on the rocks of confusion. But now ... now Sven was dead, had died saving him, and all chance of answering the questions swarming in Redknee's head had died with him. In the end, only one question remained important:

*If not Erik Kodranson, then who? Who is my father? And who, then, am I?*

For, in truth, they were the same dilemma.

Something warm, wet and spongy smothered his face. He opened his eyes and drew Silver close, feeling the outline of the pup's ribs beneath his soft coat. He would need to find his friend more food. He felt a hand on his shoulder and turned to see Sinead looking down. Her fiery hair seemed wrong, somehow, against the glaring backdrop of ice. Her eyes were too green, her lips too pink for this bleached land.

"They're arguing," she said, pointing to the group standing beside the wreck. "Olaf wants to camp here, but I fear a storm is coming."

Redknee looked at the sky. Purple clouds tussled on the horizon. She was right. The storm would reach them by nightfall. Redknee sighed. "What can *I* do about it?"

"Tell them we must find shelter. There's none on the beach."

"They won't listen to me."

"You must try."

Drawing on his last remnant of strength, he stood and walked over, squeezing past Olaf to the centre of the bedraggled group.

Olaf grinned in amusement. "Sven's whelp here to lead us?" he asked, voice dripping with sarcasm.

Redknee cleared his throat. "My uncle ... my uncle is dead. We've no leader now, but we must make a quick decision about where to spend the night. A storm is coming. We should head inland to find shelter. We can return tomorrow to mend *Wavedancer*."

196

"But we don't know where we are," Olaf said. "We're tired. Soaked through. Some are injured. And the locals could be hostile."

Several nodded at this, among them Magnus and a couple of Astrid's men-at-arms. She cast them an angry look. Clearly, *she* wanted to go exploring.

"You're right," Redknee replied. "But we can't wait out the storm here. I'm going to see if there's a pass through the ice cliffs."

"I won't leave Harold," Olaf said, folding his arms across his chest. "He's too ill to go wandering."

Redknee glanced to where Harold sat, apart from the group, on a slab of grey slate, his face as white as the ice-cliffs behind him. Redknee nodded to Olaf.

"We'll send you word as soon as we've found shelter."

In the end, everyone left with Redknee save Olaf and Harold. He led them west along the beach towards what looked from a distance to be a break in the wall of ice.

Sinead caught up with him, the *Codex* tucked under her arm. "I brought you this," she said. "The chest it was in burst open; but it's still dry—"

"That thing has caused enough death. I'm having nothing more to do with books."

Sinead stared at him in disbelief. "But we *must* find the Promised Land. We've come so—"

"Look," Redknee said, turning to face her. I was only interested in finding the Promised Land because I thought it was where my father had gone. Before my uncle died, he finally confessed Ragnar didn't kill his brother. In fact, his brother survived the fight. And what's more, he confirmed Erik *was* obsessed with the *Codex*, and wanted to find the Promised Land for himself.

Sinead's eyes widened. "Your father is alive – that's wonderful!"

Redknee shook his head. "You jump ahead. Sven also confessed he banished his brother because his obsession had grown so monstrous, he murdered a man over it."

197

*"Oh—"* She paused, then added, "But even so, you'll still need the *Codex* to find him."

"There *is* a group of men looking for the Promised Land, the ones Astrid's husband set sail with two years ago, but my father isn't among them."

"How can you be sure? Just because he was banished—"

*"Because,"* Redknee said, his voice hollow, "the last thing Sven said before the sea monster attacked, was that Erik Kodranson, his brother, isn't my father."

*"What?"*

"That's right. For me, anyway, this whole stupid search has been for nothing. Worse even, because that book was the reason our village was destroyed. It caused my mother to be killed, caused Karl, Thora and the Bjornsson twins to be murdered. Now Sven is dead too. Face it, Sinead, the bloody thing's cursed. Do yourself a favour and throw it away."

Sinead placed her hand lightly on Redknee's sleeve, "If Erik Kodranson isn't your father, Sven isn't your uncle either."

*"And that,"* Redknee said, kicking a loose sliver of flint across the beach, "is about the best thing that's come of this. Now, keep that book away from me before I throw it into the sea, where it belongs."

Sinead blanched. But she hung on to the book, wordlessly gripping it tight as she fell into step beside him.

The break in the wall of ice led nowhere. The beach was longer than Redknee had realised, snaking for miles around small inlets and sweeping bays. But two things remained constant; the high ramparts of ice blocking access to the interior and the gathering cloudbanks. So it came as a relief when, as they entered a broad bay with soft, black sand not long before sundown, Olvir stood on tiptoe and shouted, "Look!"

All eyes followed the direction of Olvir's outstretched hand. On the other side of the bay, a small wooden fort faced the darkening sky. If they ran, they would reach it before the storm hit.

198

"Do you think my husband is there?" Astrid asked, eyes lighting up.

Even from this distance, the place looked ramshackle.

"I don't see any smoke," Redknee said. "I think it's uninhabited."

Redknee pounded on the gate and waited. Silence. He glanced up. Ravens kept watch from the parapet, mocking him with their glassy eyes. One began to caw. His brothers joined in. Their screeching filled the sky. Still no movement from inside.

"There's no one here," he said, pressing his shoulder to the gate. To his surprise, it gave way.

The gate opened onto a dirt courtyard. Old, broken barrels were piled high in one corner. Behind them, a rickety ladder led to crumbling ramparts. Redknee made a mental note – someone would have to keep watch. He called to Silver. When the pup failed to appear, he turned to see him waiting by the gate. Redknee whistled. Silver tilted his head, placed his right paw across the threshold then snapped it back as if burned. Sighing, Redknee gripped Silver by his scruff and dragged him forward. The pup's joints locked, his paws digging parallel furrows in the mud.

"Come on," Redknee said, bundling him into his arms and nuzzling his ears. "There's no one here."

"The pup's right," Olvir said, sliding an arrow from his quiver and placing it on his bow. "This place rattles my bones."

The group fanned out slowly, weapons drawn, eyes alert. At the back of the yard stood a small wattle and daub hut, roofed with shingles. Old rope held a misshapen door in place. Redknee motioned to the others to stand back. He put Silver down and gave the door a kick; it flew open in a cloud of dust.

By the pummelling of his heart, Redknee fully expected a dozen berserkers to charge forth, blood dripping from their bearskins, biting their shields and swinging cudgels the size of small skiffs. In fact, the only movement came from a startled rat scuttling towards the door, its pink tail brushing Redknee's toes as it escaped.

199

The room was dark inside, and empty apart from a bench. A black circle in the dirt floor, evidence of a fire, was the only sign of recent human habitation. Redknee relaxed and lowered his sword.

Astrid peered over his shoulder. "I'm not spending the night in *there*," she said, wrinkling her nose and pulling her rabbit fur hood over her head.

"Where else do you suggest with the storm closing in?" Redknee asked.

On cue, a fat raindrop landed on his forehead, and a moment later, pounding rain filled the yard. They all piled inside the hut and Sinead set about laying a fire with driftwood she'd collected.

Astrid stood at the edge of the room with her men-at-arms. "This *can't* be one of my husband's forts," she sniffed.

"Plonk your royal arse on that," Koll said, dragging the bench in front of her. "And stop moaning or I'll throw you on the fire."

"I should have one of my men whip you for insolence," she said, wiping the bench with her sleeve.

"Watch your step," Koll said. "My wife is dead. Poisoned. You had the wolfsbane. You're the main suspect. It was only because Magnus vouched for you that you're not already dead. So I wouldn't get too cocky, because I'm watching you, and if you do anything to make me think you did it … well, by Odin's eye, I won't think twice about wringing that pretty white neck of yours."

At this, her men-at-arms stepped between them. Koll straightened to his full height. Astrid's men only came up to his chin. "Well," Koll said, smiling, "who wants to go first?"

"Stop it!" Redknee said, worried for his friend's weakened state. "We have to get along."

Koll nodded and backed away. "I'm going to find something for dinner," he said, stalking out into the rain.

Redknee sighed. Though he tried not to show it, Koll missed Thora badly.

"This place feels wrong," Olvir said, shuffling closer to Sinead's fire. "All those ravens watching us."

200

Olvir was right, Redknee thought. There was something strange about the fort. Suddenly he realised Silver was missing. He ran outside; rain blurred his vision; mud sucked at his feet. He searched the yard; found the pup cowering behind the pile of old barrels, shivering in the cold.

"*There* you are," he said, folding the slip of sodden fur into his arms. But Silver seemed more interested in staring over his shoulder at a shadowy crevice among the rain-lashed barrels. Redknee heard a scratching noise as something; a rat perhaps, disappeared into the dark. Silver squirmed as Redknee carried him inside, but the fire seemed to persuade him of the sense in staying. He made straight for the hearthside, stood in front of Astrid and, ignoring her shrieks, vigorously shook himself dry.

It was only as Redknee settled that his mind began to order what he'd seen Silver staring at – a small white face, with black, peering eyes. A boy's face. Redknee hurried back outside, searched the yard, but the boy was gone. When he returned to the hut, he asked Toki, who was sitting nearest to the door, to keep watch.

Toki nodded. No one wanted uninvited visitors in the night.

The storm rattled the shingles until the hut felt like the inside of a drum. It had been dark for some time when Koll returned with a seal draped over his shoulder. He looked better than when he'd left, stronger, his vigour restored, as if he'd drawn strength from the power of the elements. Too bright, perhaps.

"Right," he said, dropping the carcass in front of the fire and shaking his hair dry. "Let's get this feast started."

"Do you think Olaf is alright?" Sinead asked.

"Impossible to see past your nose. I was lucky to stumble upon this old lump of lard," he said, slapping the seal's hindquarters. He dug into his cloak, producing a pigskin flask. He held it out to Redknee. "Take it. The gods have been hard on you, lad."

"No more than you," Redknee said.

"Ach, take it."

201

Redknee took the flask and tipped his head back. The liquid burned his throat as it went down. He wiped his lips and offered Koll a slug.

"No. Have more. You deserve it. Besides, I've my own supply." Koll's eyes glittered in the firelight as he produced two more flasks from inside his cloak.

Soon everyone was enjoying the mead and telling stories. Koll told a tale of how Sven, when only nine, had killed a wolf that was terrorising the village, with his bare hands.

"Ah," Koll said, finishing off his flask and patting Redknee on the back. "He was a brave one, your uncle."

When his turn came, Redknee told a story about how, just last year, Thora had caught him stealing wheat cakes straight off her griddle. She'd chased him round the village and half way up the mountain with her broom. He hadn't managed more than one bite before she'd wrestled them back.

"Ah, she'd been making those for me – for our anniversary," Koll nodded sadly, remembering. "Six years since she accosted me in Kaupangen market. I'd just bought new tongs from her father – she grabbed my ear and accused me of paying with bad coin ..." Koll sighed. "I fell in love on the spot."

Redknee stared into his flask. It was nearly empty.

"Come on," Koll said, "Let's cheer the lad up. Brother Alfred, you must know some happier stories."

"Not as colourful as yours," Brother Alfred replied.

Redknee stumbled to his feet. The room spun beneath him. Faces jumped out of focus. "*She* has a story," he said, pointing at Sinead. "Tell us what the *Codex* really says."

Sinead shrank against the wall. "I thought you wanted nothing more to do with the book."

Redknee hiccupped. "I want to know the secret of a treasure so powerful it stole the life of my uncle. So powerful, Ragnar is chasing us to get his hands on it. So powerful, you won't let the book out your sight."

Sinead tightened her grip on the *Codex*. "I haven't had the chance to read it yet."

"Read it now," Redknee said. "With my uncle dead, we need to know if there's any point continuing his quest."

202

"Well," Sinead began, carefully laying the *Codex* on the floor and opening it at the picture of the unicorn. "It tells of Saint Brendan the Navigator, an Irish monk who lived more than four hundred years ago."

"We *know* this," Koll said, rolling his eyes.

"Yes. But what you don't know is Saint Brendan found a vast land, larger than all the Northlands. Larger even, than all the kingdoms of Christendom. Saint Brendan found a new world."

The little group listened to the rain as it continued to pound the timber roof. No one had expected the Promised Land to be so big. True wealth did indeed await them.

Astrid spoke first. "This must be the land my husband's man, Ulfsson, told of."

"Perhaps," Sinead said. "But that's not all. The book says the Promised Land has fields of emeralds, rivers of sapphire and streets of burnished gold."

"Ah," Koll said. "Now we get to the important bit."

"There's *always* gold," Toki said dismissively. It was the first time he'd spoken since they arrived at the fort.

"You don't believe the book?" Sinead asked.

Toki tilted his head and fixed her with a cynical look.

"Well …" Sinead sounded less certain now. "It says here: '*after enduring months at sea, and much hardship, Saint Brendan came to a land where everything was made from gold and precious jewels*' – the houses, the furniture, the plates, the barrels – every last thing."

"This reminds me of Moses' hardship in the desert before finding the land of milk and honey," Brother Alfred said.

"The one who freed the slaves?" Sinead asked.

Brother Alfred nodded.

"I like that."

"Don't get your hopes up," Astrid said. "My husband took more than twenty slaves with him to this promised land."

"I hope they've risen up and killed him," Sinead said, lunging at Astrid and knocking her to the floor.

"Girls!" Koll shouted, pulling Sinead off Astrid. "Save your fighting for Ragnar."

Astrid glared venomously up at Sinead. She called to the leader of her men-at-arms, who, having had rather a lot of mead from his own secret stash, stumbled noisily to his feet. "Egil," Astrid said imperiously, "have this slave whipped."

"I'll not be whipped," Sinead said, kicking at Koll's shins. "I'm the *only one* who can read the *Codex*."

Egil approached Sinead cautiously, as one might a rabid dog.

"I'll not read if you whip me," she said.

"Ha," Astrid snorted. "Brother Alfred can read your stupid book. *If* it holds anything worth knowing."

"Brother Alfred can't read like me."

"What do you mean?" Redknee asked.

"Ask him yourself."

Everyone turned to stare at the little monk.

"Is this true?" Redknee asked. "Can't you read?"

Brother Alfred blushed. "… A little," he said, lowering his eyes, before adding, "not really. The truth is … in the monastery … I was only a gardener. I tended the vegetables. The turnips were my pride and joy. I grew the biggest, juiciest ones in five burghs."

"But the stories you told?" Olvir asked, his voice flat with disappointment.

"My stories are all true, though I didn't learn them from books. I used to sneak inside after my duties were finished and listen to the educated monks discuss the bible."

"Why are you here, then?" Redknee asked, standing over Brother Alfred. "Do they often send gardeners to be missionaries?"

"No. I wanted to spread the love of God. I don't need to be able to read of God's love to know of its truth. Besides, no one else was brave enough to come to the Northlands. So they sent me. I would point out that Jesus was only a carpenter."

"*What*?" Koll asked. "Not a warrior?"

Brother Alfred shook his head.

"You'll never baptise me now," Koll snorted, folding his arms across his chest.

"What about the things you read from the *Codex*?" Redknee asked, leaning forwards, mead trickling from his flask onto Brother Alfred's head. "Were they all made up? Have we been following the wrong clues?"

Brother Alfred nodded slowly. "I was ashamed to admit I couldn't read – and I thought ... I thought your uncle would kill me if he knew I was of no use."

# Chapter 21

The next morning Redknee felt like a troll had used his head for kicking practice. He searched the floor for his water flask, cursing when he found it empty. He needed air. Picking his way over out-flung arms and legs, he made it to the yard. He darted behind the stack of old barrels, dropped his breeches and relaxed as a series of plops kissed the wet mud.

His first thought was that Sven would give him an earful for drinking. Then he remembered.

The bitterness of the morning whistled against his skin. Fastening his breeches, he climbed the ladder to the ramparts. The storm had cleared and he could see across the bay. He inhaled deeply; cold air was a welcome antidote to the staleness of the hut.

Memories from last night came flooding back. Sinead's insistence the Promised Land was real; Brother Alfred's admission he couldn't read. Koll had wanted to throw the lying rogue out into the storm, Redknee had persuaded him not to.

He sighed. Beyond the soft, black sands, a carpet of gleaming turquoise stretched to the horizon. It was as if yesterday's storm had never been. He pulled the remnant of his mother's embroidery from his tunic. The green of the ivy leaves shone bright as emeralds in the morning light. He thought of his mother and his uncle. He closed his eyes and recalled their faces; imagining they were still alive. But the images faded quickly; no matter how he focussed, he couldn't hold them. His breathing came fast and shallow as he struggled to fix the colour of his mother's eyes. Were they sky blue, or sea? He gripped the railing till his knuckles turned white. Perhaps they hadn't been blue at all. Just a murky grey-green.

Panicked, he turned to go inside, to lose himself in the chatter of the living. As he did so, he saw a ship enter the bay and head towards the fort. He did a double-take, but there was no need. Only one ship boasted a great yellow sail emblazoned with a scarlet and gold serpent.

Redknee slid down the ladder, ran across the yard and threw open the door to the hut. Sinead stood. She looked hung-over and bleary eyed.

"Ragnar's ship is in the bay," he said.

Her hand shot to her mouth. "But I thought—"

"You thought wrong," Redknee said, before shouting at the others to get up. He saw Toki wasn't there. He turned back to Sinead. "Where's Toki gone?"

"I don't know."

Astrid stretched her arms above her head like a cat. "Well, we can't wait for him."

Redknee glanced at the door. Astrid was right. He turned back to the others. "We have to leave here *now*."

"We should warn Olaf," Koll said, fastening his sword belt.

Redknee ran back out to the yard. "No time," he called over his shoulder. "We can't go out the gate anyway. Ragnar will see us and follow."

As Redknee spoke, the big gate creaked open. He drew his dagger.

"Hey!" Magnus said, his face full of surprise. "What kind of greeting is this? I've brought breakfast." He held up a brace of herring.

Redknee nearly collapsed with relief. "Come, Magnus. I didn't realise you'd gone. Did you see Ragnar's ship in the bay?"

Magnus nodded. "That's why I hurried back."

Redknee peered round the gate. The snake ship was only a few moments from landing. There was no escape over the ice cliffs; if they left the fort, they would have to run the length of the beach in full view of Ragnar. They were trapped.

207

The others joined Redknee in the yard, each looking as tired and dishevelled as Redknee felt. A scuffling noise came from behind the stack of barrels in the corner.

"I hate rats," Brother Alfred said, crossing himself.

Koll went to investigate. "By mighty Thor, it stinks round here."

Redknee blushed.

Koll reappeared with a smile on his face. "Come see what I've found."

"A cesspit?" Magnus offered, holding his nose and peering round the barrels.

"Come see," Koll said again.

As Redknee followed Magnus, he remembered the little white face with big black eyes he'd seen last night. A trap door lay open in the ground, near where he'd relieved himself earlier. Rough-hewn steps led down to a tunnel, the end of which disappeared in darkness.

"Do you think it's trolls?" Sinead asked, joining them.

"Or a trick," said Brother Alfred. "Maybe Ragnar already got here in the night."

As they debated the merits of entering the tunnel, a young woman with hair the colour of roast chestnuts climbed out and blinked in the sunlight. "I'm Gisela," she said, smoothing down her scarlet over-dress. "Won't you follow me?"

Koll's sword wavered a hair's breadth from the woman's throat. Silver flattened his ears and growled. Gisela merely smiled and turned back down the tunnel.

Sinead placed her hand on Redknee's arm. "Let's not go. I fear it's a trap."

"Or trolls?" Astrid sneered. "I say we take the risk. Maybe she knows something about my husband."

Redknee glanced round. The others were waiting for *him* to make the decision. He reached out and lowered Koll's sword. "We need to take the chance."

Koll nodded and went first. Redknee waited as the rest followed. He was about to go too when he felt something missing from his pouch. *His mother's embroidery.* He must have dropped it running to warn the others.

Sinead was half way into the tunnel, the *Codex* tucked safely under her arm, when she saw Redknee pause. "Aren't you coming?" she asked.

Redknee glanced in the direction of the gate. *Ragnar's men would be here soon.* Damn. He couldn't leave the cloth. "You go," he said, "and take Silver with you. I have to find something."

Sinead nodded reluctantly and called to Silver.

The pup cast Redknee a doleful stare.

"On you go," he said.

After a moment's hesitation, Silver bounded down the steps allowing Sinead to close the trap door behind him.

Hearing footsteps beyond the gate, Redknee half ran, half skidded across the yard and into the hut. Last night's fire still smouldered in the pit and hunks of uneaten seal meat lay on the floor. Ragnar would know someone had been here, but he needn't know it was them.

Seeing the scrap of yellow linen in a corner, Redknee grabbed it, stuffed it in his tunic and hurried out to the yard as the gate swung open. He dived for the barrels, rolling to a stop in a puddle of sticky mud. *Had they seen him?* He listened as Ragnar's men entered and started searching. Heart pounding; he fumbled for the latch. Footsteps approached. *Where was the damn thing?* Then a gap, no wider than his head, opened in the ground and he slid into the darkness.

Redknee landed on a soft mound of damp earth. A torch spluttered to life and he saw the almond shaped eyes of the girl in the scarlet dress. "Where are my friends?" he asked.

"They're waiting for you," she said simply.

He followed the strange girl along the tunnel. "Do you live here?" he asked, running his hands along the smooth earth walls.

Gisela nodded. "Some of the time."

Other, smaller tunnels, branched off at right angles. "Making these must have taken a lot of work."

"Oh, they've been here for years. Since before I was born."

The girl's dress was the colour of rowanberries and its gold trimmed hem swished about her ankles as she walked,

209

catching the flickering torchlight. She seemed untouched by the mud and darkness around her. "*Why* do you live here?" he asked eventually.

"You'll see," she said, glancing over her shoulder and smiling. A dimple pinched her cheeks.

Redknee knew he should be wary – afraid, even. Somehow, the hypnotic swoosh of her skirts, her smile, her calm voice, meant he wasn't.

She led him to a chamber as long as *Wavedancer's* hull and wide enough for three men to lie flat. He gauged they were deep underground, maybe as deep as *Wavedancer's* mast was high. Thick furs lined the earth floor and richly coloured tapestries hung from the walls. A large table sat in the centre, laden with all kinds of meats and fruits Redknee had never seen before. Behind the table, on a finely carved oak throne, flanked by guards, perched a boy, who was, perhaps, a couple of summers younger than Redknee. It was hard to tell, because the boy shone in the torchlight as if bathed in the very essence of the sun. His skin glowed a pure white and his hair fell across his shoulders like wisps of summer cloud. But it was his eyes that intrigued Redknee, for they lacked a band of colour round their black cores.

Amid all this, it took Redknee a few moments to realise Sinead and the others were already in the chamber, standing against the far wall, waiting for him. He relaxed when he saw they weren't manacled and still had their weapons. On seeing Redknee, Silver bounded forward.

"Please," Gisela said in a gentle, but firm, tone. "Bow before the Boy King."

Redknee bent low, removing his wool hat.

The Boy King stood over Redknee. "I am Thorvald," he said in a voice not yet broken. "Tell me – is that your ship in my bay?"

Redknee shook his head. "That ship belongs to Jarl Ragnar, come from the Northlands. Ours is damaged and lies in a bay half a day's walk to the east."

Thorvald reflected on Redknee's answer. "You're afraid of this Ragnar?"

"We believe he doesn't come in peace."

210

"And why is that?"

Redknee glanced at Sinead, the *Codex* was still pressed tightly to her chest. "We have something he wants."

Thorvald followed Redknee's gaze. "Jarl Ragnar wants that girl?" he asked incredulously.

"He wants the book she holds ... and her power to read it," said Redknee, already worried he'd revealed too much.

Gisela stepped forward. "Does the flame-haired girl have the new magic?"

Thorvald laughed. "Our Gisela is fascinated by the new magic, as she calls book reading. She's my court sorcerer, my *erilaz*. I think she's worried her divining powers will become obsolete."

Astrid bristled beside Sinead. "Can you tell me, Sir, if you have seen my husband? His name is Gunnar Osvaldson, he is Jarl of Reykjavik and I believe he may have come this way in search of Greenland, which some say is the Promised Land."

"*This* is Greenland," Thorvald said. He glanced at Gisela who nodded for him to continue. "But I haven't met this Gunnar you speak of."

"But where are the never ending fields of rye and crystal clear waterfalls?"

Thorvald smirked. "Our parents were told those lies too, so they would settle here. Unfortunately, the land is mostly barren."

"So ... there are *no* green fields here?" Astrid asked.

"There are some, but not many. Barely enough to support us."

Astrid shrank back, a frown on her face.

"Why do you live in these tunnels?" asked Redknee.

Thorvald lowered his eyes. "Because I carry the curse; like my father and grandfather before me, my skin cannot bear the sun."

"He will die if he goes outside," Gisela said, stepping up to the dais and resting her hand on her king's shoulder. "Of course, some of our subjects live above ground, so they can grow and collect the food we need. But we have all our meetings, all our important ceremonies, down here."

211

Astrid cornered Redknee in the tunnels during their welcome feast.

"Wait!" she said, catching up with him. "I would speak with you alone." Her hair shone gold in the light from the wall torches and her silvery-grey dress, though marked and muddied from their journey, still glimmered like Arab coin. She looked like a princess. She drew closer to him until her their eyes were level. She smelled faintly of lavender.

"I feel we are nearing the Promised Land," she whispered.

"Do you? I fear Brother Alfred's false clues have sent us on a wild goose chase."

Astrid shook her head. "My husband believed Greenland and the Promised Land were one and the same. But he was wrong. Instead I believe he found the Promised Land while looking for this ..." she made a derisive sweeping motion with her hand, "this *wretched* place. If we have reached Greenland, then we are nearly there. Remember what Ulfsson said in the tavern?"

Redknee thought back to Iceland, but it was the memory of their swim in the lagoon that came to him, not Ulfsson's weather-beaten face. "You don't know if the place Ulfsson went to is the same as the Promised Land Saint Brendan speaks of in the *Codex*. By Odin's eye, you don't even know if Ulfsson spoke the truth. He was a drunk."

"But it is, I'm sure of it. How many large islands can there be off the coast of Greenland?"

Redknee shrugged.

"I need to see the book for myself. We can't trust Sinead to tell us the truth. For all we know, she might be lying too. She *is* a Christ-follower."

"Why should I help you find your husband? What's in it for me?"

"I thought you wanted to reach the Promised Land."

"I did. Like you, I thought someone I cared about would be there. But now I see it was a false hope. To be honest, I wouldn't care if we turned round and headed for home as soon as the damage to *Wavedancer's* hull is fixed."

Astrid placed her hand on Redknee's arm. "You mustn't do that," she pleaded. "Don't you see? We're so close to wealth beyond imagining. You think I still love my husband, and in many ways, I do. But he left me. I don't know if I can forgive him for that. I ruled Reykjavik on my own for two years. Me – a mere slip of a girl! I had to use cunning where I lacked strength, and it made me brave. The people who settle this Promised Land with us will need leaders. It seems to me that you and I ... we would make a good team."

The torchlight flickered in the black depths of Astrid's pupils as she reached up on tiptoe and placed a kiss, gentle as falling rain, on Redknee's lips.

Footsteps echoed down the corridor followed by a loud gasp. Startled, Redknee pulled away. As he did so, he saw the hem of a green dress disappear round the corner. *Sinead.*

Astrid laughed. "Ignore the slave girl. She means nothing."

Redknee stood in the doorway of the main hall. Long tables heaved under bowls of pickled herring, smoked gull, chicken legs and platters of blackberries and rosehips. Sinead sat halfway down one of the tables, in the middle of the throng. She was laughing as she helped herself to the brightly coloured feast. Silver sat nearby, a bone between his paws. Astrid was right – Sinead was getting uppity for a slave.

Redknee slammed his hand into the wall leaving a fist-shaped dent in the packed mud. By Odin's eye, Astrid *was* right. They'd come so far, turning back when they were likely almost at the Promised Land would be stupid. Worse still, it would be a waste of so many lives, his mother's and uncle's among them.

*You give up – you die.* That's what his uncle had said. But look where it got him!

Redknee shook his head. *Damn*, he had to know what the *Codex* actually said before he could make a decision. There was only one person who could tell him that and he'd seemingly just blown it with her. Making up his mind, he brushed the mud from his fist and walked, casually as he could, towards the table in the centre of the hall.

"So," he said, his voice wavering as he slipped onto the bench beside Sinead, "are we still on the right course for the Promised Land?" Nothing like getting straight to the point.

213

The merriment disappeared from her eyes. She popped a blackberry in her mouth and shrugged. "How should I know?"

Ah. She was going to be difficult. "Because *you* can read the book," he said patiently.

"I thought you wanted to go home now you know Erik isn't your real father."

Redknee faltered. "Well, yes, I did decide that. But, now I've thought about it, I realise we've come so far, it would be stupid to turn back."

"What did *Her Royal Highness* promise you?"

Redknee inhaled sharply. "If you mean Astrid, she's had nothing to do with my change of heart." He lowered his voice so the others at the table couldn't hear him. "You're the only one who can read the book and you believe it tells the truth about the Promised Land. That's enough for me. But I need to know for certain before I commit the others to going further. I need you to show me what the book actually says."

"Before *you* commit the others to going further – how do you know they'll follow you? Olaf, for one, seems set on his own plan."

Redknee hung his head. She was right. Who was he fooling?

Sinead folded her arms across her chest. "And you make a poor liar."

"Come on," he said, changing tack. "You know you need me if you want to reach this Promised Land."

She contemplated him for a moment. "First I want to know what will happen to Brother Alfred."

"Because he lied?"

She nodded.

"The others are angry. Especially Koll. But I doubt he'll do anything about it, he's still cut up about Thora."

Sinead spun round to face him, eyes alive with excitement. "I've been meaning to talk to you about that. I came looking for you …" her voice trailed off and Redknee realised she was remembering she'd seen Astrid kiss him.

"Go on," he said, not wanting her to ask about it.

"Well, it came back to me this morning, after we left the fort. When Magnus returned with the herring for our breakfast,

214

it reminded me who provided the fish for the stew. All the other ingredients Thora added herself. I saw her do it. But not the fish. It was given to her fresh."

"So who gave her the fish?"

"Two people. Olvir gave her a fresh-caught salmon; Magnus, a brace of herring."

Redknee looked over to where Olvir and Magnus were sitting at the end of the table, their faces pink with laughter and good ale. "You think one of *them* poisoned the stew?" he asked, with more than a hint of incredulity.

Sinead bit her lower lip. *"Possibly ..."* As she spoke, Astrid crossed the room and sat between Olvir and Magnus. She whispered something in Magnus's ear. The steersman laughed and passed her a plate of food.

Sinead opened the *Codex* at the page with the unicorn. The gold leaf shone in the flickering torchlight of the small chamber Thorvald had given them for sleeping. Redknee took the remains of his mother's linen square from his tunic and placed it on the table beside the ivy border. The green trefoil shaped leaves were identical to the ones circling the unicorn, right down to their twisting stems and thick, splayed veins.

"I remember Mord talking about a map. Have you found one?" he asked.

Sinead shook her head. "But this page is interesting." She traced the outline of the unicorn with her finger. Her nails were short, chewed. Ground-in dirt etched the creases at her knuckles. Redknee was struck by how different her hands looked to Astrid's smooth, white ones. Unlike Astrid's lavender scent, she smelled vaguely of chicken stock and vegetables; a hearty winter soup rather than a spring blossom.

"In Christian mythology the unicorn represents Christ. It's said only a true maid can tame the unicorn and entice it to lay its head on her lap."

"Really?" he asked, unsure what else to say. He had no experience of maids of any sort, true or otherwise.

"But here I think it relates to finding what you seek – which in this case would be the Promised Land."

"The unicorn is a clue?"

"I don't know. If it is, it's not obvious. There's lots in the text about the places Saint Brendan passed on his voyage. Look," she said, turning the page. As she did so, her hand brushed his. Instinctively he snatched his away and immediately felt awkward without knowing exactly why.

Seemingly unaware, she pointed to a section of spidery black writing. "Here it mentions the Island of Sheep."

"Read it to me." His voice sounded dry, croaky.

She looked hesitant.

"Go on."

"All right, but I read slowly."

"I've got plenty of time."

"So ... well, here it begins about the sheep – *'On the fourth day Saint Brendan and his men reached an island. When they sailed round the island they saw large streams of water, full of fish, and deep, rocky canyons hiding secret lagoons with water the colour of newly hewn emeralds. Walking round the island, they found many flocks of sheep – all of one colour, brown. The sheep were so numerous the ground could not be seen at all.'"*

"That's the Sheep Islands," Redknee said excitedly. "Where Ivar had his farm."

She nodded. "There's more." She flipped the pages of the *Codex* to about halfway. "Listen to this – *'There appeared to the monks, through the clouds, a high mountain in the ocean, not far towards the north.'"*

"The volcano on Iceland?"

She continued. *"'The mountain spouted flames up to the ether. The whole thing, from the summit right down to the sea, looked like one giant pyre'"*

"Does it say anything about Greenland?"

She turned the page. "It's not explicit; this is the closest description I can find: *'A pillar of crystal appeared to them in the sea. When they tried to see the top of it, they could not – for it was so high. It was higher than the sky.'"*

"That's the icebergs off the coast!"

"I can't think what else it could be." She closed the book. "I think your uncle knew all this. I don't think he needed Brother Alfred at all."

216

"But how?"

"I don't know. But if he didn't, then the fact we've got this far is nothing short of a miracle."

"What happens next? Are we nearly there?"

"It seems we might be." She reopened the book a few pages from the end. "Listen to the description of the last place they visit: *'They sailed for forty days towards the west—'*"

"Wait – that's the same number of years as Moses was in the desert. Do you think it's significant?"

"I don't know."

"Is forty a magic number in Christianity?"

"I don't think so. Shall I go on?"

He nodded. Forty days at sea still to go! She'd better not tell Olaf.

"*'At the end of the forty days, a great fog enveloped them. After the space of an hour, a mighty light shone all around and their boat rested on the shore. On disembarking, they saw a wide land full of trees bearing fruit as in autumn. They walked for many days, and still they had not found the end of the land.*

*"One day they came upon a great river, too wide to cross. A youth met them, embracing them with great joy and calling each by name. The youth said: "There lies before you the land you have been seeking. At its heart lies the White Pine. You have almost reached it. Beneath it, you will find that for which you have been looking. The jewels of this land are nothing as compared to that which lies beneath the White Pine.*

*"Return then, to the land of your birth, bringing with you the fruit of this land and as many of the precious stones as your boat can carry. In many years time this land will become known the world over, when persecution of the Christians shall have come.'* – I think that means now," Sinead added, "with all the attacks on monasteries by you Northmen."

"Perhaps – but go on."

"*'The youth continued: "Just as this land appears to you ripe with fruit, so it shall remain always, without any shadow of night. For its light is Christ."'*"

Redknee stared at Sinead in silence; was this why King Hakon thought his leprosy would be cured? If even half of

217

what she said was true, it was worth sailing a little further west to find this place. He was about to ask how they found the White Pine once they landed, when—

"Come on you two lovebirds!" Redknee looked up to see Koll standing in the doorway. His beard glistened with wine and meat fat.

"You're about to miss the best part of the feast – a whole reindeer cooked in plum juice!"

Redknee edged away from Sinead slightly. "We'll be right with you." Satisfied, Koll stumbled off in the direction of the main hall.

Sinead closed the book and put it inside the chest Thorvald said they could use to store their valuables. Redknee could have sworn he saw a smile playing on her lips, but when she turned back to him, her face was serious, all hint of humour gone. "Have you thought any more about what your uncle said before he ... before he died?" she asked gently.

"No. I've been trying not to."

"Don't you want to know who your real father is?"

"Yes ... of course. But without my mother ... it's impossible."

# Chapter 22

"We can't hide down here forever," said Koll, spooning clumps of steaming porridge into his mouth. They'd risen late after the feast and were taking breakfast in the main hall.

"I'm worried about Olaf and Harold," Sinead said, handing round a basket of rye bread. "And Toki, where is he? No one has seen him since the night in the hut."

Redknee took a chunk of bread from Sinead and used it to clean his bowl. They were both right. They'd hidden in this troglodyte maze for two days. For all they knew, Ragnar had found *Wavedancer* and destroyed her, killing Olaf and Harold into the bargain, and maybe Toki too.

"I'll go and find them," Magnus said.

Redknee had been watching the young tiller-man since Sinead mentioned the herring he'd given Thora on the day of the poisoning. Was that why he volunteered now? To make his escape? Or worse, meet with Ragnar and tell him of their hide-out.

"Someone else should go with you," Redknee said.

Egil stood, already fastening the straps on his helmet. "I will," he said. "This place makes me restless."

Astrid lowered her drinking horn. "Be careful," she said. "And remember to ask after my husband."

A shadow flickered across Egil's face and Redknee suddenly understood the nature of the man's loyalty.

"We'll give you until the morning," Redknee said. "If you're not back by then, we'll come and find you."

Magnus and Egil exited the tunnels through the well in the village. Gisela told them there were four entrances: the trap door in the fort, a cave on the beach, the well in the village and a hidden door that led to a riverbank. She'd shown them the village, although Redknee thought the term 'village' rather grand for a settlement of two small longhouses and a few bare

219

fields. As far as he could gather, about twenty people lived above ground in the 'village' with a further fifteen or so sheltering in the tunnels. Thorvald, it seemed, was no more a king than Uncle Sven had been.

Redknee spent a restless day with Olvir, helping Koll make repairs to their kit. Between them, they had a handful of daggers, a few swords and axes and one bow. Hardly the arsenal of an army. He still rued *Flame Weaver's* loss. The sword he had now was old and poorly made; the tang and blade ill-fitted. Determined to enhance this paltry collection, and aware they may have to face Ragnar soon, Redknee went in search of Thorvald. As he passed their chamber, he noticed the door ajar and overheard Gisela talking to Sinead.

"You have such beautiful red hair," said Gisela in a sweet, singsong voice.

"It's very messy," Sinead replied, trying to flatten the flyaway strands with her palms.

"Nonsense," said Gisela. "Sit on the bed and let me decorate it for you." Gisela held a length of gold ribbon up to the torchlight.

Sinead gasped. "It's gorgeous. I've never worn anything so delicate."

"A trader brought it to us, all the way from a land called Persia. If you sit still, I'll thread it through your hair."

Redknee watched in silence as Gisela first brushed Sinead's hair with an antler comb and then, very carefully, began to weave the golden thread through her russet curls, starting at her crown and working round to the nape of her neck.

"Why don't you read to me as I work?" Gisela asked.

"From the *Codex*?"

Gisela nodded.

"I don't know ..."

"What harm can it do? I just want to hear you using *your* magic. And later ... I'll show you some of mine."

"Oh, all right." Sinead fetched the book from the chest and opened it at a page containing a picture of a huge pine tree with silvery-blue needles.

220

Redknee listened as Sinead read a passage that talked of the riches to be found in the Promised Land. She was reading in Latin, but every so often, she stopped and translated into Norse. He should have been angry with her for telling Gisela, but, as he listened to her soft voice dance over the words, somehow he didn't mind. It was funny, he'd always thought of her voice as whiny. Maybe he was just used to hearing the complaints of a slave.

"You shouldn't listen at doorways – you never know what you'll hear."

Redknee spun round to find Thorvald smiling up at him.

"I … I was just coming to find you."

"I can see that."

"We need weapons, and tools to fix our ship."

"Why are you here, Redknee?"

"I … I don't know what you mean."

"Come with me," he said. "I want to show you something." Thorvald led Redknee through the tunnels until they came to a cave. Rock crystals hung from the high, arched roof in green stalagtites, dripping brackish water to the floor. "Careful," Thorvald said, weaving his way between puddles, "it's slippery."

"You seem to know your way," Redknee said, following in Thorvald's footsteps.

Thorvald stopped at the cave mouth. "This is where I come to watch."

Sand, black as ashes, led from the cave to a calm, grey sea. But above, streaks of emerald, cerulean, crimson, danced high in the sky, swirling amongst a mist of deepest violet. He turned to Thorvald but the boy had a faraway look on his strange eyes.

"Do you never go outside?" Redknee asked eventually.

Thorvald shook his head. "I can't; if I do, I will die. But I like to come here and sit. Especially now, at the end of the day, when the world looks peaceful and comfortable with itself and I can see the magic lights."

Redknee stayed silent, listening to the rhythm of the waves and the occasional cry of a gull overhead. When the sky deepened to the colour of a ripe plum and he could barely see

221

his own hand in the gloom, he decided he'd indulged Thorvald long enough and stood to go back inside.

"Wait," Thorvald said. His voice sounded hollow.

Redknee paused. It was getting cold.

"What's it like out there?" Thorvald asked.

"You've *never* been outside?"

"Not since I was a babe."

"The other night, in the fort, I saw—"

"I creep around the entrance sometimes."

Redknee nodded. How did you describe the whole wide world in one sentence? "It's *big*," was all he managed.

Thorvald laughed. "That's hard for me to imagine."

"What, *exactly*, do you want to know about?" he asked, sitting back down.

"Start with your village."

It felt like a knife in his gut. He didn't want to talk about the dead, about his mother. That time was past. They were heading for a new world now. After a pause he said, "My village burned."

"I'm sorry to hear that. Tell me about something good, then. Tell me about ... tell me about the women."

Redknee smiled. "You've high hopes if you think they're all good ..."

He spoke for a long time, the words tumbling into the growing darkness. He told of his mountain, how it teemed with rabbits and deer, and wild flowers so plentiful that in spring you couldn't see the forest floor for a sea of bluebells. He talked of helping to build *Wavedancer*; of the team of men needed to make something so complex; about Koll's speed with the rivets; Karl's dexterity with the adze and his uncle's ability to find the longest, straightest oak in the forest for the keel.

"She sounds like a fine ship," Thorvald said, "I should like to see her one day."

Redknee nodded and went on. He told Thorvald about the women; about a girl who wanted more than anything to be free and about another girl who seemed to revel in her cage. But most of all, he talked about the land beyond the sea, about his uncle's dreams of a new world and of his own nascent dream,

222

of a place to live where he would be free from the shadows of his past.

"Thank you," Thorvald said when Redknee ran out of words. "You've given me a glimpse of life beyond my mud prison."

"If it's the sun that wounds you, why not go out at night?"

Thorvald shifted uncomfortably. "It's Gisela," he said.

"How so?"

"She says it's too dangerous – I could get caught in the open when the sun comes up – and there I would be – one roast piggy!"

Thorvald laughed at his own joke. "*But*," he whispered, "I did go for a walk along the beach once. I never told Gisela."

"Why do you heed Gisela? You're the king."

"You don't understand."

"Try me."

"It's hard being king. Making decisions. *Tough* decisions. My subjects don't respect me. I see it in their eyes. And Gisela is always there with her counsel. And her advice is sound."

Redknee spoke in a gentle voice. "Perhaps it's because you defer to Gisela so often that people doubt your strength."

"But is it not a sign of greater strength to be able to consider the opinions of others, to weigh them up, and to come to the best conclusion?"

"Yes. If that's what you do."

"Gisela has been good to me. She was my nurse when I was a babe – my mother died giving me life. Gisela has always looked after me, fed me, clothed me … gave me counsel when my father died. And it was Gisela who first noticed how my skin blistered in the sun. It was only my second summer, and the air was unusually warm, so I am told." Thorvald went silent and stared out at the darkness. After a long moment, he picked up his thread. "And I've been living under ground, in these tunnels, this *tomb*, ever since."

"So it was Gisela who first brought you down here?"

Thorvald nodded.

"Let's go out, let's go out now, and explore. I'll show you *Wavedancer*."

"I don't know …"

"Come on."

"But I'm *afraid*." He hung his head for a moment, thinking. When he looked up, Redknee saw a new determination on his face.

"I didn't tell you the whole truth before, when you arrived. Gisela stopped me. One of you asked, I think it was the girl, Astrid, whether we had had visitors before—"

The sound of footsteps on the cave floor startled Thorvald. Redknee turned to see Gisela picking her way round the puddles.

"What are you two talking about?" she asked, reaching them and folding her arms across her chest. Two men-at-arms followed behind her.

"Nothing … just sailing." Thorvald blushed as he stumbled over the words.

Gisela placed her hands on her hips in a vaguely threatening gesture. "Thorvald, you're needed in the great hall. Bera Helgadottir is complaining about her neighbour – the one who keeps stealing her eggs. You need to make a decision on the matter."

"What's happened?" Thorvald asked.

"Bera's son killed one of the neighbour's sheep practising with his bow. Says it was an accident."

"*Was* it?" Thorvald asked.

Gisela shrugged. "As far as I'm aware. But the neighbour says she's due compensation, and a few eggs are the least of it."

"It seems clear—"

"The neighbour is also refusing to let us sink a tunnel behind her longhouse. We need that tunnel to strengthen our defences."

"Can she do that? Refuse to allow us to sink the shaft, I mean?"

"She says she was given the land by her grandfather – one of the first settlers on the island. She says she needs the land to grow turnips for winter. But you're the King. You can take the land – as a punishment for stealing Bera's eggs."

Thorvald rose to his feet. He moved like an old man, not like a boy of thirteen summers.

Gisela went on. "If you're unsure as to the right outcome, I can cast the runes."

"Yes," Thorvald said. "That would help me."

As Redknee expected, when Gisela cast the runes, the decision was clear. Bera's neighbour must sacrifice her land for the tunnel. It was obvious who really ruled here. As Bera's neighbour was led away screaming, Bera hung back, a look of uncertainty on her face. When the screams subsided into the softness of the earth walls, Bera approached the throne again.

"Please, Sir," she said, bowing low. "What is to be my compensation for the stolen eggs?"

Thorvald began to speak, but Gisela strode across the dais until she was between him and Bera. "*Compensation?*" Gisela said, her lips curling like those of a she-wolf readying for attack. "You want compensation for a few dozen eggs after your son killed that poor woman's sheep?"

Bera cowered in fear.

"You're lucky I don't have you flogged for insolence, and your son strung up for recklessness. Now, get out of my sight, and don't trouble the king with your petty squabbles again." Gisela had raised herself up to her full height and towered over the peasant woman like some monstrous Valkyrie.

Bera nodded and scurried out the great hall. Sinead entered in her wake. "What was *that* about?" She mouthed to Redknee.

He just shook his head and motioned for her to come stand beside him. Gisela remained on the dais.

"I think," she said, turning to Thorvald, "that was a good morning's work."

Thorvald nodded glumly.

Gisela scooped up the rune stones from the bone tray she had cast them into earlier. Each stone was roughly the size of Redknee's thumb and contained one letter of futhark etched on its smooth side.

"My magic is strong today," she said, pointing to Redknee from the dais. "You," she said. "Traveller boy. Step forward."

Redknee looked about him to ensure she really was pointing to him. There were about twenty other people in the

225

room; other than Thorvald's men-at-arms, there were a few peasants, Brother Alfred, Sinead and, he noticed from the corner of his eye that Astrid had also slid through the door.

"Yes," Gisela said again. "I mean you, Redknee, or should I say, Jarl of Kaupangen?"

No one had yet referred to him by his official title. If he even had an official title. Yes, a Jarldom was inherited, but it also had to be earned. Besides, he no longer knew who his father was. Redknee was as far from being Jarl of Kaupangen as Sinead was from being the Queen of Sheba.

A finger prodded his side. It was Sinead. "Go," she said. "You've no choice."

He stepped forward. "Really, there's no point casting the runes for me. I've already had them read."

"Silence," Gisela said, raising her palm to face him. She took a small jewelled dagger from her belt and slowly drew it from the base of her forefinger to her wrist. A ribbon of scarlet blossomed across the whiteness of her palm. She squeezed her hand until several drops of blood had splashed into the bone tray holding the rune stones. She closed her eyes and stirred the tray with her finger, coating the stones in her blood.

"You've recently suffered a great loss," she said. "Two losses, in fact." Her eyes flashed open. "You've lost two people close to you."

Redknee nodded slowly. Everyone knew this.

"The runes can make the dead live again. But you must make your choice ... for I can only bring one of your loved ones back."

Brother Alfred dashed forward and pulled Redknee's arm. "Necromancy is a sin," he said.

"Didn't Jesus raise Lazarus from his grave?" Sinead asked. "And didn't Jesus himself rise?"

Brother Alfred blushed, unable to answer.

"I shan't choose," Redknee said. "Because I don't believe you can do it."

"Very well. But even if you do not believe, isn't it worth the risk? You don't have to do anything. Just think the name of the person you want to meet again."

"I don't have to say their name aloud?"

"Only in your head."

Redknee thought of his uncle, who died saving him from the whale and who'd lied to him his whole life, and he thought of his mother, who'd always loved and cared for him, and who'd died saving his uncle.

"Are you ready?" Gisela asked, a broad smile on her face. "Have you chosen?"

Redknee screwed up his eyes and nodded. He wasn't sure what he was expecting – to see a body made flesh from the air before him?

Gisela began to chant:

*"I see, up in a tree,*
*a dangling corpse in a noose,*
*I can so carve and colour the runes ...*
*that man walks and talks with me."*

Redknee recognised Odin's words. The words of the god of magic.

When Gisela stopped her incantation the room was silent. Redknee opened his eyes slowly. But there was nothing. No apparition. No flames of hell, just Gisela standing quietly with her tray of runes. He heard someone laughing, and realised it was him.

Gisela scowled. "You will see," she said. "Real magic is not fire and ice. Real magic happens quietly. That is its power."

# Chapter 23

The next day Sinead paced the main hall, her fingers moving over the edge of her cap, endlessly re-arranging it. "Where *are* Magnus and Egil?" she asked for the umpteenth time. "The sun is high, and still they haven't returned. They should have found Olaf and Harold hours ago."

"We should wait here a little longer," Redknee said, flipping a piece of meat from the table and onto the floor. Silver pounced on it greedily. "A search party could easily miss them."

"You're frightened," Sinead said.

Koll laughed. "The girl is right."

Thorvald had left his guests to eat their mid-day meal alone at the trestle table in the main hall. Everyone, save Astrid, was happy to enjoy their fill of the roast pork, mutton and bread on offer. Instead, Astrid had begged off, claiming a headache. When Redknee had told her they were still on the right course for the Promised Land; indeed, that according to Sinead's reading of the *Codex*, they were nearly there, she'd gone pale and shaky. He supposed the prospect of soon finding her husband had come as a shock.

Redknee shoved a chunk of bread into his mouth and stared at Koll. Did Koll *really* think he was afraid? He wasn't. But he couldn't see the point in giving up the safety of the tunnels to go looking for two people who could be anywhere. Not with Ragnar outside. Besides, he wasn't sure he trusted Magnus any more, after Sinead said he'd given Thora the fish for the poisoned stew. If Magnus *did* have some betrayal planned, if he *was* the traitor Sven had so worried about, they were better to stay here and face what came head on.

Koll lowered his drinking horn. "Ach, lad, it's hard making decisions. This boy king," he said, leaning in so Thorvald's men in the next chamber couldn't hear, "is ruled by the sorceress. It's a bad state. A leader must keep his own counsel. If you ask me, she's put a spell on him."

"Nonsense," Brother Alfred said, reaching for the jug of mead. "There's no such thing as magic."

Koll grinned. "When the witch started chanting you looked scared as a pig in a blood-month."

"She thinks words are magic," said Sinead, finally tugging off her cap and flopping down beside Redknee. "She means to increase her powers by learning to read Latin for herself." Sinead stared at her feet for a long moment, when she looked up her face was etched with concern. "Was it wrong of me to read to her? I mean, if she learns to read, could she really use it to increase her powers?"

Brother Alfred looked thoughtful. "It depends what you mean. All knowledge brings power. That is magic of a sort."

Sinead furrowed her brow. "I think she meant more than that."

"Well?" Koll said, rising from the table and rubbing his stomach. "I don't know about magic. All I trust is the strength in my right arm. But Thorvald shouldn't listen to the sorceress. Handsome though she is, something about her sends a chill through my bones. By Thor's hammer, this whole dark, damp turd of a place chills my bones. So what of it, Little Jarl?" he said, looking at Redknee. "Are we going to go find Magnus and Egil, and save their good for nothing, stinking hides?"

Redknee swallowed the bread in his mouth whole. *Koll had called him a Jarl!*

"Watch it there, lad," Koll said, thumping Redknee on the back. "There's no place in Valhalla for a man mastered by a loaf of bread."

Sparks flew into the air as Thorvald ground his axe along the whetstone.

"What are you doing?" Redknee asked, picking a battleaxe from the armoury walls; sliding it between the leather straps on his back. He'd decided Koll was right. They couldn't hide here forever, relying on Thorvald's favour. If Magnus *had* betrayed them, better to know sooner. Besides, if their friends

229

*were* in trouble … well, they couldn't lounge around feasting evermore; growing fat and soft.

"Isn't it obvious?" Thorvald replied. "I'm coming with you." He wore a padded leather tunic beneath an old mail coat that hung below his knees, almost reaching his ankles. He could barely lift his arms.

"But it's still daylight."

"I've been cooped up too long. I need to get out. Show my people I'm still in charge."

"This isn't your battle. It was *my* village Ragnar burned, *my* mother he killed," Redknee said, placing a hand on the boy's shoulder. He felt Thorvald's muscles tense beneath the goosedown wadding. "You've done enough by sheltering us."

Thorvald's black and white eyes stared back at him.

Redknee sighed. "You *will* go outside again, but not—"

"Seize him!"

Gisela stood in the doorway, her arm outstretched, index finger pointing directly at Redknee. He reached to draw his axe as six men-at-arms filed past her and grabbed him by the arms and legs.

"What's happening?" he shouted as they bundled him through the door and down the corridor. He hadn't time to draw the battleaxe or even grab one of the swords that stood against the armoury wall.

"I heard you," Gisela said. "We all heard you," she said, nodding to the men-at-arms as they pushed him into a dark cell. "You were inciting Thorvald to go forth during the day, an offence punishable by death." With this, Gisela turned and walked away.

"But …" Redknee shouted as the door slammed in his face and one of the guards slid an iron bar across its wake. "I've done nothing wrong!" He banged his fist against the wood. His friends would find him, they would get him out. He called until his throat became hoarse but still no one came. Gisela had taken him deep into the labyrinth.

Sometime later he heard footsteps approach along the tunnel. He peered through the small window in the door, no bigger than a child's hand. Thorvald had come and was speaking to one of the guards. Was Thorvald here to rescue him? Or to authorise his execution? He pressed his ear against the window and listened.

"Come, my man," Thorvald said in as deep a voice as a thirteen year old could muster. "This Redknee is my friend. I command you to release him."

Redknee's heart soared. Thorvald had come to free him. Everything would be all right.

"Sorry sire, but Mistress Gisela's instructions are to keep him locked up, no matter what. She said he'd tried to influence you, sire. I'm sorry. She says it's for your own good."

Thorvald nodded and shuffled back down the corridor.

Redknee slumped to the floor. Suddenly he knew what it was like to be Thorvald. To be alone in the darkness, jarl of nothing but mud and shadow.

# Chapter 24

A long time passed. Redknee listened to the sounds of the dark. Became alert to their patterns: a blacksmith hammering out his trade; snatches of disembodied voices; the drip, drip of water.

He closed his eyes and waited. Someone would notice him missing and come looking. *Wouldn't they?*

Heavy footsteps woke him. He'd no idea how much time had passed. The footsteps came from above, sending puffs of dirt from the ceiling. Voices joined them, grew louder, fought with the screech of iron on iron. He scrambled to his feet and pressed himself against the door, terrified the mud roof would collapse.

He peered through the window. His guard had gone. Damn. *Had he been left to rot?* Well, he wasn't waiting. He forced his arm through the window and tried to lift the iron bar. He couldn't reach.

"Help!" he screamed, withdrawing his arm and shouting as loud as he could. "Help me!" But the shadows at the far end of the tunnel made no reply.

The footsteps above stopped. The sound of metal scraping against rocks echoed through his cell. Digging. Maybe they were sinking a new tunnel. He listened to the urgent clawing. They were in a hurry.

A cloud of dirt blackened the air in the tunnel. He covered his eyes. Men, five of them, tumbled through a hole in the ceiling, scrambled to their feet and quickly formed a defensive line. He squinted through his cell door. Their fine helmets glittered in the faint torchlight of the tunnel. Their leader took charge.

"Spread out," he said, drawing his sword. "And remember what we're looking for."

Redknee pressed his body flat against the wall. He doubted these men were his friends. He heard them leave along the corridor. No one had thought to look in his cell. He turned to peer through the window at their retreat and came face to face with a bushy red beard and pair of watery blue eyes. Damn. He shot back into the darkness.

"Sir," he heard Red-beard call, "there's someone in this cell."

Redknee pushed himself backwards, into the shadows, as far from the clank of armoured men running his way as he could.

"Open the door, then," their leader said.

Red-beard removed the iron bar and pushed the door.

Their leader squinted in the darkness. "You sure you didn't overdo it on the mead last night?" he asked Red-beard. "I don't see anyone."

Redknee's eyes, accustomed to the gloom, saw where they could not. Their leader had long black hair and a hard jaw. He'd seen him before. Only three times, granted, but he knew him well. He cursed for not recognising the ostentatious mail coat sooner, but he'd thought its owner dead.

Mord stepped further into the cell. "It smells rank," he said, swinging his sword in a wide arc. The blade whizzed past Redknee's nose, drawing a sliver of blood, but he dared not move.

"Nothing," Mord said conclusively, turning from the cell.

Redknee remained still as Mord stalked into the corridor. *Please*, he thought to himself, *please don't secure the door*.

Mord turned to Red-beard. "Draw the bar over the door," he said. "We don't want anyone surprising—"

Red-beard had begun to shut the door, but Mord had frozen. "Wait!" Mord cried, holding the tip of his sword up to examine it.

Redknee's stomach lurched. He pressed the back of his hand against his nose to stem the bleeding. In that instant, he saw Mord turn and charge towards him, realisation on his face. He'd seen Redknee's blood on his blade.

Mord sped into the cell. "Come out my little dungeon rat," he said, brandishing his sword, "or I'll run you through."

Redknee held his breath as Mord lunged at the darkness.

"Wait, Sir," Red-beard said, handing Mord a torch.

Mord grabbed it and swept the cell with the flickering light.

Redknee blanched as the flame passed in front of his face. Caught.

Mord shoved Redknee to the ground and pressed his foot into his back. "What were you doing in there?" he demanded.

"Nothing," Redknee spluttered, truthfully. Blood ran down his face from where Mord had struck his cut nose. A hot, metallic taste filled his mouth; he tried to spit it out.

"What's that you say, boy? You *were* going to attack us! Do you know what the punishment is for that?"

Redknee shook his head. "I was imprisoned."

Mord laughed. "Ah, the great Sven Kodranson's whelp, locked up by the boy king. Tell me, mud rat, what did you do?"

"Nothing."

"It must have been something. Steal the boy king's sweetmeats, did you?"

"No. It wasn't Thorvald. It was Gisela."

"Ah, bested by a *girl*."

"She's a sorceress—" Redknee stopped. He was giving too much away. He didn't know why Mord was here, and he didn't want to give him information he could use against Thorvald. "What are you looking for?" he asked, changing the subject.

Mord removed his foot from Redknee's back. "Why should I tell you?"

Redknee shrugged. He guessed it was the *Codex*. "I might know where it is, that's all."

Mord looked thoughtful. "You're friends with the Irish girl?"

Redknee nodded cautiously.

"Well," Mord continued. "We're looking for *her*. My father is anxious to find her … and, well, anything she may have in her possession."

"I can take you to her."

234

"I don't know—"

"She'll run away as soon as she sees you. She trusts me."

"True. But—"

"Don't you want to get to her before your brother? You would please your father."

Mord's eyes lit up. "Yes. I'll show that Skoggcat," he said, grabbing Redknee and dragging him to his feet. He called after his men. "Forget the tunnel. I've a new plan."

And that was the last thing Redknee heard before the roof collapsed.

Dirt filled his mouth, choking him as he tried to breathe. He coughed; attempted to clear his throat. If he didn't, he would drown here, in this dry black sea, far from sunlight, far from Valhalla. Where no Valkyrie would find him.

He heard scraping noises coming from above. *Rescuers?* He kicked and clawed at the soil in a wretched parody of swimming; tried to call out, but the mud muffled his screams.

The noises stopped. The rescuers were going. He scrabbled frantically. They would *not* leave him. He reached something soft yet solid; clambered along it, using it as a ladder. The ladder squirmed, started to kick. Something, a knee perhaps, rammed his belly. He doubled over. A foot pressed against his head, pushing him deeper into the abyss.

Whomever he'd stumbled across was going to live … at his expense.

*If you give up – you die.* Sven's words reached him through the dark. He pushed off with renewed vigour. All of a sudden, a rod jabbed his back. He turned; grabbed what he took to be a quarterstaff. Someone began hauling him to the surface; he scrambled upwards, using the staff for purchase, pushing off unseen debris, helping his rescuer. He might die today, but it wouldn't be in a black pit beyond the Valkyries' reach.

Air rushed his lungs.

Magnus smiled down at him. "Thought we'd lost you there."

"You got back safely?" Redknee asked, surprised to see Magnus and not Mord and his warriors.

235

"Yes. We found Olaf and Harold, but I'm afraid we ran into Ragnar." Magnus looked uncomfortable. "Egil didn't make it."

Redknee thought of the captain with a soft spot for his mistress. He gave Magnus a sidelong glance. "How did that happen?" he asked.

"Just as we were returning to the tunnels, they ambushed us from behind some rocks. Egil didn't even get the chance to draw his sword."

"And you?"

"I managed to get away."

"That was lucky," Redknee said with some sarcasm, but Magnus's expression didn't falter. Perhaps Sinead had been mistaken about Magnus poisoning the fish. In any event, Magnus had just saved his life. He owed him his trust just for that. Redknee turned back to the rubble. "There are more men in there. Ragnar's men."

Magnus shook his head. "I've already checked. You were the only survivor."

"But … I felt someone else move …"

"They must have got out before I arrived. Come on. Ragnar is attacking the tunnels, we should get moving. I was careful, but I fear he may have followed me."

They hurried to the upper tunnels, to the main living quarters. There was no sign of life.

"Where is everyone?" Redknee asked.

"Fled." Magnus said. "When Ragnar came."

Redknee peered into Gisela's chamber. It was empty.

Olaf stood a short way down the tunnel, beneath one of the few remaining rushlights. The yellow flame cast a sickly glow over his pale features. Behind him, Harold cowered in the shadows.

"Looking for the slave girl?" Olaf asked.

"Have you seen her?" Redknee said, his hopes rising.

Olaf trudged forward. He held his sword in his right hand and a shield in his left. Blood smeared his arms and face. "Yes," he said, wiping the flat of his sword across his breeches. It left a dark stain.

236

Magnus edged backwards. "Don't trust him," he whispered. "I saw him signal to Ragnar as we entered the tunnels."

Redknee froze. Then remembered he'd hidden Harold's dagger in his boot. Keeping his eyes trained on Olaf, he reached down and felt for the engraved handle.

"Don't listen to him," Olaf said. "I was your uncle's most trusted man. We worked together for years. And now that you've succeeded him as jarl, I want to sail under your command."

"I thought you wanted to go home," Redknee said, holding up the dagger.

Olaf stood a sword's length in front of Redknee. Harold had followed his father down the tunnel, twisted and hunchbacked, like a malformed shadow. His face looked monstrous in the torchlight, eyes glittering with madness. Olaf saw the shock in Redknee's face.

"My son is not what he used to be," he said sadly.

"I'm sorry," Redknee said.

"I must have vengeance for him."

*"From me?"* Redknee asked, fear fracturing his voice.

Olaf shook his head. "I blame Ragnar, not you. I'll help you find the slave girl, and together we'll keep the *Codex* from Ragnar. Then, when the time is right, we'll seize our chance and—"

"He lies," Magnus blurted out from behind Redknee. "He means to kill you!"

Redknee's eyes darted from Olaf to Magnus and back again. Neither moved. Redknee saw Harold stare at his old dagger in bewilderment. His mind truly gone. Suddenly Redknee felt a rush of sympathy for Olaf. He put a hand on Magnus's arm. "You're mistaken, my friend. Olaf comes in peace. He means to help us find Sinead."

Olaf lowered his sword, the tension in his shoulders gone. "You've made the right decision. I've no idea why Magnus thinks I led Ragnar here."

"Magnus?" Redknee asked, turning to his friend.

"Yes," Magnus said hesitantly, "I must have been mistaken."

237

"Good," Olaf said, smiling. "I heard the others say they were heading for a cave. Some hidden exit?"

*Thorvald's cave.*

"Follow me," Redknee said. "I know where they've gone."

They crept silently through the tunnels, their backs pressed against the walls, torches low. But they encountered no one until they reached the cave. Voices echoed off the arched ceiling, magnified a thousand times. Redknee pressed his finger to his lips. Around twenty people stood near the cave mouth. They were arguing. Redknee searched the crowd for a familiar face, saw Sinead's auburn curls and realised they were safe. He called to her.

Sinead's face broke into a smile. "You're alive," she said, rushing towards him, Silver bounding along behind her. "I thought Ragnar had you …" her voice trailed off when she saw his bloodied face.

"It's nothing," Redknee said, kneeling to give Silver a hug. "Gisela imprisoned me for talking to Thorvald about life above ground. Probably saved my hide."

"Gisela has vanished," she said with a snort. "We're discussing what to do."

Redknee scanned the group. He saw that Koll, Olvir and Brother Alfred were amongst them. "Where's Astrid?" he asked.

Thorvald stepped forward. He looked gaunt. "Both of Astrid's men died fighting Ragnar. We think she left with Gisela."

"What do you mean, *left*?" Olaf demanded.

Sinead spoke before Thorvald had the chance. "Gisela stole the *Codex* in the mêlée. We think Astrid has gone with her." She hung her head. "It's all my fault. I should never have read the part about forests of gold."

Thorvald stopped. "I've come as far as I can." He pointed to a weathered door. "That leads out to a river. Follow the river down stream to a waterfall. Gisela goes there to cast her spells. If she believes your book contains magic, that's where she'll be."

238

Redknee said goodbye to Silver, thanked Thorvald, who had volunteered to look after the pup until they returned, then stepped out to a bright autumn day. His eyes blanched at the contrast with the dark tunnels.

The river wound through marshy brown fields edged with rush and figwort. He and Olvir helped Sinead pick her way through the mud. It was slow going. Olaf and Harold brought up the rear. Magnus and Koll ran ahead, acting vanguard.

They heard the falls long before they saw them – a thunderous, ear-splitting roar to mock Thor. When he reached the cliff edge, Redknee peered over into a swirling granite cauldron fed by a flume of water a hundred feet tall. Spray moistened his skin. He closed his eyes and revelled in the cool sensation.

Sinead stared, wide eyed. "The water looks like milk. I've never seen anything like it. In Ireland we had—"

"No one's interested," Koll said, making towards stone steps worn into the cliff.

Olaf laughed as Sinead stomped after Koll. "I don't know what *you're* so pleased about," she said. "I thought you hated the *Codex*. You wanted to sail home."

"That was before it became personal," Olaf said, drawing his sword. "Still don't care about the book – but if I find that stinking Ragnar behind these falls, I'll gut him like a herring." He turned to Harold who was shuffling down the steps behind him. "Isn't that right, son?" he said.

Harold snivelled and his mouth seemed unable to form words. Drool hung from his nose. Olaf took a linen square from his tunic and wiped it away. "There we go, lad," he said, patting Harold on the back. "A Viking doesn't go to war with snot dangling from his face."

The steps were steep and slick with water. As they descended slowly, they heard chanting coming from a ledge about halfway down. The ledge disappeared behind the curtain of water, hiding whoever was speaking. Redknee pointed to a narrow, moss-covered path that led along the cliff wall, joining with the ledge. "We can use that," he said.

Koll edged onto the first foothold.

239

Redknee turned to the others. "We have to be ready at the far end. We'll be in single file, whoever is behind the falls will have the advantage."

"I'll be ready," Olaf said, holding up his sword.

Redknee turned to Sinead. "You wait here."

"I will not."

As he stared into her stony eyes, he wondered why he'd allowed her to come this far. It would have been much safer for her back at the tunnels.

"I'll tie her up for you," Koll said.

"No need," Sinead folded her arms over her chest and reluctantly stood aside. "I'll wait."

Redknee followed Koll onto the ledge. It was so narrow he had to press his body flat against the cliff; cold rock grazed his cheek. Olvir followed him, then Magnus, with Olaf and Harold bringing up the rear. The chanting grew louder. A different, higher voice, answered. *Astrid's perhaps?* He clung to the cracks in the rock face and prayed it was only Astrid and Gisela on the ledge.

Koll disappeared behind the spray. A woman's scream echoed through the gorge followed by the sound of iron clashing against iron. Redknee froze.

"Come on," Olvir said, placing a gentle hand on Redknee's shoulder, "remember what you told me before?"

Redknee looked into Olvir's young face and shook his head. All of a sudden, he felt dizzy. He dare not look down, into that churning foam – falling would bring certain death.

"You said there was no way back – some things have to be done."

Redknee steadied himself. Olvir was right. *There was nothing for it now.* Taking a deep breath, he drew his battleaxe and leapt through the falls. Water pounded his face, blinding him for precious seconds. By the time he opened his eyes, the tip of a finely tempered steel sword pressed against his Adam's apple. *Flame Weaver.*

"Nice of you to join us," Ragnar said, grinning. "Now drop your axe." Redknee hesitated; Ragnar pushed the tip of *Flame Weaver* into the hollow of his throat. *"Do it."*

240

Cursing to himself, Redknee complied. Ragnar kicked the axe off the ledge. He was grotesque up close. The burned skin on his cheek had hardened like week-old porridge.

"Don't stare at me, lad. Just because life is yet to touch *you*. If everyone wore their character on their face, there'd be much less vanity." Redknee didn't mean to obey, but he felt himself lowering his eyes.

The ledge opened to a cave that reached back into the cliff, large enough for several people to stand. Koll was on his knees before Mord, two of Ragnar's men holding him down. Astrid and Gisela cowered behind them; Astrid's face was pinched with fear. Gisela had the *Codex* in her arms. Three other armed men crowded the ledge.

"We've more in common than you think," Ragnar continued, raising his voice above the thunder of the falls. "Did you know your mother stayed with me for a time when her husband abandoned her to go raiding?"

"Don't listen to that turd-eating troll," Koll said.

Redknee glanced at his friend, the skin around his left eye was broken; blood smeared his cheek, but Koll still found the strength to smile.

"I don't believe you," Redknee said, meeting Ragnar's eye. "She stayed with Ivar."

Ragnar smiled and shook his head. "No, no, young troll boy. Not *then*. Not once your uncle, the thieving double-crossing snake, had the *Codex*. Before. When we were all still friends. Though, what a fool I was to trust in the friendship of those brothers."

"You lie. It is you who double-crossed them. You wanted the *Codex* for yourself. My father ... *Erik* ... he was only seeking a better life. One free of tyrants like you." As Redknee spoke, he realised the irony in defending a man he knew wasn't his real father, but by Odin's eye, he wasn't going to let that affect his hatred for Ragnar.

Ragnar snorted without mirth. "And where was he going to find such a life?"

"You tell me," Redknee replied. "Isn't that why you attacked my village? Killed my mother and countless others? Chased us across the sea? All to get your hands on that bloody

241

book." He pointed to the *Codex*, still in Gisela's arms. "Are its secrets worth all the lost lives?"

At that moment, Olvir tumbled through the falls, landing at Mord's feet. Mord quickly relieved Olvir of his bow and pressed his foot into Olvir's back, pinning him to the ground.

Olvir glanced up at Mord. "I thought you were dead."

"You should be so lucky," Mord said, grinding his heel into Olvir's spine. The boy whimpered.

Ragnar turned back to Redknee. "Any more uninvited guests I should know about? Should I expect the pleasure of your *most* honourable uncle?"

Redknee shook his head but in the same moment Magnus charged through the falls, slamming into Ragnar, knocking him over. *Flame Weaver* skittered across the floor. Thinking Magnus was going to seize the chance to drive his sword into Ragnar's belly, Redknee made for *Flame Weaver*, but Magnus hesitated, giving one of Ragnar's men time to jab him between the eyes with his pommel.

Ragnar stared at Magnus's unconscious body. "Best thing you could've done," he said, patting the man-at-arms on the back. "Now," he said, collecting *Flame Weaver* and turning to Redknee. "I believe you have something I want."

"*Me?*" Redknee asked, shaking his head. "It's you who—"

"The Irish girl," Ragnar snapped. "Where is she? The one who reads Latin."

*Please*, he thought, *give Sinead the sense to stay outside*.

"Tell me where she is, or I'll …" he cast round, grabbing Olvir and hauling him to his feet. "I'll toss the boy in the drink."

Redknee glanced at the curtain of water. Where *was* Olaf? He had to delay. "Why do you need Sinead? he asked. "Is it to read Latin?"

"That's of no concern to you," Ragnar said, dragging Olvir forward until his toes met the edge and his face glistened with spray.

Olvir pressed his eyes tight shut.

Redknee remembered Mord had been looking in the *Codex* for a map. "It's just, there's a map in the book. You don't need Latin to follow a map. If you'll let me show—"

Ragnar frowned at Mord.

"The rat lies," Mord said. "I looked thoroughly. There's no map."

Ragnar turned back to Redknee. "Is she outside?" he demanded. "Shall I go see?"

*"No!"*

Ragnar ignored him. "Bring troll boy," he said to one of his men before releasing Olvir and disappearing through the spray. Reluctantly, Redknee shuffled out behind Ragnar, the tip of Red-beard's sword pressed into his back. Ragnar crossed the ledge in a couple of bounds; displaying the agility of a much younger man.

On reaching the steps, Redknee was relieved to see Sinead had gone. There was no sign of Olaf and Harold either.

"Ah," Ragnar said. "I have misjudged you. I thought you lied, but I see I measured you by my own—"

"Throw down your weapons and we'll give you the girl." Olaf appeared at the top of the cliff, holding a dagger to Sinead's throat. Harold cowered behind him, a look of twisted glee on his face.

"I knew you wouldn't have left her behind," Ragnar said, grinning at Redknee.

Anger rose from Redknee's gut. What was Olaf playing at?

Ragnar turned back to Olaf. "Don't be stupid. You're outnumbered. Hand me the slave and I'll let you and your son go unharmed."

"You and whose army?" Olaf replied.

"If I call, twenty men will rush to my aid."

"I don't believe you."

"Shall we put it to the test?"

The steps were slippery and the man-at-arms behind Redknee was young and clumsy – the kind of youth whose joints seem yet too big for their limbs. One well-placed blow would give Redknee the moments he needed. He shifted his weight, planting his feet wide apart. He would only get one chance. Twisting, he drove his elbow up and under his captor's chin. The youth fell back. Redknee lunged at Ragnar, drawing Harold's dagger from his boot; pressing it against

243

Ragnar's throat and grabbing *Flame Weaver* before the bigger man realised what had happened.

The youth recovered and hurtled forward.

"Stay where you are," Redknee growled. "Or I'll carve my name in your master's neck." Ragnar raised his hand and the youth backed down. Redknee turned to Olaf. "Leave Sinead, and go."

Olaf shook his head and lurched backwards, dragging her with him. Harold peered over the cliff. He spat in Redknee's direction then hobbled after his father until he was out of sight.

"Right," Redknee said to Ragnar, pushing him back onto the ledge towards the falls. "You have a few things *I* want." Before he went further, Redknee turned to the youth. "Stay here," he said. "If I see you so much as wriggle your little toe, I swear I'll cut off Ragnar's ears and feed them to the pigs."

"Do as he says," Ragnar said and the youth nodded solemnly.

Redknee forced Ragnar along the ledge and through the falls.

"Father!" Mord cried, his face wide with surprise.

"Stand back, son. Redknee means us no harm. We're like family to him – as I said before, we looked after his mother when she was abandoned."

"You *killed* my mother."

"An unfortunate mistake."

"Stop lying. Just order Mord to release my men and return their weapons."

Ragnar nodded. Mord pushed Olvir forward and directed his men-at-arms to release Koll.

Koll rubbed his wrists where the men had held them. "Fart-breathed puke-eaters," he said, delivering his captors an evil look.

Magnus was still out cold. "Wake him," Redknee said.

Olvir shook Magnus.

"What happened?" Magnus asked as he came round. "Did we win?"

"Just seeing to that," Redknee said. He turned to Mord. "I'm taking your father with me. You and your men will

244

remain here, and, once we are far enough away, I'm going to release him. But I won't do that if you come after us. Alright?"

Mord nodded reluctantly.

"Wait," Astrid stepped forward. "I want to come with you too."

"Why?" Redknee asked. "I thought you'd thrown your lot in with Ragnar."

Astrid shook her head. "*Please*, I didn't know Gisela was planning to meet with Ragnar. I only came with her because she told me she could help me find my husband. She said he passed through Greenland two springs ago. Said she knew where he'd gone – that she could show me if she had the book."

Gisela laughed. "You are so foolish – I know something about your Promised Land that would freeze your blood."

"We're not interested," Redknee said, motioning to Olvir to take the *Codex* from Gisela. Olvir hurried forward and tugged the book from her.

Gisela glowered at Redknee. "You think you go to an empty land where you can all live like kings. Well you're wrong. It's populated by fearsome warriors who possess the power to vanish and reappear at will. So fearsome are these warriors that only one man from the dragon ships lived to tell the tale. Ulfsson was his name."

"That's enough," Redknee said, sensing the tension rising again. He motioned for the others to start heading back along the ledge. Olvir went first, followed by Magnus and Koll. They were eager to be rid of Gisela's poisonous tongue.

"One last thing, Redknee, son of Erik," Gisela said, rising onto her tiptoes just as she had done in the great hall only the day before. "You, who seek the truth about your father. You've come far, but your journey is far from over; it will yet be fraught with danger. In this, I condemn your fate to be tied to that of your gravest enemy. For it is only from him that you will learn the truth."

Before Redknee could do anything, Ragnar shot forward, grabbed Gisela by the neck and without pause, tossed her into the falls, her screams mingling with the thunder of the river.

245

"She was bad for morale," Ragnar said, casually drying his hands on the hem of his tunic.

# Chapter 25

Redknee stumbled along the ledge. "Run!" he shouted to the others as he reached the steps. "Run … Ragnar has escaped."

"We should stand and fight," Koll said.

"No." Redknee said, charging past him. "We have the *Codex*. And we're outnumbered.*"

"The tunnels then."

They scrambled along the riverbank to the secret entrance. Redknee pulled aside the ferns concealing the door and gave a sharp knock. No answer.

"Come on," Astrid said. "Just open it."

Redknee felt for a handle, but the door was completely smooth, without a mechanism for entry.

Koll drew back. "I'll kick it in."

"No," Redknee said, "they'll see where we've gone."

Astrid pushed him out the way. "My hands are smaller, let me try." She worked her fingers between the door and the wooden frame and yanked, but nothing happened.

"Hurry," Koll said. "I can hear them coming."

"I'm doing my best. Unless you want to have a go with your big blacksmith's paws?"

"Just keep trying," Redknee said, catching the sound of heavy footsteps beyond the riverbend.

Olvir strung his bow and took an arrow from his quiver, ready to pick off the front-runners. Then, just as Ragnar came into sight, sword raised, face set against the wind … the door stuttered open and they all piled through.

"Did he see us?" Magnus asked breathlessly as Koll jammed the door shut behind them.

Redknee pressed his ear to the door; the footsteps were receding.

◊

Thorvald wept into his drinking horn. "I can't believe she's dead."

Redknee had come straight to the main hall to tell Thorvald of Gisela's death. They were alone apart from Bjorn, Thorvald's chief man-at-arms, who stood to attention behind Thorvald's throne. Redknee placed a hand on Thorvald's shoulder.

"I'm sorry," he said. But he felt uneasy saying it. Gisela had not been loyal.

Bjorn spoke into his master's ear. "What your kingdom needs now, is strength – not magic. Gisela's powers were nothing against Ragnar's fury."

Thorvald nodded. "You're right, Bjorn. I have been living under a shadow. We all have."

"You need protection," Bjorn continued. "I'll post three of my fiercest berserkers to your personal guard."

"Is that needed?" Redknee asked. "It's *us* Ragnar is after."

Bjorn frowned. "You doubt I have the best interests of my king at heart?"

"I think you're over-reacting," Redknee said, but as he spoke, the thick oak beams holding the ceiling above them shook, sending clumps of earth spiralling to the floor, like underground rain.

"What's happening?" Thorvald asked, his face pale with fear.

Redknee grabbed Thorvald's wrist. "We're being attacked," he said, dashing for the cover of the table in the centre of the room, pulling Thorvald with him.

"Is it Ragnar?" Thorvald asked as they huddled under the table.

Redknee nodded. "I should have killed him when I had the chance."

Timbers crashed all around them, smashing furniture, bringing down whole sections of ceiling, deluging the hall in waves of horrible, choking mud.

"Come on," Redknee said, "if we don't go now, we'll be buried alive."

They ran for the exit, dodging falling beams, splintered furniture and mounting piles of earth. Bjorn was just ahead of

248

them when the lintel above the door gave way, knocking him flat. Redknee and Thorvald scrambled through the small opening, and began to pull Bjorn free.

"Leave me, Sire," Bjorn said. "Save yourself."

Thorvald shook his head just as Bjorn's leg came unstuck.

"Can you manage?" Redknee asked.

Bjorn tested his ankle and nodded.

Redknee started up the tunnel. Many of the beams had already fallen in, but it was still passable on hands and knees. He'd barely gone ten feet when he heard Bjorn shout after him. He spun round to see Thorvald lying unconscious on the ground, blood gushing from his temple.

"He's been hit by a beam," Bjorn said. "You go ahead. I can manage him."

Redknee shook his head.

"Don't be daft. Look at the tunnel. There's not space for the two of us to move him."

Redknee glanced ahead. Bjorn was right. He would have to pull Thorvald through gaps in the fallen earth. It would be tough going, but Bjorn was a big man; a second person would only be a hindrance.

"Alright. But if you're not out behind me, I'm coming back for you."

Redknee burst out of the tunnel into a silvery evening. Fearful villagers huddled, waiting for their leader to emerge; Koll, Olvir and Magnus were among them.

Astrid ran forward. "I'm *so* glad you made it," she said, wrapping her arms round Redknee's neck. "The villagers say Ragnar attacked from the caves. The tunnels were vulnerable to assault. Ragnar had only to remove a few supporting beams for the whole place to cave in." She pressed a kiss onto his cheek. "I'm so sorry about what happened at the waterfall, I had no idea Gisela meant to give the *Codex* to Ragnar."

Redknee pushed her away as Brother Alfred came forward, sleeves rolled up, forearms splattered with blood. He held a strip of linen in his stained hands. He'd been assisting the injured. "This brutality will only stop when every man, woman and child is baptised."

249

"Is there no fighting in Christian lands?" Astrid asked.

Brother Alfred shifted uneasily. "Of course, there is some. But not like this … the Promised Land, we will make it Christian … and it will be peaceful."

Astrid smiled and nodded. "My husband will help us – he is a great leader and will crush any opposition to peace," she said, shooting Redknee a challenging look.

Redknee pushed past Astrid and watched as Bjorn crawled from the tunnel. Mud and sweat smeared his face. "It's hopeless," he said, collapsing to his knees. "I brought Thorvald as far as I could, but he refused to leave."

"But he's only a boy – you could have dragged him out."

"It … it is Gisela's curse …" Bjorn said quietly. "He cannot survive the daylight."

Redknee shrugged off his knife belt, his leather body armour, the straps that held his battleaxe, even *Flame Weaver* – anything that might add extra weight or cause him to become trapped. Then, carrying only Harold's ivory-handled dagger and a spade, he headed back inside the tunnel.

Koll caught up with him. "You can't go back in there," he said. "We must get to *Wavedancer* before Ragnar."

Ignoring him, Redknee continued towards the tunnel entrance.

"If we don't go now, it will all have been for nothing."

Redknee stopped and turned to Koll. "No, if I leave Thorvald to die in that hole, *then* it will have been for nothing." He lowered his head and spoke quietly. "I would do the same for you."

Koll nodded once and stood aside. As Redknee passed him, he heard his friend whisper something. It was only in the darkness of the half-collapsed tunnels that his mind strung the words together until they repeated themselves over and over, echoing the rhythm of his spade as he ploughed through the fallen earth.

*"You are your mother's son …"*

The air grew thin as Redknee pushed deeper into the man-made warren. It was close, heavy work. Some of the beams still held true; there were pockets where he could crawl freely

250

but where the supporting structure had collapsed he had to wedge the fallen beams into makeshift supports and use his spade to burrow under. Sweat oozed down his spine, soaked his tunic. He wiped his forehead with his sleeve. The whole place could cave in at any time; his heart thumped in his chest; he had to find Thorvald: *fast*.

He redoubled his efforts. Eventually, his spade broke into a cavern. It was almost in total darkness, but he realised he must be in, or near, the great hall. Wheezing, he called for Thorvald. There was no reply. He called again, his throat hoarse from the thin air. If he did not return to the surface soon, he never would.

He was about to go back, when he heard a soft moan. "Thorvald," he said. "Is that you?"

"Over here," a small voice replied.

Redknee squinted through the darkness. He saw a hand stir in the gloom and crawled towards it. A six-foot beam lay across Thorvald's legs. Redknee began to move it, but stopped when Thorvald screamed.

"Let me die," Thorvald said. "I can't leave the tunnel anyway."

"That's not true," Redknee grunted, having another go at the beam. "You only have Gisela's word you'll burn above ground."

Thorvald flinched in pain as Redknee heaved the beam from his legs and pushed it aside with a roar.

"Here," Redknee said, extending his arm. "Lean on me."

Thorvald wrapped his arm round Redknee's shoulders. He was small and light, but with his leg broken he was a dead weight. More than once, Redknee had to stop, but each time he did so he heard the groan of the few remaining beams, and forced himself to push on.

Eventually, Redknee stumbled, exhausted, through the tunnel entrance, dropped Thorvald onto the wet grass, took another two steps and collapsed. *They'd made it*. If he'd had the strength, he would have punched the air. From somewhere far off he registered screaming, but he paid it little heed, so glad was he to be out, to be alive. Instead, he revelled in the judder of his ribs as his lungs clamoured for air.

"You did it."

He looked up. Astrid stood over him; bright spots floated in front of her face. He thought he would black out – then he remembered Thorvald. He tried to turn, to see if Thorvald was all right, but found he was too stiff, too tired. Then it hit him. *The screams.* Those terrible screams. Had they belonged to his friend? Had his rescue been futile? He looked up at Astrid and mouthed one word – "Thorvald?"

Astrid glanced at a spot on the grass behind him. For a moment Redknee thought she was going to shake her head, then her face broke into a smile. "He's fine. It seems Gisela's curse was a lie."

"But the screams?"

"Not him."

Koll came over and stood above Redknee, arms folded. "Someone fetch our hero a drink," he shouted. One of the villagers scurried over with a pitcher.

Redknee reached for a sip, gladly anticipating the liquid on his parched throat. But Koll had other ideas. Instead of a refreshing swig, Redknee was drenched in cold water. He sprang to his feet, arms outstretched, seeking the blacksmith's neck. "Why you …"

Silver bounded over; began hopping on his hind legs with excitement. He liked the joke too, did he?

"Well," Koll laughed, "you seem to have found your feet again."

Redknee glowered. "You might have let me drink some of it."

"No time for that. We must get to *Wavedancer.*"

Redknee glanced to where a group of village women were clucking over Thorvald. "I have to go," he called.

Thorvald nodded feebly. His skin, pale as it was, had not shrivelled instantly in the sun. Perhaps the boy king would not lead a normal life, perhaps his exposure to the sun would have to be limited. But who could claim freedom from all bonds? Who was not bound by their abilities, by their fears, their hopes?

Redknee turned to follow Koll and, as he did so, from the corner of his eye, he saw Bjorn approach Thorvald, a look of

252

supplication on his broad face. Some things, it seemed, would never change.

Olaf stood on *Wavedancer*, Harold beside him, his body folded in on itself like a wind-ravaged tree. Harold's face twisted into a smile when he saw Redknee. Sinead sat nearby, her hands tied behind her back, mouth gagged, eyes bulging with terror.

"Let her go!" Redknee called, breaking into a run across the sand.

"Ah, the wanderers return. I bring you the slave girl, in exchange for passage for my son and me," Olaf said.

Redknee stopped at a safe distance and drew *Flame Weaver*. Every muscle in his body tensed. The father was strong and fast, the boy unpredictable. That made Harold the more dangerous of the two. "I'm not sure it's a fair trade," Redknee said, eyes darting between father and son. "You nearly got me killed."

Olaf shuffled forward.

"Stay where you are!"

"You're mistaken. I saved your life."

"You were *supposed* to help attack the ledge," Redknee said as Koll and Magnus arrived, breathless, at his side.

Olaf shook his head. "I was distracting Ragnar so you could escape. I see it worked."

"So why is Sinead still bound?" Redknee asked.

Olaf cast Sinead a wary glance. She glared at him over her gag. "Had to look authentic, didn't it? I was going to let her go when she calmed down ..."

"I wouldn't trust him," Magnus said, drawing his sword and moving closer to Redknee.

"His trick *did* save us," Redknee replied.

Magnus shrugged. "I suppose."

"And he *was* my uncle's right hand man."

Olaf's face broke into a gap-toothed grin. "Fought with Sven for fifteen years. Not much your uncle didn't know about me."

"See," Redknee said, as Brother Alfred, Olvir and Astrid arrived beside him. "If my uncle trusted him, we can too."

"Where's Toki?" Olvir asked.

"Working hard," said a deep voice from somewhere in the bowels of the ship. A moment later, Toki appeared above *Wavedancer's* prow; hammer and chisel in his hands. "I've been here since the storm finished. Fixed up the ol' dragon good and proper – she's just like new. Although that buffoon," he said, nodding in Olaf's direction, "has been keeping me off my work all morning, asking how many rivets I've used and if I've left enough hemp to mend tears in the sail."

A flicker of pleasure lit Harold's dark eyes. At first, Redknee thought it was because Toki had repaired *Wavedancer*. Then he realised Harold was staring further down the beach. Slowly, Harold raised his hand and pointed over Redknee's shoulder.

Everyone turned in unison. Twenty or so men ran along the sand towards them, their helmets glinting gold in the low evening sun. They were still some distance, but Redknee saw their armament bristling; it was a full war party.

"Alright," Redknee said, turning back to Olaf. "You can come. But you must give your weapons to Koll."

Magnus shook his head as Koll relieved Olaf of his knife and sword, but Ragnar's men were already splashing through the surf and Redknee had no time to deliberate further. As they pushed *Wavedancer* into the water and leapt aboard, Redknee found he was already regretting his decision.

# PART III

# ABROAD

# Chapter 26

They rowed. Rowed with strength born of desperation. Rowed until Ragnar's men were reduced to tiny, shadowy figures splashing angrily in the surf. Then, at Redknee's order, they unfurled the big square sail; the wind rushed to greet the bright yellow stripes like an old friend and *Wavedancer* charged through the sea with the energy of a warhorse at full gallop.

Redknee turned to face the wind and breathed deeply. He felt twice as alive at sea as he did on land. Maybe the vast emptiness of the ocean gave him room to dream. Maybe it was the work – demanding and monotonous – that freed his mind to wander. Maybe it was the motion – the water speeding by, its ever-changing surface – that made him feel that at least he was doing something. Being someone.

Until today he had thought it false progress. He had wondered if they were all making some terrible mistake. Perhaps they *would* fall off the end of the earth. Be eaten by the giant wolf Fenrir. More likely, he was leading them to an ignoble death on some distant shore where their courage would be forgotten, never to reach the ears of home.

*Home.* Was that really what they sought? And could it be found on some strange land far across the wild sea?

"I don't trust Olaf."

He turned to find Sinead standing beside him. She cast a worried glance over her shoulder. Redknee followed her gaze to where Olaf stood with Harold near the prow; one arm slung over his son's crooked shoulder, the other pointing to a spot on the horizon. He whispered in Harold's ear. The boy laughed.

Redknee turned back to Sinead. "Neither does Magnus," he said.

"I don't trust Magnus either."

Redknee sighed. Magnus was at the tiller, doing his duty as always, yet as far away from Olaf as possible. Redknee couldn't have the last stretch of their voyage descend into accusations and suspicion. Eventually he said, "You would have me trust no one. Besides, you heard what Olaf said. The trick he played with you, on Ragnar, saved us all."

"So why take his weapons?"

He remembered Magnus's allegation – that Olaf had led Ragnar to the tunnels. It was one man's word against another.

"To smooth things over," he ventured. "For the time being. I'll return Olaf's sword and dagger soon. Once we've put a good stretch of sea between ourselves and Ragnar."

Sinead looked unconvinced, though she managed a small nod.

"He didn't hurt you?" he asked, suddenly concerned there was more to her complaint.

"No. Frightened me yes, but nothing more."

Satisfied, Redknee half turned from her, braced his hands against the rail and stared out to sea. "I fear we're nearly there."

"You fear that?"

"I think I've feared reaching the Promised Land for a long time. What if it's all lies?"

"What if it's all true?"

Redknee nodded. A gust of wind whipped his hair across his face. "There's something about the winds today." He waved his hands as if to catch the very breath of the earth, and began spinning round and round, arms outstretched. "There's something favourable about them, don't you think?"

Sinead giggled as Silver joined him, barking and hopping on his hind legs. "And what about you?" he asked. "Excited? Nervous?"

She nodded. "I won't be a slave any longer. I'll be as free as the winds." She shook her hair until it tumbled from its bindings and flew about her head like fireflies.

"Truly, I don't think you've ever really been a slave."

"No?" She stopped spinning; a frown marred her face.

"Isn't it a state of mind?"

"Oh, Redknee, you've been spending too much time with Brother Alfred. That sounds like something he would say. But when you work sixteen hour days, and you're so tired you can't even make it back to your bed before you fall asleep. Then you know that slavery is more than a state of mind. It's real."

"I'm not sure I got off much lighter. My mother always set me more tasks than I could do in a day … and my uncle expected me to train long after it was dark."

"It's not the same. But listen," she said, grabbing Redknee's outstretched arms, tumbling into him, "I think I've found the map Ragnar wanted Mord to find."

Redknee stared at the picture of the unicorn with the ivy border draped around its head, straining to understand. "It just looks like a pretty picture to me."

Sinead sighed. "You're looking but not seeing." She pointed to the ivy border. "Look at the leaves; does their pattern remind you of anything?"

"Not really."

"Think of where we've been: First the Sheep Islands, to the west of the Northlands, then Iceland, a little to the north." As she spoke, Sinead traced the pattern of the ivy with her finger, pointing to each new leaf in turn, working from right to left across the top of the page. "And, lastly, Greenland," she said, resting her finger on a big, pointed leaf near the top left-hand corner of the page. Redknee squinted more closely at the drawing. It was a crazy idea, so crazy, she might just be right.

"If you look closely at the leaves, you can see they're edged in different colours. Brown for the sheep of the Sheep Islands, red for the fires of Iceland—"

"Greenland in white for the ice …"

"Yes. And, if you look to the left-hand side of the page," she said, pointing to the biggest leaf of all, "to the south-west of Greenland, you'll see that leaf, the one the unicorn's horn points to, is edged in gold."

"You think that means the Promised Land?"

Sinead shrugged. "What else can it signify?"

Redknee scratched his head. If Sinead was right, they were only days from the Promised Land, the lion's share of their journey behind them. "What are those markings beside what we're assuming are the Sheep Islands?" he asked, having given the map more study.

Sinead peered at the faint, grey crosses. "I think someone has added them later, in charcoal. Maybe they're the hermit rocks we saw before reaching the Sheep Islands."

"Could be," Redknee agreed. "Or they could just be a dirty mark."

"I don't think that matters. The important thing is, this means we're nearly there."

"We've been at sea over a week since Sinead found her supposed map, and still no land," Olaf said, staring out to sea. "We've only water enough for two more days."

Redknee had opened the *Codex* on an up-ended barrel and was studying it … with little success. Consequently, he didn't have an answer that would allay Olaf's fears.

Toki peered over Redknee's shoulder. "Let me have a look," he said. "I studied a map when I sailed down the Volga with Ragnar."

Redknee shuffled aside. Koll still thought Toki's association with Ragnar as a soldier for hire meant he wasn't to be trusted. But if he knew how to read a map, that made him invaluable.

Toki furrowed his brows, held a huge, grubby thumb up to the picture and closed his left eye.

"What's he doing?" snapped Olaf. "He looks like he's about to take aim."

"I'm measuring the distance between what Sinead thinks are the Sheep Islands and Iceland. It took seven days to sail between them, right?"

"So?" Olaf said.

"Well, on the map, the distance between the Sheep Islands and Iceland is half the length of my thumb."

"What's the distance between Greenland and the Promised Land?" asked Redknee.

Toki measured up again. "It depends where I take the distance from, but about the length of my thumb, due south west."

256

"Does that mean it should take us about another four or five days?" Redknee asked.

"I reckon so."

Olaf turned to face them properly. "If it does," he said. "We'll all be dead, for we've only water for two."

That evening, Redknee found Toki by himself, making repairs to his deerskin boots with a bone needle and waxed thread. Redknee shot a glance round the deck. Everyone was busy, they wouldn't be overheard. "I must speak with you," he said, sitting down.

"If it's to do with the map, my reckoning was very rough—"

Redknee shook his head. "I wanted to ask about my family. You knew my parents before I was born."

Toki nodded and continued sewing his boot where it had split.

"When I was at the waterfall, Ragnar said something I thought strange."

"Go on."

"He said he looked after my mother when my father left her to go raiding sixteen or so years ago. He said he and I were more alike than I knew."

A faraway look came over Toki's face; he paused in his work, his needle glinting in the fading sun. "Yes," he said eventually. "I do remember that. But it doesn't mean—"

"There's more." Redknee lowered his voice. "Right before my uncle died …" Toki leaned in. "… when he was showing me how to use his battleaxe … my uncle said that Erik Kodranson was not … *was not my father*."

Toki turned white. After a long moment, he managed to speak. "You sure he said that?"

Redknee nodded. "Do you think he meant—"

"That *Ragnar* is your father?"

"I'll not believe it."

"As you shouldn't." Toki looked thoughtful. "Have you considered Sven was lying?"

Redknee shook his head.

257

"Then again," Toki added, "there is another man he could have meant, who stayed with Ragnar around then."

"Who?"

"Ivar visited Ragnar's longhouse in the spring of that year to announce the birth of his daughter."

Instinctively, Redknee turned to look at Astrid. She was weaving silver ribbon through her long blonde hair, taking great care to smooth each section with the palm of her hand. Their colouring was the same. But a deeper resemblance? He hoped not.

They sailed due west for two more days. With still no sight of land, Olaf imposed rationing: A third of a turnip and one slice of meat per man each day. Magnus snorted at Olaf's attempt to impose order. Though, to Redknee's relief, he shied away from an outright confrontation – Olaf had his sword back. It seemed everyone was suspicious of everyone else. Koll and Toki slept with their weapons drawn. Magnus stayed, recluse-like, at the tiller. And when Olvir shot a fulmar for the pot, Sinead was quick to take it off his hands, her suspicions having remained since the day of the poisoning.

Sinead also gathered the silvery fish that jumped, twisting and flapping, onto the deck. Her haul numbered twelve and meant they enjoyed a good meal that night.

The fog landed thick and fast in the afternoon of the second day. It made Olaf more nervous than he was already and served to heighten the mood of mistrust onboard. Redknee stood at the prow, but he struggled to keep watch, hardly able to see his own right hand through the murk. He needn't have worried, for they were barely moving. The big square sail sagged against the mast like a discarded stocking, dragging their spirits with it. A brisk wind petered out to nothing; full-grown waves regressed to juvenile ripples. They crept along like this for many hours, scarcely moving, as if the sea wanted to hold them there forever. Or perhaps she wished to guard the secret of the Promised Land – her finest jewel.

The similarity with Saint Brendan's journey, as told in the *Codex*, wasn't lost on Redknee. Saint Brendan and his monks had entered a dazzling miasma right before sighting the

258

Promised Land. And it was then, when they were at their lowest point, when they had lost all hope and were about to give up, that Saint Brendan had finally found what he'd been looking for all along.

Thinking on this, Redknee sought Sinead. He found her sitting with Brother Alfred, wrapped in sheepskins, the *Codex* balanced on her lap. Sinead had learned to read by looking at the apothecary's labels, then by studying the recipes for herbal cures. Hers was not the high Latin of Church documents. Brother Alfred, on the other hand, although he couldn't read, had more knowledge of monks and their affairs. He was helping her decipher the last few passages that still eluded her understanding. It was a slow process.

Redknee sat beside them, pulling a spare fleece over his own shoulders, for the fog had brought a bitter chill. Sinead turned to the page he'd heard her read to Gisela in the tunnels, the one with the picture of the silver-leafed pine tree. He watched as her lips formed the alien sounds. He followed her eyes and the sounds began to merge with the shapes on the parchment.

"Why do you read *that* page over and over?" he asked.

"There's one part that puzzles me. Brother Alfred is helping me work it out. It comes just after the passage about crossing the river. It says: *'They crossed the river and found the land was filled with streets of gold for as far as the eye could see.'"

"Is that the part you don't understand?"

"That's just it. A street would have to be built by people. But nowhere in the *Codex* does it say the Promised Land is inhabited. Except, of course, for the youth who greets Saint Brendan. But I'd taken him to be symbolic."

Redknee remembered Gisela's claim about the fearsome disappearing warriors. He shook his head. "Maybe all the people died," he said, firmly pushing aside Ulfsson's stories in the same vein.

"Perhaps," Sinead said, chewing her thumb nail worriedly.

Suddenly the call came down the ship: "Land, land! Land ahead!"

Redknee turned. Olvir was waving his cap in the air. Everyone, Redknee included, ran to the prow as large grey cliffs loomed out the fog. "About!" Redknee shouted, rushing for an oar, using it to help Magnus steer. "Come about, now!"

Koll and Toki grabbed oars too and *Wavedancer* wheeled around. The force threw Redknee to the deck. He scrambled to his feet. Magnus was still at the tiller. "Keep her line steady," Redknee shouted. "And watch for rocks!"

Magnus nodded. He had many days experience at the helm and his hand was firm. They could rely on him. *Wavedancer* slid past the cliffs unscathed. The wall of granite seemed to go on forever.

"Where will we land?" Sinead asked.

Redknee looked up. The cliffs rose skywards until they faded into the mist. They could not drop anchor and climb them. Nor could they risk sailing too close and puncturing the hull on hidden rocks. "We need to wait until we reach a natural harbour," he said.

And so they followed the line of the cliffs south until the darkness melded with the fog. Redknee lit a torch and joined Magnus at the tiller. The yellow flames reflected in his eyes.

"I'll stand at the prow and light the way as best I can," Redknee said. Nightsailing close to shore was dangerous, treacherous in unfamiliar waters. But it was too deep to drop anchor, so they had no choice. At least the sea was calm. They didn't have to worry about angry waves smashing them against the cliffs.

Magnus nodded. Then, as Redknee started towards the prow, he added, "*Wait*."

Redknee turned. Magnus looked older than his nineteen summers; spidery lines framed hollow grey eyes, his skin sallow, the corners of his mouth pinched and dry with tiredness.

"Sometimes," Magnus said, "it gets lonely back here. Always on watch, always vigilant. Hardly anyone comes to speak to me."

"I'll stay with you," Redknee said. "I doubt my torch will do much good tonight anyway." He perched on a chest near

260

Magnus and took a crust of bread from his pouch. Magnus smiled and accepted it gladly.

Redknee spoke to Magnus as they crept through the night. He kept his torch high to get the best light they could; though it was an almost futile exercise in the eerie, fog-swamped sea.

He learned Magnus was an orphan, both his parents having died of the sweating fever when he was a boy. Since their death, he'd been looked after by the village, staying first in Karl's longhouse, then with Koll and Thora. He explained he'd been a quiet and withdrawn child after his parents died, that was why Sven had thought him suited to the long, still hours manning the helm. But Magnus, like the rest of them, had never been on such a long voyage. Enough was enough. Redknee sensed Magnus felt undervalued.

"Although no one says so," Redknee said, staring into the inky blackness beyond the halo cast by his torch, "we all know manning the tiller is the most important job on the ship."

Magnus sighed. "I know that. Sometimes it just feels like I'm invisible."

As the darkness faded to smoky grey, Olvir joined them, bringing with him bowls of steaming soup. "Is this it?" he asked, leaning against the gunwale and looking up at the endless cliffs. "I mean, is this *really* the Promised Land?"

"I think so," Redknee said, digging into the chunks of boiled turnip sprinkled with herbs. Only after he'd taken several mouthfuls did he remember Sinead's warning – Thora had used Olvir's catch in the poisoned stew. Redknee suddenly felt his throat burn. He gasped for air, clawed at the skin on his neck, knocking his bowl to the floor.

Magnus glanced up from his breakfast. "Everything all right?"

"You don't feel it?" Redknee asked, struggling for breath. "You don't feel it hot – searing your tongue, your windpipe?"

Magnus nodded enthusiastically. "Yes, it's good."

Redknee looked down. Silver was licking the spilled soup, his pink tongue working between the planks, finding every last piece. *Oh no, not the pup too.* Silver glanced up. Guilt laced

261

his golden eyes but he did not look sick. In fact, he looked quite well. Redknee dared to open his mouth, dared to breathe in. He found the action cooled his throat.

Olvir looked round from where he'd been watching the sea. "You disliked the soup?"

Redknee's eyes darted between Olvir and Magnus's bemused faces. Sinead would have him believe one of *them* was the traitor. He couldn't see it, not Olvir anyway. What did he have to gain in sabotaging their voyage? He'd volunteered to come; he knew nothing of Ragnar; had no connection with his uncle's dubious past.

Redknee found his voice, "The soup is good," he said. "I'm just feeling a little sea-sick."

Unperturbed, Olvir scratched a fleabite on his arm. Blood oozed from the scab, staining the surrounding skin. "It would be a shame," he said, "if we'd come all this way and couldn't land. I'm itching to go exploring."

Redknee cricked his neck so he was looking up to where the cliffs faded into the mist. "We'll find a way to go ashore."

Olvir smiled simply and Redknee felt an icy shudder pass through his body. What if there was no way ashore? *Please*, he thought. *Please let there be a harbour somewhere along this infernal rock.* But the cliffs stretched on.

"Here," Olvir said. "Let me take the torch."

"No—"

Olvir reached up and eased the baton from Redknee's fingers. "You can't do everything."

"Thanks," he mumbled. "Were you born in the Sheep Islands?" he asked, yawning.

Olvir nodded. "My parents were shepherds. They moved there about sixteen years ago. From the Northlands. Ivar went to the mainland to find settlers. I think they sailed with him just after Astrid was born."

Toki had said Ivar had visited Ragnar to announce the birth of his daughter. Redknee fought to keep the excitement from his voice. "Did your parents ever mention Ivar's time in the Northlands? About him visiting Ragnar, perhaps when my mother, Ingrid, was a guest of his?"

262

Olvir thought for a moment; then shook his head. "They came from an area of pastureland in the south – near the land of the Danes. I know they travelled north with Ivar before sailing. Maybe they all stayed at Ragnar's longhouse then?"

"Possibly," Redknee said. He'd thought he might learn something from Olvir, but the boy knew little about his parents' lives before they arrived in the Sheep Islands.

# Chapter 27

Later that morning Redknee stood with Silver on the sun-splashed deck, the night's fog a distant memory. Around him, crenellated rocks had bowed to creeping sands. Long, flat beaches stole, finger-like, into the sea, snaring the waves in a maze of turquoise lagoons. Beyond all this, a crown of plush hills brushed a confident blue sky.

"I believe," Redknee said, turning to find Koll had joined him, "we have found our landing spot."

Koll nodded his agreement.

A hush had come over the ship; gone was the cacophony of excitement, the clatter of voices, the robust anticipation of previous landings. Instead, wide eyes strained to devour every detail, every nuance, every colour, of this first sighting of the Promised Land.

They lowered the sail and rowed through an inky channel to a harbour as good as any Northlandic fjord. When the shore was still several ship-lengths away, Redknee leapt into the water and started swimming. He heard a splash and a moment later Silver drew level with him, his grey-tipped ears and black nose just visible above the water. By Odin's eye, the pup grew more fearless by the day.

Redknee hadn't planned to jump in. Perhaps it was Sven's voice, speaking to him from beyond the grave. Whatever the source of the impulse, Redknee powered through the water, scrambled onto the beach, and, collapsing to his knees, drew *Flame Weaver*, plunging its shimmering blade deep into the sand.

"I claim this virgin land as my own," he said breathlessly, as Silver circled him, "and in the name of my noble uncle and protector, Sven Kodranson."

Behind him, he heard *Wavedancer* mount the beach. He turned to see Harold's deformed frame blocking the sun. For a moment he thought the whelp was going to kick sand in his face, as he had done the time they were back in the Northlands, training. Instead, Harold just laughed and shuffled over to his father's side.

Redknee stood. The others were heading up the beach towards the dunes. He pulled *Flame Weaver* from the ground and followed. *Yes*, he thought, *who is the shame of the Vikinger now?* Yet behind him, the sands were already moving, healing the wound rent by his sword.

They camped on the beach that night, warmed by a fire of driftwood that smelled of seaweed as it burned. The fine weather meant they didn't need the tarpaulin from the ship for protection. Almost as soon as they'd arrived, Sinead had gone looking for food, finding a colony of big pink crabs in one of the lagoons. She plunged them into boiling water, then, with the help of Koll's smithing tongs and a wooden mallet, she prised the juicy white meat from the shells. It was a fitting delicacy for their first meal in the Promised Land.

"You know," Koll said, shoving the last of the crabmeat in his mouth, "this place doesn't look half bad – though there's a distinct lack of precious jewels. Tomorrow I'm going to take a bow and explore those hills." He pointed to the high, rolling landscape behind them that resembled the hulls of an upturned fishing fleet.

Toki sat furthest from the fire, his face half in shadow. "We should find a headland first, secure our position," he said, working a piece of driftwood with his knife. "We don't know enough about this place yet."

"You speak as if we're staying," Olaf said. "The sooner we find this damn treasure and get home, the better."

"And leave ourselves defenceless to Ragnar's attack?" interjected Magnus.

Redknee cleared his throat. "Come Magnus, no-one here really believes Olaf betrayed us in the tunnels." He turned to Olaf. "I want to find the treasure too, but Toki is right, we must make ourselves secure."

After much debate, it was decided a scouting party would venture into the woods the next day with a view to finding the best place to set up camp. Olaf huffily declared that he and Harold would stay to guard *Wavedancer*. Brother Alfred, fearful of the toll a climb would take on his soft feet, offered to keep them company.

Only Astrid seemed uncertain about what she should do. As the fire burned low, she addressed Toki, who was still carving the piece of wood in his hand. "When you say secure … do you mean from wild animals?"

"I mean wild people," Toki said, and smiled.

Brother Alfred crossed himself. "If there are heathens on this island, I will find them and tell them the ways of Christ."

"But not tomorrow?" Astrid shot back. "And you have come so far just to tell some grubby peasants about a carpenter?"

"If you're so interested in our Christian stories," Sinead cut in, "why don't you read them for yourself?"

Astrid curled her lip in disgust. "Reading is like collecting wood, or scrubbing tables. It's work, and work is for slaves."

Sinead lunged forward and clamped her hands round Astrid's throat. Astrid clawed at Sinead's face, but the younger girl was strong and able to hold Astrid down, pushing her cheek into the sand.

"That's enough!" Redknee said, grabbing Sinead by the shoulder.

But it was Olaf who gripped Sinead's hair with one hand and dragged Astrid free with the other. "There will be no killing women." he said. "If we're staying, we're going to need them." Then he turned and resumed his place beside Harold.

"She really gets to you." Redknee joined Sinead at the far end of the beach where she stood near the water. The night was clear and the new moon cast a blueish glow over her features.

"I shouldn't let her," she said, smiling.

Silver, who'd followed Redknee, slunk off to investigate an interesting orange shell.

Redknee sat in the sand. "Do you think this can work?"

Sinead sat beside him, her hands folded in her lap. "Can what work?"

266

"This … this settlement," he said, lying back and watching as a wispy cloud passed in front of the moon.

"So it's decided – we're going to stay here?"

"Yes – at least for now."

"What about Saint Brendan's treasure?"

"We need to secure our camp before we can go looking."

She lay back beside him, her shoulders level with his, her eyes trained on the greyish white of the moon. It was a while before she spoke. "Once we find the treasure, Olaf will want to return home."

She was likely right, Redknee thought. There would be nothing keeping Olaf and the others in the Promised Land once they had Saint Brendan's treasure. Nothing keeping him either. Not really. Only the draw of the land itself: hundreds, maybe thousands, of untouched acres – all for the taking. But then, there was Sven's jarldom for him in the Northlands, if he had the wit to claim it. Sinead was unique in her desire to truly start afresh. He turned on his side to face her, watched as her chest rose and fell with each breath. He hadn't noticed before, but her cheeks were spattered with the palest freckles.

"Do you still think about Ireland?" he asked eventually.

"Now that we've reached the Promised Land?"

He nodded.

"Before I was sent to work for the monks I remember a woman with bright green eyes and hair the colour of autumn leaves, much like my own. She sang to me. I think … if I try very hard … I can still remember some of the words to her song."

"Sing it."

"No."

"Go on," he said, raising himself onto his elbow. "I want to hear it."

"Don't tease me."

"I'm not."

"All right." She sat up and took a couple of deep breaths. "I think the song went something like this:

*"Where get ye your dinner, my handsome young man?*
*I dined wi' my true-love; mother, make my bed soon.*
*For I'm weary wi' hunting, and fain would lie down"*

267

Her voice soared over the water like a heron in flight, all trace of her usual harpying gone.

"You have a beautiful voice."

She stopped. "You're making fun of me," she said, shoving him in the ribs. "It's a very sad song, about a young man who dies of a broken heart."

"You can't die from love."

"Can't you?"

Redknee lowered his eyes. "I don't know … I've never been in love."

"What about Astrid? I saw you kiss in the tunnels."

He shifted uncomfortably. "There's nothing between Astrid and I. She's married, she thinks only of her husband." In truth, he *had* felt nothing when Astrid had kissed him.

"Well then … you can't talk about what you don't know."

"So," Redknee said, in an attempt to change the subject, "this woman, the one who sang to you, was she your mother?"

"I think so. The sad thing is, I'm not entirely sure. I was so young when I was sent to work for the monks, no more than four years old. I can't even remember."

"Why were you sent to work for them?"

She shrugged. "The monks told me my parents couldn't feed and clothe me. I suppose it makes sense."

"Do you ever wonder about finding her? The singing lady, that is."

"I do, yes. But how would I? I don't have the same luxury of freedom as you. There is no fine dragonship at *my* disposal, no troupe of men to do my bidding."

Redknee flopped back onto the sand. "Sometimes I think it's a curse. I wish my mother had never started me on this quest. It wasn't great, having a coward for a father, but at least I knew who he was. Believed him dead. There was certainty in that. Now I don't know what to think."

"You asked me if I'd ever wanted to find the woman I remember as my mother. And yes, I have wanted that. But at the same time, what does it matter? It wouldn't change who I am. Nor would it change how my life has turned out. My past is not my future," she laughed at this. "Heavens above, I of all people should know that; starting out as a treasured servant in a rich monastery and ending up here, beyond the ends of the earth, a slave to pagans." She leaned over him, eyes serious. "I suppose I'm saying – does it really matter *who* your father is?"

Redknee reached up and tucked a flyaway strand of hair behind her ear. "Finding my father was my mother's dying wish."

Sinead said nothing, her expression telling him all he needed to know. Instead, she lay back down beside him on the sand and stared up at the huge, star-sprinkled sky.

Just then a yelp came from a few paces off. They turned to see Silver, head down, ears flat, leaning on his back legs and growling at the strange shell. Redknee called the pup over. Blood oozed from the soft black pad at the end of his nose.

"He's been bitten," Sinead said, glancing worriedly at the shell.

Redknee checked the wound. There was a white splinter. "Hold him," he said as he gripped the splinter between his thumb and forefinger and gave a sharp tug. Silver yowled as the splinter came loose and eyed Redknee reproachfully. Redknee held him close for a moment until the shock left the pup's system, then he went over to check the shell. "It's some sort of sea creature," he said, easing it away with the toe of his boot.

When he rejoined Sinead, he found Silver sprawled across her lap. They lay side by side for a long while, not speaking, just listening to the rumble of the waves beyond the lagoon.

When the cold started to seep through his tunic, Redknee got to his feet and offered her his hand. "My lady," he said, bowing slightly. "Your world awaits ..."

She stood, but instead of taking his hand, she stood on tiptoe and planted a soft kiss on his lips. When he leaned in, to deepen the kiss, she pulled away and ran laughing along the shore towards their camp, trails of spray flying in her wake. He wasn't even going to try and catch her. That could wait.

It was then he noticed them. Across the blank sand, further out than either he or Sinead had yet ventured, a set of footprints snaking into the distance.

# Chapter 28

Redknee kept quiet about the footprints. He didn't want to admit the existence of possible challengers. This island was his. He'd been first to land, hadn't he? First to cleave the beach with steel. Nothing – and no one – was going to take that away from him. In any event, when he returned the next day to where he'd seen the footprints, they were gone, washed away by the tide. A fact he took as a good omen.

His daring, however, did not extend to recklessness and he insisted everyone arm themselves on their trip to the hills. It took the whole morning to climb the ridge behind the beach. On reaching the top, Redknee had expected to see the far side of the island and the sea beyond. Instead he saw trees. Wave after wave of burnished gold and bronze shimmered in the noonday sun, an arboreal ocean of precious metals that swept the pale autumn sky. A breeze whistled through the leaves, rippling the surface of the golden sea. Redknee felt the energy as a tingle in his fingertips. His island was huge: its depths swollen with the fruits of the earth. He – they all – would be rich indeed.

Sinead's eyes widened with excitement, her skin glowed. She took Redknee's hand and squeezed. "It's beautiful."

Redknee was about to agree, but Toki spoke first. "You still think we're the first people to find a place like this?" he asked.

Redknee shrugged. "We lost Ragnar ages ago," he said vaguely. He did not want to be reminded of the footprints on such a fine day. With any luck, they belonged to some shipwrecked beggar: no more a claimant to this magnificent island than the eagles swooping above their heads or the worms that chewed the ground beneath their feet. For if his uncle had taught him anything, it was that the spoils belonged to the quick and the strong.

The forest stretched as far as the eye could see, so they decided to push on while there was still a good six hours of daylight. Beneath the canopy, the trunks of the great broad-leafed trees soared straight and tall, their highest branches arched in cloistered avenues. The air swam with the nutty perfume of decaying leaves, lightened only by the occasional sweet note of a bough laden with sticky dark fruits. The earth was soft and mulchy with its carpet of leaves, so that their footsteps were silenced as if in reverence to their surroundings. Where a spear of sunlight pierced the thatch, it seemed to set the very ground ablaze, as if, in illuminating the dead leaves, it had struck a constellation of fallen stars.

"It's like gold," said Sinead, kicking a tuft of leaves into the air.

Silver dived amongst them, tail wagging. Redknee watched as they fluttered to the ground. *Streets of gold.* That's what Saint Brendan had spoken of in the *Codex*. He couldn't have meant ... *Could he?*

Sweat trickled down Redknee's neck and pooled at the base of his spine. He'd dispensed with his woollen tunic long ago and his skin glistened like a sea-pearl in the mid-day sun. Chopping wood was hard, but rewarding. Because of their limited manpower, they would only harvest a couple of the smaller trunks now. But they would be back tomorrow and the day after that.

Choosing the wood for the longhouse was a skill in itself. The main supports had to be long and straight. That wasn't a problem as the forest here was dense, forcing the trees to strain ever upwards to gain a share of the sun and rain.

Redknee was currently attacking a young birch with a flat-bladed axe while Silver looked on. He spotted Sinead approach with a bucket of water as he drove the axe into the fibrous flesh one last time. "Watch out," he said, pulling her backwards as the trunk swayed for a moment, then keeled over in a cloud of dust.

He looked at his work with satisfaction before taking the bucket from her, gulping down a couple of mouthfuls and pouring the rest over his head.

She folded her arms across her chest. "You'll catch a chill."

"Don't be a nag," he said, plunging the axe into the felled trunk. "What's for lunch?"

Sinead sniffed and stalked away.

So much for last night, he thought, following her towards the small cooking fire she'd started earlier. She seemed to have reverted to treating him with her usual disdain.

"Smells good," he said peaceably, settling himself down on an upturned log.

Toki and Koll emerged from between the trees and joined them. Sinead began spooning clumps of thick porridge into wooden bowls. She handed the first one to Koll. He sniffed the mixture then began slurping it straight from the dish.

"You know," he began between mouthfuls. "There are more trees on this island than on all the lands from here to home."

"Quite a treasure," Toki said, stirring his porridge with the handle of his eating knife. "Could make a man rich … if he owned it."

Redknee shuffled uncomfortably. He was beginning to feel cold and vulnerable without his tunic.

"Reckon your claim to the beach entitles you to all this?" Toki asked, taking in the forest with a sharp sweep of his eyes.

Redknee didn't want to confront Toki over this. He'd assumed Toki had understood the rules of the trip. Redknee was his uncle's chosen successor. It was his uncle's ship that had brought them here. By rights that made the spoils Redknee's to divide, in line with pre-agreed portions.

Problem was, no one had expected to find all this. How did Redknee, just sixteen summers old, defend his claim against seasoned warriors? Friend or foe, this island was an awfully big prize to give up just because of some outdated rules. Honour had a price, and Redknee was certain it was a lot less than the miles of verdant forest that stretched before them.

Before Redknee could answer, Sinead cut in. "What are you suggesting?" she, demanded, jabbing her wooden spoon at Toki.

Toki nearly spat his mouthful of porridge into the fire. "Nothing," he mumbled. "Nothing at all."

A shout came from the between the trees. They all turned to see Olvir and Magnus running towards them.

"Leave some for us," Olvir called, a big smile on his face.

The tension dissipated as the newcomers noisily took their places by the fireside.

Only when Redknee resumed eating his porridge did he see Koll's hand wound tightly round the hilt of his dagger. Something told him it had been there all along.

And so they worked on. Each day they marched into the forest and brought back timber for the longhouse. It was hard work and Redknee noticed his muscles grow. His body was changing. It was no longer that of a boy on the cusp of adulthood. Each morning, when he went to the sea to wash, he saw that coarse hair, the colour of wheat in August, brushed his chin. His torso lengthened, his legs became sturdy. And when he stood beside Olaf, he no longer faced the older man's chest. Instead, he looked steadily into Olaf's tired grey eyes.

It was with this newfound confidence that he crept into the forest on the night of the first proper frost. The longhouse neared completion. Redknee wanted to make a carving for above the door. This would be an important symbol; Redknee had not forgotten Toki's challenge that first day gathering wood.

A breeze scratched nervously at half-naked trees. Silver's ears pricked up. Redknee whistled to the pup to stay near. He pulled his cloak tightly round his shoulders. The forest closed in on a man at night. Though he'd only seen the footprints that one time, weeks ago, he was glad to have *Flame Weaver* at his side.

He chose a fine tree with thick branches and a smattering of blood-red leaves. His first blow sent a spray of bark into the night. Chopping eased his nerves. Soon his cloak lay on the ground. As he worked, he turned Sinead's song over. One bit

273

stuck in his head, something about being *sick at heart, and fain would lie down*. Strange. He didn't feel heart-sick. The deaths of his mother and uncle seemed a long way off – part of the old world, part of his old life. Instead he felt strong, invigorated – full of purpose. He remembered Sinead's kiss and smiled. He'd need to convince her she wanted to repeat it.

The branch creaked and slumped to the ground, leaving a pale gash. Redknee brought his axe down one last time to complete the amputation. He sat on the ground to shear off the bark; it flaked away easily. The grain beneath was tightly packed and strong. He'd chosen well.

As his eyes adjusted to the dark he moved with quick, confident strokes, paring the branch into a regular shape. Satisfied, he put aside his axe and slid a long, wooden-handled chisel from his bag. Wood shavings littered the grass as his chisel flew over the emerging figure of a man. Silver's amber eyes followed every stroke. Eventually he slowed – runes demanded care.

A twig snapped to his left. Silver stood; every muscle in his little body taut as a bow. Redknee peered among the branches. He saw nothing, yet he edged back until his shoulders met the tree trunk.

"Hey, little one," he called, "there's no-one there." But Silver kept his vigil.

Wanting to be back at the camp with the finished sign before the others woke, Redknee worked on. But he was alert now, listening for the slightest sound.

It was only when he was nearly finished that he heard another noise, this time a gentle rustling, like fabric brushing the forest floor. He reached for his sword as a figure in a moss-green cloak, the hood pulled over its face, stepped into the clearing. Silver rushed forward, tail wagging. The moonlight shone on the figure's hands as she, for it was clear now it was a woman, lifted them to reveal her face.

"Sinead," he said, breathing a sigh of relief. "What are you doing out so late?"

"I could ask the same of you."

274

"How long have you been here?" he asked, thinking of the noises he heard earlier.

"I just arrived. I couldn't sleep and I thought a walk would help. Then I heard the sound of your chisel working on that—"

Suddenly shy, his hands darted over the carving. "It's for above the main door."

"Show me," she said, sitting beside him on the ground. It was the first time they'd been alone together since the night on the beach. She pointed to the figure. "Is that your uncle?"

Redknee nodded.

"What does the inscription say?" Despite her skill with Latin, she still refused to learn what she called 'the pagan letters.'

*"This place is named for Sven: a warrior who knew no fear."*

She placed her hand on his arm. "I think … you miss him. More than an uncle … like a father."

For a moment he wondered if he should kiss her, but it felt wrong. Instead he stared at his carving. The work was rough. Unworthy of his uncle's memory. It took him a while to speak and when he did, his voice was tight and serious.

"He was the closest thing I ever knew to a father." He ran his hand over the crude rendition of his uncle's face. "And now I know he wasn't even my uncle."

Sinead bit her lip. He knew she was thinking of something to say that would soothe him. She should know he didn't want to be soothed. He wanted to be angry. "And he gave you no clue who your father might be?" she asked gently.

Redknee shook his head. "I don't think he knew."

"Well that's it, don't you see?"

"Not really."

"He knew you weren't his brother's child. Maybe not even family. *Still*, he wanted *you* to succeed him."

Redknee thought Sinead's logic about as convincing as a feather knife.

They arrived back at the longhouse at first light. Sinead helped him fix the sign above the door. It fitted perfectly.

"Your uncle would be pleased," she said, standing back and admiring. Redknee only nodded, he did not have the words to say what he felt.

Koll was the first to rise. He stroked his beard as he studied the new addition. At first Redknee thought he was angry. But Koll turned to him, smiling, and drew him into a back-slapping hug.

"It is a good likeness of your uncle. He would be proud of you. From now on this settlement shall be known as *Svensbyan*."

Redknee needn't have feared the others' response. Everyone, Toki included, admired the carving and agreed *Svensbyan* was a good name. After that day, the speed of their work seemed to increase. The day of the first snowfall saw the completion of the outbuildings, only the protective wall remained to be finished. Brother Alfred blessed the new settlement in the name of the Christian God. Koll, unsure as to whether such a blessing would carry any weight in Asgard, the land of the gods, declared that they should also have a feast in honour of Odin.

Brother Alfred had no objections. He liked a feast as much as anyone, and it was well known throughout the camp that Koll had just completed his first brew of Promised Mead.

And so began the preparations. Olvir took his bow into the forest and brought back a great stag. Toki, who was a better fisherman than hunter, took his lines to the shore and returned with a sackload of fat pink salmon. Brother Alfred laid traps around the camp, catching squirrels. Sinead, used to keeping a kitchen garden at the monastery, rummaged in the forest for fruits, returning with a heap of shiny red berries that tasted sharp on the tongue.

So, although they had found no chickens, cows, sheep or pigs on this new island, they had plenty to fill their table. The only missing ingredient was bread. They had searched thoroughly, but failed to find wheat.

On the day of the feast, Redknee helped Sinead decorate the longhouse with evergreen branches and pinecones. Olaf lit the fire in the centre of the room and everyone huddled round. Koll burst through the door, a barrel of mead slung across each shoulder. Smiling, and attuned to the drama of the event, he began walking slowly down the hall towards the dancing flames.

*"A better burden, no man can bear,"* he boomed, looking round the room and drinking in the rapt faces, *"than his mother's wit: and no worse provision can he carry, than a draught of mead."*

Everyone laughed at the last line, for Koll always seemed to have a stash of mead. Odin's famous poem could be Koll's motto.

Koll pretended to stumble the last few feet under the weight of the barrels, gaining one last laugh, before placing them, very carefully, on the floor. The barrels were opened and everyone began filling their drinking horns.

*"Dew of the Gods ..."*

*"Sweeter than honey ..."*

*"Fiery and true ..."* ...were just some of the accolades won by Koll's mead that night. Sinead served up the feast and soon everyone lay sleepily round the fire, their bellies full. Redknee sat beside Sinead; Silver chewing a bone at his feet. He felt warm and content, yet strangely lost for words. "Tell us a story," he called to Brother Alfred.

"Don't you want to hear of Valhalla tonight?" the little monk asked.

A cheer went up and everyone drank a toast to the gods. Once the noise died down, Redknee repeated his request. Soon everyone was goading the little monk to tell a story – and make it a good one.

"Oh, all right," Brother Alfred said, dabbing the corner of his mouth with his sleeve. "Will it be a tale of guts and gore ... or honour and love?"

"Honour and love!" Sinead called. Redknee fancied she cast him a quick glance.

"Guts and gore," Koll shouted.

Brother Alfred listened until the rest had called their preference. "Very well," he said, "I think that was a tie." He rubbed his hand over his bald head. "Let me think ... love *and* gore, honour *and* guts. That really calls for the Greeks. Then again, the Bible has its fair share—"

"Just get on with it," Olaf shouted. The festivities had done little to lighten his mood.

"Very well. I shall tell you of the homecoming of Odysseus. Odysseus was a seasoned warrior – he'd been away from home for twenty years fighting the Trojans. This war finished, he decided it was time to return to his beloved wife and son."

"Bet she'd entertained a few," Koll shouted, eyes gleaming with mead.

Brother Alfred chuckled. "As it happens, Penelope remained true to Odysseus for many years, but even her patience had its limits. In Odysseus' absence many suitors had arrived at her door. Penelope refused to hear any of them until she had woven a memorial shroud for her father-in-law. For three years, she wove by day and, at night, crept back to her loom to unpick her work."

"Canny little shrew," Magnus said, spitting berry pips on the floor. Redknee thought the comment out of character for the straightforward steersman.

Brother Alfred tilted his head thoughtfully. "But to Penelope's suitors, her guile only made her more desirable." He took a slug from his drinking horn and continued. "Now, at this point, Odysseus was ensnared by the beautiful nymph Calypso. She offered him immortality if he would stay with her forever. But Odysseus wept every day for his wife and son. So the gods helped him escape, but before he could return home, he had to travel through Hades – where the dead go."

"Greek warriors don't go to Valhalla?" Koll asked, concerned.

Brother Alfred shook his head. "Nor do they go to the Christian heaven, my friend. Of course, this is but a tale. In those days *everyone*, good or bad, heroic or cowardly; they all went to the same place – to Hades. Now, in Hades he meets his old friend Achilles. In life, Achilles had been a great warrior, obsessed with risking death for eternal glory. But in Hades he states he would rather be alive as a swine-herd than dead."

278

"No!" Redknee jumped up. "That's a lie. It could never be better to tend pigs, than to die bravely, your name on the lips of men forever."

"Perhaps it was because he was in Hades and not Valhalla," Toki offered, grinning. "I'm sure it's different for a Viking."

Brother Alfred raised his hands. "I only tell the story as it happened. I cannot change Achilles' feelings."

Sinead tugged on Redknee's arm. Deflated, he sat down and let Brother Alfred continue.

"Before Odysseus reached home, he passed the island of the Sirens. These women use their sublime singing to entice sailors ashore and kill them. Odysseus ordered his men to block their ears. He lashed himself to the mast, and though he heard the Sirens' magnetic trill, he was powerless to steer his ship aground. But what Odysseus heard was terrible. Truly so. For the Sirens promised knowledge of all things."

"But knowledge is good," Sinead said, frowning.

"Ah ... my child, but what would there be to *do*, once one knows *everything*? It would be a kind of death, for certain."

"You're saying the Siren's knowledge would kill him?" Sinead asked in disbelief.

"Well ... more that it would stop him from going home. Stop him completing his destiny."

Sinead bit her lip. Brother Alfred's explanation appeared to bother her.

"Odysseus arrived home safely," Brother Alfred continued. "Disguised as a beggar, he sets out to test his wife's loyalty. He creeps into the palace and sees how the suitors harass her to accept their proposals. He corners Penelope and tells her that her husband is still alive. She says she is holding a bridal contest ... the successful suitor must match her first husband's ability in shooting an arrow through a row of twelve crossed axes.

"The day of the test arrives. Each of the suitors tries but none can string Odysseus' great bow, let alone shoot it. Acting the drunken fool, Odysseus stumbles forward for his turn. The suitors cry in outrage. But Penelope nods. *What harm can it do? No one but her husband can wield his bow anyway.*

Grasping the familiar sweep of yew, Odysseus strings his great bow and pulls. His arrow thrums through the twelve axeheads.

"Silence falls over the room. He grabs a second arrow and spins round. He draws back; the arrow snaps into the chief suitor's throat, killing him instantly. The other suitors try to flee, but Odysseus mounts the table and reveals his identity. Then he draws his sword and sticks the soft-bellied suitors like pigs. The only person spared is the priest."

"Cowpats!" Koll shouted. "He would stick the priest too."

"No, no. It's a particular sin to kill a man of God."

Koll growled his dissent, but he let Brother Alfred go on.

"Still doubting Odysseus' true identity, Penelope asks a servant to bring their marriage bed for him to rest. But this is a trick. He stops her by saying their bed cannot be moved for it is built round a living olive tree. Penelope sinks to her knees; her hero is home."

"I'll tell you a story of real betrayal," Toki said. Everyone turned; Toki had moved closer to the fire. The flames glinted in his eyes. "It's about two brothers."

"Is there a wench?" Koll asked.

"There's always a wench," Toki said dryly. He leaned back so that half his face was cast in shadow. Everyone in the room leaned in. He commanded their attention like a true *skald*. "We will call the brothers Einnear and Sigurd," he said.

Sinead's eyes widened. "Are those their real names?"

Toki glanced sharply at her, but did not answer. Instead, he said, "Einnear and Sigurd grew up together and loved each other as only brothers can. Einnear, the elder of the two, taught Sigurd to swim, to ride and to hunt. Sigurd idolised his brother, copied him in everything. And though Sigurd proved the better warrior, he didn't show a speck of jealousy when Einnear succeeded their father as jarl."

Koll snorted.

"You doubt the strength of brotherly love?" Toki asked.

"Only its endurance," Koll blustered.

Toki laughed. "Well, one day Einnear heard about a monastery atop a rock in the middle of the sea. A place said to hold more gold than all Byzantium. This was too good a tip-off for the brothers to ignore. They gathered their men and set

280

sail. The sea swooped down on their longship, but the brothers kept their course true. They arrived while the monks were at vespers. The men of God were helpless in the face of the Northmen. Soon, only the aging abbot and a few servants remained alive."

Koll raised his drinking horn in a wide sweep. "*That's* how to deal with Christians," he shouted. "Show 'em for Verden."

Brother Alfred tutted.

Redknee felt Sinead shift uncomfortably at his side. He ventured to put his arm round her shoulder. She didn't shrug it off.

Toki smirked then continued. "The brothers searched for the famed treasure, yet they found nothing. Angry, and thinking he'd been tricked, Sigurd raised his sword and told the abbot to prepare to meet his God. Being a pragmatic man, the abbot quickly agreed to take the brothers to the vault. Provided, of course, they would spare the lives of his servants.

"A true man of God," Brother Alfred said.

"Indeed the abbot was." Toki said, flashing his coal-black teeth. "He led the brothers to a room deep in the crumbling monastery. A casket stood against the wall. Sigurd opened it; it was a quarter full of Arab coins. When he saw the pitiful amount, Sigurd struck the abbot across the face with the back of his hand and demanded to see the rest.

"Blood trickled from the corner of the abbot's mouth. He knew not of what treasure Sigurd spoke. Their most prized items, he said, were in the *scriptorium*. His voice faltered over this word as if he feared uttering it in the presence of the Northmen. Now, since the fall of Alexandria, this scriptorium knew no equal in all Christendom. And the abbot, it was said, had been lucky enough to receive many treasures from the demise of that great city.

"The brothers followed the abbot back up the stairs. Neither Einnear nor Sigurd knew what a scriptorium was. Whatever they imagined, they were not prepared for what they saw. Spread out before them, on solid oak shelves, were row upon row of leather covered blocks.

"Sigurd stared in surprise at a leather-covered block that sat open on a desk, its flesh of yellow parchment exposed. His

281

eyes scanned the strange black marks on the top page. He realised these so-called treasures were but rune-keepers. Angered, he turned to the abbot and said he would only spare the lives of the servants if the abbot could show him something truly worth his time: a rune-keeper encrusted with lots of jewels.

"A sensible demand," Koll said. "What use have monks for such finery anyway?"

Brother Alfred shifted uneasily. It hadn't escaped notice that the wooden cross he wore round his neck was inlaid with a tiny amethyst.

Toki tilted his head. "Well put Koll, and indeed, that was also Sigurd's opinion. Yet a fleeting smile crossed the abbot's face. He told Sigurd they had many books ringed with gold and silver. Others still, with peridots and opals set deep in the covers. Fine Flemish workmanship, to be sure. He took a slender volume from a shelf and held it up for Sigurd to inspect. Swirls of silver, picked out in strange green stones, glittered in the candlelight.

"While Sigurd had been speaking to the abbot, Einnear had begun wandering through the scriptorium, running his fingertips over the soft leather spines. He fancied them like silk, and his eyes glazed over, trancelike, as he stared along the shelves.

"Just as Sigurd was about to say such a quality piece would go some way towards sparing the servants, Einnear asked the abbot which of the rune-keepers had the most important story. Einnear believed such a book would be the most valuable.

"The abbot stared at the be-jewelled volume in his hand. Regretfully, he admitted that it was not his most valuable book. Sigurd's cheeks flashed red. He accused the abbot of lying."

"That's Christians for you," Koll said, burping.

Toki shook his head. "The abbot was most apologetic. Explaining he thought the brothers wanted only the books with fine jewels."

"And they didn't just kill him then?" Koll asked. "For insolence."

"They did not. For at this point, a lookout came running into the scriptorium. Now, the brothers had a friend with whom they'd agreed to share their spoils. The lookout had spotted their friend's ship approaching. Thinking quickly, Sigurd decided there wasn't enough of value to divide between the crew of two longships. He turned back to the abbot and told him to show them the most valuable book right away.

"The abbot shuffled towards the far end of the scriptorium. He stopped when he reached a small, undecorated cabinet covered in a thick layer of dust. He fished in his belt-pouch and produced a rusty key. Sigurd told him to hurry, yet the abbot remained calm. He warned the brothers he kept the key about his person, because while the book he was about to show them *was* the most valuable in the scriptorium, it was also the most dangerous. And he felt it his duty to warn even heathens such as them."

"Pah," Koll said, interrupting yet again. "How can a book be dangerous?"

"Sigurd's thoughts exactly," Toki replied a touch wearily.

"Is it like the Sirens in Brother Alfred's story?" Sinead asked.

Redknee stared at her, for he did not see the connection.

Toki tilted his head. "How so?"

"Because of the knowledge inside the book," she said.

"Perhaps," Toki said. "The abbot explained that when the book first came to the monastery it was left out for the monks to read whenever they wanted. Much like the other books. But, over time, the abbot observed a change in the monks. First came the tired, bloodshot eyes, then grumpiness and irritability. They'd been staying up late into the night, burning candles at great cost, just to read its words. Einnear remarked the story must be a good one. Perhaps a tale of heroism and adventure.

"The abbot replied it would have been fine if that was all it was. But one day a fight broke out among the novices. One of them, a lad of only fourteen summers, stabbed a younger boy. It was not a pleasant death. Bad humours, the abbot thought. The lad died in agony.

"Sigurd failed to see how the boy's death related to the book. The abbot told him they'd been fighting over whose turn it was to read it. Sigurd snorted, but the abbot shook his head. He explained the book was written by an Irish monk who, long ago, travelled to the Promised Land. It was said that whoever reaches the Promised Land will find treasure beyond their wildest dreams and more – he said that in the Promised Land no one could ever die."

"Sigurd grabbed the key from the abbot's hand. "Sounds sellable to me," he said. But even as Sigurd twisted the key in the lock, the abbot warned him the book would drive anyone who read it mad with longing.

"Sigurd laughed, telling the abbot he'd take his chances. He grabbed the book. It was smaller than he'd imagined and covered in dull brown leather. Then he hauled his brother from the scriptorium.

"The abbot cried for them to wait – he feared he and his servants would be killed if they waited for the next longship of Northmen to descend. Sigurd called over his shoulder that they could come, *if* they could keep up.

"The brothers escaped the island just as their friend rounded the headland. Their men were bitter about the lack of 'real' treasure, as they put it, and the brothers knew they would have to find a buyer for the book, and quickly. Einnear volunteered to take it to the great market town of Kaupangen to see if he could sell it. True to his word, Sigurd did not kill the abbot or those of his servants who had made it onto their longship. Instead, he allowed Einnear to take them to Kaupangen to be sold as slaves."

"Double-crossing liar," Sinead said, jumping from her seat.

"How so?" Toki shot back. "His promise was merely to allow them to live."

"It's true," Redknee whispered to her.

Sinead harrumphed and sat down.

Toki continued. "When Einnear returned from Kaupangen, he said no one would buy it, as they could not read the Irish runes."

"Pigfarts," Koll said. "That's a pigfart of a story."

284

"Yes," Harold said grinding his eating knife into a piece of venison. "Nothing's happened. Where's the betrayal?"

"They betrayed their friend," Sinead said.

Toki smiled. "That's just the background. I'm getting to the good bit *now*."

"I need more food," Koll said, rising and stumbling towards the table. "Who are these brothers anyway? This book they found – it's not the *Codex*, is it?"

"It matters not." Toki said. "The point of the story lies elsewhere."

Olaf shifted uneasily, one hand on the hilt of his dagger. "Come now Toki," he said, "you've gone far enough with this nonsense."

Toki shook his head. "This is a good story. They need to hear it. Now," he cleared his throat," it so happened that, in a way, the abbot's prophecy came true. Einnear became obsessed with the book. Just like the monks before him, he would stay up late every night pouring over the strange Irish runes, neglecting his duties as jarl. One day Einnear said he wanted to take the book to Dublin. Sigurd was hesitant. Einnear had a new wife and responsibilities at home. Besides, the old monk could have been lying. But Einnear was determined. Early in the summer, he left his wife in his brother's keeping and sailed for Dublin."

"Did Einnear learn about the book in Dublin?" Sinead asked.

Toki frowned. "I'm coming to that. On his return from Dublin, Einnear called in on his old friend to make a peace offering. Einnear was surprised to see his new wife and brother there. He greeted Sigurd warmly and told him he had learned the book was written, not in Irish runes, as first thought, but in Latin, and that it did recount a monk's voyage to the Promised Land in great detail."

"You *are* basing this on the *Codex*," Sinead said, disappointment deadening her voice.

"Wait," Toki said, "we're getting to the crux."

Olaf stood. "I think you should finish it here."

Toki stared at him. "Nervous?" he asked. "You needn't be."

Redknee thought Olaf was going to pounce on Toki. Then, as suddenly as he had stood, he turned and headed for the door.

Toki shrugged and continued. "Sigurd considered what his brother had said about the book containing directions to the Promised Land. Desire grew in him as he listened to his brother's talk of going to find it. As I said, Sigurd had never felt jealous of Einnear before—"

Koll snorted.

Toki's eyes twinkled in the firelight. "*As I said.* But now he realised his brother had everything he didn't – a beautiful wife, men to lead, and the key to this vast treasure."

"What did Sigurd do?" Magnus asked, leaning forward.

A gust of icy air filled the hall. Everyone turned to see Olaf had opened the door. "You'll regret it, Toki," Olaf said. "Sometimes it's best to leave things as they are." Then he disappeared into the night, slamming the door behind him.

"What did he mean?" Redknee asked, suddenly concerned. "What will you regret?"

"Nothing. Ignore him. Do you want to hear the rest of this or not?" Everyone nodded, so Toki went on. "Sigurd waited until the three of them: Einnear, their friend Rurik, and himself were up late discussing how to raise the funds for their quest. A lot of mead had been drunk. Rurik was going to help by supplying another ship: on a dangerous voyage, two longships are better than one. Now, Sigurd did not want to share the treasure with anyone. Not his brother, and especially not Rurik. Einnear's wife, Inge, was still up, pouring their mead. Sigurd saw the way Rurik looked at her. For Inge was a comely woman, untouched by hardships of childbirth or the ravages of illness. Suddenly Sigurd saw a way to get exactly what he wanted.

"When Rurik went outside to relieve himself, Sigurd leaned over to his brother and whispered in his ear. Quietly, so Inge, who had then gone to bed, wouldn't hear."

"What did he say?" Redknee asked.

"He asked Einnear if he'd seen how Rurik looked at his wife. Einnear shook his head. He had not. Sigurd contorted his face into a pained expression. "I hate to have to tell you this,

286

my dear brother," he said, "but we cannot allow Rurik to come with us to the Promised Land, for only yesterday I saw him lying with Inge in the long grass behind the weaving hut."

"No!" Sinead's hand darted over her mouth.

Toki laughed. "Just the response Sigurd was hoping for from his brother. And indeed, Einnear jumped from his seat by the fire and ran outside. He saw Rurik in the yard, feeding one of his favourite dogs. Einnear charged at him, dagger drawn. For a moment, Rurik stared, confused, at the image of Einnear running towards him. When he realised it was no joke, that Einnear wasn't going to stop, he moved quickly, grabbing an axe wedged in a nearby tree stump."

"Who won?" Redknee asked.

"Well, it wasn't really a fair fight. For although Einnear had the advantage of surprise, Rurik was the better armed, and frankly, the superior warrior. Einnear had let himself go to seed, reading the monk's book late into the night, neglecting his training."

"Was Einnear killed?" Harold asked, delight warping his face. "Was it bloody?"

"His anger carried him some of the way. He cut a slice down the side of Rurik's face. Almost took his eye. But anger must be channelled, or it works against you. Rurik stayed calm. Got in a good few swings. Clipped Einnear's thigh. Took a chunk from his forearm. Terrified at Rurik's superior skill, a quickly sobered Einnear decided to retreat. It was as he ran away, that Rurik threw his axe into the air. It shattered Einnear's left shoulder."

Sinead looked as if she was going to be sick. Redknee gave her hand a squeeze. She felt warm. "Did Sigurd help his brother?" he asked.

"In a way. Sigurd couldn't quite bring himself to be the cause of his brother's death. Frightened Rurik really would kill Einnear, Sigurd carried him to a cave high in the mountains where he tended Einnear's wounds."

"What about his wife?" Astrid asked. "Wives don't just forget about their husbands."

"Ah, yes. Penelope's famed loyalty for Odysseus. I'm afraid this maiden wasn't as honourable. Sigurd told her Rurik

287

had attacked Einnear in a fit of revenge, but with one crucial difference from the real events – that Einnear was dead."

"And she believed him?" Sinead asked.

Toki smiled. "Why wouldn't she? Though perhaps she grew to have her doubts."

Sinead shrugged. "What happened next then?"

Redknee sighed. "Sigurd assumed Einnear's position as jarl … and found the treasure for himself?"

Toki nodded. "The first, certainly."

Sinead frowned. "And what about Einnear? Did he live?"

"No one knows."


Later, when the fire had near spluttered out, and most were half-asleep, Olaf burst through the door. Icy air leached the hall of warmth.

"Has anyone been out?" he shouted, striding across the floor.

"No," Redknee said. "We've all been together since you left."

Olaf stopped. Sweat trickled down his brow despite the cold. "Footprints," he said, "hundreds of them in the snow."

# Chapter 29

Redknee listened carefully, certain they were being followed. Last night's snow was slowly melting and the going on the hillside was soft … quiet. Yet Redknee fancied he heard every sound – every bird, every insect, every drop of melt water.

… *the crack of footsteps.*

Surrendering to his fears, he spun round. Stared past Koll's bewildered face to the tangle of bare branches beyond. Silver's ears pricked up. Redknee followed the pup's gaze, but still, he saw nothing. He gave Silver a quick pat on the head and trudged on.

After the discovery of the footprints in the snow there had been arguments about what to do. Olaf wanted everyone to stay at the longhouse where he thought they were safest. Such an obvious trail, he said, was likely a trap. The others, Redknee included, wanted to search the forest. Without a finished wall, they were sitting ducks. Their visitors hadn't attacked this time, but it was likely they'd be back. Redknee insisted they had to know who, or what, they were dealing with.

Eventually it was decided that Olaf and Magnus would stay at *Svensbyan* to finish the wall with the help of Brother Alfred, Harold and the girls.

Redknee, together with Toki, Olvir and Koll were nominated to form a scouting party. They had set out early that morning, following the footprints as the sun rose. The thaw, however, meant the footsteps were disappearing fast.

They marched on in silence. With Silver at his side, Redknee allowed his mind to wander. Toki's story about Sigurd and Einnear bothered him. It was clearly a thinly veiled attempt to tell of how Sven and Erik found the *Codex*. Had Toki been there? Why had Olaf walked out halfway through? Redknee shook his head. He couldn't believe Sven had incited

Ragnar to kill his own brother. Wouldn't believe it. That's why Olaf had become so angry – he didn't believe a word of it either. But Toki's story suggested Erik might still be alive. *Could it be true?* Was that the origin of his mother's dying request? Could Sven ... could his mother ... have known Erik was alive all along? And if Sven had lied about Erik not being his father ...

He resolved to ask Toki about it as soon as he got the chance.

They arrived at a mighty river as the sun reached its summit. The last of the snow petered out at the water's edge. Redknee strained to see if there were footprints on the far side of the river, but there was even less snow there. Only a few daubs of white shone among the brown of dead and dying leaves. The opposite bank rose sharply to form a ridge beyond which all Redknee could see was the tops of yet more bare trees. The river marked the end of their trail.

"We'll rest here," Toki said.

"When did he become jarl?" Koll whispered in Redknee's ear.

Redknee moved a half-step away from his friend and addressed Toki. "It's too dangerous. I think we're being followed."

"I've seen no-one," Toki replied. "And that river forms a barrier between us and whoever might be on the other side of that bluff."

Redknee shook his head. "I feel it in my gut."

Toki smirked. "Let's hope that's all you feel in your gut today," he said, turning from Redknee and unrolling his sleeping fur on an area of dry grass.

Redknee went over to where Koll was unfurling his own bedroll in the lee of a big rock. The smithy's usually smiling face was set in a frown. "What's wrong?" Redknee asked.

Koll's eyes flicked over to Toki. "I don't trust him. He's Ragnar's man, remember. And he tried to challenge you that day in the forest."

"He saved my life in Iceland."

"Only after you saved his."

Realising he couldn't convince Koll, Redknee bedded down a few paces away and tried to sleep. The mid-day sun pierced his lids. Unable to settle, he raised himself onto his elbows and looked round. Toki was asleep under a nearby bush. Olvir sat about twenty paces away, on watch. He turned back to Koll.

"You awake?" he whispered.

*"The best mead,"* Koll muttered, *"is all about the bees ..."* Redknee lay down and closed his eyes. Koll was already dreaming.

"You spoke?"

Redknee turned back. Koll stared at him, bleary-eyed, his eating knife in his hand.

"Everything's fine," Redknee said.

Koll looked disappointed.

"I just wanted to ask about when you first arrived in my father's village. Was it before my father died?"

"After."

"So my uncle was already jarl?"

Koll nodded. "I heard they needed a blacksmith. So I went. Offered my services. I never met your father."

"What happened to the previous blacksmith?"

"No idea. Died, I suppose. He'd left his tools. Great stuff – bellows, tongs, beaters. All well made."

Redknee's body felt like a series of angles pressed into the hard ground. Still unable to sleep, he got up, and motioned to Olvir that he was going for a walk along the riverbank. Silver followed at his heels. The forest looked different to when they'd first arrived. Gone were the streets of gold; instead, dead and blackened trunks twisted against an empty sky.

He followed the river downstream. Silver bounced in front of him, sniffing the wet ground, tail wagging. The water sped past: a chortling foam that tumbled over glassy rocks, eddied in clear pools and then raced on, leaping boulders and fallen logs. He looked for a place to cross, using his sword to test the footing. Some rocks were spaced close enough to—

The water rushed towards him, smacked into his face. The fierce chill ripped the air from his lungs. He heard barking, grasped for the bank, but the current was strong. Trees and rocks shot past. He fought to keep his head above the water, tried to swim, to keep his balance, but everything was a blur ...

His head struck a rock and he screamed in pain. Water filled his mouth as the current dragged him on, tugging at his feet, pulling him along, *pulling him under* ...

Redknee coughed. Spewed water. He blinked to find a pair of hard, flint-coloured eyes staring down at him. Seeing Redknee conscious, the man stretched to his full height. He was tall, and broad as a bear.

Redknee shivered in his wet clothes. He was on the far bank. A small fire near his feet was giving off blueish smoke. The man turned away. A large, patch-worked bag lay next to his feet. He rooted about in it.

Wary of the stranger, Redknee felt for his sword. But he must have dropped it when he fell. His heart jumped when the big man turned back and thrust out his hand, so much so that he nearly fainted with relief when he realised that it wasn't a weapon in the stranger's outstretched fingers, but a brightly coloured blanket.

Redknee gratefully wrapped the blanket round his shoulders. Then he cried out. For behind the stranger, axe raised, ready to sever the man's neck, stood a grinning Koll. Before Redknee had drawn breath, the stranger whipped round. His foot sliced through the air, crashing into the side of Koll's skull. Koll stumbled backwards, his axe thumping harmlessly to the ground. Redknee leapt up and helped Koll to his feet.

"This man saved my life," he said. "Pulled me from the river."

Redknee followed Koll's bewildered gaze. The stranger wore a leather tunic with fringes, breeches to his ankles and soft boots. His skull shone like an eggshell, clean of hair save for a corn-coloured tail wound with red and black feathers that hung in a rope down his back. Redknee pointed to the river.

"Thank you," he said slowly. "Thank you for saving my life."

292

The man nodded with the same scarcity of movement he'd shown when disarming Koll, then turned to leave.

"Wait," Redknee said. "Are there others like you?"

The man looked confused and Redknee wiggled his fingers to show people walking.

"Ah, just leave it," Koll said. "He doesn't understand."

The stranger froze. Then he spoke in Norse. "This land is no place for you," he said. "No good will come of your being here. Death will hound you until you leave."

"What?" Redknee frowned. "This island is vast … and rich. A thousand men, more even, could live here. Each one fat as a jarl."

"Don't you see?" the stranger said, his stony eyes fixed on Redknee's face. "That is exactly what will happen. Once the world knows about this place, they will all come in their longships. It will be made in the image of the Northlands, and everything will be as it was before." The stranger lifted his bag and began to walk away.

"But," Redknee said, scurrying after him, "we aren't going to tell anyone. We just want somewhere to live, free from tyrants and taxes."

"*Really?* Is that how you think it will come to pass? Not one of you has thought about getting rich from all this timber? From the furs?"

Redknee remembered the conversation about selling logs to the Greenlanders and the Icelanders who had no trees of their own.

"I thought as much," the stranger nodded, lifting his pace.

"But *you* are a Northman," Redknee shouted at the stranger's retreating figure. "And *you* are here."

"Leave it," Koll said, tugging on his arm. "There's nothing he can do to stop us. He's only one man."

"But he got here first. Don't you see? This is *his* land. And he might know about my father …" Redknee left Koll looking bewildered and ran after the stranger. *"Wait!"* he shouted as the stranger started up the grassy embankment. "I owe you for saving my life."

"It is no matter. You ought to stay by the fire."

293

Redknee drew level with the stranger. "What's your name?"

"I'm not getting rid of you, am I? Should have left you to enjoy your swim."

Redknee shrugged. "You know, getting here was hard. We lost a lot of good people."

"And you will lose many more if you stay." The stranger sighed. "They call me Dreaming Hawk."

"Who's 'they?'"

"You don't want to know."

"Are they like trolls?"

"I've no idea."

"*You know* ... things people are scared of, but no one has actually seen. Least, no one sober."

Hawk laughed. "If only that were true. No, my young friend, the Kanienkehaka most definitely exist."

"Who are the *Kanianke—?*"

"*—haka.*" They'd reached the top of the embankment. Hawk stopped and faced Redknee. "Kanienkehaka means *People of the Flint.*"

"What does *that* mean?"

"It means, young one, that they protect this land from invaders like you."

Redknee followed Hawk in silence. After a short while, he asked where they were going.

"*I* am going home."

"Where's that?"

"You ask a lot of questions. It's half a day's walk."

"Were you following us?"

"Picked up your trail this morning."

Redknee let out a long, low whistle.

Hawk laughed. "Didn't suspect a thing?"

Redknee shook his head. "Had a hunch – but I couldn't be sure."

"That's the Kanienkehaka training. They move quick and quiet."

"Can I learn?"

Hawk spun round. Koll and Toki were running up behind them, Silver at their heels. Olvir trailed a few paces behind.

294

"Maybe *you* can learn," Hawk said, turning back to Redknee, "but those over-fed lumps never will."

Redknee faced his friends. "This is Hawk," he explained. "He saved my life. He's going to take us to his home and tell us all about the Flint People."

Koll gritted his teeth. "What manner of——"

"They are just people," Redknee said.

Koll shook his head. "It's a trap."

"No!" Redknee said, "He saved my life."

Koll snorted. "He's luring us astray – so his Flint People friends can pick us off."

Hawk folded his arms. "We're days from Kanienkehaka territory, but suit yourself. Though, if it makes any difference, others are on your trail."

Hawk led them on a twisting route, so that by the time they reached the clearing, night was already drawing a veil over the sky. A hovel of branches and mud huddled against the frozen ground.

"*This* is your home?" asked Redknee.

"It's better from the inside."

Hawk was right. Beneath the thatch of leaves and daub, the air was warm and dry. What looked small on the outside easily held the six of them. Thick furs lined the floor and woollen blankets hung from the walls. The men kicked off their boots and made themselves comfortable while Hawk lit the fire.

They had caught a couple of squirrels on their walk and once he had a good blaze going, Hawk went outside to gut the carcasses. Soon they were talking and eating. Silver, though, sat by the door, amber eyes scanning the gathering dark. Nothing, not even the sweet smell of roast squirrel, could tempt him from his vigil. Sensing the pup's unease, Redknee kept *Flame Weaver* by his side. Toki had recovered it for him after his dip in the river. *One more I owe him*, Redknee thought grimly.

"Ah," Hawk said, chewing on a piece of meat. "Tastes good."

"How long have you been here?" Toki asked.

"Two winters."

295

Redknee studied the hut in more detail. A man's tunic hung from the rafters, drying. A pair of soft, brown boots warmed by the fire. A soapstone bowl and spoon sat in a corner, half covered by a linen square. One of everything. He turned back to Hawk.

"You live alone?"

"My wife is visiting her people."

"She's a Flint Person?" Redknee asked.

Hawk nodded.

Koll loosened the neck of his tunic. "Didn't you have a wife before?"

Hawk studied the fire, the yellow flames dancing against the dull grey of his eyes. "I did," he said quietly. "But I will never see her again."

"Aye," Koll said, nodding sadly. "My woman has gone too."

Something moved outside. Silver's ears pricked up. Both Redknee and Koll jumped to their feet. Olvir grabbed his bow.

A smile played on Hawk's lips. He didn't stir. "Your stalkers have finally caught up with us."

"What?" Redknee said. "I thought all that doubling back was to lose them."

Koll marched to the door and burst into the night. He reappeared a moment later, a violently struggling woman under his arm. "Vermin!" he said, dropping her onto the floor.

Astrid scrambled to her feet and lunged across the fire, knocking Hawk backwards. She tore at him with her nails, gouging angry red lines across his cheeks.

Hawk kept perfectly still.

"Bastard!" she screeched, getting to her feet and kicking his shins. "I hate you, Gunnar Osvaldson, you're a traitor and a coward!"

Koll dragged Astrid off Hawk and pinned her arms behind her back. It was then that Redknee saw Sinead standing in the doorway, her hands folded neatly beneath her green cloak; she flashed a brief smile in his direction.

"Astrid sneaked out. I had to come with her. She would have died on her own."

296

Astrid wriggled like a salmon in Koll's arms as she tried to spit in Hawk's eyes. Koll pressed his hand over her mouth. "Can someone tell me what's going on?" he asked.

Redknee turned to Hawk. "Should we call you Gunnar, as Astrid does?" Hawk just shrugged, so Redknee continued: "Our new friend is Astrid's estranged husband. Gunnar Osvaldson, long lost Jarl of Reykjavik."

Koll howled. Blood flecked from Astrid's teeth where she'd sunk them into his finger. As Koll snatched his hand away she began shouting at Hawk with renewed fury. "You *lied*. You said you'd come back for me."

"I *tried* to build a ship."

"You didn't try very hard."

"My men were all killed … or died of the fever. And the Kanienkehaka, none would come with me … except for Running Deer."

"Ha! Your new wife? That would be a fine homecoming. Bet you didn't think I'd come to find *you*!"

"So you came all this way, risked your life, just to shout at him?" Sinead asked.

Astrid rounded on her. "Shut up, slave. You don't know the first thing about Gunnar and me."

Sinead laid a bag on the ground then marched across the room and slapped Astrid square on the cheek. "I know he left you," she said, her expression softening at the sight of the angry welt rising on Astrid's pale skin. "But be quiet, before someone really hurts you."

Tears sprung into Astrid's eyes and she went limp like an old rag. Cautiously, Koll loosened his grip, and she slunk, defeated, to the furthest corner of the hovel, drew her feet to her chest and closed her eyes.

They spent the rest of the night listening to Hawk tell of his journey to the Promised Land. He confirmed Astrid's story that just over two years ago a group of men from the Northlands had arrived in Reykjavik. Word had soon reached Hawk, as jarl, that they were asking round the port if any of the sailors had visited a land far to the west, reputed to contain more riches than the great palaces of Byzantium. Their tales

297

interested Hawk, and, disguised as an ordinary seaman in rough linen tunic and breeches, he'd gone down to the waterside taverns to talk with the travellers. Among their number was a monk. He appeared to be in charge.

"Not a Northman?" Koll asked incredulously.

Hawk confirmed the monk spoke perfect Norse. He also had a book with him, a brown leather-covered affair, weather-beaten and water-spoiled in places, and without precious jewels to distract your notice. But the monk and his men were entranced by this thing. Said it held the key to wealth and happiness beyond wildest imaginings. Fired by the monk's talk Hawk committed to join them, with two longships and seventy of his best men.

"What happened next?" Redknee asked, kneeling forward.

Hawk explained that they set sail on a fair spring day. They made good time. Within eight days they had reached an ice-capped land. Landing they discovered the locals called the place Greenland – they thought it some kind of joke.

The monk became very ill on Greenland, Hawk said. He suffered from an old injury in his arm and the pain had returned. His skin turned grey and he was too weak to leave his bed. After a month of waiting for the monk to recover, Hawk had ventured on. He reached the Promised Land after ten days at sea, but the shores did not afford a landing place, being comprised of fortress-like cliffs. Eventually, they found a suitable bay and made a camp. But many of the men had fallen prey to a vomiting illness. Soon, there were only around thirty of them left and that was when they met the People of the Bear.

"I've heard this part of your tale," Redknee said. "From one of your men who made it back to Iceland, Ulfsson was his name."

Hawk nodded solemnly. "Ulfsson was indeed known to me. I'm glad to hear he survived. The Bear People came on us in the night, quick and deadly, like the lightning from Thor's hammer. There were so many of them, we didn't stand a chance." Hawk hung his head in shame, eventually he spoke again. "Running Deer found me lying face down in a swamp."

A tentative smile formed on his thin lips. "She thought me dead at first."

"And that's how you came to be with the Flint People?" Redknee asked.

Hawk nodded. "I thought I was the only survivor out of my men. Now I know there was another."

Redknee remembered the blank look on Ulfsson's face as he lay across the threshold of the tavern, his head bashed in. He decided to say nothing. "What happened to the monk?" he asked instead. "Did he catch up with you?"

"I never met him if he did. I assumed he either died or returned to his monastery when he was well enough to travel."

Redknee thought about this. It was most likely the monk had died. "I was wondering," Redknee began tentatively, "if my father might have been among the Northmen who came to Reykjavik."

"What was his name?"

*What, indeed?*

"Erik Kodranson," Redknee said finally. It was the only name he had to work with. Something told him, if he found Erik, he would find his father.

Hawk shook his head. "I don't recognise it. But there were a good number of men. What does he look like?"

Redknee bit his lip. "I don't know."

"*Ah,*" Hawk said, smiling kindly. "It's like that, is it?"

"Wait," Redknee said. It was likely Erik looked somewhat like Sven, so he gave Hawk a description of his uncle.

Hawk shook his head sympathetically. "I'm afraid that describes half the Northmen I've known."

Disappointed, Redknee sat back and allowed the others the chance to question Hawk. Predictably, they spent the remainder of the evening asking if he'd found Saint Brendan's treasure. He said that he had not. Koll snorted at this, suspicious, it seemed, of their host's veracity. Hawk explained he hadn't had the advantage of the *Codex* – the monk had kept it. At the mention of the book Sinead glanced at Redknee, then moved to conceal her bag under her cloak. Had she brought it? Clever girl.

Turning back to Hawk he asked, "Have you been looking for the treasure these two years past?"

Hawk shook his head. "I have a new wife, I am happy—"

Astrid groaned scornfully.

"—I *am* happy with her," Hawk asserted. "And I'm no longer interested in treasure. You would do well to forget it too – I doubt it can be found."

Koll shook his head. "If anyone finds it, it'll be us."

Eventually they got to discussing the footprints in the snow. Had they been made by the Flint People or the Bear People? They pestered Hawk for information. Hawk said the Flint People, the Kanienkehaka, were proud, but fair. They were experts with the bow, which made Olvir smile, and hunted wild deer and all manner of smaller creatures for their thick, warm pelts. But Hawk had no time for the Bear People. He went to sleep insisting that if either the Kanienkehaka or the Bear People had wanted to attack them, they would have by now. The footsteps in the snow, he explained, had likely been a warning.


Redknee dreamt of a face with hazel eyes and spidery lashes. This was strange, because he usually dreamt of green eyes and hair of flaming copper; or of standing at his uncle's side, fighting Ragnar.

The face leant closer. It belonged to a beautiful woman. He felt her warm breath on his skin. This was a realistic dream. He smiled and snuggled into his sleeping fur. His dreams weren't normally this good. The beautiful woman began to speak. Her words were garbled, but she sounded panicked. His eyes shot open. A very real woman with curtains of jet-black hair leant over him. She was frowning.

Redknee leapt up and drew *Flame Weaver*. The woman looked startled.

"It's alright," Hawk said, "it's just Running Deer and her brothers." He pointed to two well-built young men standing by the door. Hawk lay on a rug, fully dressed and sipping hot soup from a bowl. He looked perfectly relaxed.

Silver still slept at Redknee's feet, paws twitching. Some guard dog, Redknee thought, lowering his sword.

300

A scream came from the back of the hut. Koll jumped to his feet, instantly awake, swinging his battleaxe in front of him, knocking over the pot of soup.

"Wait!" Redknee shouted as Toki and Olvir began to stir. "They're our friends."

The young woman with the raven hair spoke. "My name is Running Deer," she said in halting Norse. "These are my brothers, Crouching Wolf and Thinking Owl. A Bear People war party is heading this way. They know about your camp on the beach. They are coming for you. You will be safer if you come with us."

"She lies," Koll said, his battleaxe still in his hand.

Hawk uncoiled his long legs and stood. "I doubt it," he said, crossing the room and planting a kiss on his wife's forehead. "We will be safest if we go with them."

"If anyone is coming for us, we'll fight them ourselves," Koll said.

Hawk folded his arms. "Suit yourselves. But this war party is more than thirty men."

"We can't leave Olaf and Magnus to fight a war party on their own," Redknee said.

"The longhouse is two days' walk," Toki said, pulling on his boots and looking outside. "And the weather is closing in."

Thinking Owl spoke to his sister, and she translated: "My brother says if you come with us, the war party will follow your tracks – they won't go to your longhouse. You'll be saving your friend's lives."

"What about *your* village?" Redknee asked her.

Hawk snorted. "Don't worry," he said. "Running Deer's father is chief. He knows exactly what he's doing."

# Chapter 30

The village lay in a wide valley, surrounded by snow-covered meadows. A wall of tall stakes protected four longhouses. The longhouses were set out at right angles to form a large square in the centre. Wood-smoke fluttered from a central hole in each roof, a smudge on the blank grey sky.

Even from the surrounding hills, Redknee could see children playing in the snow. Old women watched, fingers ever busy with some task or other. Already, it reminded him of home – of his village in the Northlands before Ragnar came and changed everything.

"We plant the three sisters in spring," Running Deer said as they started on the path to the valley floor. Redknee must have looked puzzled, for she laughed until her eyes watered. "They're not *real people*," she said eventually. "They're crops – maize, squash and beans. We call them the three sisters because we plant them together. The beanstalk supports the maize and the squash, and they grow leaning on each other, like sisters."

"I've never had a brother or sister," Redknee said, treading carefully on the frozen slope.

"I'm sorry to hear that," Running Deer said. "I have four sisters in addition to my two brothers."

A sentry nodded to Thinking Owl as they passed through the main gate. Close up, Redknee saw that the four longhouses were made of elm bark stretched over wooden frames. They were big, each perhaps able to hold as many as forty people. He caught a whiff of a rich, meaty smell. Three women were stirring a large pot outside the nearest longhouse.

Koll sighed audibly.

"You ever think about anything but your belly?" Redknee asked, laughing as Koll loped over to the women, a hopeful grin on his face.

A group of children ran up to Sinead and Astrid. The youngest held out a small leather ball. Astrid shook her head and turned away. Sinead rolled her eyes and handed Redknee her bag. He watched as Sinead kicked the ball high into the air, and then sped after it, copper hair streaming. Silver stared after her.

"On you go," Redknee said, and the pup tore into the fray, nose down, tail wagging.

Astrid hung about awkwardly. Her eyes had never left Running Deer since they set out that morning. Redknee frowned as she made a circle in the snow with her toe. Hate seemed to rise off her like steam.

"We're going inside."

Redknee turned to see Toki standing at the entrance to the nearest longhouse, beckoning him in.

"We're going to meet their chief."

Redknee's eyes took a moment to adjust to the dark. A corridor dissected the hall in two. Stretching along each side of this corridor, at knee height, were two wide, fur-covered platforms. Sacks of food, clay jars and extra furs lined a second, higher platform beneath the roof.

Thinking Owl and Crouching Wolf emulated a small, grey haired man sitting cross-legged on the lower platform. The grey haired man indicated to Redknee, Koll and Toki to do likewise. Running Deer sat beside her father, lowering her eyes as Hawk joined them.

Sitting opposite him, Redknee saw the chief clearly for the first time. His long, straight nose was held regally aloft, as if in defiance of the world. Yet his eyes held the shrewd sparkle of ambition. Even before he spoke, Redknee sensed he was in the presence of a true leader of men, a force that could turn the wind and halt tides.

The chief turned to his daughter and spoke in the same strange language Redknee had heard Hawk use with her. She listened with her head bowed and hands folded across her lap. When her father finished, she raised her eyes until they met Redknee's. "My father, Hiawatha the Wise, wishes to know your purpose here."

Redknee cleared his throat. He'd known they would be asked this and had prepared his answer.

"We have travelled across the sea to—"

Hiawatha raised his hand for silence.

Running Deer leaned in to listen as her father spoke. When he finished, she looked awkwardly round the circle. "My father," she said, her accent thicker than before, "wants to know why... *a boy* ... speaks for ... *men*."

Hiawatha was testing him. "There is no boy here," Redknee said, glancing at Toki, wondering if he would challenge this.

A half-smile played on Toki's face. He crossed and uncrossed his arms, evidently unwilling to support or deny Redknee's statement. From the corner of his eye, Redknee saw Koll quietly draw his dagger. Running Deer's brothers looked confused, but Hiawatha studied Redknee with narrowed eyes.

Eventually, Toki flicked his hand dismissively. "The lad is right," he said. "He speaks for us all."

Redknee heard the breath rush from his lungs. He hadn't even realised he'd been tense.

Hiawatha smiled as his daughter translated, but Redknee knew from his eyes that he'd understood perfectly.

"Please," Running Deer said, turning back to Redknee, "continue with your story."

"We come from a land of mountains far from here. Our enemy destroyed our village and we sailed across the sea to find a new home. We do not want to fight you. We seek an empty land where we can be the first settlers." Redknee went on to tell Hiawatha of Ragnar, of their journey, of Sven's death and of their camp by the lagoon. All the while Hiawatha nodded as Running Deer translated.

He'd debated whether to tell them about Saint Brendan's treasure and the *Codex*. But the decision was made for him when Running Deer pointed to Sinead's bag.

"My father wants to know what you carry so carefully."

Redknee lifted out the *Codex* and placed it in front of Hiawatha, showing him how to turn the pages. Hiawatha nodded in understanding, so Redknee pointed to the text. "The markings tell a story about a monk – *a holy man* – who came

304

here many years ago. We used his tale as our guide – to help us find this beautiful island."

When they came to the page with the giant pine tree, Hiawatha's eyes lit up and he began tapping his finger on the drawing.

"Do you know this tree?" Redknee asked, his excitement rising. "Do you know where it is?"

Running Deer leaned in to take a closer look at the picture for herself. "It could be the White Pine. It's three days walk north—"

Hiawatha cut her off. She blushed and bowed her head in silence. Clearly she must have spoken out of turn. Hiawatha turned to Thinking Owl and began prodding him in the side. His son shook his head. They appeared to be disagreeing about whatever Hiawatha had asked him to do. After a few moments of this, Thinking Owl gave in. He rose and disappeared down the longhouse, re-appearing a moment later with a rectangular strip of beads in his hand.

Running Deer took the beads from her brother and placed them beside the *Codex*. "These are wampum," she said, glancing awkwardly at her father. He nodded for her to proceed. "They are made from shells. This belt tells the story of my father, but it is not yet finished."

Redknee ran his fingers over the woven beads. "Do the colours have different meanings?"

"The white shells mean purity of mind, as in forgiveness or understanding. The purple shells represent all the possibilities a person has in their lifetime, which we believe are as numerous as the stars in the night sky."

"Hiawatha wants to commemorate his great victory over the Bear People," Hawk interjected dryly.

Redknee frowned. "But, I thought—"

"That's right. He hasn't defeated them yet. He's preparing."

Running Deer looked uncomfortable as she translated Hawk's words for her father, but the older man laughed and clapped his hands together. He clearly liked his son-in-law, though his tongue was sharp.

Redknee asked Running Deer if the Bear People's war party would attack the village.

She smiled. "Don't worry. We have many warriors. We'll be safe."

Crouching Bear dragged the youth across the snow to the centre of the village. He was only a year or two older than Redknee. The gathered women and children spat at him, some threw stones. Blood trickled from a gash in his forehead and a purple smear darkened his cheekbone. Crouching Bear tossed him in front of Hiawatha and smiled.

"He's a Bear People spy," Running Deer whispered into Redknee's ear. "My brother caught him prowling outside the village."

The youth knelt, shivering in the snow. His head was bare, shaved clean, save for a knot of straight black hair that hung down his back in a braid. A band of red paint encircled his eyes.

"Is he alone?" Redknee asked.

Running Deer nodded. "Though he confessed there is a war-party less than a day away."

The women and children fell silent as Hiawatha studied the youth's face. Even under the chief's heavy stare, defiance shone brightly from his eyes. Satisfied, Hiawatha issued a command to Crouching Bear and retreated into the warmth of the longhouse.

Crouching Bear grabbed the youth by his hair, pulled him towards a tree stump and forced him to kneel. He held the youth's head in place with one hand and pointed to Redknee with the other.

"What does he want?" Redknee asked, reluctant to approach the executioner's block.

Hawk joined Redknee. "He wants to try your sword. They don't have iron here. Their axes and spears are headed with stone."

Crouching Bear jabbed his finger in Redknee's direction again.

Redknee approached the tree stump slowly. A tear trickled down the youth's cheek, smearing a trail of red paint in its

306

wake. Redknee drew *Flame Weaver*. At least his death would be quick.

But the eyes of the crowd were not on the captive. Even Crouching Bear was distracted. Redknee turned to follow his gaze. A small, white-haired man shuffled towards them, testing the ground before him with a stick.

"Who's that?" Redknee asked.

"It's Deganawida," Running Deer said. "He is a sort of holy man – like your monk. His name means *'Two rivers flowing together.'* He travels between villages, sharing wisdom."

Redknee looked again at the old man. Despite the cold, his feet were bare and caked in mud, but he didn't seem to notice. "What does he want?"

Hawk answered first. "He wants to prevent the youth being killed."

Running Deer eyed her husband sharply. "Actually, he wants us to join his great peace. My father will *not* be pleased."

Someone must have notified Hiawatha because he stormed out of the longhouse and glared angrily at Deganawida. The old man had gone over to where the youth lay sprawled across the tree stump. When he saw Hiawatha appear, he raised his eyes skywards and began chanting. Hiawatha stood awkwardly for a moment. Then he turned to Crouching Bear, issued a new order, and disappeared back inside.

"What's happening?" Redknee asked.

"I'm not sure," Running Deer said, watching with concern as her brother forced the youth's mouth open. On seeing this, Deganawida stood back and lowered his chanting until it was barely audible.

Crouching Bear reached into the youth's mouth, pulled out his tongue, and, with one sharp upward flick of his knife, severed it clean.

307

# Chapter 31

Despite Hiawatha's confidence in his warriors, Redknee could feel the villagers become increasingly on edge as they readied for the attack. He pulled *Flame Weaver* from its scabbard and ran his finger along the blade. The steel glimmered in the cold winter light.

Koll grinned. "Best steel in the world, that."

Redknee nodded and surveyed the village defences from his position on the ramparts. Men, maybe forty or more, armed with bows and arrows, lined the wall. Below, in the village, Sinead and Astrid were helping the women boil pitchers of water. The children, too young to fully realise the coming danger, excitedly gathered brushwood for their fires.

Koll whetted the edge of his axe with a stone. "He's a shrewd one, that Hiawatha," he said. "I bet he wanted us to fight the Bear People with him all along. Been watching our camp. Knew about our steel weapons. Wants to see us use them. That whole rescue thing was just a way to put us in his debt—"

Redknee shook his head. "He said he knew nothing about the footprints—"

"Getting cynical in your old age, Koll?" Toki approached along the rampart. He carried something small in the palm of his hand, hidden from view. Silver followed the movement of Toki's hand with interest.

"Only since I met you," Koll replied.

Further along the rampart, Olvir looked worried. Redknee went over to him. "Don't worry," he said quietly. "You're the best archer here."

Olvir bit his bottom lip. "My fear of blood has returned. I feel sick."

Redknee placed a hand on Olvir's shoulder. There was nothing to say. Sensing his distress, Silver sidled over and pressed his body against Olvir's legs. Olvir reached down and rubbed the pup behind the ears.

"Look at him," he said, "only a pup, yet he fears nothing. He'll make you a good fighting dog in time."

Redknee nodded, but he didn't want the pup anywhere near the fighting. He was still too small. Redknee pointed to where Sinead was helping the women light a fire and told Silver to go join her. Sinead laughed as Silver leapt into her arms. Redknee smiled. They would keep each other safe.

Redknee went back over to Koll and Toki.

"Look at this," Toki said, holding up the flint arrowhead he'd been hiding in the palm of his hand."

"Shouldn't be a problem with our steel weapons," Koll said.

Toki shook his head and stared over the wall, into the dark of the forest. "After Hawk's tale I'm not so sure … I think it's no bad thing we're here to see off these Bear People. The experience might come in useful later … if we ever have to face them on our own."

Although his reasons were different, Redknee agreed with Toki. For his part, he couldn't stand to see another village destroyed.

Lights flickered in the forest, between the trees, teasing, terrifying. The Flint People fought hard, but eventually, the Bear People, through sheer force of numbers, and the use of long ladders, had breached their defences. Fire engulfed the village, and Hiawatha had ordered the warriors out into the darkness to face their enemy head-on.

Not long after, Redknee had become separated from the others.

He wiped blood from his cheek and looked at the boy lying on the ground. His first win. He raised *Flame Weaver*. It hovered mid-air. Uncertain.

"You haven't killed before?"

Redknee looked up to see Hawk standing beside him. He shook his head and dug his foot into the boy's chest.

"Make it a quick one to the gullet," Hawk said.

309

He raised his arms above his head and this time let gravity propel his sword, blade down, towards the boy's throat. Damp brown eyes stared through a mask of sweat and war paint. Redknee froze, the blade tip a hair's breadth from the kill.

*He couldn't do it. By Odin's all seeing eye, this was no time to lose courage.*

A steel flash caught the moonlight. The boy's skull burst open. Redknee stood, *Flame Weaver* motionless in his hand as blood and brains drenched his face. He spat a piece of bone from his mouth. Koll jerked his axe free and placed a hand on Redknee's shoulder.

"Never, never, never, look in their eyes," he said. "and," smirking, "always close your mouth."

"The Kanienkehaka say a prayer for the souls of those they kill," Hawk said.

Koll spat. "No time. There's more Bear People heading this way. Besides, the lad was a warrior. He'll go to Valhalla, never mind me trying to make myself feel better."

A terrible cry pierced the forest. Then, suddenly, a mass of painted warriors emerged from between the trees. Redknee looked round. The three of them were on their own.

"Stick close to me," Koll said to Redknee.

He didn't argue.

Still screaming, and beating on their war drums, the Bear People spread out, encircling them.

"If they rush us, we're dead," Hawk said, waving his sword about as if it were a torch.

Redknee watched as the warriors began to ease closer. "There must be at least twenty of them."

Koll grinned. "I took out twelve Saxons on my own once. Think you two can manage four each?"

"Toki was right about you. You're all bluster," Hawk said.

"We'll see who's hot air!" Koll said, charging at the nearest warrior.

The warrior sped forward to meet Koll, tomahawk raised high. Koll feinted and, at the last moment, ducked, sending the warrior tumbling headfirst onto the grass. A second, younger, brave emerged from the circle carrying a spear. He thrust it at Koll's stomach, but the big Viking was quicker than he

310

looked, dodging each jab before leaping into the air and slamming his axe down on the youth's neck.

From the corner of his eye, Redknee saw an archer take aim at Koll. *Coward*, he thought, rushing to cut the man down. But he was too late. The arrow sliced through the night air, lodging in Koll's shoulder. The blacksmith dropped to his knees with a bellow. Redknee cried out. He would *not* lose his friend. He spun round, blind with anger. *Flame Weaver* light in his palm, twitching for blood.

The archer's arm came away surprisingly easily. Like removing a chicken leg. *Flame Weaver's* hunger was insatiable. It greedily chomped through four fingers, one thigh, two shoulders and an oak sapling, the latter being an unfortunate mistake that cost Redknee vital moments. Gorged but not sated, the blade fell to the ground still cradled in its master's hand.

Redknee's head hurt. He tried to massage his temple, but found his hands bound. Pain shot through his shoulders and he realised he was slung beneath a sturdy branch carried by four thickset warriors.

*He remembered attacking the archer... and then, nothing.*
*Why hadn't they just killed him?*

He craned his neck to see if they had Koll and Hawk too. But all he could see in front was a pair of sweaty buttocks, and behind him, two grinning faces. Then he saw the clumps of hair. Not on their heads, but on belts round their waists. Hair clogged with blood and patches of skin. *Scalps*. And among the black tufts was a streak of yellow.

His head didn't hurt that much, did it? Panic rising, he twisted his wrists and ankles until they burned. He had to get free. The two warriors at his feet sniggered. He was bound fast.

Blood trickled down his left arm, pooled at his throat. He looked up. He had a deep cut just below his wrist. *Damn*, but he hurt all over.

*"You give up, you die,"* that's what Uncle Sven had told him. So he tried to form a plan. But with no weapon and no

idea where he was going, or why, any attempt at planning seemed futile.

One of the warriors stumbled, jolting Redknee forwards. Pain shot through his wrist. He glanced at the cut again. A sliver of white protruded from his skin. He almost passed out with fright. Then his heart quickened, and he sent up a prayer of thanks to Odin, for it was then that he realised, the sharp sliver of bone hanging from his arm … well, it wasn't his.

The walls of the Bear People village loomed overhead. The light of bonfires cast strange shapes on the walls. The sound of drums echoed in Redknee's chest. Excitement thrummed through the warriors; some ran ahead, breaking into a war dance as they reached the open gates.

*This was it.*

He got ready to act; he would have only moments to make his escape.

Inside its walls, the Bear People village looked much the same as the Kanienkehaka one. And, for that matter, Redknee's village in the Northlands, only larger. Upwards of ten bark-covered longhouses surrounded a huge fire. Women holding babies, small children at their skirts, stared at him with a mixture of fear and confusion. Scraggy dogs scavenged for scraps in the snow. Old men chewed wads of tobacco, the years etched on their wary faces like tree rings.

He was dropped unceremoniously in front of the central bonfire. The heat from the flames warmed his skin. Curious villagers crowded round. A small boy, no more than four summers old, ran up and prodded his belly before scurrying away to hide behind his mother's legs. The crowd parted and a pole bearing Hawk was brought into the circle, followed by another bearing a very angry Koll.

"You're alive!" Redknee said. "Do you know about Toki and Olvir?"

Koll could only snarl through gritted teeth. He was in pain from his arrow wound. A little girl followed the boy in taking a closer look. She approached Koll on tiptoe. Koll opened one eye and growled and the child screamed and kicked him in the shin.

312

"What are they going to do with us?" Redknee asked.

"No idea," Hawk said.

Redknee's head still hurt. "How does my hair look?" he asked.

"By Thor's hammer," Koll roared, "this is no time for vanity!"

The crowd parted suddenly and Deganawida shuffled forward.

"That old goat gets about," Koll said.

But it wasn't Deganawida who sent shivers through Redknee's spine, it was the unnatural creature crawling behind him. Skoggcat's orange skin glistened in the firelight, his face a rictus of unholy pleasure. He slithered up to Redknee, raised a finger in the air, licked it and slid his sharpened nail across Redknee's throat.

Redknee gagged. How could he have let this abomination live? Skoggcat leaned in. Redknee was about to spit in his face, when a man's voice boomed from beyond the crowd.

"Show me the prisoners," it demanded. Skoggcat shrivelled fearfully, then skulked away, between the tan clad legs of the crowd, but not before giving Redknee a conspiratorial wink.

Redknee was still processing Skoggcat's wink as Ragnar, followed by Mord and half a dozen men-at-arms, marched through the crowd.

"We meet again," Ragnar said, removing his leather gloves and kneeling by Redknee's side. "You seem to be leaving a trail of destruction in your wake, young Erik-son. Volcanoes in Iceland, cave-ins in Greenland. What next, I wonder? If I were the Bear People, I shouldn't like to have you here at all. But as it is, I'm rather pleased to see you again," he said, placing Redknee's hard-won ivory-handled dagger against his throat and leaning in. "For you and I are more alike than you realise."

"No ..." Redknee mouthed. "I am *nothing* like you."

Ragnar laughed. "We shall see. Now, tell me, where is the girl with the book?"

Something moved in the maze of hide-clad legs and snow-soaked moccasins. It wasn't much, a pair of amber eyes and a

313

flash of white fur; a glimmer of copper, perhaps, amongst a sea of jet, but it was enough to catch Redknee's eye.

Ragnar had seen it too.

Redknee raised his chin in defiance. "I will never lead you to the book."

"Pah. You're as dumb as a mule." Ragnar turned to Mord and handed him the ivory-handled dagger. "This is one of yours, I think. Now search the crowd. I've a hunch troll boy has brought his little friends."

# Chapter 32

Eventually the curious onlookers began to disperse. The night was cold and nothing much had happened for a while. People drifted off in little groups, some returning inside the longhouses, others to talk on the sidelines. But it was clear; interest in the newcomers was waning. Soon, only the chief and a handful of his men stood round the fire. It was time. Koll let out an enormous cry and began rolling sideways, quickly gaining speed as he reached a shallow slope. The chief gave chase, but Koll was quick, and even with his hands and feet tied to a pole, he made it halfway across the village before anyone caught up with him.

It was all Redknee needed. He sucked at the cut on his wrist, easing the sharp sliver of bone between his teeth. Fresh blood oozed down the inside of his arm as he wrenched the sliver loose. Ignoring the pain, he began sawing the bindings at his wrist. The bone was sharp, a good tool, and with his hands soon free he quickly untied his feet.

Koll was standing now, free of his pole, his snow-daubed body surrounded by Bear People warriors jabbing at him with spears. But the big Northman wouldn't stay still long enough for the Bear People to skewer him. It gave him the bizarre appearance of dancing. Deciding his friend could survive another moment or two without his help, Redknee hurried over to Hawk and loosened his bindings.

Hearing the commotion, three of Ragnar's men ran, swords drawn, to help the Bear People fight Koll, but changed course when they realised Redknee and Hawk were free.

Redknee grabbed his discarded stake. "So thoughtful of the Bear People," he said, spinning his new quarterstaff in the air.

"Still think we should have tried negotiating?" Hawk asked, clobbering the first of Ragnar's men between the eyes. The force of the blow sent the attacker flying backwards onto the ground.

"Ever see a lamb talk its way out the pot?" Redknee said, swinging his staff low and taking out two sets of legs at once.

Hawk shook his head as, again and again, oak slammed against steel. "Deganawida is a good man. Most of the people believe in the peace he is trying to bring. Except my father-in-law. He thinks prolonging this war keeps him in power."

"Fancy telling them that?" Redknee pointed to a new group of approaching Bear People warriors. He glanced over to where Koll was still fighting off the chief and his men, make-shift staff in one hand, a flaming torch in the other. "I must find Sinead," he said, "before Ragnar does."

As Hawk nodded, an axe thundered at Redknee's head, he ducked and it whizzed past his ear. The warrior who threw it drew his knife and slashed wildly at Redknee's chest. He dodged the flying blade before smashing the man's hand with his staff. The knife skittered to the ground.

"Go!" Hawk said, stepping between him and four more warriors, each armed with stone axes. Hawk swung his staff in a wide circle in an attempt to keep them at bay, but he couldn't fend them off forever. Suddenly he had a partner; Koll had broken through the circling warriors and was swinging his staff as if Ragnarok, the battle at the end of days, had come and Odin himself was calling for men to fight by his side. One by one, their attackers fell back.

"We'll keep them busy," Koll said, grinning.

Redknee took his cue, slipping into the darkness between the longhouses. After several paces, he looked to see if he'd been followed. But it appeared Hawk and Koll were keeping the Bear People warriors occupied. His heart slammed against his rib cage. He didn't have long.

He crept along the back of the longhouse beside the waste pits. A groan came from the shadows. Judging by the stink, someone was having an argument with their bowels. Redknee tried to edge past unseen, but the man turned. It was one of Ragnar's men, his face the colour of a ripe plum. Without thinking twice, Redknee jabbed his staff into the man's jaw and he slumped to the ground, breeches still round his ankles. Redknee took the man's sword, slid deeper into the shadows and waited; making sure no one had heard the man fall. He felt

316

a tug on his tunic. Thinking it was Ragnar's man recovered, he raised his staff, ready to …

He stopped. It was the young boy who'd prodded his stomach earlier. Wide eyes gazed up, his thumb stuffed into his mouth. Redknee didn't want to hurt a child. Thankfully, the boy remained silent. He tugged on Redknee's sleeve then vanished into the darkness.

Redknee hesitated. Did the boy want him to follow? What if it was a trap? He decided to take the risk. What choice did he have? He could hardly go round asking if anyone had seen an annoying redhead. He chased the boy to the end of the longhouse and down a narrow alley under the village wall, when suddenly the boy disappeared into the ground. Redknee thought the boy had fallen. Then his head popped up and Redknee realised he'd climbed down a hole.

The boy beckoned Redknee to follow. Redknee shook his head. He would never fit into a child's den. But the boy persisted, and Redknee downed his staff and burrowed, head first, into the frozen earth.

The den was surprisingly roomy. Redknee was able to sit up and look round. The boy pointed to a sheet of bark over one of the walls. Redknee went to remove it, but the boy's hand shot out, stopping him. The boy slid the bark aside with care.

Redknee gawped. They were right beneath the longhouse. He could see Ragnar and Mord: they were standing in the middle of the floor having a conversation. A girl's voice joined them. She spoke Norse. Redknee strained to see who it was, but she was just out of sight. He had to get closer.

He eased his head through the hole, trying to keep hidden behind a stack of baskets. Mord's foot was only inches away. The girl started talking. It sounded like she was reading. Redknee looked round, searching for the source of the voice. Then he saw her. Happily ensconced on a thick bear fur, the book open in her lap and a cup of something hot at her feet, Sinead looked like queen of all she surveyed.

Silver sat a short way off on a multi-coloured rug. He growled every time Ragnar or Mord came close.

*"Beyond the great sea, go west to where the mountains bow to the trees…"* Sinead said, her voice calm and clear.

317

*"where the jaws of two great serpents lock, and between their teeth, an apple of the greenest hue. Beneath the Great White Pine you will find treasures enough to bring peace to all the earth ..."*

Redknee sat back, stunned. She was telling Ragnar the location of Saint Brendan's treasure, and without him so much as laying a finger on her. Astrid was right, slaves weren't to be trusted.

Mord spun round, nearly kicking Redknee in the head. Just then, Silver rose and trotted over. Redknee raised a finger to his lips, but the pup kept coming, tongue lolling, pleased to see his master. The boy tugged on Redknee's tunic and he slid back into the safety of the burrow. He'd heard all he needed to hear. He had to get the *Codex* from Sinead.

Footsteps echoed across the packed earth floor. He looked up. Ragnar and Mord were leaving. This was his chance. He nodded to the boy in thanks for his help, scrambled out of the den and collected his sword. The night shook with war cries and the sound of steel on stone, but Redknee kept hidden in the shadow of the longhouse as he crept round to the entrance. He threw the curtain back and ducked inside before being spotted.

Surprise registered on Sinead's face. "Redknee," she said. "I didn't expect you." She clutched Silver as he trotted torwards Redknee and held him close to her, like a shield.

"I'll bet," he said, edging forward. "Now, give me the *Codex*."

Sinead frowned. "Why ...?"

"I heard you talking to Ragnar. *Telling him everything*."

"You don't understand."

"I understand perfectly. Astrid was right. A slave can never be trusted."

She picked up the *Codex* and held it to her chest. "It's not what you—"

Cold air blasted his back. Redknee spun round. Ragnar stood in the doorway. When he saw Redknee, his eyes widened. Taking the advantage, Redknee sprung at the bigger man, and, using his own weight against him, flung him inside.

Ragnar fell heavily to the floor and Redknee pressed his stolen sword into Ragnar's throat.

"Go on," Ragnar sneered. "Kill me, send me to Valhalla. But then you'll *never* know the truth."

"Don't give me lies," Redknee said. One sharp jab would end it all. "I want my face to be the last thing you see before you die, hate the last thing you know. This is for my village, for my mother, and for my—"

"Stop it," Sinead said, rising from her seat. "You're choking him."

"Stay back – that's the idea."

Ragnar's eyes' bulged, his blank eye especially throbbed, spittle appeared at his lips, but he still managed to croak out a few words. "Do it for your village ... and your mother. But your father ... I never touched a hair on his damned head."

"Liar! I heard you admit it. In the forest, before you attacked my village."

Ragnar laughed without mirth, a dry raking sound. "You've got me. It was worth a try. I did fight Erik Kodranson. But he was still alive after the fight. Though rather the worse for it. Sven spirited him away." Ragnar paused, looked up at Redknee's face, his good eye narrowed. "You know, you're more like me than you realise."

Redknee hesitated. Perhaps this *was* his one chance to discover the truth about his father. Perhaps Ragnar knew more ... was more ... than he'd thought. Toki's strange story had spoken of two brothers and their friend, and the love each had for a beautiful woman. Had it been more than a story...?

"*You*," Redknee said, hands trembling, mouth dry. "*You* are my real father?"

Ragnar's laugh turned into a desperate rasping for breath.

Sinead grabbed Redknee's arm. He shrugged her off, but relaxed the pressure on Ragnar's throat a touch. He had to hear this. Had to face this new nightmare.

Ragnar gulped for air before focusing his watery eye on Redknee. "Not sure if that question is a compliment, young warrior. But, no, I am not your father."

Tension seeped from Redknee's body. He knew what he had to do.

319

"Well then," he said, knuckles whitening on the sword-hilt, "it's time to pay your dues."

"Stop!" Sinead called out, her face white with fear. "He is *my* father."

# Chapter 33

Redknee's mind reeled. How could Ragnar be Sinead's father? *How?*

"The monastery," Sinead said, reading his expression. "Ragnar visited the monastery just after your father and Sven. They were meant to go together, share the pickings. But Erik and Sven betrayed Ragnar, went on their own. That was when Ragnar met my mother. Toki's story was for me."

"But—"

"It's true," Ragnar spluttered. His face had turned grey. "Your father and uncle double-crossed me."

The curtain flew open. Mord entered, followed by Skoggcat. As soon as Mord saw Redknee he drew his sword.

"*Don't ...,*" Ragnar said, eying his sons, "*...do anything stupid.*"

Mord hovered nervously in the doorway. His face glistened with sweat. Skoggcat stood perfectly still.

Redknee kicked Ragnar firmly in the shoulder. "Stand," he said, adding, "*Slowly.*"

Ragnar hauled himself to his elbows, watchful of the blade at his throat. Sinead eased backward, gripping the *Codex* to her chest, her eyes flicking between the men.

"What should I do father?" Mord asked, fear shaking his voice.

"Watch your good for nothing brother."

Skoggcat made a hissing sound. It was the first time he'd drawn attention to himself. Mord scowled at him in disgust.

Redknee prodded Ragnar in the back with his sword. "On your feet, old man." Ragnar glowered at Redknee as he struggled upright.

"Where are you taking my father?" Mord asked. "Are you going to kill him?"

321

Was he going to kill Ragnar? He hadn't thought that far in advance.

"Not if you get out my way," he offered.

Mord glanced at his father. Ragnar nodded, and, reluctantly, Mord stood aside.

"You know," Redknee said to Mord, pushing Ragnar forward. "Don't believe a word your father says. You think he's going to share Saint Brendan's treasure with you? I'm betting he didn't tell you this slave girl is his daughter." He motioned to Sinead with his elbow.

Mord sneered. "Of course I know that. But what does it matter to me? Her mother was an Irish peasant. I am his legitimate firstborn. I will inherit everything."

"Think about it," Redknee said. "Why was he so keen to find her again? A daughter can be worth a hundred sons when it comes to marrying time."

Mord stared at his father. "You mean to form an alliance?"

"No," Sinead cried. "He lies!"

Mord's eyes darted between Redknee and his father, as if trying to find the truth in their faces.

"Stand back, son. You're making this worse."

"Who is it?" Mord asked, his face suddenly red with anger. "Who is to take my place at your right hand?"

"You know King Hakon's eldest?" Redknee asked cautiously.

*"Princess Asa?"* Mord said.

Redknee bit his lip. This was quite the gamble. Did King Hakon even have a son? "I meant his *heir*."

"Prince Halfdan?"

Redknee nodded.

Mord slumped. "Then it *is* true."

"Ragnar needs your share of the treasure for her dowry," Redknee said, praying there was a shred of truth in this guess. Redknee thought he had Mord with this last comment; he was nearly out the door with his hostage and Mord looked as if he was ready to kill his father himself. Skoggcat had been slinking in the shadows, watching his brother, watching Redknee, but still keeping his distance. Redknee was going to do it. He was going to get away.

322

Then the curtain opened and Olvir burst in, his bow drawn and ready. But it took him vital moments to assess the situation. Mord, however, reacted with animal efficiency, grabbing Olvir by the neck and slicing his windpipe from left to right in one sharp, fluid motion. Blood sprayed Mord's face. Olvir raised a hand to stem the flow. His attempt was useless. Blood drenched his hand, bubbled from his mouth, streamed down his chin and arm. He gurgled wordlessly before sliding towards the floor.

Redknee pushed Ragnar aside and flung out his arms to catch his friend. He was too late. Olvir's lifeless body lay in a blood-soaked heap, fingers still curled round his prized bow.

His father out of danger, Mord lunged for Redknee. Numb with shock, Redknee could only watch as Mord aimed for his belly. There was a flash of orange, Mord stumbled, his speed his enemy as he tumbled headlong towards Redknee's boots.

Recovering his senses, Redknee grabbed the *Codex* from a stunned Sinead, leapt the spread-eagled Mord and made for the unguarded door. As he sped into the night, he heard a hissing sound from the shadows. Skoggcat had repaid his debt.

# PART IV

# HOME

# Chapter 34

Redknee burst into the night, Silver darting behind him. Together they turned from the orange glow of the bonfire and hurried back along the shadowy alley. He heard the jangle of a mailcoat, the thud of heavy boots behind them. Then silence. Whoever it was hadn't followed them down the alley. They'd gotten away.

His mind reeled with questions. Big questions. *If Ragnar hadn't killed Erik, what had become of him?* Both Toki and Ragnar had said the same thing – Erik Kodranson, the man he knew as his father, was still alive after his fight with Ragnar. But their stories raised yet more questions. If true, then *Sven* was the last person seen with Erik. And that raised one terrible possibility … a possibility Redknee was fighting to push from his mind. He needed to speak to Olaf. No one else knew his uncle as well as the old warrior. He would make Olaf tell him the truth. He'd come this far, now he needed answers.

Redknee skirted the longhouses, climbed over an abandoned stretch of wall and landed softly in the darkness of the forest. He needed to forget about the Flint People and their war. Olvir, he couldn't forget. He felt responsible. *Was* responsible, for the boy's death. If only he hadn't hesitated when Sinead claimed Ragnar as her father …

Four days later Redknee heard the sea, long before he saw it. For a sailor, a Viking, that deep rumble gave the strength to push on. It seemed to have the same effect on Silver, and he bounded onto the sand, ears pricked, ready to chase whatever seabirds might be foolish enough to venture landside.

The longhouse still stood on the high side of the bay, guarding the lagoon. Why Redknee was surprised to see this, he didn't know. He'd only been gone eight days. Yet it seemed like a lifetime. He ran beneath the *Svensbyan* sign, threw open the door and strained his eyes in the dark, searching out Olaf's familiar features.

"Olaf," he called, "it's Redknee. I must speak to you." Silence. The hall was empty. Magnus and Brother Alfred must be outside too, he thought. He turned, ready to run back out to the yard, and slammed into a solid wall of muscle.

"Ah, there you are," Olaf said gently, placing his hands on Redknee's shoulders to steady him. "I thought you'd be back sooner or later."

Redknee caught his breath. Then the words came tumbling out. "We found people – lots of people. And Ragnar too—"

"I know," Olaf said, a smile forming on his lips. He moved aside.

Redknee blinked. Was he hallucinating? Ragnar stood a little way off, Toki and Sinead at his side. Silver growled. "*What?*" Redknee began to ask, "... *what's happening?*"

Olaf held him by the arms. "Be still," he said. "Nothing's *happening*. Ragnar arrived earlier this morning. He thinks he knows where the White Pine is. It's sacred to the Bear People. He's asked for our help to find it because it's in Flint People territory. Apparently you have friends among the Flint People. I believe you also have the book."

Ragnar smiled wolfishly.

Redknee shook his head. "*No ...*"

"We're going to help him. We're going to join together ... this is the best offer we'll get. I don't want to fight him. Don't you see ... otherwise this whole trip – your mother's death, my daughter Aud, Karl, Thora, even your uncle – all these deaths will have been for nothing? This way we can rescue something from it."

Ragnar and his men, about twelve of them plus Skoggcat and Mord, made themselves at home in *Svensbyan*. Redknee watched in disgust as Olaf fell over himself to make them welcome. Helped by Harold, his uncle's second-in-command fetched wood, boiled water and generally did everything he could to make Ragnar feel like a jarl. Redknee reckoned there was no point trying to speak to Olaf now: he had a new master. One he seemed just as happy serving as he had Sven.

326

*Traitor.* The word rose from Redknee's guts like bile. On Ragnar's command Olaf had relieved Redknee of the book and his weapons and tied his hands behind his back. Now the question spun in Redknee's mind: was Olaf just playing a clever game ... or had he always been in Ragnar's pay?

So much for Olaf's promise to seek vengeance for Harold.

Sinead too, seemed different. She kept her distance from Redknee, only casting him the occasional wary glance. Well, damn her, Redknee thought. If she wanted to throw her lot in with the likes of Ragnar, so be it. Only Silver and Brother Alfred paid him any notice.

When Redknee bedded down for the night on the cold earth floor, far from the fire, he'd never felt quite so alone. But before sleep claimed him, Mord stumbled over. Bloody flecks still crusted his mailcoat. He pressed his face against Redknee's, his breath smelled of mead.

"Try anything tonight and you'll go the way of your weedy little friend," he said, drawing a finger sharply across Redknee's throat. Then added in a slurred voice, "though, it's not me as wants you dead," before lurching away towards the fire.

According to Sinead's reading of the *Codex*, the White Pine was two days north from where Hawk had pulled Redknee from the river. Led by Ragnar's guide, they set out to find it the next day. This was, as Olaf kept telling Redknee, the point of coming all this way, and they would be fools indeed if they didn't take this chance to discover Saint Brendan's treasure.

Sinead muttered the directions from the *Codex* as she walked: "*Go west to where the mountains bow to the trees ... where the jaws of two great serpents lock, and between their teeth, an apple of the greenest hue. There you will find the Great White Pine. Beneath its boughs lie treasures enough to bring peace to all the Earth.*"

By mid-morning Redknee was fed up with her prattle. Unable to hold his tongue, he snapped round. "Won't you be quiet?" he said. "We must have heard that a hundred times now."

327

Sinead opened her mouth to retaliate, but Ragnar raised his hand, cutting her off. He turned to Redknee.

"Remember your place, troll boy," he said, a smile edging across his face. "If it was up to me, I'd have you whipped, gutted and your gizzards hung out for the birds to peck. But my daughter has a soft heart. It was she who begged me not to. And who am I to deny my long-lost daughter?" he asked, raising his arms skyward as if thanking the clouds for delivering Sinead to him.

Redknee glowered at Ragnar's back. He'd slit the bastard's throat right now, if his hands weren't bound. He watched Sinead follow her father. She seemed to be walking more erect, almost with a swagger. She wore a bronze pendant round her neck. And someone, Ragnar presumably, had given her a white fur cloak to replace her worn green one. Snow fox. He grudgingly admitted it suited her.

Still, he hated being in her debt. The only reason he was staying with this doomed expedition was because he had to know what manner of treasure lay at the end of Saint Brendan's journey. *Was that a weakness?* Had the *Codex* got to him? Its promises finally woven their spell … And maybe, just maybe, he still believed he would find something beneath the White Pine, some clue that would lead him to his father, whether alive or dead.

He trudged on through the forest, dead undergrowth crunching beneath his feet. Silver stuck by his side, ears alert, wary of the strange new dynamic. Sometime later, when Ragnar and his men had pulled ahead and Redknee's weariness caused him to lag, Toki dropped back beside him.

"I was sorry to hear about Olvir," Toki said as they fell into step. "I'm afraid Koll didn't make it either."

*Koll hadn't made it.* The news lodged like a blow to the guts.

"The two of us didn't see eye to eye, but he was a good man, worthy of Valhalla."

"Look," Redknee hissed, spinning to face Toki. "I don't need your false sympathy. Was it you who led Ragnar to our camp?"

328

Toki didn't answer.

"Was it Sinead then?"

He sighed. "What choice did I have? Koll and Olvir were dead. The Flint People retreated into the forest. They just left me. I think Astrid stayed with them. You were gone, I didn't know where. I sailed with Ragnar for years, remember? If I hadn't helped him, he would have been damned suspicious. Besides," Toki said, drawing Redknee back a little as the others walked on, "Olaf greeted Ragnar like an old friend. Almost as if ... as if he'd been *expecting him.*"

They spent the night inside a limestone cave with the kind of echo children love. It was no place for a private conversation.

Ragnar called to Redknee as they sat down to eat. "Troll boy," he said, "didn't I first meet you in a cave like this one?" Redknee narrowed his eyes and turned his back on Ragnar's laughter. It was going to be a long night.

Brother Alfred brought Redknee some food. The monk held out a plate of bones and meat scraps. "It's all that's left," he apologised. "I've given you some of mine too. Help keep your strength up."

Redknee motioned to his hands bound behind his back.

Brother Alfred blushed and lifted a scrap up to Redknee's mouth. Redknee shook his head. Brother Alfred left the plate and slunk away. Damn their charity. He wasn't hungry. Besides, he'd just seen the person he wanted to speak to slip outside.

Redknee counted to twenty before following Toki into the night. A rustling noise came from behind a nearby bush, a moment later, Toki appeared.

"I need to speak to you in private," Redknee said.

Toki glanced towards the cave mouth. They were outwith earshot. He nodded.

"The story you told; about the two brothers who double-crossed their friend. Sinead thinks it was aimed at her. Was it?"

Toki shrugged. "As much as anyone."

329

"But was it a true story – based on real events, the events of my father's ... of Erik Kodranson's death?"

"No-one died in my story."

"That's what's been annoying me," Redknee said. "If Sigurd is my Uncle Sven – not very well concealed, I have to say."

"It wasn't meant to be. By Odin's eye, I thought you'd have worked it out long ago. When I realised you hadn't, that you were still rooting around in the muck and coming up with nothing, I knew I had to set things straight somehow. That yarn was my best attempt."

"Why not just tell me outright?"

"Because I wasn't certain. I'm still not."

"Not certain about what?"

"What happened to Erik, to your father—"

"— *if* he was my father."

Toki nodded. "I'm not certain what happened to Erik Kodranson after Sven took him off to recover from his injuries. All I know is he was never seen by anyone again. At least, no one who knew him before."

"That's it," Redknee said. "That's what I've been thinking about. And it's obvious, isn't it?"

Toki shook his head.

"Sven killed him. *Sven* killed my father."

# Chapter 35

They followed a mighty river up stream on foot for the next two days, keeping the roar of the water to their left. Sometime towards late afternoon on the second day, the landscape widened. The river slowed, turning from a deep churning blue to silt-laden brown. A huge flood plain stretched before them. Gulls swooped across the big grey sky, dived among the reeds. Silver pricked up his ears, instantly excited.

*"Where the jaws of two great serpents lock, and between their teeth, an apple of the greenest hue,"* Sinead said, staring at the slow marshy water. When she turned round, her face was set in a smile. "We're looking for another river," she said.

"Another river?" Redknee asked. "Why've we been following this one for two days then?"

Sinead shook her head. Her copper curls snagged on her white fox fur. "We're looking for where another river meets this one."

They walked on, skirting the edge of the river, now so wide and slow it could now almost be called a lake. The waters were deep. Unfathomable. And then they saw it. *An apple of the greenest hue.* Sitting in the current from a new river that entered the lake at right angles to the river they'd followed, was an almost perfectly circular island. Evergreens covered the banks, but, even from five hundred paces, they could see, rising from its dark core, the uppermost branches of a tree that dwarfed the rest.

"The stalk in the centre of the apple," Sinead said.

Ragnar came up behind her. "Never mind that," he said, looking for a place to cross. "We're going to have to build a raft."

The air beneath the Great White Pine, as the *Codex* called it, was still and dark. In truth, its needles were a shimmery blue-

331

green, not white at all. Nonetheless, the Great White Pine stood as tall as forty men, and at least three times as high as any tree Redknee had seen. Its trunk was straight, and so thick it took five men with outstretched arms to circle it.

Redknee walked around it, agape. Five huge roots emerged from the ground, like a giant's legs meeting its torso, seeming to heave the earth up with them. It reminded Redknee of the tales his mother told of Yggdrasil, the world tree. The tree that connected the realm of men to the realm of the gods. The place where Odin hanged himself to learn the secret of all things. Redknee's heart quickened. He stumbled on a long snaking root, skidded across the loamy earth. This was no normal tree, but a gallows. A place where knowledge leads only to death.

Brother Alfred hurried over and placed his hand on Redknee's shoulder. "You're pale. What ails you?"

Redknee stared up at the Great White Pine. Its boughs stretched far above his head, like the bars of a prison wall. He blinked. He saw the faces of the others looking down at him. His eyes regained focus. He saw that it was only a tree. A simple, stolid, tree.

"Nothing," he said, gathering himself together. "I thought I saw someone … a body … hanging from a branch."

Sinead stared doubtfully at him, then, seeming to decide he wasn't worth the trouble, turned to Ragnar. "The *Codex* says the treasure lies beneath the tree," she said, then added in a brusque voice, "we should dig."

Mord handed out spades, and everyone except Redknee started digging.

"You'll need to cut me loose," Redknee said, "if you want me to help."

Ragnar hesitated, then nodded his agreement. Magnus, hurried over. He fumbled with the rope for a moment before managing to cut Redknee free. Redknee saw a flash of pity in his old friend's eyes.

"I'm watching you, troll boy," Ragnar said. "So don't try anything stupid."

"Are we supposed to be digging in any particular place?" Mord asked.

332

Sinead shook her head. "The book doesn't say where exactly. Just that the treasure is beneath the tree."

"We'll never cut through these roots," Mord said, prodding one with the toe of his boot.

Ragnar stared at his son. "Just get on with it. We're nearly there. Think about what you'll spend your share on."

Mord grinned. "Aye, father, I'll buy myself the best looking wife in all the Northlands."

It was slow work. The earth was cold and hard. Sweat soon dripped from Redknee's brow. Eventually Ragnar said they could stop to eat. The hole Redknee had dug was little more than waist deep. He put down his spade, climbed out and sat on the grass, nestling between the giant roots of the White Pine for warmth. Sinead handed him a skin of water. He took it from her without a word.

Despite digging all afternoon, and making a good number of pockmarks in the ground, they'd found nothing. Redknee doubted the Bear People guide could be trusted. They only had the guide's word this was the White Pine of the *Codex*.

He took a swig from the pigskin, leaned back and looked up. The sensation was dizzying. A river of grey bark stretched, almost endlessly it seemed, towards the heavens. He closed his eyes. The fear that gripped when they first arrived had gone. But in its place came a growing doubt. Even if this was the White Pine, did he really expect to find the key to his father's whereabouts here? Beneath some old tree? No. Sven had killed his father. That was all there was to it. There was no mystery to be solved. No clue to be found. Telling Redknee Erik wasn't his father was just another one of Sven's lies.

*Yet ... did he really believe his uncle capable of killing his own brother?*

Silver moseyed over to him. He stroked the pup absently behind the ear. "Eh," he said in a low voice, so the others, who sat not far off, wouldn't hear. "Am I the biggest fool that ever lived? Searching for a father who, if he isn't dead, likely abandoned me. A father I've never known. And looking for him here, of all places, so far from home?" Silver stared back

333

uncomprehendingly, then began licking Redknee's face. Redknee grunted and gently pushed the pup away.

"Perhaps Sinead is right," he said, glancing over to where she sat laughing with Ragnar and Olaf. "What difference does it make if I ever find him, or even who he is? It won't change anything. I need to start planning for myself."

Then he saw it, barely visible among the natural lesions in the bark. He looked again. His eyes did not deceive him. He stood. Raised himself on tiptoe for a better look ... etched into the trunk, faded and worn, but definitely there, was the crude outline of a unicorn followed by a series of what Redknee now knew to be Latin script. He called to Sinead before he could stop himself.

She rushed to his side and he pointed to the carving, surprised no one had seen it before.

"It's Latin all right," she said.

Ragnar joined them, a piece of half-cooked fish in his hand. "What does it say?"

Sinead squinted. "It's faded. It's a long time since Saint Brendan came here – *if* he wrote it. But I think it says *Deus providet.*"

Ragnar frowned. "Speak Norse girl, we don't all have the advantage of a monastery education."

"I think it means ... 'God provides'."

"What does *that* mean?" Ragnar asked.

Brother Alfred opened his mouth to speak, but Mord cut him off. "It means," Mord said, picking up his spade and starting to dig again with renewed vigour, "that not only are we in the right place, but we're going to be very, very rich."

"Well, everyone," Ragnar said turning to the others, who by now were all listening. "This is confirmation. You've seen the Christian monasteries. How wealthy they are. Their God provides. It says so here. What are you waiting for? *Fall to!*"

Mord threw his hand in the air. "Look what I've found!" He held up a stone, as big as a man's hand and so black it shone in the gathering dusk. Everyone stopped digging and crowded round. Silver's tail wagged.

"What is it?" Sinead asked, taking the piece from Mord and examining it for herself.

"Isn't it obvious?" he said.

Sinead looked at her newfound brother with a blank expression.

Mord turned to Ragnar, his face aglow. "Father, I have found the first piece of Saint Brendan's treasure."

Ragnar frowned. "Why does it have such a sharp edge?"

"Because it's a spear head," Sinead said. "It's not a jewel at all."

Someone in the small group sniggered. Redknee thought it was Skoggcat. Mord snatched the stone back. "You'll see," he said, slipping it into his leather pouch and picking up his spade, "this is just the first of many."

"The Irish girl is right."

Everyone turned. Hawk stood at the edge of the clearing. Running Deer, her brothers and Hiawatha were with him.

"Who is this speaking the Norse tongue?" Ragnar demanded.

Hawk stepped forward, his hand placed lightly over the hilt of his sword. "I speak the Norse tongue because I was once a Northman," he said. "I sailed to this place two winters ago with my fellow Icelanders. I too came looking for Saint Brendan's treasure."

Mord's eyes narrowed. "Did you find it?"

Hawk shook his head. "And I doubt you will either."

"You lie," Mord said. "Tell me where you have hidden it, or I'll slice you open from nose to knee."

Hawk fastened his hand round his sword and grinned. "I'd like to see you try." As Hawk spoke, a band of about twenty warriors carrying tomahawks and bows filtered into the clearing behind him.

Ragnar's own men-at-arms stepped up behind Mord. "Enough of this," Ragnar said, waving Mord down. He turned to Hawk. "Did you follow us here?"

Hawk shook his head. "Hardly. This tree has been known to the Kanienkehaka – the Flint People – for many years. It is sacred to them. A peace council has been called—"

Running Deer placed a hand over her husband's arm. "This concerns my people," she said, "I should explain." Hawk nodded reluctantly, and Running Deer turned to face Ragnar and the other Northmen. "Many years ago, my ancestors ... and the ancestors of the other peoples that live in this land ... were always fighting. Many died, until a great man whose name has been lost to memory, convinced the six great chiefs to agree a peace. As evidence of their intentions to keep to their promise, the six chiefs agreed to bury their weapons beneath the tallest tree in the forest." Running Deer looked up at the White Pine. "This was the tallest tree."

"So ... there's no treasure buried here?" Mord asked. "Just some old weapons?"

Running Deer nodded.

Mord's lip curled in anger. "You lie. You *have* followed us here. You want to keep the treasure for yourselves." He stamped over to Sinead, grabbed the *Codex* from her and held it up. "It says in here," he said, shaking the *Codex*. "It says Saint Brendan travelled to a land in the west where he buried a great treasure beneath a white pine marked with Irish runes."

Running Deer glanced at Hiawatha. "My father ..." she began hesitantly, "he ... he didn't want me to show you this at first. But I think ... well, you should see it for yourselves." She reached into a beaded pouch and a pulled out a piece of crumpled vellum.

"What's that?" Sinead asked, stepping forward.

Running Deer handed the page to her. "I don't know what the patterns mean. It has been in my family for many years. Some say it was left by the man who made the peace here all those years ago. When you brought out the book, the one that led you here, I remembered. I thought you should see it ... in case it explained."

Redknee watched Sinead as she scanned the page. She frowned as she reached the end.

"What does it say?" Mord asked.

Sinead looked up. She smiled slowly.

"Don't hold us in suspense," Ragnar said. "I've waited over sixteen years for this."

"It's a list ... an inventory, if you like."

336

*"What?"* Ragnar marched forward and grabbed the sheet from her.

Mord grinned hungrily. "Does it list the treasures buried here? Swords inlaid with rubies, brooches of purest gold—"

Sinead shook her head, her curls bouncing from side to side.

"Tell us," Redknee urged, unable to hold his tongue any longer.

"It is certainly in the hand of the scribe who wrote the *Codex*. But this is a more … *prosaic* document. Laughably so. It lists the items needed to build an Irish *curragh*. There's even a drawing."

"What's a *curragh*?" Redknee asked.

"It's a boat made of leather. It must be what Saint Brendan used to sail here. Remember, I told you about them before? They're stronger than you'd think."

Mord rubbed his hands together in glee. "This means Saint Brendan was really here."

"But not that he buried any treasure," Sinead said.

"Why else would he go to all the trouble of writing such a long book?" Mord scoffed, picking up his spade.

Redknee didn't recognise her at first, so much had she changed. She stood at the very edge of the clearing, behind Hiawatha's warriors, half hidden by greenery, seemingly unsure whether to stay or go. Once lustrous skin hung dully over sunken cheeks, grey circles ringed her eyes and her lips were bitten raw. Astrid was a changed woman. But it wasn't this that sent a shiver through Redknee's spine; it was the fact that since he had noticed her … not once had her eyes left Hawk.

337

# Chapter 36

Mord dug long into the night. He found five axe heads, four spearheads, a wampum headdress, a deerskin drum, six flint knives, a leather sling, four bows, two woven quivers and maybe fifty or sixty flint arrow tips. Ragnar remained unimpressed. He lit a fire, told everyone else to stop digging, and sat down.

Sinead joined him, the book open in her lap. Her new bronze pendant glimmered in the firelight as Redknee took his place opposite. Hiawatha and his warriors sat a little way off. They hadn't tried to stop the excavation, merely watched from a distance, wry grins twisting their faces.

"Tell me, daughter," Ragnar said gently, "tell me again what the book says about the treasure."

Sinead turned the pages, stopping when she found the right part. "It says … *They came to a great white pine, so tall, Saint Brendan could not see whence it touched the sky, but he was certain that it did. The youth said: 'This tree lies in the centre of the Promised Land, so that all peoples may reach it, and none are further away than the other.' Saint Brendan nodded, for he understood. He took his most treasured possessions and buried them beneath the roots of this tree, the greatest of them all.'"* Sinead stopped reading and scratched her head. "Wait, I don't think that translation is quite right. It's not his most treasured possessions that he buried, but the things he treasured most."

"What's the difference?" Magnus asked, his calm steersman's eyes unblinking in the flickering firelight.

Sinead sucked in her cheeks. "I'm not sure … shall I read on?"

Ragnar nodded.

*"'Then he turned to his fellow monks, and told them to do the same. And, so it came to pass that many treasures lay*

*beneath this tree, treasures great enough to bring peace to all the Earth.'"*

Ragnar wearily massaged the spot just above his blind eye, as if that blank orb was the source of all his pain. When he looked up and saw that Running Deer was tentatively approaching the fire, he waved her over.

"There is no mention of Saint Brendan brokering a peace," he said.

Running Deer nodded slightly. "We think of this tree as precious because of what it stands for. I think that is what your book is trying to say. It's not real treasure."

Ragnar inhaled sharply. He turned to Sinead. "Is that what you think?" he asked, his lips curling in disgust. "That this has been a … a *symbolic* journey?" He spat these last words.

Sinead bit her lip and stared at the open page in front of her. A tear began to trickle down her cheek.

"Pah," Ragnar said, standing. "I never should have trusted Sven. He's still leading me a merry dance, even from beyond the grave." He called to Mord. "Come, son," he said. "It is time to rest. You can try again in the morning, but I think we have to accept defeat on this one."

Mord looked up from the pit in which he stood. Mud splattered his face and clothes, only the whites of his eyes shone clean in the moonlight. He gave a low, desperate growl.

Ragnar sighed. "There will be other journeys, and other treasures. We will be rich yet. And King Hakon will keep his promise to us about the jarldom. I'll make sure of it."

Mord climbed out reluctantly, as if his limbs were made of stone. Ragnar threw his arm round his eldest and led him to the warmth of the fire. Mord slumped to the ground, fished a small piece of bone from his pocket and began working it, almost obsessively, with his knife.

Redknee bedded down near Hawk and watched the others. Even with Silver at his feet, he couldn't fully relax. Something was wrong. Ragnar had accepted defeat too easily. Had he known all along that there was no treasure? What about the stories in the *Codex* about a land where the flowers were made of rubies, raindrops of pearls and the rivers flowed blue, the product of a hundred thousand sapphires?

Had it all been lies? Or, as Running Deer called it – *symbolic*. Which, if you asked him, was just about as good as lies.

Redknee listened to the rumble of Olaf's snores, worse now they were no longer at sea. He turned over, trying to block his ears. Mord had moved a little way from the others. He was still awake, still working on his piece of bone, carving an intricate design on its smooth face. It looked like it was going to be the handle for a small eating knife or dagger. Even from this distance, Redknee could see the workmanship was good. Mord held it up. It caught the light. Redknee saw the design clearly – a pair of interlaced snakes.

Suddenly he realised where he'd seen such craft, such a design, before. His head spun with the revelation. He slid from his sleeping fur, grabbed a discarded spade and pressed the iron tip into Olaf's throat.

"You!" he whispered, shaking with anger. "*You* were the traitor all along."

Olaf's eyes flew open.

"*You!* My uncle's right-hand man. You have been in league with Ragnar from the beginning and I can prove it."

"What's happening?" Ragnar demanded, stumbling groggily to his feet.

"I know who your snake was," Redknee called back, pushing the sharp tip of the spade into Olaf's throat until a droplet of blood sprung forth.

Olaf's eyes bulged in his fear pinched face. "Not me," he croaked.

Redknee laughed bitterly. "It's all so clear now. Why didn't I see it before? When my uncle went to Kaupangen the month before Ragnar's attack, you and Harold went with him. Sven went to see if he could find a buyer for the *Codex* – or at least if anyone there could read it. Harold returned from that trip with a fine ivory-handled dagger. He boasted you got the dagger from a Frankish merchant. I now know that to be a lie. For it was Mord who carved the fine decoration on the handle. *You* met Ragnar when you visited Kaupangen, he gave you the

340

dagger as a gift for agreeing to be his spy, and you gave it to your son."

Olaf tried to shake his head despite the pressure of the spade at his throat. "It's not true," he said. "Harold won the dagger in a game of dice. I didn't see Ragnar when I went to Kaupangen. Didn't even know he was there."

"You lie. You were against this voyage from the start. Always telling my uncle to give up, to go back home. You were working for Ragnar – *tell me the truth*."

"No – I truly thought the voyage futile—"

The blow to his head knocked Redknee sideways. His vision blurred. When he stumbled round, Harold stood opposite him, sword and shield in hand. Harold stood tall and straight, all signs of frailty gone.

"*You?*" Redknee said, more accusation than question.

Harold raised his sword. "My father was always in your uncle's shadow. Serving him like a faithful dog. He's the one who organised this voyage. He readied the supplies. He oversaw the building of *Wavedancer*. Hell, he even checked the sea routes. Without my father, your uncle would have been nothing. And what thanks did he get?"

"Come, son," Olaf said, gripping the necklace of blood at his throat. He too was on his feet now, along with most of the camp. He held out his arms, beseeching Harold to desist. "I respected Sven. We had our differences, but he treated me well. Like the brother he'd lost."

Harold shook his head. "No, father, Sven didn't treat you like a brother. Did he reward your service with land, with power?"

Olaf's silence was answer enough for Harold. He jabbed his sword at Redknee. "*And him* – one day *he* would be jarl! Despite being a better warrior, I would never inherit anything. I *had* to do something."

"And you thought *Ragnar* would give you what you want?" Redknee asked.

Harold laughed; sparks danced in the pits of his eyes, the mania had not left him. "It was *Mord* I found at the Kaupangen docks. Trying to sell a boatload of slaves from the Rhineland. He wasn't having much luck. Surly bastards,

341

Germans. He was drunk, throwing dice with some Frankish merchants. Gambled away half his cargo. When I heard who he was, I told him about the book Sven had come to Kaupangen to sell and how he could make his money back a hundredfold. Provided he saw me right. The dagger, however, I won. Always did have a fast hand."

Ragnar cut in. "Is this true?" he asked, staring at Mord.

"I told you I had my spies," Mord said, stepping closer. He'd been keeping his distance in the shadows, but came forward to answer his father. The light from the fire danced across his mailcoat. He still held the bone carving in his hand.

"I meant about losing half the slaves – you told me they'd died from sea-fever."

Mord shrugged. "They were weak and would've died anyway."

Harold banged on his shield. "Come on, Red-knee," he said, drawing the name into an insult. "Are you a coward like your father? Going to run?"

Redknee tilted his head and smiled. "Only to hunt you down." He'd learned a lot since that hot day in the village when Harold had beaten him at sword craft. He shifted his weight. Tossed the iron tipped spade from hand to hand. This time he would win … and the outcome would be final.

Harold swung first. The blade nicked the edge of Redknee's sleeve. Damn, he thought. Enough talk. He'd have to be quicker.

The others stopped gawping and stood back, forming a wide circle round them. Torches flickered between the faces. Hiawatha's warriors joined the onlookers. Olaf tried to intervene, but Ragnar held him back.

Redknee burned with anger. Harold was the traitor; he'd killed Karl and Thora, he was to blame for his mother's death. He let out a roar and charged, swinging his spade at Harold's head. The crowd gasped, but Harold snapped to, and Redknee's blow glanced off Harold's shield. Before he could pull back, Harold thumped him between the shoulders with his pommel. He lurched towards the ground, only stopping himself falling flat at the last moment.

"*Catch.*"

He chanced a sideways glance. Toki smiled at him from the sidelines then threw a shield in the air. He caught it, sliding his arm through the metal handle.

*Keep your shield high ... like a jug of mead* ...Yes, that's what Uncle Sven had taught him. *And watch for the snakebite* – that, he had learned himself.

He spun round and stared into Harold's eyes, certain the hatred he saw there was reflected in his own. This time he met Harold's blow with his shield, dropped his right knee and swung low, catching Harold's ankle with the tip of his spade. He grunted with pleasure as Harold recoiled. The blow had little power, but it served as a warning.

"You've improved," Harold said, lunging forward again, and again, and again, his face set in a wolfish snarl.

As each blow smashed into Redknee's shield, he struggled to catch them with the iron boss and not the fast disintegrating wood. As he was pushed backwards, sleeping furs snarled his feet. Seizing on this, Harold attacked harder, his face glistening with sweat. Redknee didn't think he could hold out much longer when he saw Sinead push to the front of the crowd. He wished she'd stay out the way. Didn't need the distraction.

They were near the White Pine now, among the snare of roots. Being backed against it would be suicide. Redknee faked a stumble. But he'd judged it wrong – fell flat on his back.

Sinead was above him, pressing something into his hand. *Flame Weaver.* He rolled away as Harold's sword whizzed past his ear and twanged against the hard earth. *She came through for me,* Redknee thought, rounding on Harold with renewed energy. This was his chance for revenge.

*Lead with the sword, follow with the body.* Sven's words echoed in his head as he propelled *Flame Weaver* through the air, shattering Harold's shield into splinters. It was a decisive blow. Redknee moved in for the kill, smashing the iron husk of his own shield under Harold's chin. Blood and teeth spewed from Harold's mouth as he flew back, into the trunk of the White Pine.

Redknee stood over him, poised to bring *Flame Weaver* down, to send the traitor to his grave. Silver must have seen it first. The pup sprung into the air, throwing himself between Redknee and Harold's knife.

The scream was no less terrible for not being human. Silver fell to the ground, blood streaking his white fur. Redknee crumpled over the pup's body. *How could this have happened? He had defeated Harold – hadn't he?*

Harold smirked down at Redknee, the bloodstained knife still in his hand. "I've wanted to do that for a long time," he said. "Now, I'm going to have my other wish." He swung his sword at Redknee's neck, but Redknee was already up, moving. The swing missed Redknee completely; Harold's sword plunged deep into the trunk of the White Pine. Harold tugged. It was stuck. Redknee raised *Flame Weaver*—

"Stop!" Olaf demanded. "I won't allow my son to be killed."

Redknee looked round at the horrified faces staring at him. Suddenly he realised just how outnumbered he was amongst Ragnar's men. If he killed Harold, there would be many to exact revenge.

Olaf stalked over and pulled Harold's sword from the tree trunk. Redknee thought Olaf was going to fight in his son's stead but he knelt over Silver and bundled him into his arms.

"Sinead," Olaf asked, "do you have medicine that can help? I know you worked for the monks in their infirmary."

Sinead hurried over and stroked Silver's head. The pup whimpered. The wound in his side was large, ragged; he'd lost a lot of blood. A tear sprung to Sinead's eye. "I'm afraid I have nothing here."

"Wait," Running Deer said, stepping forward. "I think I can help."

Olaf laid Silver on the ground beside the White Pine. Running Deer took a sharp blade from her belt and sliced into the bark, using the cut Harold's sword had already made. Thick, sticky sap oozed forth. Running Deer scooped as much of it as she could with the edge of her blade, and, very carefully pasted the greenish-white paste over the wound in Silver's side. The sap soon hardened to form a sticky poultice.

"There," Running Deer said as she finished, "that should stop the bleeding. But we'll have to wait until morning before we'll know if he'll live."

# Chapter 37

Redknee sat with Silver, well away from the others. He kept his sword by his side: no one would take it from him again while he lived. He nudged the pup gently. Nothing. No response.

"How is Silver?"

Redknee looked up. Sinead stood over him, concern in her eyes. Was she really still his friend? "Why do you care?" he asked.

She knelt and gently traced the grey circle on Silver's forehead with her fingertip. Silver's paws twitched a fraction.

Redknee felt a sudden pang of jealousy. "You care more for that pup than you do for me."

She drew back. "I gave you *Flame Weaver*, didn't I? And when you arrived at *Svensbyan* Ragnar was all for killing you – even told Olaf to do it. But I—"

"Olaf wants to speak to you."

Redknee looked up to see Toki standing over him. He glanced back to Silver; a fine mist trailed from the pup's nostrils. The paste Running Deer applied had hardened to a crust. He appeared to be out of immediate danger.

"I'll watch him," Sinead said.

Redknee hesitated then got to his feet.

"Word of advice," Toki said as they approached where Olaf sat near the fire, "don't lose your temper again."

Redknee shook his head in dismay. If Olaf wanted a fight, he wasn't going to be the one to back down.

Olaf motioned for Redknee to sit beside him. Harold was standing a short way off, talking to Mord and Ragnar. He cast Redknee a defiant look. Before Redknee could draw his sword, Olaf was on his feet, standing between them.

346

"Don't even think about it," Olaf said. "Now sit, before I kill you myself."

Redknee reluctantly did as he asked, but sat so as he could keep one eye trained on Harold at all times. Olaf told Redknee he had to stay away from Harold, or leave the group.

Redknee protested. "Your son killed good people, murdered them in cold blood. He has to pay."

Olaf shook his head. "He says he didn't kill Karl or poison the stew. And I believe him. Yes, he admits giving Mord information about the location of our village, about the fact we had the *Codex* and were going to seek Saint Brendan's treasure. But that's all he did."

"But even that—"

"Come now," Olaf said, placing a hand on Redknee's shoulder. Redknee guessed it was meant to be reassuring, but it felt like a threat. "I'm as sorry as you are about what happened to the village," Olaf continued. "By Thor's hammer, I lost my daughter. I'm sorry Harold had a part in it. But I'm not going to punish my son. He's suffered enough. And let me warn you now against seeking your own revenge, because I don't believe Harold capable of the terrible crimes you accuse him of."

"But he attacked *me*."

"You forget he was trying to save me from your temper. Look, Redknee, I never thought it would come to this. I respected your uncle. Loved him even, like a brother. I always said I'd look out for you, if anything happened to Sven, but the time has come for us to part ways."

"But it is Harold who—"

Olaf raised his hand. "Let me finish. Ragnar is leaving here now. He doesn't want to be around when the other clans arrive. To be honest, you're lucky Ragnar hasn't already killed you. You have the slave girl to thank for that. Now you can do what you like. Stay with the Flint People, or go your own way. But you can't come with us. I won't have my son's life endangered." He sighed, "One day you'll understand I've done you a favour."

When Redknee left Olaf, anger burned in his veins. Whether Harold had actually slit Karl's throat, or put the

347

wolfsbane in Thora's stew was only a detail. Harold was a traitor, and traitors deserved to die.

Redknee rejoined Sinead at the edge of the camp. She had Silver across her lap, her arm curled protectively around his stomach, her fingers balled into a fist, tufts of white fur protruding between her mud-stained knuckles. Silver was still sleeping, but every breath seemed to wrack his too-thin body with pain.

Sinead looked up. "He's a fighter," she said, her eyes glassy.

Redknee knelt beside her. He spoke quietly. "Ragnar is moving out. He doesn't want to be here when the other clans arrive. Olaf and Harold are going with him … I'm not welcome."

"I'm sorry."

Redknee shook his head. "I've no wish to serve Ragnar."

"What will you do?"

Redknee shrugged. He hadn't thought about it. He wanted to ask Sinead to forget her father, to come with him. But the words sounded stupid, jumbled in his head. Instead he watched as Running Deer approached them carrying a bowl of water.

"I thought Silver's wound might need—" she began, her voice drifted off. She was staring at a spot just behind Redknee. He turned. Deganawida stood in the shadows. The old man shuffled forwards, his footsteps silenced by the carpet of moss. A shaft of moonlight caught him and his white hair gleamed like ice against his weathered skin. How long had he been standing there, Redknee wondered? Listening to their conversation, taking stock of the camp.

Ragnar strode over. "What's *he* doing here?" he demanded.

"He's come for the peace ceremony," Running Deer said. "The weapons you dug up – they must be reburied."

Deganawida sat cross-legged beneath the White Pine and closed his eyes. Ragnar's men cast curious glances his way as they readied to leave, but they didn't taunt him; despite his years and apparent frailty, he had the other-worldly power of a sorcerer. Hiawatha also kept his distance. But every so often Redknee saw him cast an equally wary glance the old man's way.

Redknee recognised the beat immediately. It echoed through the trees, shook the very ground. His chest tightened. He would know it anywhere. The sound of Bear People war drums.

"I thought it was a peace meeting," he said to Running Deer.

"It is," she replied, her eyes anxiously seeking out her father.

Hiawatha heard it too. He ordered his warriors to stand in a circle round the White Pine, bows at the ready. Only Deganawida remained perfectly still. Though Redknee could swear he saw a flutter of excitement behind the old man's lids.

The chief of the Bear People entered the clearing ahead of his tribe. He carried a war club in one hand and a tomahawk in the other. His warriors fanned out behind him, facing Hiawatha's braves. Ragnar, far from fleeing, strode over, and greeted the Bear People chief as an old friend. It seemed Ragnar had changed his mind.

They didn't have to wait long for the other four clans to arrive. Running Deer explained for Redknee as each new clan filtered into the uneasy space between Hiawatha's men and the Bear People: the People of the Standing Stones with their alleged power to vanish at will; the People of the Great Hill with their single-feathered hats; the People of the Hills with their two feathered hats. Last to arrive were the People of the Swamp, who were easy to identify because of their mud-caked feet. Running Deer said they made up for this by having the fanciest headdresses of all.

When everyone was assembled, Deganawida stood on a small mound beneath the White Pine and began speaking. Silence crept over the gathering, as one by one, the clans stopped to listen. He didn't raise his voice above a whisper, but every syllable was delivered with the sweet crispness of a mountain stream. When he eventually stopped, Redknee turned to Running Deer and asked what he had said.

"He said the White Pine is a good place to meet because the spirit force, which runs through all things, is strong here. He wants to stop the fighting between the clans. He wants to set up a council of leaders – or *sachems* – one from each clan, who will meet here twice a year. He likened the land to a great longhouse – with each clan given a role. The Flint People, my clan, will be Keepers of the Eastern Door, the People of the Great Hill keepers of the Western Door and the People of the Hills keepers of the Central Fire. He was asking permission of the spirit force to hold the councils here."

"Will the clans agree to this?" Redknee asked.

Running Deer shrugged. "I don't know. It's been done before, a long time ago, as you know. But it's never lasted. And now we're on the verge of full-scale war."

"What about your father, Hiawatha. Will he agree to be part of this council?"

Hawk stuck his head between them. "Hiawatha only ever agrees to what suits him."

"That's not true," Running Deer said.

"He promises his warriors land, women, furs, if they'll fight for him. How will he keep his power if there is no war?" Hawk asked.

Running Deer shook her head. "My father is a very spiritual man. He *wants* peace. He *wants* to please the spirit force."

Hawk snorted and turned forward to face the proceedings.

Hiawatha had joined Deganawida on the mound. He began addressing the crowd. He spoke faster than Deganawida, moved his hands forcefully. Suddenly, a great cheer went up among Hiawatha's men and the People of the Great Hill. The other clans drew their weapons.

"What did he say?" Redknee asked.

Running Deer opened her mouth to speak, but Hawk cut her off. "Hiawatha believes the Flint People and People of the Great Hill, as protectors of the Eastern and Western Doors are more likely to encounter hostile tribes and should be allowed additional *sachems* at the council," he said dryly.

350

The Bear People started stamping their feet on the earth and chanting. Clouds of dust rose into the air.

"Oh no," Running Deer said, glancing fearfully at her husband, "that's their war cry."

Redknee watched as a chasm opened in the crowd, the Bear People and People of the Hills on one side, the rest of the clans on the other. Insults were lobbed at Hiawatha and his men. A Bear People archer raised an arrow to his bow and took aim. Everything seemed to slow ... the archer uncurled his fingers ... his arrow thrummed through the air with dreadful finality. The scream that came from the Seneca warrior as the flint tip lodged in his thigh sounded through the forest as a call to arms.

Deganawida moved with an efficiency that belied his age. Gone was the shambling old man welcomed in every village. He stood tall and straight, the years melting away as he leapt between the two forces and held up a large strip of purple and white wampum as if it were a shield of steel, fit to repel all foes.

The warriors watched him as he spoke. His words rang scornful and proud. Running Deer translated as quickly as she could, *"Is this what you want? To paint your story in blood? One day you will be the ancestors. When your children's children come to you for advice, will you tell them to slaughter their brother? Or will you tell them to live in peace, rich in land, and children and time?"*

A murmur rippled through the crowd as this was discussed. Hiawatha stepped forward. He looked uneasy. Again, Running Deer translated. *"Perhaps I was hasty, the Bear People and the People of the Hills will bring much to the council. Their representation should be the same as ... my people. What's more, Tadodaho, esteemed chief of the People of the Hills, should lead the council."*

The Bear People and People of the Hills stared at each other, confusion writ large on their faces.

"Why is he doing that?" Redknee asked. "Doesn't he want to be leader himself?"

Hawk smiled. "My wife's father plays a dangerous game."

351

Tadodaho stepped forward. He wore his hair in many braids that hung down his back and squirmed like snakes when he walked. *"I thank Hiawatha for his proposal. He thinks it will convince me to join with him against my friends."*

Hiawatha laughed. *"The Bear People are not your friends. Only yesterday their chief tried to convince me to join with them in an attack against your lands."*

This time the Bear People warriors drew their weapons alone. Tadodaho looked uneasy. The air crackled with energy. Redknee could almost see the Tadodaho arguing with himself.

*"Come, wise Tadodaho,"* Hiawatha said, *"I have already spoken with the other chiefs. They would be glad if you were to lead the council – as first among equals. Without the People of the Hills, whose lands lie in the centre of our great longhouse, the confederacy of clans cannot work. You must take this role."*

Tadodaho nodded. It was a small movement, but it was enough to send a wave of cheers through the crowd. Only the Bear People remained silent. Although sorely outnumbered, Redknee thought their chief was going to order his warriors to attack. He even glanced at Ragnar to see if the Northmen would fight for him. Ragnar pointedly avoided eye contact.

The Bear People chief turned from the clearing and motioned for his men to follow. The Bear People would not be part of Deganawida's great peace.

They called Deganawida the Great Peacemaker. Running Deer said this event would be remembered for a long time. New weapons were buried beneath the White Pine and the tree itself was renamed the Tree of Peace. Deganawida asked all gathered to send thanks to "He who Holds the Sky" for allowing the peace to be agreed.

Only the absence of the Bear People cast a shadow. But Hiawatha seemed pleased as he danced and sang with his warriors.

Hawk joined Redknee where he was sitting quietly beneath the White Pine, still holding Silver.

"Why didn't Hiawatha want the Bear People in the confederacy?" Redknee asked.

352

Hawk shrugged. "I assume he didn't want his own influence diluted by such a powerful faction."

The other Northmen were joining in the celebrations. Sinead danced with Thinking Owl, laughing each time he linked his arm through hers and spun her round. Even Mord was trying to learn the steps of their intricate dance, despite the weight of his mailcoat.

Redknee nodded in Sinead's direction. "You think she'll be happy with her father?"

"She won't be with him for long; I hear she's to be married to a Norse prince – one of King Hakon's sons. Thought I doubt he'll mention her former slave status. Probably say she's an Irish Princess – so often the facts are in the telling."

Redknee flashed a wry smile and rubbed Silver behind the ears. The pup blinked. He had regained consciousness, but was still in a lot of pain. "Do you know who?" Redknee asked, thinking how his words of warning to Mord had been fatefully prophetic.

Hawk shook his head. "But I could find out for you ... if you want to know."

"No. That's all right."

Hawk nodded and moved off to join his wife who was dancing round the fire.

Redknee leaned back against the trunk of the White Pine. He'd failed. In every respect. There *was* no treasure. He'd hadn't found his father; had failed to fulfil his mother's dying wish. His search had only brought him further from the truth. Now he didn't even know *who* his father was, never mind where he might be, or if he was alive. His attempts had fallen on deaf ears. No one, it seemed, either knew, cared, or would admit to knowing.

Sinead was right. *What did it matter?* It wouldn't change who *he* was. He would still be a nobody; with no friends, no land ... no future. He could see his life stretch before him ... an itinerant wanderer ... perhaps he should join one of the brotherhoods who raided the southern shores of Britannia, who welcomed anyone with a strong arm and their own sword.

Of course, Sinead had changed her attitude now she'd found her own father. Never mind that he was a murderer, a henchman for King Hakon. Now she had a home, and a family, a place in the world. Things that had been taken from Redknee.

"Deganawida wants to talk to you."

Redknee looked up to see Running Deer standing over him, Deganawida at her side. The old man sat opposite Redknee and stared straight into his eyes as he spoke. Unnerved, Redknee didn't know whether he should look away. Instead, he held the old seer's gaze.

When Deganawida stopped, Running Deer translated. *"War, the glory and riches it brings, is a desire my people have long nourished. Today they have buried their enmity with their weapons."* She hesitated. Deganawida nodded that she should go on. Her voice sounded almost apologetic. *"When you seek one truth with all your soul, it is easy to forget the good things that have been around you all along. False idols must be buried before you can find your destiny. Take Hiawatha. He'll finish his wampum now ... now that he has put thoughts of war behind him, he will become the great peaceful leader he was meant to be."*

When Running Deer finished, Deganawida stood, made a little bow and shuffled away. "It is a great honour," she said as Redknee watched the old man's retreating figure, "that he wanted to speak to you."

"Thank you. His words are those of a true visionary," Redknee said. Running Deer smiled and went to rejoin Hawk in front of the fire.

Redknee slumped against the tree trunk. Deganawida was right. This voyage, this quest for treasure, the search for his father, had all been a waste of time ... a distraction from the real truth. He looked up at the canopy. The moonlight seemed far away through the tangle of branches. He thought again about Deganawida's words. Perhaps there *had* been value in the journey precisely because it had failed ...

He watched as Astrid moved through the crowd, a basket of seeds and nuts slung under her arm, offering handfuls to whoever was hungry. It wasn't like her to be so thoughtful. Perhaps she'd caught the festive mood.

"Can I sit with you?"

354

Redknee looked up to see Toki smiling at him.

"Do you remember what I said that first time we came into this vast forest?" Toki asked.

"About how it could make a man rich?"

Toki nodded. "Ragnar is going home. Returning to the Northlands with his men."

"I thought you were one of Ragnar's men."

Toki laughed. "I'm my own man, lad. Thought you knew that by now. And I knew your mother well ... as a friend. Which is why I've come to *you* with this idea."

"Go on."

"Ragnar is going to sail home in his clunky, iron-clad ship. It's an ugly thing, if ever there was. And it's slow and sits low in the water. He might allow you passage if you asked nicely – you *are* a favourite of his daughter, after all. But I got to thinking, *Wavedancer* is a very different sort. She's long and light in the water. She won't carry a lot of cargo – she isn't a *knar*, but she would do for exporting timber. The Greenlanders and Icelanders have none of their own – we'd be rich as kings!"

Redknee scratched his head. When they'd first arrived he'd wondered if Saint Brendan had meant the land itself and its fruits when he talked about finding a great treasure. Certainly, this island was vast, vaster still than Iceland or the Sheep Islands combined. Perhaps something real and tangible *could* still be garnered from their voyage. Something more than a *lesson*.

"Come on," Toki said, giving Redknee a friendly punch on the shoulder. "How could we lose?"

The feasting lasted well into the night. Redknee watched with Silver from the sidelines as Hawk, filled with mead and rosy cheeked, went to Astrid and put his arms round her waist. She tried to shrug him off, but he persisted. "I'm sorry," Hawk mumbled. "I did love you once—"

"I don't want to hear it," she said.

"Come on – one kiss, for old time's sake. I've seen you watching me." Hawk strained to press his lips to her cheek as she fought to push him away, eventually giving up and allowing him to plant his kiss. "There," he said, "that wasn't so bad."

Astrid grimaced as Hawk staggered away. Then she seemed to change her mind. "Wait," she called after him, placing her basket on the ground and fishing in her pouch. "Have something to eat."

Hawk smiled. "Don't mind if I do," he said, taking the seeds from her and supplementing them with another handful from the basket. Then he stumbled merrily into the throng, whistling a jaunty tune Redknee recognised from home.

Bright morning light shone on Hawk's peaceful features. If he'd died in agony, Redknee couldn't tell. Running Deer knelt beside her husband's body, weeping into her apron while her father and brothers consoled her.

The events of the night before were foggy in Redknee's mind. The last thing he'd seen Hawk do was kiss Astrid. Wait. He'd taken nuts from her basket. But *everyone* had eaten from it – and no one else felt ill, at least, no worse than to be expected after a night-long celebration. Then he remembered. He turned to Hiawatha. "She did it," he said, pointing to Astrid. "She killed your son-in-law."

Astrid's face turned pale. "No! I swear I didn't."

"Check her pouch," he said. "She keeps the poison in there."

Crouching Bear grabbed Astrid and handed the pouch she kept round her waist to Hiawatha, who emptied its contents on the ground. Three black seeds, the size of peppercorns, fell out. *Wolfsbane.* Everyone gasped.

"Did you poison Thora and the Bjornsson twins too?" Redknee demanded.

Astrid raised her chin in defiance. "I swear I didn't."

"I *saw* you give these to Hawk last night," Redknee said.

"Only yesterday you thought Harold poisoned Thora and the Bjornsson twins. Now you point the finger at me. It is *you*, Redknee, who is hard to believe. Let us see what's in your pouch."

No one spoke; they just stared at him with wide eyes. They couldn't think he'd done it … *could they?*

356

"This is mad," Redknee said, tipping his pouch upside down. "I had no reason to kill Hawk or any of the others." But as he finished speaking a large handful of black seeds, identical to those from Astrid's pouch, fell out. "Wait!" Redknee said, horror drying his throat. "I know nothing about these!"

Thinking Owl whispered in Hiawatha's ear. When his son had finished, Hiawatha nodded.

"What did he say?" Redknee asked.

Running Deer spoke between sobs. "He says ... that you were the last person my ... my husband spoke to before he bedded down for the night, before ... before he was *murdered*."

"What? But I saw him talking to Astrid."

"No one else saw that," Running Deer said quietly.

Toki pulled on Redknee's arm. "I think you should leave now. Before things turn nasty."

"No," Redknee said. "I'm innocent. I want to prove it." But as he looked round, only hard faces stared back. He started to edge away. Maybe Toki was right, maybe he should run.

"Come on," Toki said, "remember what I said to you last night, how we can make our fortune. Let's go."

Redknee held his hands up. "I didn't do this," he said. "But I'll leave now, if that's what you want." He turned and went over to where Silver lay, still recovering beneath the White Pine. Running Deer had saved the pup's life, and now she thought he'd killed her husband. With great weariness, he scooped Silver into his arms and set off after Toki.

He'd gone no more than twenty paces when he heard his name being called. He turned round. Sinead ran towards him, her hood of copper curls bobbing between the trees. She had her big leather bag with the shoulder straps in her hand.

"I don't think you killed all those people," she said as she caught up with him.

"*Thanks*."

"But I do think you should go ... there's nothing for you here ... with these people."

"Nothing?"

357

Sinead glanced over her shoulder.

"Won't you come with me?" The words were out before he could stop himself.

"You know I'm going back to the Northlands with Ragnar."

Redknee nodded.

"I can't be your slave forever, can I? I have a future with Ragnar, with his family. He knows King Hakon. He wants me to marry his son, Prince Halfdan."

Redknee tilted his head. "How can I compete with that?"

Sinead laughed nervously. "You can't."

"How do you know you'll like him?"

"I don't. But being married to a Prince must be better than milking cows, kneading bread, grinding corn and emptying the cesspit."

"Yes," Redknee said, leaning closer. He felt her warm breath on his face, "I suppose it must be." Her lips felt soft beneath his. He remembered their kiss, on the beach, under the stars. He'd thought that would be the start of something …

"It wasn't meant to be," Sinead said, pulling back, her eyes over-bright.

Redknee could only nod mutely.

"Here," she said, holding out her bag. "It has a solid base, you can carry Silver in it until he's better – it will hold."

She helped him tuck Silver into the bag, which wasn't easy as the pup kept trying to lick her face. Eventually, with Silver bedded down safely, his white nose peeking out, Redknee slung the bag over his shoulder, and, without a further word, turned and left.

If Sinead had run after him, she would have seen his tears. But she didn't. His only solace was the occasional sad snuffling coming from the bag on his back.

# Chapter 38

Magnus and a slightly wheezing Brother Alfred caught up with Redknee and Toki in the forest. The steersman had heard of their plan to import timber to Iceland and wanted to help. The little monk felt he still owed Redknee for saving him from the Blood Eagle.

And so the five of them, Silver stowed safely in Sinead's knapsack, struck out for the coast. With each step away from Ragnar Redknee felt more optimistic. He had a new plan. He would make money as a trader, perhaps even petition King Hakon for Sven's Jarldom. Though he suspected Ragnar would try and get in a claim as part of a deal with Prince Halfdan.

Redknee tried to push Sinead's marriage from his mind. It was less than a year since she'd come to their village, and yet, he felt like he'd known her forever. Every time he heard a crackle in the trees he would turn, half expecting it to be her, come after him, just like she did that day so long ago when she'd tracked him up the mountain. Of course, it was always just a wild deer or a bird taking flight. Sinead would not follow him. Not now she had Ragnar. He doubted he'd ever see her again.

At the end of their first day's trek, when Redknee opened the knapsack to let Silver out and stretch his legs, he noticed something heavy at the bottom. Sinead had said the base was reinforced, but this seemed something more. He reached in, dislodged whatever it was and pulled it out. He stared at the *Codex* in puzzlement. Why had she given it to him?

He didn't need it now they were going home. Perhaps she just wanted rid of it? He thought about throwing it away, for it was heavy to carry, but decided against it in the end – it might have value still.

Silver seemed stronger, more alert on the fifth day. And when they stopped to eat lunch, Redknee let him out to stretch his legs.

"How you've grown," he said, opening the bag on the ground. Instead of sniffing round for a few minutes then lying down to sleep, Silver bounded off, tail wagging, into a thicket of saplings.

Magnus laughed. "I hope you haven't lost your friend."

Redknee hurried after him; they were in an unfamiliar forest and Silver was still weak. He pushed through the young trees and into a small clearing dappled with sunlight. He found he could hear the distant rumble of the sea. They'd nearly made it back. Silver must have heard the noise and thought there'd be gulls for chasing, a sure sign he was getting better.

Redknee heard a movement behind him. He spun round, ready to grab Silver into his arms, instead he came face to face with a broad chest. He stood back.

"Thought you were dead, lad."

Redknee stared up at Koll's smiling face. "Likewise," Redknee said, throwing his arms round his friend. Something squeaked and struggled between them. Redknee stood back. Koll had Silver in his arms; the pup started licking Koll's face with vigour. Redknee laughed. "They told me you were killed by the Bear People."

"*Hardly*. Nah, stabbed a few of them in the guts after you ran off to rescue Sinead. Lots of Flint People arrived; there was a bit of a scrap, then everyone started clearing out. That's when I lost you all. Thought the best thing to do was head back to the longhouse at *Svensbyan*. But when I arrived, there was no one left."

"How's your shoulder?"

"Fine. It was only a flesh wound."

Redknee told Koll how Olaf had agreed to help Ragnar find the treasure. Koll was sorely disappointed to learn there was no treasure to speak of, but he didn't seem surprised to learn Ragnar was Sinead's father.

"Why not?" Redknee asked.

Koll shrugged. "Because she's just about the most difficult woman I've ever met."

"There's one other thing," Redknee said, as they emerged from the forest and onto a wide, sandy beach. "Harold is the traitor."

"*That whelp!*"

Redknee nodded. He could see the longhouse in the distance, no more than a short walk away.

Koll came to a standstill, his gaze drifting out to sea. "So that's who poisoned my Thora," he said quietly. It wasn't the reaction Redknee had expected. There was no cry of anguish, nor protestations of revenge. Just sad acceptance.

"*There* you are!"

Redknee turned to see Magnus running to catch them. The steersman smiled when he saw Koll. "We all thought you were dead," he said.

Koll grunted distractedly.

"I was just telling Koll about Harold," Redknee explained.

Magnus nodded. "Can you believe it?"

Koll shook his head and resumed walking, his face set hard against the sea-breeze. "I do find it hard to believe Harold slit Karl's throat and poisoned our food."

"Of course, he denied the killings," Redknee said.

Magnus snorted. "He would. But then, people are hard to read." They'd almost reached the longhouse. Magnus hurried ahead and threw wide the door. The smell of stale wood smoke filled the air. He called over his shoulder: "I'm happier reading the waves."

"A man after my own thinking," Koll said, laying Silver on the floor and slipping a skin of mead from his cloak.

"So Ragnar just let you leave – knowing you were planning on starting a new trade route with Iceland?" Koll asked, laying down his axe and standing clear of the tall pine from which they'd just hacked out a wedge near the base.

Redknee nodded. They'd been out in the forest since early morning and the sun was almost full in the sky. Three long pine trunks lay nearby, waiting to have their branches cleared. Toki and Magnus were working together a little way off, Koll had instigated a competition to see which team could fell and clear the most trees by noon. Judging by the infrequent shouts

361

of excitement from where Toki and Magnus worked, Redknee thought he and Koll had a good chance of coming out on top. It was important – Koll's last skin of new-island mead was at stake.

Koll pushed the trunk of the tall pine and shouted "Timber!"

Redknee fancied he heard cursing through the trees.

"What I don't understand," Koll shouted above the noise of the pine crashing to the ground, "is why he let you live at all."

"I won't take that comment personally," Redknee said. "I believe Sinead begged for my life. I don't think there's any more to it."

"Seems unlikely that would influence a man like Ragnar," Koll said, starting to clear the larger branches from the pine trunk with a small stone-headed hatchet. Redknee smiled – it was a Flint People piece.

He jumped up beside Koll, adding his own muscle to the job. "I think," Redknee said between axe strokes, "that Ragnar knew Uncle Sven had Sinead all along … I think he knew she lived at the monastery, and when he heard Sven had been back and taken slaves he wanted to know if his daughter was among them. I think it was one insult too many."

"Aye," Koll said, pausing to wipe the sweat from his brow. "That's as may be, but money and power are more important to a man like Ragnar than family – especially a bastard daughter he's only just met."

They left the Promised Land on the spring equinox. They would have left sooner, but for the need to wait for the right winds. *Wavedancer* had required a few minor repairs to her hull, but she looked as good as new when she greeted the sea that bright morning.

Once they had the sail up and were underway, Redknee moved to the stern. He wanted to watch as the Promised Land, with its green hills, long sandy beaches and sheer cliffs, disappeared out of view. There was something sad about leaving – about returning home. It was as if everything that

362

happened, since they set sail from the Northlands almost half a year ago, had been a dream.

If he closed his eyes, he could almost believe Ragnar's attack on his village had never happened. Any moment his mother would call him in from the training yard; Uncle Sven laughing as he tried to carry his sword, spear and shield together.

"We don't call you Redknee for nothing," his uncle would say. "You're the clumsiest Northman I've ever seen."

How he'd hated the teasing then. He knew now that it was all in jest. That the real world, outside his village, was so much tougher than his family had ever been. And it was Ragnar who had brought that hard, cruel world rushing in. How he wished he'd taken his revenge – and to hell with Sinead and *her* new-found family.

They arrived at Greenland a mere ten days later. Redknee was glad to see Thorvald settling in well to his responsibilities without Gisela looking over his shoulder. Thorvald was glad to see them too, laying on a feast of spring lamb and herring. Although most of his wealth was lost when Ragnar destroyed the tunnels, the boy king still bought almost all their cargo. He had plans to build the greatest palace ever seen this far north, one filled with light and air, in contrast to the dark earthen warren where he'd grown up. And, he told Redknee, he would have need for a lot more timber … if Redknee could supply it.

The journey from Greenland to Iceland with the last of the timber was harder. Huge waves, as tall as the mast, threatened to overwhelm them. Only Magnus's skill with the helm, and Toki's quick lowering of the sail ensured they stayed afloat.

When they arrived in Reykjavik harbour, wet and battered, they were amazed by the change in scene since they'd left. Redknee had expected to find a busy hub, desperate for timber to rebuild their shattered town. Instead, they found a wasteland, barely populated and still smouldering from the volcano's fire. He sought out Ivar, who they'd left sheltering, with most of Reykjavik's unfortunate inhabitants, on an island just outside the harbour. Redknee was unsure what he would tell Ivar about his daughter. He still thought Astrid had murdered Hawk. But as for the others … Karl, Thora and the

Bjornsson twins, he couldn't be sure. Ivar had been good to Redknee, he deserved more than supposition when it came to news of his only daughter.

Redknee needn't have worried, for Ivar was nowhere to be seen. The poor wretches who were trying to rebuild Reykjavik said they thought he'd gone back home, to the Sheep Islands, others thought he'd died, drowned, when Mount Hekla had erupted for a second time.

Much to Toki and Magnus's annoyance Redknee offered the last of their timber to these wretches for free.

"But we've risked our lives for this wood," Magnus said. "We can't just give it away."

"These people have nothing," Redknee said. "Thorvald gave us a lot of coin – a full case – for the wood he bought. We can afford to be a little charitable."

Brother Alfred grinned. "I see you are becoming a Christian."

"It's nothing," Redknee said, shrugging, for in truth, he felt no affection for the ways of the Church.

Eventually, the others agreed to give away the timber, and they decided to spend the evening celebrating having rid themselves of their cargo. They found a small stone tavern on the edge of town. Being one of the few places to have survived the volcano, it was packed. A mixture of stale sweat and hops filled the air.

Koll took a deep breath. "When you can't find mead," he said smiling, "ale's the next best thing."

They found five seats near the back and ordered. Silver slipped under the table and settled on top of Redknee's feet. His injuries attracted the sympathy of the serving wench who surreptitiously slipped him a morsel of her master's best ham.

It was a long night, replete with dancing, games of dice and stories of bygone times. None were as rich as their tale of the journey to the Promised Land and the fierce warriors they met there. Even the sea-wizened merchants who claimed to have been as far as the exotic desert city of Baghdad, listened in wonder as Koll, helped by Toki and Redknee, told the tale of their voyage.

As the night drew to a close, Toki pulled Redknee aside. "Aren't you upset about Sinead?" he asked.

"Why should I be?"

Toki shook his head. "Just thought you had your eye on that little one, that's all."

"She's going to be married well ... to Prince Halfdan. I can't compete."

"Didn't his last wife die in a riding accident?" Koll cut in.

Toki shrugged. "I didn't know that."

"Yes," Koll said emphatically. "She did.' He turned to Redknee. 'Before I came to your uncle's village, I used to work in a smithy near Prince Halfdan's fort. He's not that young – maybe five and thirty. And there were rumours."

"What kind of rumours?" Redknee asked.

"Well ... the horse that threw his wife. Some say he startled it deliberately."

Too tired to make it back to *Wavedancer,* Redknee fell asleep in a space beneath the eaves. He'd had to pay the landlord extra for the peace. But it was worth it, he thought as he dozed off, Silver at his side. Brother Alfred had left the tavern early to sleep on *Wavedancer.* Redknee wasn't sure where Toki and Magnus had gone, but Koll was sleeping downstairs with the chest of coin. It would be safe.

Redknee awoke to the sounds of a busy household: the milling of corn; squawking chickens; children playing. For a moment he thought he was back home in his uncle's longhouse by the side of Oster Fjord. Then everything came flooding back. He rose and went downstairs. Koll was out in the yard washing his face in a bucket of water.

"Morning," Redknee grunted. "Are the others awake?"

"No idea," Koll said as Toki staggered, blinking, into the daylight.

"Anyone seen Magnus?" Toki asked.

Koll shook his head. "Thought he was with you."

Redknee's stomach sank. "Koll ... do you still have the chest ... with Thorvald's coin?"

"Yes ..." Koll said. "I hid it beneath the floorboards—"

They went to check where Koll had hidden the money. Koll stamped his foot to find the loose board.

"Here it is," he said, kneeling.

Redknee stared into the hole. It was empty.

Koll's face fell. "I don't understand."

Redknee ran to the door. "If we go now," he said, we might still catch him."

"But no one saw where I hid it."

"You were right, Koll," Redknee said, banging his fist on the doorframe, "Ragnar didn't allow me ... *any of us* ... to go so easily. He sent his spy."

Koll scratched his head. "I thought Harold was his spy?"

"Harold was Mord's spy. Of course Ragnar wouldn't leave his information-gathering to little more than a child," Redknee said. "I should have realised there would be someone else – someone under his direct authority. Magnus went with Uncle Sven to Kaupangen; he must have met Ragnar then."

"Do you think he killed Hawk ... and the others?" Koll asked.

Redknee shook his head. "I still think Astrid killed Hawk. That it was always her intention. But if I'm right, she got the wolfsbane from Magnus."

"Then you think he killed Thora ..."

Redknee nodded. "Yes, I do," he said gently.

"Well then, by Thor's hammer – what are we waiting for?"

Redknee, Koll and Toki hurried to the docks, but they were too late. A *knar* had already left for the Northlands that morning with a new crew member on board matching Magnus's description.

# Chapter 39

Sailing *Wavedancer* with just four men would be a struggle, so they asked around the docks if anyone wanted free passage to the Northlands. Three burly Icelanders took up their offer.

The mood on board *Wavedancer* the day they sailed from Reykjavik was low. They'd discussed returning to the Promised Land for more timber, but the three Northmen were in consensus – they'd had enough and just wanted to go home. Brother Alfred, too, was keen to return to Winchester and tell the leaders of his church about the new land and strange people he'd found. He believed there might be an abbacy in it for him, which he explained to Redknee, was a bit like being a jarl for holy men.

Their plan was to press on for home, avoiding a stay on the Sheep Islands. They had plenty of food and water for the seven men and Silver.

The weather held for four days but on the fifth day ugly black clouds gathered on the horizon. On the sixth day, the skies broke, sending hard, lashing rain. The sea rose until the waves towered above the mast, then crashed with terrifying power across the deck. This time, lowering the sail made little difference and the storm tossed poor *Wavedancer* about as if she were a child's toy.

They fought to tie down their belongings while the storm shrieked in their ears. Barrels smashed against the gunnels. The last of their food was lost over the side. The strakes in *Wavedancer's* hull groaned as she battled to stay intact. Brother Alfred crossed himself; sure their end was near. Koll kissed his Thor pendant. Silver cowered beneath a rolled up sheet. One of the Icelanders started puking. Toki shook his head and got on with helping Redknee secure the deck – a fruitless task as the waves climbed ever higher, breaking over the side with a new ferocity.

One huge wave sent everyone skittering on their backs. The retching Icelander flew over the side. Redknee only stayed onboard by grabbing hold of the rigging. After this, he put a whimpering Silver into his bag with the *Codex* and tied the straps across his chest. Then, drenched and with numb fingers, he tied a rope round his own waist and fixed the other end of it to the mast, tugging on the knot to make sure it would hold. He saw Koll and Toki do the same as another huge wave pounded the deck. Brother Alfred vanished over the side in a flurry of black sack-cloth and flailing limbs.

Redknee and Silver stayed lashed to the mast for what seemed like hours. *Wavedancer* plunged bravely on, her red and gold dragonhead set proudly against a furious sea. And then Redknee saw them. Rocks; lots of them, like teeth rising from the deep.

There comes a time when we must leave the things we hold dear. The promise of a new life, a love, a beautiful ship, must each be abandoned in the fight to survive, lest we drown from the weight of our dreams. Redknee took out his dagger and, as he saw the first great rock loom overhead, sliced clean through the rope tethering him. It was the last he saw of *Wavedancer*.

When Redknee woke, his left cheek had been scraped raw and every bone in his body ached in a way he'd not thought possible. He groaned - his throat felt like he'd swallowed a vat of ashes. Coughing, he hauled himself to his feet. He was on a long sandy beach surrounded by high cliffs. Gulls arced overhead. The storm had passed. The air smelled fresh. He felt his back, the bag was still there with the *Codex* inside, but Silver was gone. He stared down the beach. It was empty, save for the body of a man lying nearby, face down in the sand.

Redknee stumbled across to the man and turned him over. It was Koll. His face was blue and puffy and his eyes rolled white in his head; a deep gash split his forehead. Redknee shook him hard.

368

Koll spluttered awake. "Where are we?" he asked, looking round.

"I don't know. I think we must be near the Sheep Islands though. Do you remember the storm?"

"Aye," Koll said, "she was fearsome as a Valkyrie with toothache."

"*Wavedancer* is gone," Redknee said, staring out to a grey-blue sea. "Smashed to pieces on the rocks."

Koll shook his head. "A sore waste."

They headed along the beach with Redknee calling for Silver at the top of his voice. The island was small, barely more than a boulder dropped into the high, foamy sea. Sharp cliffs climbed away from the beach. As they reached the south side of the island, the cliffs became less steep. Presently they saw smoke coming from inland.

"Let's see who's home," Redknee said, making for a path that led up the hill.

"Wait for us!"

Redknee turned to see Toki and one of the Icelanders running towards them. They were both barefoot and their clothes were torn. Redknee realised he must look a sight himself.

"We thought you were dead." Redknee shouted back, his words carried on the blustery air.

"We thought the same." Toki said as he reached them.

The path rose to form steps cut into the rock. "These have taken someone a lot of work," Toki said, puffing as the climb became steeper. Redknee wondered what sort of people – fishermen or farmers, lived in such a remote, yet well-appointed place.

The steps circled the exterior of the island, twisting upwards, affording dizzying views of the sea. Whoever lived here valued safety over easy access to the water.

When they reached the top and saw the dwellings that created the smoke, Redknee sighed. He'd hoped for a grand monastery, or, at the very least, a finely carved longhouse fit to hold a hundred warriors. What stood before him, in a little hollow at the top of the island, were eight small roundhouses,

369

made of stone and roofed in chipped slate. They looked like peasant hovels.

"Are we dead?" Koll asked, staring at the strange buildings. "Is this Valhalla?"

Redknee shook his head. "We didn't die in battle."

"If Valhalla's like this, I'll be sorely disappointed," Toki said.

Koll laughed, the first time since arriving on the island. "Aye, there'll be no feasting in this wretched place."

As they debated the likelihood of adequate refreshment, the door of the nearest roundhouse burst open. A tall man dressed in a brown habit ran forward. He held his arms out in greeting and Redknee saw his left arm was smaller than the other, like a withered branch.

"Welcome, friends," he said in Norse. "We are poor hermit monks with nothing to offer you but our fireside and a little ale. I pray you come in peace."

Redknee told the monk their ship had been wrecked in the storm and that they did indeed come in peace.

Relief lit the monk's face and he beckoned them inside. The room smelled of whale oil and animal skins. "We are a hardworking monastery," the monk said, clearing rolls of vellum from a table. "My name is Brother Luke. Please," he said, pointing to some stools by a roaring fire, "warm yourselves."

It took a moment for Redknee's eyes to adjust to the dark. A group of monks were already by the fire. "Brother Alfred!" Redknee exclaimed recognising him from amongst their number.

As Brother Alfred stood, a leather ball fell from his lap and rolled across the floor. Before Redknee had finished thinking how it looked like the one Running Deer had given Silver, Silver himself shot from behind Brother Alfred and leapt into Redknee's arms. The pup covered Redknee's face in licks.

"Aw," Redknee said, holding him tight. "I thought I'd lost you."

"I found him washed up on the beach," Brother Alfred said. "He was unconscious but came round well enough when

370

I got some heat in his bones. He's been pining for you ever since."

Redknee thanked him and set a reluctant Silver on the floor. He learned Brother Alfred had been washed ashore on the south of the island and that he'd been alone. They agreed Silver must either have been swept from Redknee's bag or swam out himself for he'd been found near Brother Alfred.

"But isn't this wonderful?" Brother Alfred said, gesturing to the dark, smoky room. "Can you believe? We're in one of the foremost scriptoriums in all Christendom! When the Lord takes with one hand, he gives with the other."

Brother Luke caught Redknee's doubtful expression. "It's true about the scriptorium," he said, setting a bowl of hot porridge on the table.

Redknee noticed the monk's fingertips were stained purple. "I don't see any books here."

"We keep them in a separate room," Brother Luke said. "Do you have a particular interest in books?"

"I've only ever seen one; so I don't know about others. Do they all tell of treasure and adventure?"

Brother Luke stirred the porridge slowly. "*Not all*," he said, after some thought. "But reading a book, even one on mathematics or philosophy, is *like* an adventure – and as for what you learn, or experience through reading … that is the greatest treasure of all."

Brother Luke held out the ladle. Redknee took it, filled a bowl and put it on the floor. Silver gobbled ravenously. Redknee turned back to Brother Luke. "I don't think I know what you mean," he said, "about books."

"Where did you learn to speak Norse, Brother Luke?" Toki cut in. He had gone straight to the fireside where he was warming his bare feet. "I feel I've seen you somewhere before."

Brother Luke laughed nervously. "Well, I grew up in the Northlands."

"And you became a Christian," Brother Alfred said, impressed, "and a monk, no less?"

371

Brother Luke tilted his head. "Yes. I do not find that surprising. The teachings of the Nazarene have something to tell us all."

Toki frowned. "Where in the Northlands did you grow up?"

"Oh, I grew up in a very small village. Perhaps, if I can say so, I have been at a monastery you have raided?"

Toki shook his head. "I doubt any monastery I've raided. We always killed the monks."

"I would like to see your scriptorium," Redknee said, casting Toki an angry look. "If I may."

After they had eaten and dried their clothes by the fire, Brother Luke showed Redknee to the scriptorium. From the outside it looked the same as the other roundhouses – small and squat and dark. But as soon as Brother Luke opened the door, the stench of lime hit Redknee.

"It's really two buildings in one," Brother Luke said. Scraped sheepskins hung from the rafters. Beneath them sat large barrels of the foul smelling liquid. Brother Luke stirred one with a paddle. Hides bobbed to the surface. "We treat the sheepskins here. Our sister monastery on the mainland has a large farm. They send us the hides; we make them into vellum – for writing on."

Redknee coughed and nodded.

Brother Luke laughed. "Don't worry," he said, "the next room smells better."

Brother Luke led him through a low door and across a covered yard. The next roundhouse was even smaller and sadder looking than the one before. Brother Luke pushed open the sea-weathered door. As soon as Redknee stepped inside, he knew he was somewhere special. It wasn't the furnishings, for the room was bare save for three small desks and a large cabinet against the far wall. Somehow the place had an aura of serious study and reflection.

The doors of the cabinet were closed, but a whale oil lamp and quill sat on each of the desks.

"Where are the books?" Redknee asked.

372

"This is where we write them. Every book we make has to be copied from an original by hand. Mostly, we make copies of the Bible. It can take as long as two years to finish a single volume. And that doesn't include the illuminations."

Redknee looked puzzled.

"The illuminations are the pictures," Brother Luke said patiently. "They take the longest and require a great deal of skill. Often we use precious materials like gold and lapis lazuli for an important scene. We make books for some of the great monasteries of Europe; each year a boat comes to take our work to them. That is why we have only a few books here."

Brother Luke walked over to the cabinet and opened it with a key he kept on a cord round his belt. The top shelves were filled with sheets of vellum; the lower ones with seven large volumes bound in midnight-blue leather. He pulled the top sheet of vellum from the uppermost shelf and laid it on a desk. "We lock our work away each night in case it gets damaged," he explained. "But it is not private."

Redknee gazed at a beautiful picture of a unicorn, its tail woven round the letter *'H'* at the top left of the sheet. "I've seen work like that before," Redknee said. Brother Luke watched Redknee in confusion as he rooted inside his knapsack and brought out the *Codex*, still dripping from its immersion in the sea.

"Careful," Brother Luke cried, whipping away his sheet of vellum. "Water will destroy the work."

Redknee opened the Codex at the page with the unicorn illumination. "Oh no," he said, staring at the smudged mess of colours in disbelief, "it's ruined!"

He flipped through the rest of the book. Every page was the same. Where once neat black writing had stood, like an orderly shield wall across the page, there was now only the smeared confusion of a terrible rout.

"Wait." Redknee fished in his leather pouch. "I can at least show you a copy of the border." He pulled out his mother's embroidery. It wasn't much, but the colours had survived the shipwreck, the ivy leaves intact.

373

Brother Luke took the linen scrap; studying it closely. He didn't speak for a long time, just rubbed the fabric between his thumb and forefinger as if he didn't quite believe it was real.

Redknee shuffled awkwardly and cleared his throat, readying to ask for it back.

"That book," the monk said, his hand starting to tremble, "before it was ruined, what was it?"

"*The Codex Hibernia*." Redknee held out his hand, he was becoming concerned about the monk's state of mind. "Can I have my embroidery back, please?"

"Oh, yes," Brother Luke said, seeming to snap out of his reverie. As he handed it back to Redknee he asked in a low voice, "Is she still alive?"

Redknee edged towards the door. "Is *who* still alive?" Brother Luke was behaving strangely. He wanted to get back to the others.

"My wife … Ingrid … she sewed that when we were newly married. I remember her working on it as clear as if it were yesterday."

Redknee's mouth turned dry. "Your … *wife* … made this?"

Brother Luke nodded. "I wasn't always a monk. I used to be a Northman – a Viking – a pirate. My brother and I, we used to sail across the sea, looking for easy targets to plunder. But then, one day, just like you, my ship was washed up here. And well, I liked the life so much … found it was my true calling …"

"The woman who embroidered that was my mother. But she is dead, murdered by Jarl Ragnar."

Brother Luke leant against a desk for strength. "Even after all this time, I still believed she might be alive." He looked up at Redknee, his eyes bright with tears. "And you lad, how old are you?"

"Sixteen summers this year." The import of the monk's questions was beginning to dawn on Redknee.

"It cannot be possible …" he said, squinting at Redknee, studying his features, "but miracles *do* happen … my work here has taught me that. *My son*," he said opening his arms

Redknee hesitated. "*You* are Erik Kodranson?"

374

Brother Luke nodded slowly.

"But you are a monk."

"A young man goes out to conquer the world, to change it in his image, yet finds, as he grows older, that he is the one changed by what he has seen, by what he has done."

"I don't understand – what happened – I thought you died."

"At Ragnar's hand?"

"Or at Uncle Sven's."

Brother Luke frowned. "Why do you say that? After Ragnar wounded me in our fight, Sven helped me, hid me in some caves and tended to my wounds." He raised his withered arm. "This is my reminder. As for Sven, he saved my life, for Ragnar wanted me dead. I'd dared to challenge him for making eyes at Ingrid – your mother. Even then, Ragnar had a fast temper, and an even faster blade."

"What happened next? After Sven took you to the caves no one in the village saw you again. They thought you dead."

"Ah yes," Brother Luke said, slumping onto a stool. "Sven told me Ragnar was still after me. That he would hunt me down and kill me. I thought it wrong to return to the village; putting the lives of others at risk. But I was also in the grip of a madness of my own. That book you carry – *the Codex Hibernia* – Sven and I stole it from a monastery not unlike this one."

"I know," Redknee said. "I've been to the Promised Land."

Brother Luke sat up straight. "You have?"

Redknee explained how Ragnar had attacked his village and stolen the *Codex*; instigating the chase across the high seas. "Sven died trying to find the Promised Land, and when we got there, there was no treasure … things were no better than in the Northlands, except for a few more trees."

Brother Luke sighed. "When I was a young man, I became obsessed with the stories in the *Codex*. I'd learnt a bit of Latin from my trading days and this was enough to ignite a passion in me. I'd spend days poring over the words, trying to work out what Saint Brendan had meant. So when Sven proposed I take a ship and actually look for this Promised Land, I'm ashamed to say, I jumped at the chance."

"But your wife?"

"Sven said he would take care of Ingrid. And remember, I was a marked man. Ragnar has always been a favourite with King Hakon. And I didn't know she was with child."

"How did you end up here?"

"The ship Sven put me on was washed ashore here in a storm. I was the only survivor from the shipwreck. The monks took me in, clothed me; taught me to read; told me of our Lord. I learned that my fascination with the *Codex* lay with its deep expression of faith. So, with my ship at the bottom of the sea, and no way to return home, I was baptised and changed my name. Not long after, I took holy orders."

"Did you ever see Sven again?"

Brother Luke nodded. "About seven months after the shipwreck. He'd worked out where I was from asking around. He must have known Ingrid was with child by then. That must have been what he came to tell me. But he found a very changed man – I was no longer the fighting, drinking Northman he had known. I told him I wasn't coming back. He said he would take care of Ingrid as if she was his own wife. He never told me she was with child. I think he did the right thing, because, by then, I don't think I could have left."

"And you never saw Sven again, after that?"

"Once, about two and a half years ago Sven came here. Asked if I still had the *Codex*. Apparently the tales of Saint Brendan and his Promised Land had been haunting him. I told him I still had the book. Indeed, the old abbot was particularly interested in Saint Brendan, and without his support I never would have been able to go."

"Go where?"

"Sven helped me prepare a ship to sail to the Promised Land. He didn't come himself. Said it wasn't the right time to leave the Northlands. I made it as far as Greenland, where I fell ill. The Jarl of Iceland had joined our quest and the others sailed west with him. Without a ship or men I was forced to return home."

Now Astrid's story made sense. Brother Luke had been the monk who'd gone to Iceland.

376

"When I returned to the monastery I was welcomed by the other monks as a hero. I never made it to the Promised Land of Saint Brendan, but it was then I realised I'd found my own right here."

"And that was the last time you saw Sven?"

"He came one more time. I gave him the *Codex*, I had no use for it any more."

Redknee exhaled. The past was starting to make sense. "My uncle never married. He looked after me as a son."

A tear sprang to Brother Luke's eye. "I'm so sorry I wasn't there for you," he said, holding out his arms. "But I never knew ..."

"No," Redknee said, stepping into the embrace. "My uncle never told you ... I wonder why."

Brother Luke held Redknee away from him. "I'm so glad to have found such a fine son, so late in life," he said, smiling broadly.

*My brother, Erik Kodranson, is not your father.*

Redknee tried to push Sven's words from his head, but found that he could not. Sven had been trying to tell him something more. Of that Redknee was sure. But what? The dates added up ... in truth either Kodranson brother could be his father ...

As tears of joy streamed down Brother Luke's cheeks, Redknee came to a decision. "Yes," he said, gripping Brother Luke by the shoulders, "I, too, am glad ... to have finally found a father."

377

# Epilogue

The *Codex* could not be saved. Redknee was secretly glad. Its promises of glory and riches had ruined too many lives. They would ruin no more.

Seeing Redknee's interest in books, Brother Luke taught him to read the Latin that was so important to Sinead. It was slow work. Unused to sitting still and concentrating on one thing for such a long time, Redknee found it difficult at first. Soon though, as the words and their meanings blossomed into rich, interwoven tales and philosophies, he found himself looking forward to the time he spent reading and talking with Brother Luke each day.

If it was cold or wet, they would read inside, often in the refectory. But if the weather was good, they would take long walks on the beach, finding a quiet spot, out of the breeze, to sit and study a particularly difficult passage. Redknee found that, while he enjoyed the bible stories of Moses and David, the Greeks were his favourite, especially the voyages of Odysseus, an adventurer like himself.

He thought about Sinead a great deal – how she would have loved to explore the scriptorium and discuss book-ideas with Brother Luke. But it was more than that, he found he missed her. Silver did too, for whenever Redknee spoke her name, the pup would spin round, searching for her familiar features among the rocks.

Redknee knew he couldn't stay on the island, little more than a rock, forever. The others were restless too. Brother Alfred wanted to tell leaders in the Church about the Promised Land, convinced there would be an abbacy in it for him. Toki and Koll spent their days fishing and trapping wild birds, but such a small island held nothing more for them; they were restless. They needed to return to the world.

A small amount of timber from Wavedancer had washed ashore, but not nearly enough to make a boat. The island was treeless, save for a few small shrubs. Brother Luke said they could wait for the annual visit of the ship from their sister monastery on the mainland – but that could be months away.

One day, when Redknee was sitting on the beach, trying to understand Pythagoras' theorem, he remembered the story of Saint Brendan. Not the intoxicating tale where he reaches the Promised Land, but its humble beginning where he spends weeks constructing a boat from animal hides.

Of course, with the *Codex* ruined, Redknee had no way of knowing how to go about this. Then he remembered the list Running Deer had given them. He ran, as fast as he could across the beach, taking the steps up the hillside two at a time until he reached the top. He'd left the *Codex* in the scriptorium because the monks thought they could perhaps reuse the vellum.

When he burst through the door, the monks looked up from their desks, startled. He rushed to the back of the room and pulled the *Codex Hibernia* from the cabinet.

Brother Luke got to his feet. "What are you looking for?" he asked.

Redknee ran his finger along the inside edge of the book boards. The leather gaped open. He gave the *Codex* a shake and a small piece of vellum fluttered to the floor.

He knelt down and unfolded it. The writing and diagram of a *curragh* were in perfect condition, protected by the leather boards from water damage.

"I think," Redknee said, smiling up at his father, "I have a wedding to stop."

# GLOSSARY

| | |
|---|---|
| **arboreal** | of or relating to trees |
| **ascetic** | someone who seeks spiritual purity through self-denial and meditation |
| **Asgard** | the land of the gods in Norse mythology |
| **adze** | a kind of chisel |
| **Berserker** | fierce warrior who dresses as a bear |
| **blood-month** | the month domestic animals were traditionally slaughtered for meat before the winter, November |
| **boss** usually | reinforced area in the centre of a shield, metal, which protects the hand |
| **casket** | small chest for keeping jewels |
| **crenellated** | jagged-like battlements |
| **cacophony** | loud jarring noise |
| **caldera** | basin-like depression at top of volcano |
| **Fenrir** | a giant wolf in Norse mythology |
| **Frankish** | denoting someone from the land of the Franks, broadly modern day France |
| **Freya** | Norse goddess |
| **Furthark** | the Norse alphabet |
| **gunnels** | side rails of a ship |
| **Hela** | Norse god of the underworld |
| **helve** | axe handle |
| **ignoble** | dishonourable |
| **insolence** | disrespect  · |
| **Kaupangen** | Viking name for the modern Norwegian city of Trondheim, means 'market place' |
| **knar** | A Viking merchant ship |
| **mailcoat** | A flexible armour tunic made of riveted iron rings or links |
| **mead** honey, | An alcoholic drink made from fermented drunk extensively in Viking times |
| **nascent** | new born or rising |
| **necromancy** | the magic of bringing the dead to life |
| **novice** nun | an inexperienced person; a trainee monk or |

| | |
|---|---|
| **Odin** | Father of the Norse gods. God of wisdom and war. Exchanged his eye for the knowledge of |
| all | things. |
| **parchment** | scraped and treated animal skin (mostly sheep, goat or cow) used for writing before paper became widespread |
| **pommel** | heavy knob at the end of a sword's handle |
| **prosaic** | ordinary, dull, like prose, rather than poetry |
| **rictus** | unnatural grin |
| **runes** | letters of the Norse alphabet, sometimes used for fortune telling |
| **scriptorium** | room where manuscripts are stored, read or copied |
| **seer** | one who can see the future |
| **shingle** | wooden roof tile/ stones on a beach |
| **skald** | Norse poet |
| **skerling** | Norse word for wretch, used by the Vikings to refer to the Native Americans in a derogatory way. |
| **skiff** | row boat |
| **strake** | horizontal plank in the hull of a ship |
| **sunstone** — | a stone used to determine the height of the sun used to aid navigation |
| **tang** | part of a blade that reaches into the handle of a knife or sword |
| **tangible** | something that has real physical existence i.e. can be touched, held etc. |
| **Thor** | Norse god of Thunder. Son of Odin. |
| **tomahawk** | type of throwing axe used by Native Americans |
| **Valhalla** | the great feasting hall of the gods in Norse mythology. Located in Asgard |
| **Valkyrie** | female warrior in Norse mythology who collects the battle dead |
| **Vanguard** | the leaders/those out front or first |
| **vellum** | the best quality parchment |
| **Verden** | location of AD782 massacre by Charlemagne, a Christian king, of 4500 Saxons who refused to convert to Christianity |

| | |
|---|---|
| **veracity** | truthfulness |
| **vespers** | evening prayer service in Roman Catholic church, often involves singing |
| **whet/ whetted** | to sharpen a blade with a stone/a sharpened blade |
| **White Christ** | a Norse name for Jesus, 'white' meaning cowardly, as opposed to warrior like |
| **Yggdrasil** | the tree of life in Norse mythology. |

# Discussion Questions

1. At the end of Chapter 1, where Redknee saves Skoggcat from falling off a cliff, he thinks of himself as having been weak. Do you agree? What are your reasons?

2. In Chapter 7 Redknee thinks going on the whale hunt will help him become a warrior. Do you agree? What are your reasons?

3. A thousand years ago the concept of a book – then called a codex – was quite new. Previously information was written on long scrolls that had to be unwound to the right place. Books were seen as a technological leap. Today, we are in the midst of another technological leap in the way we distribute information through computers and the internet. Do you think physical books, as we know them, will exist in a hundred years? What about computers? How might such changes affect our society?

4. Several times in the story, Ragnar tells Redknee that 'they are more alike than he knows.' Do you agree? Can 'baddies' and 'goodies' ever share traits? If so, what differentiates baddies from goodies, both in real life and in fiction? It could be said Sven is an ambivalent character – one that possesses good and bad traits – in the end, did you think he was mostly a goodie, mostly a baddie, or somewhere in between?

5. When they are talking together on the beach, Sinead asks Redknee if it really matters who his father is. Do you agree with her? How much does someone's background, whether that be their parents, their hometown, or their education, matter to their future? What do you think about the quote from the poem *Invictus* at the start of the novel?

6. Deganawida suggests people can learn from failure – do you agree?

7. Did Redknee do the right thing when he agreed with Brother Luke's assertion in the last chapter? Why do you think Redknee did this?

8. In the novel, the Promised Land means different things to different people. Sinead is seeking a new home where she can be free. Redknee is seeking the truth about his father and acceptance from his peers. Do they find these things? To what extent can such concepts as 'home,' 'freedom' and 'acceptance' be found? And if they can't be found, are they worth looking for?

9. In the story of Saint Brendan, the search for the Promised Land can be taken as a metaphor for the quest for spiritual enlightenment. In the last chapter, Brother Luke says he's found his own promised land in his scriptorium. Do you believe him? Do you see parallels in the search for such enlightenment and Sinead's search for 'home,' and 'freedom' and Redknee's search for 'the truth'? The novel also draws on the connection between knowledge and enlightenment. Do you think they are the same thing?

10. What do you think might happen next?

## Author's Note

It is believed by historians that Leif Eriksson, a Viking explorer, was the first European in historical times to reach North America, and that he did so around AD1000. What remains disputed is to what extent the Norse travelled within America, established settlements and interacted with the native population. To date, the stone longhouses at L'Anse aux Meadows in Newfoundland are the only agreed upon evidence of a permanent, or semi-permanent Norse presence. In Viking Gold, I chose to push the boundaries of established history somewhat by allowing my Vikings to travel further south on the American continent to the area believed to be then occupied by the tribes of the Iroquois language group – somewhere around modern day New York State. I chose to do this for two main reasons: Newfoundland, the site of the proven Viking settlement, was probably sparsely, if at all, populated by native people around 1000 years ago due to its harsh climate.

Secondly, I fell in love with the Iroquois tale of Hiawatha and the Tree of Peace, and believed this to be a fitting end-point for my main character's quest. I must point out that the story of Hiawatha, Deganawida and the Tree of Peace, as told in Viking Gold, necessarily only draws briefly on the rich tale of the founding of the real Iroquois Confederacy – an early parliamentary system that must vie with the Icelandic All-Thing, for the honour of being one of the earliest such electoral systems. I must also confess to moving Hiawatha and Deganawida a little earlier in time than it's thought they existed, with the lunar eclipse of AD1159 currently thought of as the earliest possible date for the real founding of the Iroquois Confederacy.

While I am making my confessions, I might as well admit there is no evidence of people living below ground in Greenland – this was pure authorial invention, in part to reflect the dark times in the characters lives at this point in the story, and partly to add a bit of variety in setting. I feel I must also mention that 10th Century Iceland was a mostly egalitarian society – with no jarls or over-lords, and Reykjavik, at that time, was little more than a farm or small village, not the large trading town I describe.

However, while the Codex Hibernia I describe in the novel is entirely made up, there really was a 6th Century Irish monk called Saint Brendan who it is believed sailed to a place far to the west he called the Promised Land, and did so in a leather curragh. Saint Brendan's legendary voyage is documented in a very real medieval text called The Voyage of Saint Brendan, and certain of the passages quoted in the novel as coming from the fictional Codex, are in fact taken from this work, although in most cases I have made certain amendments to the quoted passages to facilitate the plot (for example, there is no mention of the Great White Pine in The Voyage). In this regard, I would like to offer a special thanks to Colin Smythe of Colin Smythe Limited for allowing me to use The Voyage in this way, and also to thank, John J. O'Meara, the late translator of this work, without whose scholarship I would not have had access to this fascinating tale.

So, the question remains – Did Saint Brendan reach the Americas four hundred years before Leif Eriksson and his band of Vikings? Unfortunately, this is probably something to which we will never know the answer, though some claim the early Irish Ogham script has been found on stones in New England. That, however, is another story …